MW01004164

BOOKS BY ISAAC HOOKE

ATLAS Series

ATLAS

ATLAS 2

ATLAS 3 (Coming 2015)

Caterpillar Without a Callsign

(A novella about Snakeoil's heroism on his first deployment)

Just Another Day

(A novella about Facehopper's encounter with the infamous privateer Mao Sing Ming)

Forever Gate Serial

Forever Gate 1

Forever Gate 2

Forever Gate 3

Forever Gate 4

Forever Gate 5

Forever Gate Compendium (Parts 1–5)

Other Works

Finding Harmon (Short Story)

ISAAC HOOKE

47N⬤RTH

Text copyright © Isaac Hooke 2014
All rights reserved.

Published by 47North, Seattle

www.apub.com
Amazon, the Amazon logo, and 47North are trademarks of Amazon.com, Inc., or its affiliates.

ISBN-13: 9781477825969
ISBN-10: 1477825967

Illustration by Elliott Beavan

Library of Congress Control Number: 2014910353
Printed in the United States of America

"Is space big?"

"Space is as big as humanity's imagination."

—Teacher Unit 52950

PROLOGUE

The morning of Lana's twenty-fifth birthday, she was out window-shopping with her best friend, Shui, on the pristine streets of Shangde City, Tau Ceti II-c.

She would have preferred to spend her birthday at home, but she worked for Juneyao Spacelines, a local service responsible for chartering passengers between the moons of the gas giant Yihuà (Tau Ceti II), and she went where her job took her. She was a commercial pilot, really just a fancy term for a babysitter since the shuttles flew on autopilot most of the time. Of course, if a shuttle crashed, the port authorities always blamed the human pilot.

In addition to the official and rather boring name of Tau Ceti II-c, the moon was also known as Hong Caodi (Fragrant Meadow), and was one of three terraformed satellites orbiting the gas giant. Yihuà resided in the habitable zone of the star, allowing all three moons to become beautiful places of sprawling forests and vast meadows whose trees were filled with birds and whose grasslands fed buffalo and wild horses. The animals were bioengineered from Earth stock of course.

Shangde City was the only major population center on the moon, and was built on the permanent light side. Though "light" was a bit of a misnomer, since the sky resided in a state of perpetual twilight, somewhere between dawn and morning. Stars twinkled on one half of the sky, and the other half was filled with the swirling, blue storms of the gas giant Yihuà, constant companion and watcher. Although in the city, that "watcher" was often blotted out by the many buildings and skyscrapers.

Despite the tall buildings, there was only one level of road system, unlike the typical Sino-Korean megalopolis found on Earth, with streets sometimes composed of up to five different levels. But since the moon's population was only one million (with most of that in the city proper), there was no real need for the multilevel roadways found on Earth.

Yes, Lana knew all about Earth. Though she had been born in Tau Ceti system, Lana had made the expected pilgrimage to humanity's homeworld for schooling, as many Tau Cetians did (on the government's tab) when they turned eighteen. Lana returned at twenty-four, enlightened, cosmopolitan, but mostly glad to be home. Earth's gravity had felt oppressive to her—on the moons of Yihuà the gravity only ever got as high as 0.92 G. Add in the stinking press of humanity and the cold throng of robots that filled every street, and sometimes she'd felt like she was literally being crushed on Earth.

No, Lana was glad to leave the heavy air, the massive crowds, and the long waits far behind.

Not to mention the bigotry. If she told someone she was from space, every eye in the room turned toward her with an envious, hateful gleam. It was even worse in the United Countries. She didn't even have to open her mouth because people realized at a glance she was Sino-Korean. They closed doors in her face, shoved her on the subway, and generally treated her poorly.

Earth.

She didn't plan on ever returning.

Shangde City was pedestrian-friendly in the downtown core, allowing Lana to walk to every destination. There were whole zones where vehicle traffic was disallowed, both air and ground. The pedestrian nature of the city explained why, despite the vast real estate available, most of the buildings were closely packed. A typical street was only about five meters wide.

Because the layout favored foot traffic, the shops and restaurants repeated with predictable regularity. On one block alone, Lana could find a grocer with 18.9 liter jugs of bottled water stacked outside for purchase, a fashion store with typically wacky outfits decorating the mannequins (popular at the moment were bright orange jackets with lightning-shaped protrusions from the shoulders, and jeans covered in colorful dragon scrollwork), a meat shop extolling the aphrodisiacal virtues of donkey balls, a gym promising new members a month's supply of free gear (the steroid kind), an electronics store offering aReal deals and hacks, a massage parlor pledging the greatest foot massage in town, a traditional Chinese noodle shop, an Italian restaurant, a Turkish "halal" kebab diner, a dessert shop, a pawn shop, a flesh parlor, and so on. Higher up, the glass-and-steel structures of the condominiums and office towers connected to the shops ate up the twilit sky.

As soon as she reached the next block, all the retail outlets repeated. Different names, same promises.

Lana stopped at Fatt's Place, "an eating and drinking establishment," and ordered Wednesday's Spicy Fingers. The chicken proved a bit mild for "spicy," and Lana was forced to add a healthy dose of chili to suit her palate.

Shui, a stewardess for the spaceline Lana worked for, purchased a burger and a Shangde specialty ale. Shui was a relatively small woman, and because of her stature, she liked to wear her hair in a vertical bun. In addition to the perceived height boost, she claimed the hair also gave her a more "traditional" look, though to Lana, the hairdo only made her friend seem a bit snobbish. As far as Lana was concerned, if Shui wanted to increase her height she should just throw on some heels. Lana of course always let her locks flow long and free, but she had the advantage of being tall.

The two of them sat on the stools by the window for some people-watching. Human beings shared the walkways with errand robots. The men outnumbered the women. And the robots outnumbered them both. Lana could pick out the visitors from Earth by the *kouzhao* masks wrapped around their noses and mouths. Earthers were afraid of the "impure" air of the colonies, and seemed to enjoy the false sense of security the masks provided. Some wore fashionable cotton *kouzhao* with cute designs, while others wore the more "practical" surgical and higher-end filtration models.

It was a little surprising how many locals were out and about today, because most of the time they preferred to stay home, either enjoying the latest interactive games provided by their aReals or Implants, or just relaxing and enjoying life. The government gave them room and board, and the robots performed the hard work, keeping the economy chugging along.

Work was optional.

But not for Lana. She was never the type to sit back and let the Paramount Leader feed her. She wanted to contribute to society. Make a difference, in her own small way.

Lana had always looked to the stars, and knew since she was a child that she would become a pilot. Sometimes during take-offs and landings she felt like an eagle, soaring free. She often disengaged the autopilot while landing (something her supervisors frowned upon), specifically because she wanted to evoke that feeling of sheer freedom.

She had a small eagle tattooed to the inside of her wrist to remind her of that feeling. To remind her of who she was, and why she would never consider work optional. To her, work *was* freedom.

Across the street, a small crowd had gathered around one of the shop windows. Bringing their meals, Lana and Shui approached, passing a man who was walking his pet bird (he gently swayed the birdcage to and fro as he walked). Reaching the shop, Lana and

Shui peered through the glass and watched as a robot made Misua noodles in the traditional fashion.

Made of high-grade polycarbonate, the black and yellow robot was humanoid in shape, with blocky arms and legs. The connecting joints—elbows, shoulders, knees, ankles, fingers—were composed of circular servomotors. The head looked like the inverted scoop of a small power shovel, complete with serrated prongs along the bottom. A yellow bar divided the middle of the face, and above it, two small glass discs stacked one atop the other formed the vision sensors. A red dot in the center of its forehead provided depth perception, and a small antenna protruded from the very top of its head.

The robot was hanging the long noodle threads between perpendicular rods separated by about three meters each. The strands drooped precariously low between those rods, and almost touched the floor.

"If they want to show how noodles are made traditionally, they shouldn't use a robot," Shui complained.

Lana could only laugh. The irony wasn't lost on her. "Maybe the shop owner is a robot."

Shui chuckled. "That would explain a lot."

Most people believed that robots were inhabited by good spirits. Lana knew the truth of course. An AI that could pass the Turing test might be conscious and self-aware, but it was still an AI as far as she was concerned, not a spirit.

A delivery drone buzzed past overhead, just out of reach. With a baseball bat and a flying leap, anyone could take down the drone and pilfer its contents. But since drones (and nearby robots) were equipped with cameras and RFID nodes, the vandal would be tagged immediately by embedded ID, and eventually sent a "repair and downtime" invoice, as well as a bill for the full cost of the stolen goods. If the vandal didn't pay, he would find himself transported to a penal colony.

Lana had finished her chicken fingers, and she dropped the empty carton inside a roaming garbage collection robot.

The streets darkened. Between the gaps in the buildings overhead, Lana saw black clouds consume the sky. That was somewhat odd, given that no storms were scheduled for that day. Oh well. When rain came on the moons, it usually only lasted a few minutes anyway.

Hoping to avoid the storm, Lana led Shui into a nearby fashion mall. She hadn't really intended to buy anything, but soon browsing turned to purchasing. She supposed she could've done her shopping in the hotel room, but today was her birthday. Time to be out and about, and to splurge and have fun.

The stores didn't have any physical inventory, and instead utilized an app that let the customers model clothes via their reflections in a mirror: Lana would strip down to her underwear in the change room, look at herself in the mirror, and the provided aReal visor overlaid fashionable items from the store's virtual catalog over her body. She was able to quickly cycle through the tops and bottoms, as well as hairstyles and entire looks (the hippie punk look gave her a good laugh). Once she picked out something she liked, the sales robot helped her use the dedicated fabric-on-demand technology to print it up in her size.

An hour later Lana found herself leaving the mall with three large bags stuffed to the brim with clothes and shoes. Ah, the joys of a paycheck.

The rotunda outside the mall entrance was shielded by a metal half dome. Beyond, the sky was as black as ever.

"*Chùsheng!*"—Damn! (Literally: Beast!)—"I wanted to miss the storm." Lana paused beneath the metallic edge of the dome.

Shui sighed. "Me too."

"Maybe if we run, we can make it back before the rain starts," Lana suggested.

An air-raid siren sounded in the distance. The noise startled Lana. Chills ran up and down her spine. The whining, ever-shifting tone evoked a kind of primal fear inside her. It was like the city itself was screaming in terror.

Shui stared up at the black clouds. "Lana, listen to the news. Now."

Shui wore prescription aReal glasses, the vision-correcting kind, so though she didn't have an Implant per se, she was always jacked in. Lana meanwhile had twenty-twenty vision, like almost everyone else. Her augmented reality device was definitely not prescription, and she wore it only sporadically.

Lana set down her shopping bags and removed the aReal from her purse. To anyone watching, it would appear she donned a pair of sunglasses.

She navigated to the Xinhua News Network.

"A massive, unidentified object has entered orbit around Hong Caodi," the newscaster said. "It appears to be of alien origin."

Lana frantically reached out, searching for Shui's hand, and when she found it, she gripped her friend's palm fiercely. It was her lifeline to the world she knew. The world of sanity and order.

"The object has not responded to our communications," the newscaster continued. "The government has assumed hostile intent."

Her eyes burned with tears. No. This could not be happening. Not now, on her birthday. Why did the spaceline have to send her to Hong Caodi today? *Why?*

In the background, the siren continued to wail, mocking her.

"Residents are advised to stay indoors. If you are at home, do not go outside."

It started to rain.

Lana was protected from the downpour by the half dome of the rotunda, which was a good thing, because this was no ordinary rain.

The fat droplets were glowing.

The screams began then.

A woman near Lana, hurrying beyond the half dome, was literally incinerated. All that was left of the woman was a smoking, organic mass on the pavement.

Other human beings who were out in the rain suffered similar fates.

Lana would have thrown up, but she was too utterly shocked.

She shut off the news.

Thus far, the half dome continued to protect Lana and Shui from the deadly droplets.

But for how long?

A part of her mind noticed the glowing rain formed puddles on the asphalt.

Puddles that *moved*.

The robots in the street abruptly froze. Though the droplets didn't incinerate them, the rain seemed to affect them in other ways. Some of the robots began to glance down at their bodies. They lifted their polycarbonate hands, examining their fingers as if for the first time. They took tentative, shaky steps. Some of the robots actually stumbled and fell to the pavement.

One robot spotted Lana and the growing group of bystanders sheltered beneath the half dome. The robot jerkily turned toward them and advanced, reminding her of a zombie from a B movie. Other robots followed the example of the first, shuffling toward the confused people.

The pavement echoed with the clang of polycarbonate feet. The robots became less zombielike with every moment. Shuffling, hesitant steps became confident strides. They were a troop of robotic hunters, marching to meet their prey. Some of the robots still tripped and fell, but many more continued unabated.

On the pavement, the glowing puddles of rain moved of their own accord, as if alive, and slowly edged up the ramp toward the rotunda.

"Shui, we have to go!" Lana tugged on her friend's arm. "Shui!"

Their shopping bags forgotten, Lana and Shui turned around and ran back toward the mall.

Lana glanced over her shoulder and watched in horror as robots from the street attacked the slower bystanders, many of whom still lingered near the edge of the dome.

Hard polycarbonate slammed into flesh-covered bone. Blood sprayed the pavement.

Maybe the people thought they were safe. Maybe they thought the robots just wanted to help. They were right to believe that, in a way. It shouldn't have been possible for the robots to do what they were doing, not with the Constitution . . . it was as if the good spirits in the robots, the spirits Lana didn't believe in, had been replaced by something malevolent. Evil.

More screams came.

The ground began to shake as an earthquake of some kind struck the city.

"Lana, what's going on?" Shui said.

"Just run!" Lana said.

A moment before she reached the mall entrance, something plowed into Lana from the side.

She fell forward and skidded onto the concrete; she felt the skin scrape off her left knee and elbow.

A weight pressed against her hips, pinning her.

She tilted her torso and stared up into the emotionless shovel-like face of a robot. The red laser above its vision sensors flashed into her eyes.

The weight of the thing was crushing, even though the robot was only partially on top of her. Lana thought her hip bones would shatter at any moment.

Lana screamed, as did Shui beside her.

The robot brought its arm far back, servomotors whirring wildly. A polycarbonate fist aimed at Lana's head—

She lifted an arm to protect herself—

From nowhere a second robot slammed into the first, sending it flying off Lana.

Saving her.

The two robots rolled away, wrestling.

Some of the good spirits remained, then. Or rather, some of the robots still obeyed their internal Constitution.

All robots, even military-grade ones, were hard-coded to protect civilians: the preservation of civilian life overrode everything else. It was called the Machine Constitution. If any harm befell a human being on the open streets, any nearby robots were supposed to come to the aid of said human. There were no conflicting instructions. Nothing that could prevent the Constitution from engaging. Helping a human being in distress was the first priority, and overrode any other task.

A street filled with robots was a safe street, the saying went. No one need to ever fear a mugging, or a heart attack. If someone robbed you, the robots would come to your rescue. If you collapsed in the street, a robot would issue CPR and call an ambulance.

Which was why it was so shocking that the machines, the most devoted supporters of humanity, would attack in the first place.

Shui helped Lana rise. The pavement still shook and rumbled.

It was getting cold, so cold. Lana's breath misted.

Behind her, robots still flooded the rotunda from the street. The rain was becoming slush.

Lana turned toward the mall entrance—

More robots emerged from the doorway and headed straight for Lana and Shui.

Trapped.

It was over. There was nothing she could do. Not now.

Lana grabbed Shui's hand, and held perfectly still, waiting for death.

Shui whimpered beside her.

The robots from the mall rushed right past them to meet the robotic attackers emerging from the sleet.

Lana laughed in disbelief, and felt joyous tears trickle down her cheeks.

Behind her, polycarbonate fists met polycarbonate chest pieces, and the clangor sounded like some medieval reenactment battle.

Lana and Shui didn't wait around to see who would win. Not with those glowing puddles creeping up the rotunda.

The two of them rushed inside the mall. They stumbled occasionally, because of the quaking floor. Once inside the arcade, the air became pleasantly warm.

The mall was connected to the underground pedestrian walkways that formed a warren beneath Shangde City. Those pedways saw little traffic in the summer, and were meant more for the winter months. (Yes, the government had programmed three months of snow into the weather system to better mimic the seasons of Earth, which helped transplanted colonists adapt, according to the scientists.) But at that moment, people rushed toward those distant pedways in droves.

Robots waded through the throng toward the exits. Like most people, Lana and Shui gave the robots a wide berth.

The earthquake abruptly ceased.

Lana paused beside a window. Outside, the rain had been replaced by drifting snow. Gusting winds whirled the flakes across the eerily empty streets. The snow seemed normal, she noted, and wasn't glowing.

"Let's go!" Shui said, dragging her onward.

Lana tuned in to the news as she ran.

"The clouds of dust thrown up by the impact have completely occluded the sky. The temperature outside is plummeting, and some areas of the city have reported snow. Reports continue to trickle in regarding robot attacks and deadly rain. The City Defense Corps has issued a bulletin: We are under attack. Stay indoors. Do not leave your place of work or residence. If you are not at home, or in a safe place, take shelter immediately. Stay away from the robots and the glowing liquid if you can."

That wasn't helping.

Lana shut off the newscast.

Random people around her abruptly collapsed to the floor: men and women pressed their palms to their ears and squeezed their eyes shut.

Lana had the impression those people were seeing and hearing something no one else did.

Something that drove them mad.

Lana knelt beside one such man. He had the smooth, ageless features and glowing skin of someone who had undergone the rejuvenation treatments. He was rich, then. Probably had an Implant. "What's wrong? Sir?"

Shui tugged at her shoulder. "Lana! Leave him! Let's go!"

Lana spoke again, but the man proved unresponsive.

Shui was glancing back nervously. "Leave him!"

Lana decided she would carry him. "Shui, grab his right arm."

Lana slid her shoulder beneath his armpit and the man rewarded her with an elbow to the face.

She fell backward, landing on her butt. The man was whimpering now, but kept his hands firmly pressed to his ears.

"See?" Shui said, helping her up. "Forget about him!"

Glass broke behind them as a robot leaped through a shop window.

The robot malevolently turned toward them.

"Lana . . ."

A "good" robot intercepted the "bad" one, hurling it to the floor.

Shui and Lana ran. It felt wrong, and rotten, to abandon the man and those others who had fallen, but what was Lana supposed to do? Especially if she was attacked by the very people she intended to save.

Lana proceeded down the wide, shop-lined concourse, finally arriving at the escalators to the lower pedways. She wanted to hurry down, but the press of humanity ahead of her ruled out that option. It was like she was back on Earth all over again.

She and Shui were among the last ones onto the moving stairway. There were a few stragglers who pushed and shoved behind them, but otherwise that was it.

The moving stairway slowly shifted downward. Lana kept her eyes glued to the top of the shaft behind her: she kept expecting a "bad" robot to step onto the escalator.

Lana's scraped knee and elbow started to throb now that she had stopped moving. Some of the shock was wearing off. She was still scared, but her mind was starting to work again.

The robots were turning against everyone. The world as she knew it was ending.

What was she supposed to do when something like that happened? She needed time to think. Time to decide what to do.

The robots. There was something about them that tugged at a forgotten memory. She thought of the errand bot that had pinned her down, with its fist raised to strike. The glowing droplets of rain seemed to have accumulated around the chest piece, where the robot's brain was housed. None of the liquid resided anywhere else on the polycarbonate body, save for a few droplets around the neck.

What did that remind Lana of?

Yes. Now she had it.

She had seen leaked pictures on the Undernet of UC special-forces soldiers who had gone to an unspecified, faraway planet and awakened the *Yaoguai,* demons from the underworld. These demons had consumed the souls of the soldiers, and possessed their support robots. In the pictures, when a Yaoguai had taken a robot body as its own, a glowing vapor surrounded the chest piece, just above the brain case.

So this was the fault of the evil, bigoted UC, always going places it shouldn't be going, stirring up trouble better left alone.

It didn't really matter whose fault it was now though, did it?

The Yaoguai were here, and the people of Shangde City were dying.

Lana tried to bring up the news, but got a "Connection Time-out" error.

"Shui, are you still online?" she said.

"No," her friend answered.

The crowds thinned out in the multiple corridors of the claustrophobic pedways. The white LEDs on the ceiling gave the underground passageway a washed-out, eerie look.

The problem with the pedways was that they weren't well labeled. People were expected to access the online map via their aReals, but since the InterPlaNet was down, only those who had their routes memorized made any real headway. Thankfully, Lana had made this journey many times, mostly to avoid the rush-hour crowds on the streets above, and she knew exactly where she was going. Shui followed, trusting her implicitly.

They finally reached a properly labeled branch. Lana glanced at the signage. She was precisely where she had thought she would be.

Lana immediately took the rightmost passage.

"Lana, wait," Shui said, pointing at the label. "The left passage leads to the port. The right leads downtown."

"I can read."

"But you're going the wrong way!" Shui insisted.

"I *want* to go downtown."

"Why, what's there?" Shui said.

"The hotel."

"No! We have to get to the port!"

Lana bit her lower lip. "I can't leave the flight crew behind."

"We don't need the crew!" Shui said. "You can pilot the shuttle on your own, can't you? With the autopilot?"

"I'm not abandoning the crew."

Shui gritted her teeth. "How do you know they haven't left already? How do you know they're not *dead*?"

Without access to the Net, Lana couldn't ping the crew to determine either. She wished she'd thought of that earlier, while the Net was still operational.

"I'll meet you at the spaceport, if you want," Lana said.

She didn't have to worry about Shui trying to activate the autopilot on her own. As a stewardess, Shui didn't have the authorization. That said, the copilot Keai *did* have authorization, and it was possible he'd already reached the shuttle and abandoned them all. There was no way to know until the Net came back online.

Shui worked her jaw. Finally: "We have to stick together. We retrieve the flight crew, then we go."

"I'm glad you agree." Lana found it hard to keep the sarcasm from her voice.

Lana and Shui hurried from pedway to pedway, staying well away from any errand robots they saw. The few humans Lana encountered kept to themselves, the fear plain on their faces as they moved with purpose to wherever it was they were going. Usually she'd find buskers perched beside every underground intersection at this hour, but they'd all packed up and left, save one brave old man who played Beethoven's "Moonlight Sonata" to the empty corridor on his violin-piano.

Lana tried tuning in to the news again, but the local InterPlaNet node was still down. Implants and aReals were supposed to form adhoc wireless networks with each other when out of node range, bridging the gap to the nearest working node, but the signals those devices produced were weak, and the bridging only worked when a lot of people (or robots) were around to disseminate the packet data.

Lana and Shui reached a wider underground section.

There was one other person present, a woman cradling a baby in her arms. She cowered in one corner, wearing an aReal visor.

When the woman saw Lana, she scrambled over.

"You're a spaceline pilot," the woman said in a rush. "It says so on your profile." Obviously she was using her visor to read the public data Lana had made available on her embedded ID. That was something anyone could do if they got close enough to you, courtesy of the aforementioned adhoc wireless network.

Lana didn't deny it. Though not for the first time, she wished she had hidden her listed occupation.

"Please, give me and my baby a ride off this moon," the woman said. "Please."

"I—" Lana didn't have the heart to say no. "You can come with us if you want. But there's no guarantee we'll make it off this moon. We're going to the Jinjiang Hotel first, then the port."

"Thank you." The woman fell in behind them.

"I'm Lana, and this is Shui."

The woman nodded. "Mei."

"We don't have time to babysit her, Lana," Shui hissed in a muted tone.

Mei overheard. "I can take care of myself and my baby. I won't slow you down."

"You better not," Shui said. "Or we're leaving you."

It was a cold thing to say, but Lana knew she wouldn't be able to abandon her if it came to it. Shui's words seemed to have the intended effect however, because though burdened by the baby, Mei kept pace.

The three eventually reached the underground entrance to the hotel. The escalator leading to the lobby no longer had power, so Lana and her companions warily climbed the metal stairway. Their footsteps sounded overloud to Lana's ears.

The lobby was deserted. Usually the higher-end hotels kept at least one Artificial at the check-in desk at all hours, but not so today. All that remained in lieu of people were the uncanny paintings lining the walls. The subjects were women, dressed in traditional Chinese garb, posing with open fans so that the lower halves of their faces were masked, emphasizing the eyes.

Those paintings made Lana feel like she was being watched.

Not the best decor to have in an abandoned hotel lobby.

She shivered, and not just from the paintings: it was freezing inside.

Lana's eyes were drawn to the far side of the lobby, where the glass doors of the main entrance had been smashed. Snow drifts formed eerie white piles just inside the doors, while outside the blizzard had intensified to near whiteout conditions.

"This isn't good." Shui's breath misted. "Not good at all. Let's go back. To the spaceport."

The port was probably entirely shut down now, given the conditions outside, but she wasn't about to tell her friend that.

Lana checked the Net.

Still offline.

The hotel would have had its own InterPlaNet node. The fact that the aReals and Implants of the hotel guests didn't form a data bridge to the next node told her that the hotel was nearly empty of both humans *and* robots. Assuming the robots hadn't simply disabled their network nodes.

And also assuming that the InterPlaNet nodes weren't down citywide . . .

Lana had to know for certain whether the flight crew was here, so she tiptoed into the lobby, making her way toward the elevators.

In the middle of the lobby she passed a toppled luggage cart. Travel bags were scattered on the floor alongside it; one of the suitcases had broken open, leaving clothes splayed across the dark tiles. There was a small pool of blood beside the cart.

So far, Mei managed to keep her baby quiet. Lana hoped that would continue to be the case; their lives could very well depend on it.

Though the main lights remained on, the power had been cut to the elevators, so the three of them were forced to take the stairwell. Lana and Shui set a good pace, and to Mei's credit, she kept up.

On the eighth floor, Lana opened the exit door and peered out. The long hall seemed empty. The doors lining either flank were shut. A ninety-degree bend at the far side led to the remaining rooms.

It was somewhat warmer up there, but Lana's breath still misted slightly when she spoke. "Here we go," she said.

She led her companions to door number 801, the room of her copilot, Keai. She knocked. No answer.

She tried again. "It's Lana," she said, softly.

The main hallway lights abruptly flicked off, and the emergency lights kicked in.

"Lana . . ." Shui said.

Lana checked the Net one last time.

Still down.

She tore off her aReal sunglasses: she could see better without them in the dim light.

She hurried now, moving from door to door. The spaceline crew had reserved the first nine rooms on this floor; she knocked on each and every one of the designated doors and quietly identified herself, but no one answered.

A beam of light appeared at the far end of the hall, coming from around the bend.

Lana heard the characteristic whir of a servomotor.

"This way," Lana whispered. She led her companions to the room she shared with Shui. The door unlocked immediately at her approach, which meant the hidden sensors in the door still had power, thankfully.

They all piled inside and Lana shut the door behind them. The curtains were closed, and the scant sunlight that managed to filter inside gave the room a gloomy quality.

The baby whimpered, seeming on the verge of an all-out bawling session. Mei perched on the edge of the bed and made desperate cooing sounds as she rocked the child.

Lana didn't think it was going to work. She was positive the baby sensed the frantic mood of everyone in the room and was going to reveal them to the approaching robot outside.

But then the child miraculously calmed down.

Shows how little I know about babies, Lana thought. Maybe children had a sixth sense of some sort, warning them when danger was near. Whatever the case, the baby did not cry.

Lana and Shui listened by the door as the heavy footsteps heralding the approach of the robot grew in volume.

When the footsteps were right outside, the robot halted.

Lana and Shui remained very still. Neither of them dared gaze through the fisheye lens of the peephole.

Mei had clamped her hand around the baby's mouth, and Lana was afraid the child might suffocate. She almost moved toward the bed to force the woman's hand down.

But she did not.

Her own self-preservation instinct had kicked in, and she couldn't move or make a sound if she wanted to.

She hated herself in that moment.

The footsteps resumed, continuing toward the stairwell. Those heavy thuds receded as the robot descended to the floor below.

Lana slumped against the door.

Shui let out a long breath.

Mei lowered her hand. The baby coughed and resumed breathing. The child seemed fine. Thankfully.

Utterly relieved, Lana went to the bed in the dim light, and sat down. She wanted to scold Mei, but what did she know about babies? Maybe there was no chance the child would have died.

Lana saw a shadow standing in the corner of the room, near the curtain. The shadow's eyes glowed yellow.

Lana started.

Shui had seen the shadow too. "Lana, we have to get out of here!" Her friend ran toward the door.

The robot made no aggressive movements.

"Shui, wait!" Lana said. "Wait. It's just Dong. It seems to be operating normally." She turned toward the robot: "You scared me, Dong." "Dong" was a common name people gave to the loaner robots found in hotel rooms.

The baby started crying.

"Calm your baby!" Shui said.

Mei tried to silence the child, to no effect.

Was the baby's sixth sense trying to tell them something?

Lana stared at the dark form of the robot.

She realized something.

The room had an outdoor balcony, hidden behind the curtain.

"Dong?" Lana said. "Have you stayed in the room all this time? Or have you gone out on the balcony?"

Dong emerged from the shadows.

Glowing blue droplets surrounded its chest piece.

CHAPTER ONE

Rade

You could tell how a man died by the smell.

A man who died of a gut wound smelled the worst, followed a close second by a man who'd suffered a grenade wound. Burn deaths smelled like roast pig. Cranial wounds smelled strangely of fish (someone told me that it was the eyes). Sometimes lung wounds smelled of tobacco. Heart wounds smelled like blood: metallic, coppery.

The man on the ground below me had died of a head wound, and the fishy smell of him filled my nostrils.

I was dressed like the dead man, wearing a privateer's black, strength-enhancing jumpsuit, with an open faceplate. Holographic lighting units were arrayed along the bottom rim of my helmet and projected an image over my face so I looked like an SK (Sino-Korean) thug.

I was on Pontus, a colony world in Gliese 581. The system itself was officially owned by the Franco-Italians, but the SKs had purchased and developed Pontus primarily because of its proximity to

Tiàoyuè De Kŏng Gate, whose Slipstream led to Tau Ceti and the heart of SK space. (Slipstreams were the only way starships could "jump" the vast gaps between systems, and required the use of Gates to enter safely. These Gates led to and from fixed locations, so you couldn't simply jump anywhere you wanted.) Tau Ceti was where the UC (United Countries) had built the secret Gate to Geronimo, eight thousand lightyears away. A Gate that was now dismantled.

Pontus. A small pocket of SK space in a system that was otherwise neutral. The planet was basically enemy territory, and off limits to the UC. If I were captured here, let's just say the United Countries would be in a world of trouble. Actually no, that's not true. They'd merely disavow my actions and call me a rogue asset. So *I'd* be the one in a world of trouble, at least until my platoon brothers came to the rescue.

And they would.

That was what most of my missions were like. Direct action: getting up close and dirty with the enemy. Ah, the wonderful life of a MOTH (MObile Tactical Human).

The SK terraformers had done a bang-up job here on Pontus. The air contained twenty percent oxygen, pressing down at a comfortable 1.07 standard atmospheres, while temperatures planetwide averaged a balmy 30 to 35 degrees Celsius (86 to 95 Fahrenheit). The surface of the planet was roughly ninety percent water, and sandy atolls populated with palm trees made up the remaining ten percent, giving the entire world a tropical island air.

It was almost paradise.

Tell that to the dead man in the flora below me.

I lay chest down on the edge of an elaborate wall of thick stone that surrounded a sprawling palatial compound. The wall's copestone proved wide enough to comfortably hold a prostrate sniper such as myself. A slight berm along the inner rim of the wall formed a sort of parapet, offering a convenient hide.

My platoon brother Lui was our inside man in the palace. He posed as an SK manservant, placed two weeks before. He'd had some minor cheek and nose reconstruction done to fool any facial scans (moles in Big Navy had leaked sensitive data to the SKs, and our classified files had ended up in the hands of privateers on more than one occasion).

Lui was the reason we had full blueprints of the palace. This morning he'd also deactivated the perimeter sensors, which were cleverly embedded into the many statues of the Paramount Leader that ornamented the wall I lay on at this moment. Trace, Ghost, and I had circled the perimeter and sniped all the cameras and other sensors anyway, just to be safe. Since Lui had replaced the camera outputs with vid feeds, the security algorithm shouldn't notice the difference anyway.

We'd also taken down all the outer sentry robots, leaving them in shot-up piles at various points outside the wall. Snakeoil's Node-jammer had prevented the robots from sharing telemetry data, so we didn't even have to eliminate them in unison.

The dead privateer below me, just inside the wall? One of the few human sentries inside the compound. He'd decided to take a piss at the wrong time and Trace had been forced to shoot him.

There were five more sentries—three robot, two human—patrolling the compound grounds within, but they weren't my concern just now. I wouldn't be able to harm them anyway, not with this weapon—I'd switched out my sniper rifle for a tranquilizer gun hours ago.

I was gazing through the scope of the tranq even now, aiming at the palace. Specifically, through a certain window, at a certain door. Lui had left the window open at our request. It wouldn't do for bulletproof glass to get in the way of a tranquilizer dart.

Because of the dictates of the mission, I couldn't look away from that door, not for a moment. I did keep my other eye open for situational awareness purposes, but other than that, all I'd known for the past three hours was the feel of the tranq gun in my arms, the sight of the closed door in my scope, and the fishy scent of the dead man below. The palace itself was just an unfocused blur in the background, this brown lump of a pagoda with dragon statues guarding the entrance (though they looked more like giant worms than dragons to me).

The palace, and the island it was built on, was owned by the privateer financier Lóng Xiōng, or Serpent Heart. He was responsible for financing some of the most infamous privateer crews out there, including the crew of Mao Sing Ming, the murderous "Malefactor of the East," who my leading petty officer, Facehopper, had personally taken down. Lóng Xiōng procured the ships and weapons, and the privateers gave him half their profits.

From the looks of it, he'd become a very rich man. Blood money. It'll buy you the world. But what it won't buy you is a modicum of decency. Nor protection from those who would see your kind forcibly removed from the world.

Today, our financier was having some sort of pool party. Scantily clad women and female Artificials lounged on the pool deck. The Artificials were obviously Skin Musicians—gorgeous, sensual robots too perfect to be actual women. They looked like they were straight out of a porn vid: long hair, flawless skin, curves to die for, shaved in all the right places. Their every movement oozed sensuality and coquettishness, and I knew they were well versed in man-pleasing.

The financier himself wasn't present at the party. Not yet, anyway. He was inside the palace, behind the door in my sights, meeting with a privateer captain whose shuttle had arrived this morning. With Lui's help, we'd positively ID'd the second man as Hóng Húxū, or Redbeard. He was almost as notorious as Mao Sing Ming had been. With his arrival, the operation had been greenlighted.

And here we were.

"I'm getting a cheeseburger when we get back," Ghost transmitted subvocally, via his Implant. The albino was staring into the scope of a tranquilizer gun beside me. His job was to take out the privateer captain, while I was to handle the financier. Once we got them, we'd switch back to our Mark 12 sniper rifles.

Earlier, Snakeoil had carefully measured out the tranquilizing dosage required for the two targets. The financier was heavier, so my dart had more of the tranquilizing agent meted out. Even so, if the dosage was even slightly off, the stuff could cause death in minutes via heart-lung stoppage. Which was why we all carried the antidote.

I resisted the urge to look at Ghost. I had to keep my eye on the closed door. "How can you think about food with that smell?" I sent back. "I've almost retched three times."

"What smell?" Ghost returned.

"The smell coming from the dead guy."

"Ah," the albino sent. "Hardly even noticed it. All I smell is barbecued meat."

"Bro, there's no barbecue down there."

"When you've been staring into your scope for three hours straight and your stomach starts to growl with enough force to give away your position, all you can think about, and all you can smell, is grilled cheeseburger. It's my greatest dream right now."

"Ghost, if your greatest dream is to eat barbecued cheeseburger, you've got some self-improvement to do."

Eight months ago I would have never dreamed of talking to Ghost that way. As a friend, I mean. I was the new guy. The guy who had to prove himself.

But my platoon brothers respected me now. I'd proven myself in battle. I'd covered their asses, taken bullets for them, patched them up while hell rained down on us. When the fecal matter hit the fan, I was the one who kept my wits and found a way out of the situation. More often than not, that involved strategies and tactics no one else had thought of, such as turning off said fan and letting the fecal matter drip right back at whoever had thrown it.

Still, I've had my doubts about my abilities. I lost two very important people in the past, and a part of me still thought it was my fault. If any more of my brothers died because of something I did, I'd never forgive myself.

"I can has cheezburger?" Trace said subvocally, mocking Ghost from his own position on the wall ten meters to my left. He was equipped with a sniper rifle, not a tranquilizer gun. Trace was East Indian, Bengali to be exact. He'd shot me in the arm during training as part of my Combat Resiliency Qualification. I didn't hold it against him—he was just doing his job.

"Har har," Ghost sent back.

"You know, it's too bad we can't just terminate both targets," Trace said. "Why the UC wants to capture scumbags like these alive is beyond me."

I kept my eye on the door. I didn't have to look at Trace to know he was aiming his rifle into the compound at this very moment, ready to snipe with lethal accuracy. I knew I could trust him with my life.

I heard Tahoe shift behind me. He was watching our backs, heavy gun in hand. "You know the political situation," Tahoe said via his Implant. "There's been way too much backlash lately. We take them alive or we don't take them at all."

Tahoe Eaglehide was Navajo, with a wife and two children back on Earth. A good friend. The best. I'd known him from the beginning. He, Alejandro, and I had enlisted together. Officially, I was supposed to call him by his callsign, "Cyclone," but it never really stuck. Not for me.

"Hey, I'm just saying, things would go a lot more smoothly if we could just drop the two of them," Trace said. "Send in a drone, and we're done. Or have Lui do the deed from the inside, and make it look like an accident. But noo, we have to take them *alive*."

The last three drone assassinations didn't go over too well with the media. The political fallout was intense, with the SKs threatening to declare all-out war if another "innocent" SK citizen was executed by a drone launched by "UC cowards."

"Moe just passed checkpoint Wheat Lager," Trace said, this time over the platoon-level comm. "Should be coming up on your two o'clock, Facehopper."

Moe was one of the three remaining privateer robots patrolling the inner grounds. All three were military-grade humanoids, armed with assaults. Basically equivalent to the UC's Centurion-style combat robots. Trace had nicknamed them after characters from his favorite Net comics, while the two human privateers on sentry duty got the names of the Golden Age pirates Blackbeard and Kidd.

"Confirmed," Facehopper said over the comm. His four-man fire team was positioned on the opposite side of the courtyard. "Moe in sight, checkpoint Pale Malt. Blackbeard is up next."

The seconds ticked by.

Facehopper's voice came over the comm again. "Rage, Ghost: How are you blokes holding up?"

"Mighty fine, sir," Ghost said, chuckling slightly. He was just as tense as I was.

"Hang in there."

"Yes, sir," Ghost said. "You know how much we love hanging."

"I do indeed. Balls in and tits up."

Twenty minutes later, the door I had been watching so carefully through my scope finally opened.

When you acted as a sniper, waiting for your target, the moment of action always arrived unexpectedly. And if you blinked, or you sneezed, you missed it. Which is why you always had your finger on the trigger, and your eyes on the target. But you had to be careful, because sometimes—actually most of the time—things didn't quite go according to plan.

I almost pulled the trigger of the tranq gun.

Thankfully, I didn't.

Because it wasn't the target: a woman had walked out, and she didn't match any of the profiles.

"Uh, who's that?" Ghost sent over the comm.

"The financier's girlfriend," Facehopper sent, obviously viewing our vid feed. "Look sharp, people."

No one else emerged from the room. The woman sauntered down the hall, toward the window Lui had left open for us, and once she was there she rested her elbows on the windowsill. She leaned out dreamily, looked at the pool, and waved at one of the girls, who waved back. After a moment the woman retreated from the window.

But then she turned around, and cocked her head as if considering something.

Then she closed the window.

"Are you guys seeing this?" Ghost sent. The disbelief was obvious in his subvocalization.

Bulletproof glass now resided between me and the doorway.

Tranquilizer darts couldn't penetrate bulletproof glass.

The woman took the stairs and vanished from view.

"Trace, we're going to need you to poke some holes in the window when the targets emerge," I said. Which could be any second now, given that the door in my sights remained wide open. "Transmitting visual data." I sent him a snapshot of my current point of view, so he'd know where to make the hole. Ghost sent him a snapshot, too.

Modern bulletproof glass didn't shatter when armor-piercing rounds hit. All you could do was poke holes in it, if you had the right rounds. Some armor piercers wouldn't penetrate on the first try, and merely caused a messy crater until you fired two or three times. MOTH sniper rounds always penetrated on impact of course, passing through and continuing on the same trajectory, striking any objects beyond with roughly two-thirds the original energy, which was more than enough to kill. So he'd have to make sure the target wasn't in the line of sight when he fired.

Still, since the glass didn't shatter, subsequent shots at different targets were made harder by the artifacts left behind on the surface. Which was why it was important that Trace made his holes in just the right place.

"Received data," Trace responded. "Two new assholes coming right up."

"Try not to kill the targets in the process," I said.

"Mmm," Trace sent. "I'm going to have to reposition. Widen my angle."

"Do it. We don't know when—" I broke off as the financier emerged from the room and ambled into my sights. He was all smiles, as was the privateer captain at his side. "Targets in sight. Repeat, targets in sight. Trace, we need those holes!"

"On it."

The financier and the privateer captain were walking toward the staircase that led down from the hall. I was going to lose my target in seconds . . .

"Trace . . ." I said.

The Bengali fired his silent rounds, and three fresh holes appeared in the glass, the bullets striking the wall just inside.

I aimed through one of the bullet holes—

The financier was starting to react to the perforated glass—

I took the shot.

Direct hit.

Beside me, I heard the muffled sound of Ghost's tranquilizer gun going off.

Both targets toppled to the floor.

29

The tranquilizer darts were equipped with medical sensors. I glanced at the heartbeat monitors assigned to the targets on my HUD (Heads-Up Display). Their hearts were beating, albeit slowly. So far, so good.

"Targets tranquilized and stable!" I said over the comm, though everyone else would see the vitals on their HUDs by now.

I rested the tranquilizer gun on the copestone beside me and brought the strap of my sniper rifle down from my shoulder.

"Moe and Blackbeard are in my sights," Trace sent. "Taking them down."

It was only necessary to capture the two main targets alive. Anyone or anything else with a weapon was considered an enemy combatant and engageable by the ROE (Rules of Engagement).

Trace let off two quick shots with his sniper rifle. Like our weapons, his muzzle was silenced, and no one poolside yet noticed.

"Targets down," Trace sent.

While the sound of a silenced rifle might be unnoticeable, two sentries toppling to the ground and bleeding out, on the other hand, was very noticeable.

Sure enough, I heard the high-pitched scream of a woman, and all hell broke loose.

Gunfire homed in on me from the courtyard.

I flattened myself against the stone, ducking behind the inner rim of the wall. Chips of concrete flew past my head.

"F2 taking fire from the courtyard!" I said. F2 stood for Fire Team Two. We'd gone for simple names today.

I switched my viewpoint to a nearby support drone.

The women by the pool continued screaming and running. The Skin Musicians with them did the wise thing and simply dropped.

I heard return fire from the far side of the compound, and the incoming bullets abruptly ceased. I switched back to my helmet point of view, and glanced over the rim: the remaining three combatants had fallen. Their bullet-ridden bodies lay scattered at various points along the concrete pool deck.

"F1 moving in," Facehopper transmitted.

I glanced at my HUD map and saw four green dots approaching the palace entrance: Facehopper's fire team was closing in to secure the targets.

A few tense moments passed. I scanned the palace windows with my sniper rifle, occasionally flicking my eyes to the HUD map to keep apprised of the situation. Trace had spotted combat robots on patrol inside the palace earlier. Passing in and out of view beyond the windows, the robots had moved in a semirandom pattern that made it impossible to predict where they would show up next.

I caught a flash of movement beyond one window, then a second flash at nearly the same time from a different window farther back. I rewound my vision feed a few seconds, repositioned it in the upper right of my HUD, and played it back at a quarter of the speed.

At that slower playback, I was able to discern exactly what had sprinted past the windows. I saw the blur of box-like shapes; light glinted off black and yellow polycarbonate skin.

Combat robots, as suspected.

"Facehopper," I sent over the comm. "Combat robots are rushing toward the palace entrance."

In reply, distant gunfire erupted from the palace.

"F1 taking fire," Facehopper sent. "Sending in HS3 drones." HS3 stood for Hover Squad Support System. HS3s were basically basketball-sized, jet-propelled robotic scouts. The little round bastards were tricky as hell for human snipers to target because of their jerky movements, but they were relatively easy for robot snipers to take down. Either Facehopper wanted to get some limited telemetry on the combat robots, or he wanted to distract them. Maybe both.

On the HUD map, blue dots representing the HS3s fanned outward from behind Facehopper. New dots appeared, these ones red, as the HS3s transmitted the locations of the enemy combatants to our Implants.

I couldn't get a bead on any of the targets from where I was perched. The combat robots inside the palace had positioned themselves well, and they'd taken into account the lines of fire from the windows in addition to the foyer.

The blue dots of the HS3s abruptly blinked out, and the red dots froze. The scouts had been shot down. Like I said: easy targets for robots.

"We're pinned!" Facehopper sent. "Three combat robots! Palace foyer. Snipers, can you take them out?"

"Negative," Trace sent.

"I got nothing," I said.

"Same," echoed Ghost.

"Lui?" Facehopper sent.

"On my way," Lui transmitted.

On the map, I saw the green dot representing Lui move away from the servant's quarters on the far side of the palace, where he'd been lying low.

Three red dots abruptly blocked his path.

Lui paused, as if answering some challenge.

One of the red dots faded to black, indicating a terminated target, then the dot representing Lui dodged to the right, ducking within what looked like a side hallway.

"I'm pinned," Lui transmitted.

"Dammit," Facehopper sent. "We have to administer those antidotes or the targets will die."

I glanced at the heartbeat monitors overlaying my vision. I hadn't noticed during the mayhem, but the vitals associated with our two main targets had dipped.

Not good.

"I'm on it." I dropped down from the wall, into the flora that grew along the inside of the compound, and landed beside the dead sentry whose smell I had complained of earlier. I raced toward the pool area.

The moment I hit the concrete deck I started taking fire. I dove behind one of the potted plants that bordered the pool area. Had the automated defense systems reactivated?

Shards of clay broke away from the urn that held the plant, and I crouched lower. Suppressive fire came from my platoon brothers on the wall behind me, giving me a chance to peer past the rim. That's when I realized my attacker wasn't part of the automated defense system at all, but rather one of the scantily clad "party" women. Crouched behind the diving board, she'd produced a powerful 9-mil, and she knew how to use it. Likely a privateer, then.

I was about to take her down. But something stopped me.

I remembered what the job counselor had told me when I first signed up: someday there might come a time when I'd have to shoot a beautiful woman to save myself or my platoon. I'd told the counselor I'd have no problem doing that. I promised him I'd be able to perform my duty without question, no matter who got in my way.

And yet now that it came to it, I hesitated.

"Rage," Trace sent. "I can't get a clear shot on the diving-board shooter. Can you take her out?"

"I'm going to go back for my tranq gun," I said. "Ghost, toss it down when I get to the wall."

"That's a negative, Rage," Ghost sent. His voice sounded strained. "You'll get hit if you leave cover. The shooter's good. She already got me in the shoulder. Use your rifle. Take her down."

Damn it.

I aimed past the edge of the potted plant while my platoon brothers laid down covering fire. I had a partial shot—I saw the woman's hair just beyond the diving board, outlined in red by my Implant.

Dark hair.

Now I knew what it was that prevented me from firing.

She reminded me of Shaw.

The woman I had lost in Geronimo system, eight thousand lightyears away.

"Rage!" Trace said. "Our targets are dying!"

Forget about the financier and the privateer. The two targets didn't matter right now, nor did the mission objective. All that mattered was the life of my teammates. And every moment of hesitation on my part might cost a teammate his life.

Already Ghost had been shot in the shoulder, probably because of my inaction.

Who else would have to suffer, maybe die, because I was too afraid to shoot a beautiful woman?

I took the shot.

The woman slumped, her temple hitting the concrete, her arm splaying out beside her. Blood poured from an unseen head wound onto the deck.

I hunched.

I felt like an executioner.

A murderer.

I wanted to give up right there.

I'd killed a woman.

For no reason.

Wait. I was being too hard on myself. She *was* shooting at me and my platoon mates. That was reason enough.

No one tries to kill my platoon brothers.

No one.

I got up.

If I didn't get to our main targets and administer the antidotes, the woman's death would be for nothing.

I reached the back door and flattened myself against the wall beside it. Ghost remained in overwatch position, but Trace and Tahoe joined me to take up positions on the opposite side of the door. The holographic projections from their helmets made them look like SKs, and if it weren't for the green outlines around their bodies and the labels provided by my HUD, I might have shot them.

"I don't think our disguises are keeping the bullets away," Trace commented, subvocally.

"As long as the surveillance cams record privateers kidnapping privateers, we're fine," I returned, maybe a bit too forcefully.

Trace's holographic face gave me a considering look. "She wasn't a civvie, Rage."

"I know."

"You had to shoot her," Trace pressed. "It was either her or us."

"I know." The irritation was obvious in my subvocalization. I don't think Trace realized I was more angry at myself than him, though. "Now, are you ready?"

"Go for it," Trace sent. "ROE say we're good. None of the civvies came this way. They all fled the compound."

"What about the financier's girlfriend?"

Trace shrugged. "Either she fled, or she's still in there. It's not going to change the ROE. If she shoots at us, we shoot back. If she doesn't, she lives."

"Yeah, unless we mistake her for an enemy," I said, sarcastically.

Well, there was no time to argue about ROE now. The main targets were dying in there. I just hoped whatever we did here today didn't come back to haunt us later.

I waved my hand over the motion sensor and the door slid open.

I made a last glance at the HUD map to confirm no friendly units resided in the room beyond, then I cooked a grenade.

"Frag out," I said over the platoon-level comm, and threw the grenade into the room.

The explosive detonated.

Keeping crouched, Trace and I entered the room. I positioned myself to the left of the entrance, against the wall, while Trace took the right. I went high, Trace low.

I scanned the room from left to right. I fired a few preventive shots at a cabinet in the hall beyond, in case any enemy combatants had taken cover behind it.

"What you got?" Trace sent in response to my gunfire.

"*Nada*," I answered. "Tahoe, left."

"Coming in left!" Tahoe plowed inside and positioned himself against the wall behind me, and began scanning the room.

"Making a circuit!" Trace said.

I waited for Trace to complete his circuit of the room. The Bengali moved quickly past the outgoing doorways, ducking from furniture piece to furniture piece. In a moment he was back at the entrance.

"Clear!" he said.

I nodded, and marked the room as clear on the map.

"Tahoe and I will administer the antidote to the targets upstairs," I told Trace. "Make your way to the foyer and see if you can help Facehopper."

Funny how small microdecisions can lead to big disasters. Looking back, I realized I should have kept Trace with us. But when you're riding the adrenaline high of the moment, it can be tough to see the bigger picture.

Trace nodded, then hurried toward the westside doorway, which would eventually take him to the foyer, as per my instructions. I could hear the distant, steady exchange of gunfire coming from that direction.

Tahoe and I cleared the next room in much the same manner, and then carefully proceeded up the ornate spiral staircase on the far side. We kept our rifles trained on the balcony above. It seemed free of combatants, at least from down here. Ordinarily I would've launched a preemptive grenade just in case, but I couldn't do that because our main targets were unconscious up there.

Luck was on my side that day, because when we were about halfway up those stairs I spotted a rifle muzzle slinking between the upper banisters.

"Down!" I said.

Tahoe and I dropped where we were. A grenade bounced down the steps.

Tahoe and I looked at each other, then we activated our jetpacks in full horizontal reverse.

The grenade went off seconds after we'd left the stairwell.

The explosion hurtled me into the far wall, and I slid to the floor.

Gunfire erupted from upstairs. I rolled behind a small cabinet, feeling groggy. I was vaguely aware as Tahoe took cover on the floor across from me, beyond the lower banisters of the spiral staircase.

I blinked away the dizziness long enough to say over the comm, "Taking fire from upstairs!"

We could've really used Trace right then.

"Hold on!" Facehopper sent.

I glanced at Tahoe's vitals. Bright green, as before. The vitals representing the financier and privateer captain, conversely, were a dark green tinged with red—it wasn't them shooting at us. They were still unconscious, and we'd lose them, soon.

Pieces of the cabinet broke away beside me as bullets from above traveled right through the thick wood. I may as well have hidden behind papier mâché for all the good it was doing me.

"Rade," Tahoe said. "Armor piercers!"

"Kinda figured that," I said. "I'm a bit vulnerable here. Some cover?"

Tahoe let loose a wave of suppressive fire and I dove deeper into the room. I landed behind a couch.

"Well, this mission has gone downhill fast," I said.

"Got one of them!" Tahoe sent. Then: "Ugh!"

"Tahoe!" I peered out from behind the couch. "You okay?"

I saw him lying flat on the floor behind the banisters, unmoving. His vitals had taken a dip, and had suddenly grown very dark.

I fired suppressive rounds at the balcony. "Tahoe?"

Still he didn't move. Now I was getting worried.

I fired off more shots, getting ready to make a mad dash to his side. "Tahoe you son of a bitch, answer me!"

Finally he stirred. His vitals brightened. "Just got the wind knocked out of me is all."

"Where are you hit?"

He lethargically resumed his position behind the lower banisters. "The shoulder. Suit absorbed half the impact. I'll live."

"Shoulder wounds seem to be popular today." Better than head wounds.

I made a quick mental evaluation of the situation. I could still hear gunfire coming from the foyer, and I doubted help was coming from that side of the palace any time soon. Facehopper was relying on us to reach the main targets on the balcony by ourselves, if we could.

I wasn't about to let him down.

I examined the map of the second floor. I thought I saw a way to outflank the upstairs attackers. "Tahoe, can you cover me again?"

"Yeah." He sounded winded.

I instinctively glanced at his vitals again. Hadn't changed.

"Then do it. I'm going to make a break for the rear entrance."

He glanced at me from across the room. I thought he was going to ask me why I was going back again, but then he obediently laid down suppressive fire with his heavy machine gun.

He trusted me to the core.

I dove through the doorway into the adjacent room. I landed, rolled to my feet, and took cover beside the doorway. I made a quick scan of the room with my rifle, even though I'd already marked it as clear (MOTHs were cautious like that), and then I hurried to the rear door.

Outside, the pool area seemed quiet.

"How's it look, Ghost?" I sent, wanting to be sure.

"Not a creature is stirring, not even a mouse," Ghost replied from where we'd left him on overwatch. There was no hint of pain in his voice. He was carrying on his duties to his brothers despite his wound. Like any of us would.

I could still hear the roar of Tahoe's heavy machine gun behind me. "Tahoe, bro, let them return fire for a minute."

The heavy gun cut out.

I waited until I heard the sound of small arms fire from the next room, then I vaulted outside, spun around, and activated my jet-pack. I landed on the ledge just beside the upstairs window.

Grasping one of the eaves above me for balance, I carefully peered around the window frame.

It looked like I'd interpreted the map properly: this was the same window I thought it was. Beyond, I could see the assailants. They were privateer sentries, dressed in black jumpsuits. Two alive; one dead and bleeding out on the floor, thanks to Tahoe. The unguarded backs of the living two were exposed as they aimed down at Tahoe's position through the banisters.

Amateurs.

I was glad to catch a break here. If those buffoons had been combat robots, they wouldn't have made the mistake of leaving their rear unguarded.

Now I just had to figure out how to get a shot off through the bulletproof glass. The three bullet holes from Trace's earlier shots marred the center of the glass. I couldn't just ram the barrel of my rifle into the holes and fire, because there wasn't enough room to aim from the ledge. Nor could I create new holes from here, for the same reason.

But if I leaped backward, out into the empty air, and initiated a continuous burst from my jetpack . . .

I programmed the desired trajectory into my jetpack, using the position of the two privateers in relation to the window, and directed the autopilot to fire the appropriate nozzles to put me in position half a meter up and two meters away from the ledge and hold me there for three seconds. It would take me about two seconds to aim and fire at each target. If I missed, the privateers would likely reposition, and possibly snipe me before I landed.

I'd just have to make sure I didn't miss. Hopefully the artifacts in the glass from Trace's bulletholes wouldn't interfere with my aim.

Since this was going to be a relatively close shot, I made a mental note to use the iron sights built into the barrel, which would be visible through the translucent scope mounts.

I took three deep breaths.

One.

Two.

Three.

I leaped backward and engaged the autopilot.

The jetpack brought me to the designated position in midair, and held me there.

I aimed and let off two quick shots, moving the barrel between targets—

The bulletproof glass perforated twice beneath my powerful armor-piercing rounds—

I scored two successive head shots. The privateers died without even knowing what hit them.

"Tahoe, the upstairs hallway is clear," I transmitted as I soft-landed on the courtyard below. "I say again, the upstairs hallway is clear!"

"Proceeding to main targets," Tahoe returned, rather stiffly.

When I got upstairs, I hurried down the hall to Tahoe, who was crouched beside the financier and privateer captain.

Two empty syringes lay on the rug beside him—Tahoe had injected the antidote into each man.

It hadn't helped: neither of them was breathing.

Tahoe was attempting to restart the heart of the financier. Blood poured from Tahoe's shoulder wound and onto his jumpsuit as he worked, but he ignored it, staying focused on the resuscitation.

He glanced up in despair at my approach.

"We're too late," he said.

———

We confiscated all the computer equipment we could and returned to our jury-rigged privateer ship, the *Royal Fortune*, via the MDV (Moth Delivery Vehicle). After passing through the airlock and de-suiting, we were ordered directly to the briefing room.

Ghost and Tahoe bid us good luck and headed to the Convalescence Ward to get their shoulder wounds treated. I almost wished I was injured too, just to avoid the epic chewing out I knew the Lieutenant Commander was going to give the rest of us.

"Lóng Xiōng had the bank codes of every privateer he funded stored in that tiny bundle of neurons known as his brain," Lieutenant Commander Braggs said. He was the officer in charge of Alfa and Bravo platoons, MOTH Team Seven. He towered over us from his position at the front of the room, and though he was fifteen years my senior, he still had a full head of thick, brown hair. His face was mostly hard, angular planes, like the chisel-work of some Olympian statue. Speaking of Olympian, he had the body of an athlete despite his rank, and often joined us for PT (Physical Training).

"With Lóng Xiōng's cooperation," the Lieutenant Commander continued, "we could've identified those privateers at the ID level, and had our cyber attackers seize all their assets and shut them down without ever having to Gate into SK space. With one blow, we could've bankrupted half the privateers in the region, leaving them without any money to pay their crews. But now we're back to square one.

"What a debacle. Team Seven is supposed to harbor the best of the best. We're supposed to be the ace up Big Navy's sleeve. The Commander-in-Chief knows that if he has a mission whose success is critical, he can rely on us. Well guess what? He can't rely on us anymore. You failed. You're not the best. Not now. And you're not going to receive the most pivotal missions. Other task units are going to get called in a whole lot more, and we'll be the ones given the drudge work.

"Well done, people. Bravo Zulu. I hope you're proud of yourselves. I really do. What part of our warrior credo—'failure is not an option'—did you not understand? Because *failure is not an option*. And yet you failed. You better damn well hope the data we recovered from Lóng Xióng's computer systems contains the IDs and bank codes of the privateers he funded. And you better damn well hope we can decrypt that data in the first place. Now get the hell out of my sight."

We returned to the berthing area of the ship and did our best to prepare ourselves for the long voyage back.

Wasn't fun. The mood was abysmal throughout the platoon. None of us liked to fail a mission.

I couldn't help but feel it was my fault. Firstly, because of my hesitation when faced with a woman target, a delay that had cost precious moments. Secondly, because I had ordered Trace away just before Tahoe and I encountered the balcony shooters. If Trace had stayed, we would've eliminated the shooters faster. More lost moments. Finally, I should have triple-checked the tranquilizer dosage. Snakeoil had prepared it, but I was the one who had loaded the darts in the end.

I was starting to think I wasn't cut out for this anymore.

Did I mention I'd lost the two most important people in the galaxy to me eight months ago?

Well that was my fault too.

I wasn't a MOTH anymore. I don't know what the hell I was.

42

I was broken, that's all I knew.

I still had another eleven and a half years in my service term. I couldn't quit, not unless I wanted to get deported back to my native country. But I could always request a transfer to a different task unit. And being deported wouldn't be so bad anyway . . .

Bender and TJ, our drone operators, and two very smart guys, worked with the fleet cryptologists to decrypt the data we'd recovered from Lóng Xiōng's computers. On the third day, Bender returned to the berthing area early. The black man wasn't wearing his usual jewelry, and instead bore the puffy eyes and cracked lips of a man long deprived of sleep, but for all that, he had a big smile on his face.

"We cracked it, bitches," Bender said. High fives were exchanged all around. Mine were only halfhearted.

So disaster had been averted by a few very smart people in our midst. We got lucky. But that wouldn't always be the case. A time would come when the rest of the platoon wouldn't be able to cover the mistakes of the broken people like me.

The overall mood of the platoon improved markedly in the following days, though there was still a dour undercurrent to everything we did. By the time we reached the neutral space that was the rest of Gliese 581 and docked with the station *Divertimento Grande* above Gleise 581b, we were more than ready for our much-needed liberty.

But by that point, I'd already decided I wasn't going to hold these good men back anymore. These better men.

I was going to request a transfer out of MOTH Team Seven.

———

The Chief refused my transfer request.

"Give it a few weeks," Chief Bourbonjack said. Our fearless leader, Bourbonjack reported directly to Lieutenant Commander

Braggs. He was a grizzled man, with streaks of gray running through both his hair and beard. His dark eyes were always observing, taking in and measuring not only the situation at hand, but the temperament of the men around him. His nose matched those hawkish eyes—hooked, like a beak.

"If you still want to transfer to a different task unit or an entirely different Team two Stanmonths from now," the Chief continued, "I'll arrange a meeting with the Master Chief of Team Seven, and you guys can work something out."

"Thank you, Chief," I said.

"Dismissed."

That night found me in the space station's only flesh cantina (what they called strip clubs in these parts), where I partied it up with the rest of my platoon, though inside I felt like I didn't really belong anymore.

We all wore dorky badges printed up by Lui, labeled "Stripper-Advisor Top 500 Reviewer." Though we had no affiliation with the aforementioned Net site, Lui said it would work wonders for customer service. I think it had the opposite effect though, because the dancers paid most of us way less attention than the last time we visited—scared of getting bad reviews I guessed.

We'd brought along the two caterpillars recently assigned to our platoon, and they were paying for the beers tonight by unanimous vote (the two of them didn't get a vote). So, as you can imagine, we ordered more than a few drinks each.

I'd had about seven beers so far, but Manic was the current leader at nine. He'd pulled a passing dancer into his lap a few minutes before, and was blabbing his mouth off to her. He was bad enough when sober, but when inebriated, well, he wouldn't shut up. Also, he liked to move his hands a lot when he talked, and in his drunken state the movements were even more exaggerated. It was like he was conducting some symphony that only he could hear.

The most prominent feature of his face was the port-wine birthmark above his eye, vaguely reminiscent of a moth (the insect).

Manic was bragging to his girl about the mark even now. "See, I always knew I'd become a MOTH because of my birthmark." I could almost feel my brothers cringing around me. Flaunting our MOTH status to civilians was frowned upon. "It's why I signed up in the first place. But I bet you—"

The girl interrupted him, placing a finger on his lips. "You talk a lot. Would you like a dance?"

"What? No, I'd like to talk. It's what I do best. So anyway, as I was saying—"

The girl pouted. "Maybe later then?"

"Later? Yeah sure. Here, I'll buy you a drink. Stick around."

"I don't drink." She got up and turned away. She was dressed in a bikini, and her long, straight black hair reached the small of her back. As she lithely walked off, she looked over her shoulder and gave him a flirty wink, flicking that long hair of hers.

Manic threw up his arms when she was gone. "What did I do?"

"It's what you didn't do, dude," Bender said. "You were basically jabbering about yourself the whole time. You gotta give them time to talk about themselves, you know? It's like you're in love with the sound of your own voice or something." Ah Bender. He was always one to give unsolicited advice on picking up dancers, most of which only worked for him.

"What are you talking about?" Manic said. "This is a *flesh cantina*. They're here to listen to us. She sits down for two seconds and then asks me for a dance. Ridiculous. They're like sharks here. I think I'm going to head next door and rent myself a Skin Musician for the night instead."

"Two seconds?" Bender said. "She was with you for at least five minutes." The well-muscled black man had worn every last item of gold jewelry he owned: chains around his neck; big, hooped earrings; piercings on the outer tip of each eyebrow; labret stud beneath his lips; and multiple rings on each finger. Basically he'd pimped himself out to the max for the benefit of the dancers, and he looked like one tough dude. Which he was.

Bender was one of our drone operators who operated the robot support troops embedded with the unit. He'd suffered from a severe headshot wound on the Geronimo deployment. The same deployment where we'd lost Alejandro, Big Dog, and Shaw.

Anyway, the doc had worried Bender might experience an altered personality from the head wound, but he had made a full recovery, his charming persona completely intact.

Manic downed his ninth beer, spilling some on his beard, and waved for another. "I've been thinking . . ."

"Don't do that," Bender said. "It's bad for you."

Manic ignored him. "What a mess the Pontus raid was. The Lieutenant Commander was right. Completely right. We botched it big time. Even if we did fix things in the end."

"Thanks to me," Bender said.

Manic's tenth beer arrived and he took a long pull. "Course, if we'd been allowed to bring a few ATLAS mechs down with us, there wouldn't have been any problems in the first place. But oh no, we don't want to reveal that we're UC. We have to pretend we're SK privateers. I still think we should've brought along some SK-model ATLAS mechs. It's not like we haven't captured our fair share of them.

"Or we could've spray painted our own ATLAS mechs to look like the SK equivalents. The mechs are manufactured by the same company after all. Sure, there might be some slightly different parts, some different decals here and there, but they're basically the same. Speaking of SK mechs, you know what really pisses me off?"

"Yeah," Bender said, snickering. "When a girl rejects you."

Manic ignored him. "The SK military has quite a few ATLAS 6s in their inventory, while we're still stuck with the older model fives. It's not like the SK government has more money in their treasury or anything, but rather, they understand the value of investing in their military. I hear they pay their soldiers better, too. Of course, they don't feed their citizens, don't give out free robots and housing and all that, so obviously they can afford better ATLAS mechs and pay grades for their fighting men."

"That's not true at all," Lui, our resident Asian American, said. Like Bomb and Manic, he was one of the official ATLAS pilots of Alfa platoon. "The SKs feed their people, and give them servant robots. Don't be spreading lies about—"

Manic spoke right over him. "Maybe that's what the United Countries should do: stop giving away free food and housing to everyone, and—"

Bender leaned forward and grabbed Manic by the back of the head. "Manic," he said.

Manic looked at him, blinking rapidly, like he'd just woken up from a dream. A bad one. "Yeah?"

The black man slammed Manic's face down onto the table. Hard. "Shut up."

Manic recovered, and blinked his eyes rapidly. "Okay."

Bender sat back.

Manic opened his mouth to say something more.

Bender shot him a look.

Manic clamped his teeth down. He got up instead, and walked to a girl dancing on a table nearby. He held up his arm, likely transferring some bitcoins to her. She immediately bent down and let him motorboat in her cleavage. I thought he needed it.

"Manic does have a point," Bomb said. The other black man in our platoon didn't wear a single item of jewelry. His head was shaven on either side, and he'd dyed his short mohawk blond again. He had spiked it too, probably for the dancers—everyone had done a little extra grooming tonight. "We should've taken ATLAS mechs with us. I mean, come on, we were supposed to be privateers. They've stolen a few ATLAS 5s here and there."

"I wanted an ATLAS for myself down there too, but I'll have to play devil's advocate on this one," Lui said. "Mechs would've only gotten in the way. For one thing, an ATLAS 5 would have never fit in that palace. For another, the mechs would've made easy targets for the robot snipers."

"Hey, it's called a ballistic shield," Bomb said. "Learn to use it."

Lui frowned. "Not many privateers have ATLAS mechs anyway. Except for the richer ones."

"Well, that's about perfect," Bomb said. "We could have implicated one of the richer, more renowned privateer captains in our attack. Killed two birds with one stone."

"Maybe," Lui said.

"If the dimnuts in Brass would grow some balls and let us use the tech we were trained for . . ."

"Hey," Facehopper said. "That's enough. I won't have any of you dissing Brass today. Different topic, please. We've already talked the mission to death. What we could have done. What we should have done. It's pointless. It's over. We're on liberty now. And we're going to have fun. I know it's a strange concept to a MOTH. Fun. What is that? Well, you're going to learn to have fun mates, or die trying. Stop sitting around and pouting like a bunch of spoiled children who've had their expensive toys taken away. We don't need rifles and mechs every moment of our lives. We're surrounded by beautiful women. Let's enjoy this." Our Leading Petty Officer crossed his arms and sat back. He had a look in his eyes that said, "Go ahead and defy me on this, I dare you."

Fret started laughing. "You guys should listen to the LPO. This place is a hottie haven." Fret was the tallest member of our team, with a long neck like a giraffe's. His eyes were locked on the main stage, where a girl was gyrating sinuously around a pole to hippie metal music. "The strippers choose the songs they dance to, right?"

Facehopper nodded. "They choose the songs, yes, mate."

"I love her already." Fret wouldn't look away.

"You *would* like hippie metal," Bender said with a grimace.

"She's gotta be, what, four foot two?" Snakeoil said. He and Fret were our communicators. Snakeoil was the opposite of Fret in terms of build: he was about half Fret's height, and where Fret was lanky, Snakeoil was all muscle. "It's not going to work out. She's too short, dude. What, are you going to kiss your pillow the whole time you're having sex? Guys are visual creatures. You can't get turned on by a pillow. She's more my size, bro."

"If the pillow is soft, and moist, and furry, I'll get turned on, I guarantee you," Fret said. "Besides, the shorter ones have lots of energy. They bounce around a lot, especially when you let them go on top. Just the way I like it. I'll be getting my visuals, don't you worry."

Snakeoil shook his head. "She's tiny, man! She'll look like your kid when the two of you walk down the street together."

"I don't care." Fret kept staring, just rapt.

The girl on stage had noticed his stares, and she started shooting him wanton looks. I knew she'd be making a stop by our table when she finished her set.

Lui had ordered chicken wings earlier, and the basket arrived then, on a tray carried by a box-like robot on treads. It was kind of funny because, when you asked for drinks, one of the sensual waitresses delivered them, but when you ordered food, they sent in an old-school robot. It was almost like they were trying to discourage people from buying food.

"Finally." Lui shook his head. "Almost forgot I ordered these. Stupid robos. Have no appreciation for customer service. But of course they don't care. Most of them don't have emotions, and those that do, well, it's not enough."

"What do you know about robos?" Bender said. "They got more emotions than most people I know. Course, I mostly know MOTHs, so that doesn't say very much about you bitches, does it?"

"I apologize for the delay sir," the robot said.

"Yeah, yeah." Lui placed the basket in his lap, and his eyes defocused as he completed the transaction with his Implant.

"Thank you." The robot left.

"What do I know about robos?" Lui sat back, and promptly forgot about the basket of wings in his lap. "I'll tell you something, Bender. Back when I attended the University of Tennessee with Snakeoil, I worked part-time at Nova Dynamics. Postal Robotics division. Biggest provider of postal delivery robots. The bipedal ones, anyway. They make flying delivery drones too, but have a smaller market share in that area.

"You'd think we wouldn't need mail these days, what with the pervasiveness of 3D printers. But while those printers can photopolymer up almost anything people order online, the printers can't make food. Last time I checked, there weren't any nutrients in thermoplastics or polymers or clothing fabrics, not any that a human's gastrointestinal tract could safely absorb, anyway. Besides, a lot of the time it's cheaper to purchase a traditionally manufactured item over a 3D-printed one. And printing larger items like furniture is impractical at best, and cost-prohibitive at worst. Who can spare a room in their homes just to print up furniture, not to mention the cost of the printer and materials? So yes, we still need mail delivery.

"Anyway, my job at Nova Dynamics was programming the cloud computing resources the delivery robos used. Petabytes, and I mean *petabytes*, of information were collected on every customer in the country, storing every kind of point-of-sale information possible. Every purchase the customer had ever made was stored: the who, the what, the when, the where, the why, and the how. And I'm not talking just food purchases, but *every* purchase. Online purchases for the 3D printers, retail purchases at the store down the street, the take-out order from the local pizza joint, the lap dance from your favorite stripper. That's right, Nova exchanged cloud data with all the other merchant clearinghouses. Probably still does. Part of the 'fair use' policy when using their web properties. Cloud algorithms are in place to tag money launderers and other tax cheats, but a lot of the time that data is misused, and sold to other retailers so Net ads can be targeted to your buying habits, for example. Just hope you don't get a stalker working at Nova Dynamics.

"The age of robos heralded the end of the age of privacy. It's a dangerous age, where robotic eyes observe your every movement. With robots and security cameras everywhere, you're constantly recorded and analyzed by cloud computing resources, one wrong word or action away from being flagged and arrested. Let's just say, it wouldn't be a good thing for the robots to turn on us."

The unsaid reference to Geronimo was foremost in all our minds, I think. Because out there, eight thousand lightyears from home, our robot support troops had done just that, and turned against us.

Snakeoil tried to lighten the mood. "And here I always thought Fret was our regional provider of doom and gloom."

Fret was still staring at the woman on stage as she gyrated to the hippie metal music. The lanky communicator was enraptured, and hadn't heard a word of what was said as far as I could tell.

"No, he's just our village idiot," Bender said.

"That's getting cold by the way." I nodded at the basket of wings untouched in Lui's lap.

"Oh yeah. I sometimes forget about my stomach when I'm talking about things I'm passionate about." Lui retrieved a light stick from his side pocket and flashed a bright beam at the chicken wings.

"Are you taking pictures of your food with your Implant again?" Skullcracker said. The heavy gunner was relatively slight of build, but the daunting, realistic-looking human skull tattooed onto his face made up for any impression of weakness. You'd think the tattoo would repel girls. Not so. They were fascinated by him, and he had two dancers in his lap right then, though he didn't seem all that interested in them, which was probably an act. "Sure, I could understand if we were ordering filet mignon or some exquisitely arranged sushi. But greasy, deep-fried barbecue wings piled into a basket at a strip club?"

"Hey, I like food okay?" Lui said. "When we're in space, cooped up for months on end, these pictures get me by. They give me a chance to plan out my food itinerary for when I get back. What buffets to hit. What diners. You know."

Skullcracker chuckled, the skull tattooed onto his face bending into a ghastly shape. "Food itinerary. I like that."

"I'm a foodie," Lui said. "I admit it. And this is what we foodies do. Cuisine and the art of eating, the presentation of the food, it's all very important to us. Even if it's just a basket of wings. Besides, being a foodie is part of my cultural inheritance. You know that 'how are you' in Korean-Chinese basically translates to 'have you eaten yet,' right?"

"You greet each other in Korean-Chinese by saying *have you eaten yet*?" Skullcracker shook his head. He turned to TJ, who sat beside him. "Hey, have you eaten yet?"

TJ, our main drone operator, had a girl giving him a microcoin dance in his seat. That night he wore his usual tight tee that showed off the groove between his pecs and his bulging biceps to good effect. The olive skin of his left arm was tattooed to look like the arm of an ATLAS mech, replete with rivets and servomotors and swappable weapons. His right arm was inked with other military robots like the Centurion and Raptor, which competed for every square inch of skin. He also had an Atlas moth tattooed to his neck, the wings extending down his chest.

The girl's hand was also reaching down his chest as she ground against him . . .

"TJ, bro, you eaten yet?" Skullcracker asked again.

TJ leaned past his girl, spread his fingers in a V, and darted his tongue through the crack.

Skullcracker glanced at the rest of us, an amused light in his eyes. "That means no," he joked.

My gaze was drawn to Ghost behind him, who, in the black light, looked like a glowing demon with his pale skin and white hair. He had attracted his own type of woman: a lithe, pale beauty with black hair. She lay in his lap with her eyes closed, her head resting on his chest, a contented smile curving her plump lips.

The woman's smile reminded me of Shaw. It was the same smile she would wear after our lovemaking.

On the main stage, Fret's girl ended her set and the cantina band took over.

"You've been pretty quiet tonight, Rade," Tahoe said abruptly, leaning close so that his voice carried to my ears alone. He was seated beside me, and up until this point he'd had his eyes unfocused, a sign that he had been inside his Implant.

"What about you?" I said.

"Writing the wife. My little girl turned three yesterday, you know."

"That's great."

Tahoe nodded slowly. "Is it? I sometimes feel like I'm missing out on her life."

I had nothing to say to that.

"But enough about me," Tahoe said. "Obviously something's got you down tonight."

I pressed my lips together and looked away.

"We all miss them," Tahoe said suddenly.

I was glad I'd looked away, because I didn't want him to see the rapid blinking those words brought to my eyes.

We all miss them.

He didn't have to say who. I knew. I'd always know.

I heard laughter to my right. From Dyson and Meyers. They were the new caterpillars assigned to the platoon, and they sat apart from everyone else.

I didn't like them.

Actually, that was too mild a term.

I *hated* them.

What right did they have to come in here, thinking they could replace Big Dog and Alejandro? No one ever could.

I had to remind myself that of course the caterpillars didn't believe that. They were assigned to Alfa platoon by Lieutenant Commander Braggs and Chief Bourbonjack. But still, whenever I looked at them, I felt anger. I truly resented them.

Dyson had two girls sitting in his lap at this moment, and he was smiling and joking away with Meyers. Skullcracker was allowed to have two girls in his lap, but not Dyson. Never Dyson.

He thought he could laugh and have fun, did he? When good people had died so that he could be here?

I'd see about that.

I got up.

"Rade," Tahoe said, warningly. "Leave it."

I ignored him and stalked over to Dyson.

"No girls for you tonight," I said, forcefully hauling the dancers off him.

"Hey!" one of the girls said.

"Here." I transferred some microcoins to her via my embedded ID. "Go play with yourself in the corner or something."

Dyson stood up angrily. "What are you doing?"

"Who the hell do you think you are?" I said, shoving him back down. "What right do you have to be here? You're laughing, huh? It's all fun and games, huh? What right!"

Dyson stood up again. "I've paid my dues to get here," he said carefully.

My hand curved into a fist and I almost punched him right there. "You haven't."

We stared at each other, our faces only a few centimeters apart as the cantina band played in the background. His Asian American features were bunched up into a scowl.

I was seconds away from starting an all-out brawl with him. Seconds.

My fist tightened—

Then his face softened, and he looked down. "Sorry, sir."

"That's right. You're a little caterpillar and I'm a seasoned MOTH. Now sit down and shut up." I shoved him back into his seat and stormed away.

I went to the men's restroom and splashed my face in cold water.

"You've had too much to drink." Tahoe's voice came from behind me.

I dried half my face, and stared at my reflection in the mirror. "I don't know who I am anymore."

Tahoe's reflection smiled sadly. "You're Rade Galaal. A man of dignity. A man of honor. More than a man. A MOTH."

"I was," I said. I looked so much older. Had my face always had so many lines? "But not anymore. I left a part of myself behind on Geronimo. And I'm never getting that part back. I feel hollow inside."

"We all left a part of ourselves behind on that planet, Rade. We paid for our victory in blood."

My eyes had a haunted look now. The same look I had seen in Alejandro, when he was alive. He'd watched his whole family get gunned down. I finally understood his pain. "Was it a victory? I thought it was a loss. We were bloodied, and we ran away with our tails between our legs. We should have attacked that alien ship. We should have blown it out of the skies."

"If we'd tried that, none of us would be here today," Tahoe said. "The deaths of our friends would have been for nothing."

I didn't answer. I couldn't bear to look at myself anymore, so I lowered my gaze, and watched a drop of water trickle from my chin into the sink.

"You should really give the caterpillars a chance," Tahoe said.

"No I shouldn't."

"They seem like good kids." Kids. It was funny. They weren't that much younger than us, though it seemed a lifetime separated us from them.

"They'll never replace who we lost," I said. "Never."

"They don't have to," Tahoe said. "They only have to be there for us, when we need them most."

"Yeah." I closed my eyes. "Just like I was there for Alejandro when he needed me most, right?"

I felt Tahoe's hand on my shoulder. "Rade. You have to stop blaming yourself. I know it's hard. Hell, I still blame myself from time to time, even all these months later. But I take consolation in the fact that Alejandro wouldn't have wanted us to keep grieving like this. He would've wanted us to move on, and live our lives."

And what about Shaw? I felt like saying. *What would she have wanted? She died for us, too . . .*

Instead I said, "Yeah Tahoe. I hear you." I patted his hand, then lifted it from my shoulder. "Gotta start living." I don't think I sounded too convincing, but maybe he'd buy it and leave me alone.

"To that end, I believe it's time you made some new female friends." Tahoe dragged me from the restroom. I remembered a time when I called every restroom a "head" thanks to the indoctrination of Basic Training. Those were the good days. When Shaw and Alejandro were alive. Probably the best days of my life. Strange how when you're living the best days of your life you don't actually realize it at the time, not until it's all over. And once you do realize it, you yearn for those moments more than anything, but they never come back. Not ever.

"Come on, Rade. We're going to introduce you to Misty Mindy over here." Tahoe pulled me toward one of the dancers, who was performing atop a nearby table.

I resisted. "I don't want to meet Misty Mindy. I don't want any new female friends."

"Which is exactly why you have to do it," Tahoe said. "Besides, you're not going to be mere friends with Misty Mindy. When you're done with her, the Rade Galaal charm will have converted her into a fan."

He tore off his StripperAdvisor badge along with my own, then finished dragging me to the table where "Misty" was performing her little show.

She was dressed in a skimpy bikini. Her hair was dyed purple at the top, transitioning to blue at the tips. She had random sparkles glued all over her tanned, athletic body, and she had tiny blue-and-white stars tattooed along the right side of her face. She wore sparkling white makeup around each eye, which was supposed to look like mist, I guess.

Tahoe waved her over.

The dancer slithered down toward us, and smirked. "Hey boys." She rubbed a spot on her breasts just above her bikini top, suggestively circling her finger around the region. I made a point not to look.

"Gonna buy my bro here a lap dance," Tahoe said.

"I'll find you when I'm done with the table," she said, giving me a wink.

"This offer is time-limited and nonnegotiable," Tahoe said. "You give him a dance, and you give it to him right now."

She frowned at Tahoe.

"Do you see that 'incoming bitcoins' request on your Implant?" Tahoe said. "Do you see the size of it? I suggest you accept right now, because if you don't, I'm going to cancel it. The house is going to be very disappointed when they review their logs and see the amount you declined."

Misty's eyes defocused as she checked her own Implant. All dancers had civilian aReals implanted directly in their heads. Firstly, because they could afford it. Secondly, because they didn't want to wear an augmented reality device that detracted from their looks.

Misty glanced over her shoulder, waving with feigned regret at the other customers she'd been entertaining around the table, then she lowered herself to the floor.

"Let's go to the private dance room, honey." She grabbed me by the hand and dragged me away. I glanced at Tahoe helplessly.

The "private" dance room in this club was basically a shared room in the back of the cantina, with small partitions placed between stalls. There were no curtains or anything like that, so I could see into every stall as I walked by. I passed Fret on the way to my stall. He was getting a dance from the short girl he'd lusted over, and he slapped her naked behind while moaning, "Incoming!"

Yikes.

Misty sat me down, and started to take her skimpy top off.

I held up a halting hand. "Keep your clothes on. I'm not a client."

She grinned suggestively. "Okay."

She plunked herself squarely in my lap and wrapped her arms around my neck. "So, what brings you to our quaint little station?"

"Oh, you know," I said. "I'm part of a traveling space circus."

She giggled. "You're not in the circus, silly."

"Yeah, how do you know?"

She pouted, and brushed my cheek as she leaned forward to whisper in my ear. "Circus performers aren't quite so handsome."

I ignored the compliment, which was probably fake. "I'll have you know, I happen to be the greatest fire juggler who ever graced this side of the galaxy."

She sat back and smirked. "Really? What's your stage name?"

"Gaul the Great."

Her nose wrinkled up. "Gaul? What kind of a stage name is Gaul? That's like, an ancient region in France."

France.

Where Shaw grew up.

The thought made me suddenly depressed again, and I felt the smile leave my face. Strange, how a word, or mere reference to a place, could bring all my feelings for her rushing to the fore again.

I almost left.

The dancer sensed it. "What's wrong?"

I hesitated. "Have you ever felt regret?"

"That's random," she said.

"Yeah. Never mind." I became suddenly very aware of her arms wrapped around my neck, and I felt guilty.

Apparently sensing my discomfort, she removed her hands and sat back in my lap.

"So you're a MOTH," she said. It was a statement, not a question.

I didn't say anything, though I wondered how she knew. I wasn't wearing any badges, or a Navy uniform. As far as she was concerned I was just a heavily bearded civilian.

"I can tell," Misty said. "I meet a lot of people in my line of work. And men like you have a certain aura about them."

"An aura."

"Yes. A dangerous aura." She ran a hand through my beard. "You've killed a lot of men."

I sighed. That was the kind of thing most people thought when they found out I was a MOTH. "So is this what you talk about with all your customers?"

She twirled her hair with one finger. "I'm just making conversation. You won't let me give you a proper dance, so . . ."

I looked away, trying to think of a way to excuse myself without offending her. Although, I guess if I really wanted to go, I could've shoved her off and left.

But I didn't.

Deep down, I yearned for female company, even if I wouldn't admit it to myself.

"What was the worst thing that ever happened to you as a MOTH?" Misty said.

I met her eyes.

"Asking a man about his worst experience isn't the greatest stripper technique to use on a client, is it?"

"You're the one who said you didn't want to be a client, remember? So come on, tell me."

"You don't want to know," I deadpanned.

"*Come* on." She continued twirling her hair, like a schoolgirl with a crush. Oh she was good at faking attraction, all right.

"You're quite the hustler," I said. "Bet you have all the guys here under your spell. But I'm not buying it."

She frowned. A smile definitely suited her face better.

"Okay, let's make it easier," she said. "Tell me the third worst thing that happened to you."

I felt my jaw tighten. "You really want to know, don't you?"

"I do."

"Third worst thing that ever happened to me?" I didn't even have to think about it. "Killing a woman while on duty. Happened just the last mission."

Those words gave her pause. She stopped twirling her hair. There was a momentary flash of emotion in her eyes. Doubt and fear, mingled with . . . excitement?

"What was it like?" she said.

"As I said, one of the worst things that ever happened to me. A really bad feeling, right in the pit of my stomach. Like I'd just done something inconceivably wrong. She was so beautiful. She could have been a model. And I took her life. I took her whole future away from her." I couldn't believe I was telling Misty this. I'd never really talked about the privateer woman's death with anyone. I couldn't bring it up with my platoon brothers. It was just too painful. I preferred to wear a mask of toughness, no matter how fake it might be. Tahoe was the closest to sensing my real emotions, and even he usually kept his distance, though that night had been an exception.

"She deserved it?" Misty said.

I sighed. "No one ever *deserves* to die. Well, unless we're talking war criminals. But she was shooting at my platoon brothers. I had no choice. So I took the shot."

Neither of us spoke for a long moment. The distant music from the cantina band played on in the background.

"So what was the worst thing that ever happened to you, then?" Misty finally said.

Maybe I should have been insulted at this invasion of privacy, offended that this stranger would dare ask such personal questions. But instead I answered right away. No hesitation. No pussyfooting around. I guess revealing the other bit had allowed me to open the floodgates, and to be honest I was glad to have someone outside the platoon I could finally talk to this about.

"The worst thing was losing the two people in this galaxy who meant more to me than anything else," I said. "A man who was more than a brother to me. And a woman who was my world. My universe."

She stared into my eyes for a long moment. She must have seen the grief there, because she began blinking rapidly, like she was on the verge of tears. "What happened?"

"The woman sacrificed herself for my ship, staying behind so we could get away, while my brother gave his life for me on a planet when we were under attack. That's what it really means to serve, you know. You're not giving up your life for your country, or some ideal. You're giving it up for those who fight by your side. For your brothers in battle. You wouldn't let them down, not for a heartbeat. You'd die for them. And that's what these two did for me."

She was silent, just looking into my eyes, pondering what she saw there, I guess.

"You said this woman stayed behind," Misty said, eventually. "Why didn't you go back for her, when all was said and done?"

"You don't understand. There was no way to go back for her. The Gate leading to her region of space was dismantled. The Gate was hidden deep in hostile territory in the first place, so to go back for her would've required the coordinated efforts of multiple military branches, at a cost upward of tens of billions of bitcoins. There was just no way."

I said it like I was trying to convince her, when in reality I was trying to convince myself.

I should have found a way to go back for her. I should have. Now she's dead.

"You blame yourself," Misty said.

I didn't answer.

She pulled away slightly. "I'm going to tell you something, and you're probably not going to like it. But it needs to be said."

I felt one of my eyebrows rise. "Oh?"

"Because you're a MOTH, because of your training, and the missions you undertake, you believe the safety of those closest to you is your personal responsibility. Whenever something bad happens to someone close to you, it's your fault. You missed something. You overlooked some possibility or outcome that could've saved them. *You should have saved them.* But you didn't.

"Well I'm here to tell you that it's not your fault. It can't be. It never was. You can't view the world as a MOTH, not in this, not if you want to get over their deaths. Your friends made their own choices. They chose to give their lives for you. And who are you to take that sacrifice away from them, and place the blame for their deaths on your own shoulders, when they're the ones who made the choice? They wanted you to live. Don't cheapen their sacrifice by blaming yourself. Don't you dare."

I regarded her in a new light. "And you claim to be a dancer? You're more like a counselor, bartender, and therapist rolled into one."

She laughed. "That basically sums up my job description."

"Let me guess," I said. "You're dancing to put yourself through school?"

"Hardly. I dance for the money. Quite a lot of lonely guys out here on the colony worlds. But I do read a lot of books, I admit. Psychology, mostly. And philosophy. Helps me talk to men about their relationship issues."

"Well that's a relief," I said. "For a moment there, I thought you were going to tell me you were an Artificial."

"I am an Artificial," she said with a completely straight face. Then she shoved me. "Just messing with you."

It was my turn to laugh. "A dancer who reads philosophy on the side. I wasn't expecting that."

"Never believe in stereotypes. Nine times out of ten they're wrong." She extended her hand. "My real name is Claire." She'd finally dropped the stripper mask and all the pretenses that went along with it.

I shook her hand. "You don't look like a Claire. 'Misty' kind of suits you better. What with the tattoos and makeup you wear . . ."

She grinned widely. "They're temporary. So what's your real name?"

I hesitated, and almost wasn't going to answer, but I relented. "Rade."

"And you certainly don't look like a Rade."

I felt my brows draw together. "What's that supposed to mean? Who do I look like, then?"

"A Pete, maybe. Or a Frank."

"Frank? I look nothing like a Frank."

"How would you know?" she said. "Have you ever met a Frank?"

"Yeah, in fact I have. This guy in MOTH training. Skinny like you wouldn't believe. Toothpick arms and legs. Dropped-On-Request the first week."

"Sorry to hear that."

"Don't be. He didn't deserve to be there."

She cocked her head, as if listening to something only she could hear. "Time's up." She gave me her vid conferencing number. "Vid me if you're ever looking for a girlfriend."

She walked away in that sexy G-string of hers, hips swinging suggestively with each step.

I couldn't help but stare.

"I might just do that," I said quietly.

———

Liberty ended prematurely: the next day the Lieutenant Commander recalled the platoon to the ship bright and early, with an order to report to the briefing room at 0700 for an "important announcement."

Most of us slept right through the shuttle ride. When we arrived, we stumbled aboard the *Royal Fortune*, and stopped by the galley for coffee. From the drooping eyelids and jerky movements around me, it was obvious that most of us were still slightly hung over. I myself had a splitting headache.

"What do you think this important announcement is going to be?" Manic said to no one in particular as he grabbed a steaming cup of coffee from the vending machine.

"Dunno," Trace said, moving forward, zombielike. "Must—have—coffee."

"Maybe Braggs is announcing he's finally decommissioning your sorry ass," Bender told Manic.

"You know, that's almost funny," Manic said, smiling sardonically. "The word is *discharging*, by the way, not decommissioning. You decommission a warship. You discharge a soldier."

"Yeah, but you ain't human, dude, so you get to be decommissioned."

"Whatever."

Fret plugged an ancient-looking device into the ship's power system via a wide-brimmed adapter. Then he slipped two pieces of bread into the device's cooking slots.

Bender stared at Fret like he was crazy.

Fret shrugged off the look. "Burnt toast. Best hangover cure there is."

"Where in the *hell* did you get a museum piece like that?" Bender said.

"Manic's house."

Manic looked up from his coffee. "You stole my toaster?"

Fret ignored him.

"Hey, you stole my toaster? My mom gave me that."

Bender pantomimed wiping a tear away. "Aw, Mommy going to cry now?"

I wrinkled my nose. "Are you sure you have the power adapter set properly, Fret? Smells like you're charring the bread. Probably should take it out."

Flames burst from the two slots in the device.

Fret unplugged the device and fanned the top with his hands. Wasn't helping.

"Blimey!" Facehopper said. "Put it out before the SAFFiR comes in with its extinguisher grenades!" SAFFiR stood for Shipboard Autonomous Firefighting Robot.

Facehopper grabbed a nearby extinguisher and discharged fire-retardant foam all over the device.

"I didn't think the *Royal Fortune* had a SAFFiR," Fret said.

"Oh, she does." Facehopper said. "Fleet installed one. Cause a false alarm, and the Brass will dock the response costs of the SAFFiR from your salary."

Manic came forward and cradled the foam-covered remains of his bread device. "My toaster. You ruined my toaster."

Facehopper's eyes defocused. I thought he was checking the time. "Drink your coffees and down your aspirins, mates. The briefing is in ten minutes. You're lucky, because otherwise I'd make you hungover blokes all drop and do PT. In fact, hell with it, we got a minute to spare. Drop!"

Groans were heard all around, but we dropped.

"Come on!" Facehopper said. "You're MOTHs. Push 'em. Push 'em! Hump the floor! Hump! We work through hangovers. We've been through hell and back again. This is nothing. A little headache, a little dehydration, is minuscule compared to what we've been through. Come on you pussies—push 'em, push 'em, push 'em!"

The galley staff regarded us with amusement.

We completed precisely two minutes of hangover-busting push-ups. Gotta love PT (Physical Training).

Then we downed our coffee, took our aspirins, and rushed to the briefing room, arriving five minutes early. I felt wide-awake now. I still had a headache, but it wasn't so bad. Amazing what pumping the blood can do for you.

Lieutenant Commander Braggs arrived at 0700 on the dot.

"I'm sure you've heard the news," the Lieutenant Commander said, after he'd assumed the podium. "You're all extremely well connected, after all."

I exchanged uncertain glances with my platoon brothers.

"Sir," Fret said. "Respectfully, the only news we've heard is from the girls we took home last night."

The Lieutenant Commander was an easygoing kind of guy, and normally a comment like that would have elicited a laugh. But his face remained dead serious. Maybe he was still upset about the near-failure of our last mission.

No way! Tahoe sent on his Implant, via the platoon-level channel. *Check the main news feed!*

You'd think one of us would've bothered to check the news before now. But seriously, the last thing on our hungover minds was news.

I reluctantly pulled up my news feed. My eyes felt really scratchy, and focusing on the icons overlaying my vision only made the headache worse. Thankfully the Lieutenant Commander spoke before I got too far.

"We're being called back into action, men," Braggs said gravely. "Something has suddenly become a whole lot more important than tracking down privateers. In fact, the SK government has just outlawed privateering, so it's not even a problem anymore."

"A truce has been struck between the United Countries and the Sino-Koreans," Tahoe announced. "They're opening up their space to one another, for a select number of vessels."

That was indeed news.

"Correct," the Lieutenant Commander said. "But you haven't heard the why. There's a news lockdown. Won't last long, though. You can't hide something like this. Though speculation in the general public is running rampant. Some vids have already leaked out." He slid a hand through his thick, brown hair. A trembling hand. The Lieutenant Commander never trembled. Something was very wrong. "We all knew this would happen one day. I guess we just hoped it would come further down the road, well beyond our lifetimes. Not now, not when we were so blatantly unprepared."

He left the podium and walked down into our midst.

"Men. My men. Our greatest trial awaits." He looked at each and every one of our faces, as if he wanted to remember us in this moment, while we were still innocent and naive, while we still held on to our youthful idealism by however small a thread. As if he wanted to burn our features into his mind one by one, before he told us what had happened and changed our lives forever. As if he believed that only a short time from now, there might not be very many of us left alive *to* look at.

"Do you remember the alien vessel we encountered at Geronimo?" Braggs said. "The big one that looked like a giant skull?"

"How could we forget, sir?" Fret said.

"It's finally arrived in human space."

CHAPTER TWO

Shaw

So this was what prison was like.

Isolation from the world you once knew. Isolation from your favorite foods, your favorite places. Isolation from the friends, family, and loved ones you once spent time with.

Isolation from the very air of the world, living apart from it, inside a thin shell of multilayered fabric.

I wasn't the first person in the galaxy to experience such things. Many people lived in prisons. A lot of the times, those prisons were of their own making.

As mine was.

Yet, for all that I named this life a prison, at the same time I was free.

There was no one holding me back. No guard to check that I stayed in my cell. No watchman to wake me in the morning. No sentry to call for lights-out at night.

I was free to roam the vast empty spaces of this dying world.

Free to discover what I would, when I would.

Free to kill.

I was getting rather good at it.

I had criticized Rade for taking life in battle. But I understood now what he did and why he did it. When it became a necessity, when it became kill or be killed, that's when morality went out the window.

Rade was a warrior.

I had become one, too.

I had to.

When the will to live, the burning fight inside you, was stronger than anything else, especially those who wanted to kill you, then you'd ascended to the level of warrior. That was all there was to it.

Accepting the warrior mentality was what separated those who survived from those who did not.

And I would survive.

I'd sworn I would.

Queequeg and I were on the hunt. My faithful companion had sprinted far ahead, having picked up the scent of our wounded prey. Inside my pressurized suit, all I could smell was the musty scent of recycled air—not that I'd be able to match Queequeg's sense of smell even if I *could* breathe the atmosphere. I simply followed along behind him, keeping to the path of misplaced shale and trusting to Queequeg's nose. There wasn't any blood I could track, because all liquids boiled away when exposed to the atmosphere of this inhospitable world.

Queequeg was a hybear—a bear with a hyena's head and an uncharacteristically long tail, bioengineered by the SKs to survive the hostile environment of Geronium. But to me he was just a very big, very loveable dog.

I glanced at the map overlaying my helmet lens. My Implant was deactivated, of course. I had turned it off months ago as a safety precaution (the alien mists of this world could use it to scramble my vision and hearing), and I relied solely on the aReal built into my helmet.

On the map I confirmed I wasn't deviating too far from the original path I'd plotted. I should still be able to make the Forma pipe by tomorrow afternoon. That would leave me around eight hours of oxygen.

Assuming everything went well.

I pushed the very real possibility of running out of O_2 from my mind: I was starving and had to eat. When a meal presented itself on Geronimo, you embraced the opportunity with open arms.

Today, hybear was on the menu.

Queequeg topped a rise ahead and vanished from view.

I sometimes worried that eating the flesh of his own kind would do Queequeg psychological harm. I supposed it helped that he thought of himself as human, and probably didn't count the act as cannibalism. Still, it didn't change the fact that it *was* cannibalism.

I topped the rise shortly thereafter and spotted our prey. It was a stroke of luck to find a hybear alone; the things usually attacked in packs.

It limped along in the valley below, trying to run, an act of extreme will made difficult by the fact it had only three legs. Earlier, when the starving animal had attacked, I'd cut its forelimb off with my rifle-scythe, a weapon I had cobbled together from a standard-issue rifle and the long, sharp mandible of one of the beasts. I could see the slight green steam of blood wafting from the severed end of the limb even now.

Queequeg was already far down the incline, running at full-tilt and eager for the kill.

By the time I reached the bottom, my faithful companion was shaking the last dregs of life from the prey, his jaws wrapped firmly around its neck.

I sat back and waited until Queequeg was done killing it. Then I watched as he ate.

That was one of our rules: whoever made the kill, ate first.

When Queequeg was satiated, he sat down beside me and contentedly rested his head on his forepaws.

I got to work on preparing the meat. One of the nice things about having grown up on a farm on Earth was that I was familiar with the farmer's trade, down to the butchery and cleaning of animals. Although it was a cider farm, my parents had believed in natural living. So in addition to the apple trees, we grew crops and raised livestock.

First I jabbed a syringe into the skin to drain the green blood. A tube led away to the collection device built into my rucksack. I remember when I used to call the sacks "spacebags" thanks to the indoctrination of Basic Training—that seemed three lifetimes ago. Anyway, my suit recycled most of the water I excreted from my pores, bladder, and whatnot, but it wasn't enough, and the blood would augment my supply. Not that I drank it raw—the collection device extracted the water from the blood plasma. The first time, I wasn't sure the extraction process would work, because these were bioengineered animals after all. But apparently hybear blood plasma was fairly similar to normal mammals, coming in at roughly ninety-two percent water. I wasn't sure where the animals got their own water from, however. Other than from eating each other.

Ideally, I would have preferred to hang the hybear first, for proper skinning, but obviously I didn't have a winch or tractor handy, which meant I had to keep rolling the carcass as I peeled the skin away with my utility knife. Bits of shale stuck to the exposed muscle and fat; I removed the small rocks by wiping one of my gloved hands down the surface. It would've been nice to have some water to wash away the excess hair and rocks with, but the liquid would have merely boiled away, like most of the remaining blood did.

I'm not going to go into too much detail on the cleaning, like how I removed the anus and intestines and other internal organs after skinning it, or how I cut off the head, cracked open the sternum, and carved away choice portions of meat with my knife (wishing the whole time I had a meat cleaver). I'll just wrap by saying I collected a nice bundle of meat and secured it to the storage compartment of my rucksack. That meat would keep me and Queequeg fed for the next few days.

The cleaning done, I covered the offal and skeleton in shale, forming a cairn of sorts. That might keep other hybears away for a couple of hours, but eventually the scent would drift to them, and the hybears would close like sharks.

Once the cairn was built I hiked to the next rise, putting some distance between me and the offal in case any nearby hybears picked up the scent early. Then I sat down and retrieved a cut of meat.

Queequeg was whining beside me, already hungry again.

I sliced away a small portion and tossed it to him.

Queequeg caught the meat in midair with his jaws, and swallowed it in two bites. Then he looked at me, panting, those puppy dog eyes begging for more.

I cut off another piece and tossed it to him. "No more. I have to eat, too, you know."

And so I did.

First I cooked the meat with the surgical laser built into the index finger of my gloves. I had to keep pulsing the laser, and since my Implant was disabled, I couldn't vary the depth of those pulses. I held my laser finger different distances from the meat to vary the cooking depth. Heat radiation helped roast the surrounding meat, but I still had to rotate the cut to ensure I cooked it thoroughly. It took a lot of time, which only seemed all the longer because of my hunger. I kept an eye on my power levels, because if I wasn't careful the laser could exhaust the suit batteries.

Eventually hunger and impatience got the best of me, and I decided the meat was cooked enough, though it couldn't have been more than extra-rare. I reached into the cargo pocket of my left leg, retrieved the suitrep (suit repair) kit, and fetched the reusable "Seal-Wrap" funnel from inside.

The SealWrap was meant to form a seal between suits when a soldier needed to perform an impromptu operation on another soldier in a hostile environment—very useful for tactical combat casualty care, otherwise known as battlefield medicine, when the war zone just so happened to be on an inhospitable world, or in space. I'd found an alternate use for it though: with the SealWrap I could transfer food from the lethal environment outside to the pressurized confines of my suit.

It was a little messy, but it worked.

With the hunk of laser-cooked meat situated in the center of the funnel, I placed the edges of the SealWrap against the outer perimeter of my face mask. I strictly ignored the rumbling of my stomach: I had to take good care here, because if I got the positioning off, I'd die. I activated the sealant, and felt the suction pull my hand toward the mask.

I tied off the other end around my wrist, then I held my breath, and said: "Suit, release face mask."

The glass plate descended inward slightly, breaking the seal between the glass and the helmet. The SealWrap abruptly inflated as the atmosphere of my suit expanded to fill the available space.

I could still breathe.

I hadn't made a mistake.

I sighed in relief.

I could already smell the roasted meat, and I salivated.

"Suit, lower face mask." The glass plate slid down.

I tilted my head back and let the hunk of meat fall toward my mouth. As expected, it wasn't cooked well at all. It was very rare actually, cold and bloody. But I bit into it, chewed, and swallowed. I had to. Tasted like raw, wet beef.

I remembered the first time I ever did this. I'd run out of rations, and was starving. I'd returned to the shuttle with a big piece of meat from a fresh kill (this was when the shuttle still had power). I cooked it thoroughly, draining as much blood as I could. The smell was amazing—I'd been living on meal-replacement rations for months before then. Still, I was hesitant to take a bite. I was convinced the meat was going to be toxic in some way. I had to remind myself these animals were bioengineered from Earth stock, so when it came down to it I was eating meat that was theoretically compatible with my stomach. Exotic meat, sure, but edible nonetheless. Eventually my stomach had overruled me, and I'd dug into the cooked hybear. Tasted great. Unfortunately, a few hours later I suffered intense abdominal pains. It got so bad I thought I was going to give birth to an alien life-form or something. The cramps lasted for days, as did the diarrhea, but eventually I got over it.

And I never got sick on hybear again.

Still, the meat was tough, even when barely cooked, and eating it made the gums of my back molars sore. My molars had always given me trouble with the tougher meats, and now I regretted not getting those teeth removed on Earth. The pain was getting worse lately. My gums didn't have a chance to recover, not when my entire diet consisted of meat. The whole area was probably infected at this point.

That day while eating, the pain got so bad I gave up halfway through. There was still a sizable portion of meat remaining, but I left it half-chewed in the funnel and broke down and wept.

There I was, bawling like a child, one hand SealWrapped to my face, a half-eaten piece of meat pressed against my chin. I rued my lot in life. Rued the day I ever came to this forsaken planet, and the day I ever signed up.

"I just want to go home!" I said aloud, sobbing. "I just want to live again!"

Queequeg lifted his head beside me, and pricked his ears in concern.

I continued to blubber away.

Queequeg lowed softly in commiseration.

I lowered my free hand to his head, and petted him.

The movement soothed me, though I could scarcely feel anything through the fabric of my glove.

"I'm sorry, Queequeg," I said, composing myself. "Sometimes, the situation seems so bad, so hopeless, like there's no way out. And it just feels like the weight of the whole world is pushing down on me. It makes me want to give up. But that's the easy path, isn't it? To lie down, vent out my suit, and let it all end.

"But I *can't* give up. I won't. I'm just not capable. My friend Rade told me something, once. That the human spirit is resilient in the face of adversity. And I'll let you in on a secret, Queequeg: I'm one of the most resilient people there is."

I shifted my head toward a small tube on the inside of my helmet, and took a long sip of water.

I could do this. I could live.

But I was done eating for that day.

I shut my helmet and removed the SealWrap, packing it away with a promise to clean it later. I tossed the leftover meat to Queequeg, and then I continued onward toward the Forma pipe.

I'd had it with self-pity. I wanted to get on with my journey. I couldn't let myself look too far into the future, too far past the now. Couldn't let the despair of my situation overcome me. I had to focus on reaching the next Forma pipe. One attainable goal at a time.

The landscape before me was bleak, barren, slightly blanched by the too-bright sun. Geronium-275, the precursor to the radioactive fuel that powered starships, filled the view from horizon to horizon, looking for all the world like black shale. Or perhaps black dunes made of flattened fingers of rock was a better description. My boots were covered in utility tape, because those sharp rocks were a perforation hazard, and had already worn away the outer fabric.

My suit protected me from about fifty percent of the radiation the Geronium-275 emitted. Before I'd abandoned my shuttle for good, I'd installed the last two subdermal anti-rads beneath my skin, which were timed to drip-feed the necessary radiation poisoning treatments into my blood.

I only had about one week of treatments left. I wasn't looking forward to suffering from rad sickness. I supposed, on the bright side, the radiation wasn't as bad as some places farther north, where the SKs had detonated powerful nuclear warheads in their attempts to clean out the beasts. Still, only one week of treatments left . . . I reminded myself not to look too far past the present moment.

That night I slept under the stars, with Queequeg on watch beside me. He didn't actually remain awake, but the animal had ears so sensitive he may as well have. He'd shoot upright if a pin dropped ten meters away, and the warning laugh he'd unleash would rouse me from the deepest sleep. Not that I slept very deeply. Not anymore.

I woke up late that night, drenched in sweat. I'd had the nightmare again. Rade and I were fully suited, on a spacewalk outside the hull of the *Royal Fortune*. A red-orange gas giant floated above us. Somehow, I lost my footing, and the line that tethered us broke. Rade caught me before I floated off. His gloved hands wrapped around mine, and he promised he wouldn't let go. Still, I was slipping away. Rade became frantic. I wasn't sure what frightened me more: the fact I was about to die, or that Rade was going to be forced to watch. Finally I fell, plunging toward the gas giant, which had become a black hole . . .

Queequeg lay beside me, watching me. Even the slight change in my breathing as my body shifted from sleeping to waking was enough to rouse him, even though the sound was muffled by my helmet.

I gazed at the stars. At first they had seemed so foreign to me, these stars eight thousand lightyears from anything I'd ever known. But I'd seen them so many times by then that they had become my new normal. I'd even invented constellations for them. There was the Robed Witch, holding the Apple. Retina, the eye, looking down on me. And there, the Claw—whenever I traveled by night, its bright red tip guided me.

While I had grown accustomed to these new stars, I truly missed the old ones, the constellations of Earth I had grown up with as a child in the warm summers of France. Aquarius, Hercules, Lyra. Sagittarius.

I missed the bright yellow moon.

The murmur of the ocean waves.

The salty, warm kiss of—

I closed my eyes.

Those days were gone. Best to forget them. I had fought with regret and melancholy many times before for this day, and nearly lost. I had sworn never to do so again. Such emotions only interfered with my survival.

Still, I was so alone . . .

No. That wasn't true.

"I have you, Queequeg, don't I?"

Queequeg lifted his head inquisitively.

I scratched him above the nose, and closed my eyes. "I have you."

The next morning Queequeg and I made good progress toward the Forma pipe. In about four hours, the structure grew from a slim finger flipping me the bird on the horizon, to a vast concrete chimney stabbing the heavens, its long shadow devouring the landscape and making the dark ground darker. The pipe extended even farther underground than it did skyward, its telescoping limbs expanding like an organic root system, its acids breaking down the mineral impurities in the crust to extract oxygen for later release into the air.

This pipe, and the forty-nine others that circled the equator of this planet, comprised merely the first phase of the terraforming process. There were other Forma pipes designed for the sole purpose of scrubbing the atmosphere and filtering out toxins, but those would be installed in the later phases.

I had to laugh. There wouldn't be any later phases. Not anymore. The SKs and UC had completely abandoned this planet, and destroyed all Gates leading to and from the system. Heck, I'd destroyed one of the Gates myself. There was no way back, not even if I could somehow get into orbit. Not even if I could somehow reach the Slipstream. Because without a Gate, I was trapped.

I knew this would happen when I'd volunteered to stay behind. And I chose this. To save the ship. And the crew.

To save Rade.

I shut my eyes.

Get out of your head, Shaw. You'll find only despair there.

As predicted, at this point I had about eight hours of oxygen left, including the contents of my bailout canister. I would've preferred to have more, but this definitely wasn't the worst low-oxygen scenario I'd found myself in.

I walked into the shadow of the Forma pipe, making my way toward the base of the structure.

The Forma pipe was constructed entirely out of concrete poured into a rebar frame. If you imagined an arch-gravity dam on Earth like the Hoover Dam, you wouldn't be far off from what I was seeing in terms of composition and scale. Except take that dam, turn its half-circle arch into a full cylinder, and send it towering into the sky, and you had a Forma pipe.

At the base, a corroded metal staircase led to a door roughly three meters above the black ground. There was no door handle or key code box—entry was entirely via embedded ID. Of course, I was never on the list of recognized IDs. That didn't stop me from climbing the stairwell and attempting the door anyway.

It didn't open. The way the steel panels smoothly irised shut gave me no purchase to pry it apart. The surgical lasers in my gloves might have been able to poke needle-sized holes after ten minutes or so, but my suit would run out of power long before cutting away anything useful.

There was another way inside though.

A ladder scaled the outer surface of the concrete chimney, all the way to the top. I ran my gaze upward, watching the perspective lines of the ladder recede into the sky. I couldn't see it from here, but a ventilation shaft/maintenance tunnel near the top offered a way inside. Why they would build the maintenance shaft so high was beyond me. Even if I had a working jetpack (which I didn't), I'd only be able to reach maybe a tenth of the way to the top before I ran out of fuel. I suspected the ladder was more a leftover artifact of the construction than anything else, kept in place as an unessential afterthought, because of course the main door would never malfunction, right? And if it did, the crew could just send a maintenance robot up the ladder.

Fortunately, once I was inside, it was easy enough to program the door to accept my ID. I had the SACKER installed in the internal database of my embedded ID, which was the Swiss army knife of privilege escalation kits. I'd taken a cyberwarfare elective back at my rating school, which gave me the clearance and training to use the kit. The SACKER was loaded with hundreds of known software exploits that allowed me to obtain administrator access on a variety of platforms, assuming any potential backdoors on a given system hadn't been patched. Thankfully the door sensor unit inside the Forma pipes utilized outdated software—all I had to do was interface with the sensor, run the privilege escalation kit, load the software's admin interface, and add my embedded ID to the list of accepted entrants. Then I could come and go from the Forma pipe as I pleased.

But first I had to get to that door sensor unit.

I doffed my rucksack and retrieved a universal charging cord for my suit battery. I tied the cord around my utility belt, then set the rucksack down beside the door. I didn't need the sack burdening me the whole climb, and I knew I could count on faithful Queequeg to guard it.

I took my rifle-scythe and secured the strap over my shoulder. Then I started the climb.

Queequeg was whining and hopping to and fro, trying to figure out how to join me. He always did that.

"Hang tight, Queequeg. I'll be back in no time."

I did my best to sound hopeful, for Queequeg's benefit, but to be honest I had a bad feeling about this one.

Scaling a ladder in a jumpsuit could be tricky, because the bulky gloves and boots caused the mind to misjudge the thickness and position of each rung. Sometimes I'd step or reach too high or low, and I'd momentarily miss a rung. It was easy enough to recover of course, but still somewhat terrifying when you were so high up. Also, I was squeezing each rung a bit too hard, and the tendons below my wrists were killing me. The wider grip forced on me by the thick gloves didn't help matters. Nor did my fear of heights.

The tendon pain eventually got so bad I had to pause. Swinging the crook of my elbow over one of the rungs, I shifted my body weight and rested. I didn't dare look down, or even toward the horizon. I always got vertigo when I did that. I was an astrogator, used to the empty, heightless void of space. I honestly didn't know how planetary pilots could constantly land and take off without getting sick. Sure, I'd passed my Planetary Shuttle Qualification in training, but only after heavily medicating myself. The instructor was a flirtatious petty officer who ignored the fact I seemed slightly inebriated because I gave him my vid conferencing number. My fear of heights was why I was partially glad my shuttle's autopilot hadn't awakened me for the crash-landing on this world—I wasn't entirely sure I could've done a better job.

I was about one kilometer up when I came across a missing rung. It had probably broken off some time after construction, because the robot workers certainly wouldn't have missed it. The winds gusted quite strongly up here, and I supposed it wouldn't take much to break off a shoddy component.

Still, that missing rung made me leery. How many more had fallen away farther up? What if a rung broke off while I was putting my weight on it, and I plunged to my death?

Curse all designers and engineers.

I wanted to turn back, but it wasn't like I had a choice. I needed the oxygen inside this Forma pipe.

I reached past the missing rung, stretching my body, and wrapped my fingers around the next one. Straining because of the awkward position, I pulled.

Don't break don't break, I chanted in my head.

When my chin was level with the rung, I folded the gloved fingers of my other hand around it, then I shoved off from the lower rung with my boots and yanked myself upward.

The winds buffeted me extra hard, and the strap securing the rifle-scythe to my back decided to break just then.

I reached behind as the weapon fell away, and tried to grab it with one arm.

Missed.

I watched the weapon plunge. It became pin-sized in only half a second.

My eyes focused on the continent far below, and an incredible sense of vertigo filled me. The winds continued to gust, swaying me, and I froze up. My gaze was locked on the distant ground, which looked like an expanded version of a Heads-Up-Display map. My vision swam, and the continent turned round and round below me.

The jumpsuit wouldn't cushion a fall from this height. The suit would puncture of course, but that was the least of my worries. All the bones in my body would break at the same time, and the impact trauma would pulp all my organs, including my brain. Especially my brain.

I was still only gripping the rung with one hand, and my entire arm was burning. Physically, that lone hand was incapable of holding on much longer, despite the strength-enhancement of my suit. I knew I had to get my other arm up there, helping out . . .

But I didn't move. Couldn't.

The winds gusted, trying to tear me from the ladder.

The ground below continued to rotate. As did the Forma pipe.

I became momentarily disoriented.

Where was I? In space? On a spacewalk?

My fingers slowly slipped . . .

I shut my eyes.

Fight on, Shaw. Fight!

Without looking, I slammed my other hand upward, and fumbled with my gloved fingers until I gripped the rung with both hands.

When I opened my eyes again, I was gazing straight ahead at the cement.

The vertigo was gone.

I pulled myself to the next rung.

And the next.

One rung at a time.

The moment of crisis was over.

Still, I'd lost my weapon.

I hoped it didn't matter.

An hour later, I reached the entry shaft and pulled myself in. I paused inside the rim to catch my breath. I only gave the outlying landscape a fleeting glance, because I was worried I'd trigger my vertigo again.

Thirty meters above me the Forma pipe ended. When operational, the pipes belched a circular stream of oxygen from their upper rims. The expelled oxygen was visible as a heat haze of sorts, due to the temperature differential. I didn't see any haze today however, which meant this Forma pipe had already failed.

That shouldn't be a big deal—the tanks stored a month's worth of oxygen. Still, I was beginning to wonder if the Forma pipes planetwide had been shut down.

The previous Forma pipe I had relied on for oxygen had mysteriously ceased operating two months after I started using it. My camp had been two klicks away from that pipe, so I didn't see what had disabled the machinery. Maybe it had just failed on its own, from lack of regular maintenance. Or, more likely, one of the alien mists had sabotaged it. What Rade had called the Phants.

In any case, after I'd exhausted the failed Forma's monthlong supply of oxygen, I set out for this next pipe.

And here I was.

I clambered on my hands and knees through the shaft, arriving at the hollow, cylindrical inner core of the Forma pipe. A ladder led down into the dark depths. There was no lighting, not in a failed pipe, and the stray daylight from the shaft only illuminated a short way inside.

I kept my focus on the topmost rung of the inner core, lest the vertigo return. I stared at that rung with trepidation, keenly aware of my missing weapon.

What if there was something waiting for me down there?

I turned on my helmet lamp. Suppressing the feeling of terror that was slowly rising inside me, I swung my feet over the ledge and onto the ladder. I almost expected a tentacle to latch on to my leg from the depths.

Making a point of not looking down, I started the descent.

The intensity of my helmet lamp was low—my suit power was reduced to ten percent by all the climbing—and only a small cone of light surrounded me. I could see the ladder in front of me, and the concrete walls in the immediate vicinity, but everything else was pitch-black.

It felt like I was descending into the dark heart of hell itself.

The climb took about an hour.

Since I never looked down, the floor came up rather abruptly. One moment I was lowering myself down into the empty air, rung by rung, then the next my heel struck solid ground.

I froze as the thud echoed up and down the pipe. When the sound faded, only dead silence remained.

I lowered my other boot and stepped fully onto the concrete floor.

Weaponless, I slowly turned around and scanned the area. I was ready to throw myself onto the ladder at the first sign of trouble, but all I saw were the various machines slumped about. Most of the machines were inactive, though weak LEDs did shine from a few of them. The illumination from my helmet was really dim at this point, so I couldn't see all that far. Still, I was satisfied that the area was clear of any beasts (other than those found in my imagination) because they would've attacked by now.

As I had hoped, the servers that harbored the door sensor still had power, so I installed my SACKER privilege escalation kit. It used a brute force approach to crack the admin password, which could take anywhere from ten minutes to an hour.

Leaving the kit do its work, I moved off to one of the machines that still had a working LED. I retrieved the knife from my utility belt—so perhaps I wasn't entirely weaponless. With the knife I opened up a side panel in the machine, revealing the terminals of a magnesium-ion battery pack.

At this point I was in far greater need of power than oxygen, so I retrieved the charging cord from my utility belt, and attached one end to the universal charge port on my wrist and the other end to the battery.

I sat down and rested while my main battery pack recharged. My helmet lamp grew stronger, but the darkness around me didn't seem to recede. I was getting this creepy, tingling sensation at the back of my neck, like someone or something was watching me.

When my battery pack was charged, I disconnected and stowed the cord, then hurried over to the oxygen storage tanks. I just wanted to replenish my O_2 and get the heck out of there.

I examined the nearest oxygen tank. What the . . .

Impossible.

The pressure gauge read zero PSI.

It was empty.

I moved on to the next tank.

Empty.

The next.

Drained as well.

The remainder all proved empty, down to the last one.

I didn't understand it. The tanks were supposed to store a

month's worth of oxygen, even after the Forma pipe failed. There was no way every tank could be drained like that.

I opened the valve of the closest, thinking there was some readout malfunction, but the sniffers in my gloves detected nothing. I backtracked, opening the valves of three other tanks.

The oxygen was truly gone.

Someone, or something, had drained the tanks already.

No no no.

And that's when I saw the beast.

It was crouched at the edge of my light cone, between two oxygen tanks.

One of the "crabs."

Sharp spikes over a black carapace from which protruded eight pairs of legs, with pincers and crushing mandibles on all sides. About one meter tall by two meters wide. Black, semitranslucent skin.

I stepped backward, reaching instinctively for my rifle-scythe—which I didn't have anymore.

I unsheathed the knife from my utility belt instead. The blade seemed pathetically small against the claws and mandibles I now faced.

The crab had remained motionless the entire time.

I kept still, waiting for the alien to make the first move.

The ladder was roughly ten paces away behind me. Could I make it in time? Doubtful.

Neither of us moved.

I don't know how much time passed. Thirty seconds. A minute.

The crab still didn't move.

Could it be . . . ?

I approached. Cautiously.

Keeping my eyes on the motionless creature, I knelt and retrieved a loose pipe. I took three more wary steps, then slowly lifted the metal tube toward the beast.

I touched the pipe to the crab, and shoved.

The carapace shifted lifelessly. I shone my helmet lamp directly onto the body: through the translucent skin I could see its three hearts.

They weren't beating.

Yup. Dead.

I ran my helmet lamp over the thick cord that trailed away from the alien corpse. The cord led between the large machinery to a sinkhole in the concrete floor, about three times as wide as the crab itself.

I squeezed past the dead crab and carefully approached the opening.

Spent shell casings lined the perimeter. Some military personnel could read the marks on shell casings to determine the make and model of the weapons that fired them, but I wasn't one of them. Nor did I have the necessary app for my aReal, unfortunately.

Slowly my angle of view increased until I found myself peering straight down the hole.

Inside resided more dead crabs. A whole bunch of them.

There was no host slug that I could see, but the bodies of the bigger creatures usually evanesced after death.

I crouched at the rim, letting my light illuminate deeper. I realized a cave-in blocked the tunnel's lower recesses. Good.

I stepped away from the hole, edged past the dead crab, and hurried to the door sensor. The SACKER hadn't cracked the administrator password yet, so I went to the ladder and sat down. There I waited, keeping my eye on the lifeless crab and the sinkhole beyond it. I was ready to vault up the ladder at a moment's notice.

The moments passed, and I relaxed somewhat. Enough to ponder the puzzle of the missing oxygen, anyway.

There were no signs that the tanks had been punctured in any way. So the crabs hadn't done it.

Still, *something* had drained the oxygen. Likely it was the same thing that had killed the beasts in here. The spent shell casings pointed to either another human being, or a robot. A robot wouldn't need oxygen of course, but there was always the possibility that the Forma pipe had never been active in the first place, and the tanks had never filled.

Robot, or human being, I supposed I'd never find out. I only had five hours of oxygen left, and the next Forma pipe was about a week away.

As I waited for the SACKER to work its magic, my mind concocted fantasies: Rade had found a way to reach this planet, and he was actively searching for me, fighting his way from Forma pipe to Forma pipe. He'd been here in this very pipe mere hours before, and would soon return. When he found me, he'd take me back to Earth. Once there, we'd quit the Navy, and after we were deported we'd move to France and live out our lives in peace.

I had to laugh. It was a pleasant fantasy.

Unfortunately, Rade wasn't coming for me.

No one was.

The chime of the SACKER kit informed me it had attained administrator access to the door sensor.

I went to the sensor and added my embedded ID to the list of recognized entrants, and the steel panels of the door irised open.

Queequeg was waiting for me outside, jumping up and down with his typical irrational excitement at seeing me.

"My weapon, Queequeg," I said. "Show me where it fell." I pantomimed the plunge of my rifle-scythe from the heights.

The animal led me toward the weapon in great exuberant leaps.

Despite the fall, the rifle-scythe seemed intact—all the tape and superglue had held up.

Now if only *I* could hold up.

"All right, Queequeg. Let's go."

Queequeg led me onward. I didn't care where he went, just as long as it was away from here. His lope was ebullient.

I wished his joy was contagious. I really did. But it wasn't.

Five hours of oxygen left.

Maybe I'd find another source of O_2 somewhere.

Right. It would take a miracle.

I marched after Queequeg, unable to shake the sense of impending doom.

I'd already used up all my miracles.

CHAPTER THREE

Rade

The war that had hung over all our thoughts and deeds these past eight months, the war we had dreaded, the war we had never talked about yet knew was coming, had finally arrived.

It didn't take long for the media to disregard the news lockdown. You couldn't really hide disaster on a planetary scale, not when everyone and their dog had a camera.

It was all over the networks. Every station on the Net and Undernet. There was no escaping it: an entire moon had been invaded by an alien species.

Seemingly from nowhere, the Skull Ship had appeared in orbit above Tau Ceti II-c fifty-five days ago. It was a black starship about one-fourth the size of the moon itself, and vaguely shaped like a human cranium—the SK news media frequently referred to the ship as the "Great Death" in their commentary.

The orbital defenses proved useless against the alien vessel. The Skull Ship proceeded to power right into the crust, unleashing a black cloud that enveloped half the planet and inflicted an unseasonal blizzard on the only major city.

Tau Ceti II-c sent out an emergency distress call, which was nearly masked by the powerful EM interference from the Skull Ship. The combined naval defensive capabilities of the system responded to the call. SK capital ships, battlecruisers, battleships, destroyers, and frigates gathered near the moon for a unified assault.

The Skull Ship destroyed or disabled them all. It was equipped with some sort of coronal point defense weapon. Get too close, and the hull would erupt with a sweeping, superheated gaseous envelope, similar to the coronal discharge from a star. The eruption was capable of disintegrating anything in its path, from torpedoes to supercarriers.

On the moon itself, meanwhile, things were quickly going downhill. From footage pieced together by armchair broadcasters, a grim story emerged.

A deadly rain fell when the black impact cloud consumed the sky, a rain that disintegrated any people unfortunate enough to be caught outdoors. The survivors called the rain the *Yaoguai*—demons from the underworld with a particular bent for the souls of men. The rain also happened to turn most of the robots against the inhabitants, and the machines systematically hunted down the survivors. The rain became a blizzard, and when the storm lifted one week later, few survivors remained amid the melting snow.

All communications with Tau Ceti II-c ceased one month ago. The remote scans weren't pretty. Shangde City was overrun, and the outlying farms and bases had been razed. It was unclear how many of the one million colonists had escaped. With its coronal weapon, the Skull Ship had incinerated many of the fleeing vessels, and destroyed the ship lots and ports.

According to surface probes, Shangde City was patrolled by robots and ATLAS mechs, and defended by automated anti-air weapons. The streets crawled with the infamous crabs and slugs my platoon had first discovered on Geronimo, with sinkholes leading to vast subterranean caverns below the city. The lower parts of the buildings were caked in black bulbs of Geronium-275, like the swollen protrusions of some disease. The snow was gone, and recent atmospheric readings returned by probes had indicated elevated levels of carbon monoxide and chlorine, which told us the invaders were terraforming the moon in some way.

In addition to the crabs and slugs, and the roving bands of robots, stagnant pools of glowing liquid had collected in some of the city streets. The Yaoguai. What I called Phants, because when I'd first encountered them on Geronimo, the alien entities had appeared as a ghostly mist. The Phants on Tau Ceti II-c were in liquid form presumably because of the more Earth-like atmosphere. The SKs reported that bullets went right through them. Explosions temporarily dispersed them, but they simply re-formed. My platoon had experienced exactly the same effects during our own brief encounter with the alien entities.

No one really knew what the Phants were yet. How sentience could be bottled up in some liquid or vapor was completely beyond our comprehension. Fleet scientists postulated that we saw only a small fraction of the entities, the tip of the iceberg so to speak, while the remainder of the beings resided in some higher plane or dimension.

Species X25910 was the working designation for the alien race, of which the Phants were X25910-A, or X-A for short. If you wanted to get into more detail, a purple, faster Phant was X-A i, while a blue one was X-A ii. Crabs were X25910-B, or X-B, and slugs were X25910-C, or X-C. There were alternate naming conventions for the bigger crab and slug variants. Crabs were also called Workers, because they were the ones who laid down the deposits of Geronium-275 that coated the buildings of Shangde City. And the slugs were called Burrowers, because of their tunneling abilities. The vast subterranean network beneath the city? The handiwork of the slugs.

X25910. The fleet scientists must have thought it a brilliant idea to give the alien race the most impersonal name possible. That way there would be no chance we'd feel empathy for them. A nice sentiment on the part of Fleet, but entirely unnecessary as far as I was concerned. The things looked like giant crabs and slugs, so I don't think any of us would be developing feelings for them. For me, it didn't matter what names Big Navy came up with, because those aliens would always be evil butchers in my mind.

They'd murdered my brother in life and best friend in the world, Alejandro Mondego. And they had taken Shaw Chopra from me, the only woman I'd ever cared about.

During the initial stages of the Tau Ceti II-c attack, eleventh hour negotiations had taken place between the SK and UC governments on Earth, culminating in a peace treaty that ended all extra-solar aggression between the two space-faring empires. With the flipping of a few bits in a rad-shielded, error-checking-and-correcting memory chip, privateering was outlawed, economic sanctions repealed, and borders opened up.

Humanity had united against its common foe.

I never thought I'd see the day, but we were actually going to help the SKs. They *needed* us. Just as we would probably need them in the coming days. Though I had to wonder just how long this "alliance" would hold.

Because of our proximity to the necessary Gate, my platoon was part of the second wave of responders. We were teaming up with a battalion of Marines who were also in the region. We'd be working with them in more of a traditional combat capacity, rather than a direct-action-type role. At least at first. Meaning we'd be taking part in the heart of the fighting.

Just the way we liked it.

For me, I was just glad the war had finally come.

It was payback time. My misgivings, my feelings of inadequacy, had lessened with the announcement of the war. I still wanted to transfer to a different task unit eventually.

But first I wanted some payback.

The *Royal Fortune* dropped us off at the *Gerald R. Ford*, the lone UC supercarrier in Gliese 581. With a crew complement of five thousand, it was basically a mobile space city.

We proceeded through *Tiàoyuè De Kǒng* Gate to Tau Ceti. It felt odd, traveling through the Gate in a full-blown UC warship, given that previously we'd had to sneak past inside the cargo hold of an SK bulk carrier.

More starships and troops were on the way of course, from all of humanity's space-faring empires. No one wanted this alien plague spreading beyond Tau Ceti.

The *Gerald R. Ford* spent the next few weeks crossing Tau Ceti. Giving the enemy vessel a wide berth, we arrived at the gas giant Tau Ceti II roughly two months after the Skull Ship's arrival. The *Gerald R. Ford* took up a position in orbit around the massive planet near the orbital station *Lequ* ("Pleasure" in Korean-Chinese), a merchant hub that had been appropriated and transformed into a forward operating base. There the *Gerald R. Ford* joined the remnants of the SK Navy in the system, alongside other United Countries and Franco Italian (FI) warships. The location had the added benefit of stealth, because *Lequ* orbited the gas giant in a position directly opposite the Tau Ceti II-c moon, masking the heat signature of our fleet from the enemy.

The remaining orbital stations were being used as staging centers for the evac of the other two moons. An evac of this magnitude took time, and only a quarter of the populations of the moons had departed so far. More rescue ships were on the way from outside the system.

Anyway, a few days after our arrival, the commanders held a fleet-wide teleconference. A plan of action was conceived. The troops were mobilized.

The day before we dropped, I found myself in the mess hall with half the platoon. We'd just finished a war game sim with some Marines, and we were chowing down on much-needed carbohydrates.

My eyes drifted to Dyson, seated beside me. He hadn't said a word the entire meal. He stared straight ahead, and from the glazed look in his eyes, I knew he was inside his Implant.

He was Asian American, like Lui, but I suspected he had at least one parent from a different nationality because of the blond hair and Romanesque nose. Or maybe he'd merely had reconstructive surgery. His brow bore the scar of a botched tattoo removal, and though he never said what the tattoo had originally depicted, I thought it looked like a Chinese dragon (though most of us told him it must have been a penis). Dyson had grown his beard out, and its thickness matched the beards of the other MOTHs. Well, except for Tahoe, whose inability to grow a decent beard earned him daily jibes.

None of the Marines here had beards, by the way. They simply weren't allowed. Beards were the cachet of the Special Forces.

"Must have some great porn in that embedded ID of yours," I told Dyson, not one to miss an opportunity to ridicule him. I didn't really care if the Marines listened in: they knew we fought among ourselves just as much as they did.

Dyson's head jerked up and he stared at me. His eyes smoldered. Finally he forced a smile. "Hey, Rage."

"So come on, what's your deal?"

He frowned. "What do you mean? Nothing. I was just listening to the 'Star Spangled Banner.'"

"The what?"

"You know, the old anthem? Before Unification?"

"Ah." I nodded slowly. "That's a good song. But have you heard 'Al Grito De Guerra?' One of the best anthems out there."

"I haven't," Dyson said. "Different lewds for different dudes, huh?"

"I think he just called you gay," Tahoe told me, jokingly.

"Quiet, Tahoe," I said. "We're trying to have a conversation here."

"Why do you call him Tahoe?" Dyson said. "Everyone else calls him Cyclone. That's the callsign programmed into my aReal . . ."

"Only I'm allowed to call him Tahoe," I said. "And we'll leave the explanation at that." I decided I'd try to treat him as more of an actual human being. At least for today. So I said, "Tell me, Dyson, are you looking forward to the upcoming battle?"

"I'm here to do what I signed up for. Kill some baddies. Save the world. You know how it is." Dyson could fake bravado with the best of us.

"I do indeed."

"Just never thought I'd be fighting side by side with stinking SKs."

I regarded Dyson thoughtfully. "Interesting. I thought you *were* Chinese."

"*Half* Chinese," he said. "The other half is Swedish. The better half."

I shook my head. "No wonder Lui doesn't want you to hang out at our table."

"Hey, I'm only telling you the truth."

"And what's the truth? That you hate your heritage, your origins, your ancestry? That you hate your own genes? Not a lot of sense in that. If you're going to fight with us, you have to put aside your own self-hatred. I'm surprised you even made it through training with an attitude like that."

"Yeah, well, this attitude of mine was exactly what got me through training," Dyson said. "My hatred for my Chinese half. It kept me going. Made me want to prove to myself I was better than that half. And I am. I'm not some weak Chinese."

"Who says the Chinese are weak?" I stared at him incredulously. "You're lucky, you know. You're going to be fighting alongside the Sino-Koreans today. Try fighting *against them* sometime. Just ask Tahoe."

"Hey, don't drag me into this," Tahoe said. "I'm not touching this conversation with a seven-foot pole."

Dyson glanced between Tahoe and me. "You don't understand," he said quietly. "I've been fighting the Chinese my entire life."

"What do you mean?" I said, though I had a good idea.

"Try growing up in the UC when you look like a member of its greatest enemy," Dyson said bitterly.

"You don't really look all that SK to me," I said.

"Not anymore."

Ah. Reconstructive surgery, then.

I swallowed a particularly large serving of rice.

"Thanks, by the way," Dyson told me.

"For what?"

Dyson hesitated, then: "For being so nice to me."

I laughed. I really laughed. "I've hardly been nice to you."

"No, you have," he said. "I want you to keep hazing me. Keep testing my mettle. Even when I get my callsign. It keeps me on my toes."

"You're the strangest caterpillar I ever met," I said. "Of course, I haven't met very many. Did you hear that, Tahoe? I think we've been too soft on our boy Dyson here. He *likes* our hazing."

Bender leaned forward, and pointed at Dyson threateningly. "I'm going to keep hazing you, don't you worry. Gonna teach you that you ain't never going to fill the shoes of the man you came to replace. Not ever."

Bender surprised me. I thought I was the only one who felt that way.

Dyson crossed his arms. "I never said I wanted to replace any-one. I'm here to offer my sniping skills to the platoon. Use me as you see fit."

Facehopper rested a hand on his shoulder. "We've all been where you are, mate. All of us. Don't mind them. We've lost good people, and you're a convenient outlet for the grief we all feel. You'll make it through, just don't let them get to you. You survived MOTH train-ing, and that's half the battle. It takes a certain kind of man to get where you are now."

"I'm not an ordinary *man*," Dyson said. "I'm a MOTH. And I know I'll make it through, sir. I'm in my element out here. This is what I trained for. Besides, with you guys at my side, I'm invincible."

I exchanged a knowing glance with Tahoe. I used to think exactly like Dyson. Because of who I was, and the friends I had, I actually believed none of us would ever die. I was wrong.

But we were MOTHs. We were supposed to believe we were invincible. Yet despite the brave faces, all of us here, MOTHs and Marines alike, knew what was coming. And we were afraid. You could feel it in the air. It was always like this, the day before a battle.

And yet I also sensed excitement. We were, in the end, doing our jobs. Doing what we were trained to do.

Dyson was looking at Bender, as if expecting him to make some gung-ho comment in agreement with what he just said.

Instead, all Bender had to say was, "Don't look at me with those beady little Chinaman eyes of yours."

Charming, as always.

Dyson started to look away, but he shot Bender a withering gaze as the words registered. "What did you call me?"

Bender smirked. "You heard me. Chinaman."

"That's it." Dyson stood up from his seat.

I was there to catch him. "Sit down, Dyson."

He tried to shove his way past me.

On the other side of the table Bender stood too, and was egging on Dyson. "Let him go! Let him go! I got some things to teach this caterpillar!"

"All right," Skullcracker said, in a voice so quiet I had to strain to hear. "If y'all don't sit yourselves down real soon, you're going to find out why I'm called Skullcracker."

Dyson and Bender regarded the man's skull-tattooed face warily, and then they returned to their seats.

"Thank you, Skullcracker," Facehopper said.

Skullcracker inclined his head.

"Tomorrow we fight," Facehopper said. "And we're doing so as a team. I need you guys to present a unified front to the world. Do I have to tell the Chief we can't work together? That he has to assign you two to different drops?"

"No, Facehopper," Dyson said.

"Bender?" Facehopper glanced at the black man.

Bender had a defiant look in his eyes, but then he lowered his gaze, and said, "No."

The next day I found myself sitting inside a Delivery Vehicle, waiting to be dropped onto the invaded moon. I wore my pressurized jumpsuit alongside the dozen Marines and five MOTHs from the wargame sims: Facehopper, Tahoe, Skullcracker, Bender, and Dyson. I would've preferred if the caterpillar Dyson had been assigned to a different Delivery Vehicle in the end, but I had no say in the matter. I knew it was wrong to resent him, that it wasn't his fault two good men had to die so he could be here. Still, knowing that didn't change my attitude toward him.

The remaining members of Alfa platoon, including Chief Bourbonjack, had been similarly spread out among the battalion. Our purpose was to give advice and offer leadership to the Marines. No one else, other than the SKs, had faced a threat like this before.

As if we really knew anything more just because we'd fought the enemy once before. These Marines were briefed. They knew what to expect. My experience and that of my platoon's wasn't going to make a whole lot of difference, in my opinion. You shot the crabs and slugs. They went down. Unless they were really big, in which case you left them to air support. As for the Phants, well, you ran from those flesh-incinerating and robot-possessing mists for all you were worth.

Lieutenant Commander Braggs was stationed in the CDC (Combat Direction Center, or operations room) of the *Gerald R. Ford*, and he would coordinate with us via Chief Bourbonjack while we were on the surface. Like the rest of the crew, the Lieutenant Commander had his Implant disabled, as Fleet hadn't found a way to shield direct-brain aReal devices from the crippling electromagnetic emissions of the Phants. So he was relying on an external aReal for his HUD and platoon connectivity. There was no chance of these HUDs overloading like had happened to us on Geronimo, not with the Implants offline. Anyway, while in the CDC, the Lieutenant Commander temporarily gave Chief Bourbonjack access to the audio and video feeds of his aReal, and the Chief in turn shared those feeds with the rest of Alfa platoon.

"What I'm sending you now, boys," the Chief sent over the private comm channel, "is shared with the understanding that you won't show it to anyone else. I hope you appreciate that common soldiers and embedded reporters aren't allowed access to such feeds. But you are MOTHs, and there's nothing common about you. You can handle scenarios that would have other men pissing in their military-issue undergarments. It's debatable whether this is a breach of Operational Security or not, but if it is, to hell with op-sec. As far as I'm concerned, you deserve to see the Commanding Officer and his XO bring this carrier into battle. Especially when you're going to be dropping out the hangar bay in the middle of it. If you're going to die, then you damn well deserve to see what hit you. Out, goddammit." The Chief was stationed in a different drop craft, but I could imagine the grim expression on his face as he said that.

I halved the size of the video feed that the Chief supplied, and moved it to the upper right corner of my helmet's aReal. On it, I saw the layout of the CDC as perceived from Lieutenant Commander Braggs's perspective. He was staring at the tactical display, which was a holographic representation of the battle space projected in 3D at the center of the room. The data for the display was filtered and collected via the multiple terminals manned by operations specialists around it. The specialists wore old-style translucent aReal visors, the kind with the red LEDs that strobed at different frequencies, giving the overhead cameras positional data for proper linking of the real and virtual worlds. The specialists wore hand straps with similar strobing LEDs, and used them to interact with their consoles (without an aReal those consoles appeared as blank plates of glass, unless the backup systems were running).

The XO (Executive Officer) of the supercarrier, *Captain Tom Linder*, was the officer overseeing the CDC. He, like everyone else present, wore an aReal visor. He had his own seat at the heart of the command center.

On the tactical display (which, I was told, could be viewed via aReal anywhere on the ship if you had the appropriate access), I saw the green dot representing the *Gerald R. Ford*, and the darker green dots representing our frigate escort, which included a handful of FI ships, three SK ships, and two other UC vessels. One of the escorting vessels was the *Royal Fortune*.

The Captain studied the display. I could see the red dots representing the enemy flotilla (comprised of captured SK ships), with the Skull Ship indicated as a sphere roughly four times the size of the others. The moon and gas giant were represented as bigger spheres, not to scale, but large enough to illustrate their positions in relation to the rest of us.

Our vessels were coming toward the moon from the far side. Like most carriers, we were decked out in LIDAR absorbers and background-rad pass-throughs, but all that was moot when you considered our heat signature would've enabled us to be spotted from millions of kilometers off. The moon wasn't big enough to shield our signatures, not given our angle of approach. But I didn't think stealth was our objective.

A small alert sounded. On the 3D display, the smaller red dots had begun moving away from the Skull Ship.

"She's seen us," an operations specialist said. "The enemy flotilla is breaking away from Bandit 1." That was the Skull Ship.

Captain Linder nodded calmly.

A voice came over the CDC comm. "Give me an ETA on weapons range." I recognized the voice as belonging to Commodore William Hanson, the CO (Commanding Officer) of the *Gerald R. Ford*. He was directing operations from the main bridge, where most of the tactical decisions would be executed. The whole point of the CDC was to analyze the battle space and advise the Commanding Officer. But if the bridge fell, the CDC could continue the battle— it was a fully operational backup command center.

Captain Linder glanced at one of the operations specialists.

"Two minutes, sir," the specialist said. "So far, only the flotilla is moving. Bandit 1 remains stationary, as predicted."

When we were about ten minutes away from the drop waypoint, designated by a flashing blue indicator on the tactical display, more red dots began to appear. These were needle-sized.

"Enemy vessels just launched fighters," an operations specialist said.

"I see them," Commodore Hanson said over the comm, from the bridge.

"Your orders, sir?" came another voice over the comm. I assumed it must be the Tactical Officer, Lieutenant Commander Miko, who was also on the bridge.

"Hold present course and speed." Commodore Hanson answered.

"Confirm fighter class," Captain Linder said.

"Avenger class, sir," one of the operations specialists answered. "Unmanned and remotely operated."

"Why launch them so early?" Captain Linder said. "By the time those fighters are in range, the communications lag with the host ships will force the onboard AIs to do most of the work."

"Unless the fighters are operated by Phants," Commodore Hanson said from the bridge.

A few tense moments passed.

"Enemy flotilla within mortar and torpedo range, sir," Miko said over the comm.

"Lock mortars on target," Commodore Hanson said. "Spread fire evenly among the enemy carriers and frigates. Order our escorts to do the same."

"Locking mortars on target, and notifying escorts," Tactical Officer Miko answered.

Launched by rail guns, mortars were true fire-and-forget weapons. Comprised of iron or other minerals, mortars had no propulsion systems of any kind, and never deviated from their initial trajectory, or their initial velocity, after launch. You didn't need a warhead to cause damage with a mortar—at the velocities starships moved in space, a hit from a mortar could tear a ship in half. Also, since the projectiles were mined from asteroids and other planetoids, they were cheap and easy to replenish.

There was no real defense against mortar projectiles, which were basically mini-asteroids. You could launch a nuke, if you were willing to waste one, but that was about it. The chances of hitting an incoming mortar with one of your own were minuscule, and the Gatlings of point defense systems hardly scuffed the surfaces. The best thing to do was steer out of the way, which made them very effective for target herding.

After a moment, the Tactical Officer's voice could be heard over the comm. "Mortars locked. The *Gerald R. Ford* and escorts are ready to fire."

"Fire," Commodore Hanson said from the bridge.

"Muting the bridge." Captain Linder leaned forward. "Now comes the moment of truth. Will our SK allies fire on their own countrymen?"

On the display, yellow lines that represented mortar projectiles streamed out from each of our ships, with dashed lines indicating the intended targets. Four projectiles were headed toward each of the seven enemy vessels.

The three SK vessels on our side had all fired.

"Looks like they came through for us," Commander Bane said. He was Linder's second. "Maybe they believe none of their countrymen are alive on the captured vessels."

The Captain rubbed his chin. "Maybe."

"Thoughts, Captain?"

Captain Linder bit his lower lip. "The alien beings we face aren't omni-powerful, despite what some of you might believe. They can't simply board human ships and expect to know how to navigate them, let alone the strategies to employ in combat. There are SKs on board those captured vessels, fighting for their alien masters, don't you worry. There have to be."

"But if Phants possess their fighters, as the Commodore suggests, how did the alien beings learn to pilot them?"

Captain Linder frowned. "I don't know. But piloting a fighter and operating a carrier lie on two very different ends of the complexity scale."

Mortar projectiles appeared on the display, coming from the enemy ships. The dashed lines of the computed trajectories converged on the *Gerald R. Ford*.

All of them.

"Interesting strategy." Captain Linder continued rubbing his chin. "What do you make of it, Bane?"

"We *are* the most dangerous threat," Commander Bane said.

"Yes, but assuming they do disable us, our escorts pack more than enough punch to take down the rest of them."

"The battle has only started, sir," Commander Bane said.

"Yes indeed."

"Alter trajectory to avoid mortar projectiles," Commodore Hanson said over the comm. "I want a starboard burst of thrust, followed by a countering portside burst the moment those projectiles are cleared."

"Initiating starboard burst, sir," another voice said. Presumably the astrogator. Female. That made me think of Shaw. I forced her image from my head. Now was not the time to let thoughts of her consume me.

"Miko," Commodore Hanson said from the bridge, "lock torpedoes on target. I want the nuclears from us and our escorts to form a constricting noose around the enemy flotilla. Give them only one safe path, down the middle, straight toward us."

Some moments later: "Ready, sir."

"Fire."

I watched purple dots leave each ship. Combined, the dashed lines of their computed trajectories formed a cone whose smaller end faced the enemy. Our SK allies had once again participated, contributing their own nuclear torpedoes.

Small orange dots erupted from the enemy flotilla; their computed trajectories led toward our nukes.

"They've launched antinuke countermeasures," Tactical Officer

Miko said over the comm. Antinuke countermeasures were small missiles designed to seek out and destroy nukes well before they hit their target.

"We are clear of incoming mortar projectiles, sir," came the voice of the astrogator. "Initiating countering portside burst."

"Good," Commodore Hanson said. "Scramble Avengers. I want those antinuke CMs taken out. And I want the enemy fighters blown from the void."

"Scrambling Avengers," Tactical Officer Miko answered.

I felt the hull of the drop vessel shudder as the *Gerald R. Ford* launched its own fighters through the launch tubes.

On the display, multiple blue dots appeared on either side of the *Gerald R. Ford* and the escort vessels.

The F-35 Avengers were fast, sleek, general-purpose drones remotely operated via fighter pilots who remained aboard the carrier. These pilots had numerous AI tools to aim and fire the weapons at their disposal, and to compensate for any delays in reaction time due to the distances the Avengers operated from the ship. The downside of Avengers was that the farther the starfighters traveled from the ship, the more they relied on the internal AIs due to communications lag. Hence the Captain's surprise when the enemy flotilla had launched their fighters so early in the game.

Roughly half of our Avengers accelerated toward the antinukes launched by the enemy; the other half headed on an intercept course toward the enemy fighters.

"Fire mortars again," Commodore Hanson said. "I want those ships boxed in. Everywhere they turn, they're going to face either mortar projectiles, nukes, or Avengers."

Space combat was really just a bunch of cow herding. You kept steering the cows until you got them precisely where you wanted them: in line for the slaughter.

The 3D display lit up with more lines and extrapolated paths as the enemy flotilla responded in kind with their own mortars. Actually no, some of those weapon paths were dark violet. That meant some of the incoming projectiles were nuclear torpedoes, not mortars. I counted twelve of them.

As usual, everything was aimed at the *Gerald R. Ford.*

"Commodore . . ." Captain Linder said.

"I see them," Commodore Hanson responded over the comm. "Launch antinuke countermeasures."

"Launching antinuke CMs," Tactical Officer Miko answered from the bridge.

Roughly one-fourth of the enemy starfighters diverted to intercept our countermeasures. Eliminating a countermeasure with the Gatling in a starfighter was safe, since antinukes didn't have sizable warheads. The Gatlings in starfighters could be used to take down nukes themselves, but the blast radius would destroy the fighter. Avengers were remotely piloted, so there would be no loss of human life; however, each Avenger cost as much as an ATLAS mech to produce, which was why antinukes were the preferred method of nuclear torpedo elimination.

"Alter trajectory to put some distance between us and the nuclears," Commodore Hanson said from the bridge comm. "Move us up the Z plane."

"Sir, that will put us in the path of the incoming mortars," the astrogator's voice came.

"I am aware of that," Commodore Hanson answered.

The dot representing our ship shifted subtly to the left. Cow herding indeed.

"Muting the bridge." Captain Linder rubbed his chin. "That's got to be their entire nuke arsenal." He glanced at Lieutenant Commander Braggs. "Again they target everything at the *Gerald R. Ford* and ignore the others. You've dealt with these alien beings before. Thoughts, LC?"

The Lieutenant Commander stared at the display. "I'm wary to suggest anything, sir. We're facing an alien intelligence here. Their thinking is going to be completely foreign to our own. But I could swear they were trying to get us to focus on the nukes and mortars. It's like they want us to forget about their starfighters. If it's true those fighters are piloted by Phants, all a Phant has to do to board us is ram its fighter into the carrier. I have a sinking feeling that the enemy wants to capture the *Gerald R. Ford*, sir, using those fighters."

Beside him, Captain Linder nodded slowly, but his face was unreadable. That was a commander's job. Never show fear. Always present a calm front.

On the 3D display the various dots and curves slowly closed on us.

"Things are going to get messy," Commander Bane said.

"Win or lose, the enemy flotilla is committed now," Captain Linder said. "We've done half our work. Take a look. Already the remainder of the fleet is closing the noose on Bandit 1."

Green dots had appeared behind the Skull Ship, spread out in a flanking, half-sphere pattern. Now that the *Gerald R. Ford* had drawn the enemy flotilla away, the remaining allied ships in orbit were taking the fight to the Skull Ship in a multipronged attack.

I counted twenty carriers in total, from three of the four major space-faring powers. All allied against a common foe. It was truly a significant moment. We were watching history unfold here, before our eyes. Whether they could actually do anything against the Skull Ship's coronal weaponry was another story however.

The Avengers met the enemy starfighters aimed at our carrier. In moments it became clear the enemy fighters were refusing to engage, because most of those red dots streaked right past and continued on toward the *Gerald R. Ford*. Some dots winked out, but most of the enemy broke through and continued on.

Our Avengers performed high-energy turns and flipped back to pursue them.

"You said they intend to board us, LC?" Captain Linder said to Braggs. "You're about to see why they'll never get the chance. The point defense of a fully powered supercarrier is not something to be taken lightly."

The moments ticked past.

"Enemy starfighters are in range of our point defense," Tactical Officer Miko said over the comm. "Automatic Gats engaging."

The red dots closing on the *Gerald R. Ford* started to vanish.

"Keep those fighters away from the hull," Commodore Hanson said from the bridge. "I don't want any Phants coming aboard."

Something struck the hull not far from the hangar bay where I resided; the impact was violent enough to be felt inside the Delivery Vehicle.

"What the hell was that?" Commodore Hanson said from the bridge.

"Sir," Tactical Officer Miko answered. "An enemy fighter managed to momentarily breach our point defense. Its Gat fire struck hangar bay three. We destroyed the fighter, but not before a cascading explosion consumed the hangar. It looks like . . . it looks like we lost the ten drop teams stationed in that bay."

Captain Linder slammed his chair's handrest in anger.

The CDC abruptly fell away as the Lieutenant Commander changed his point of view to a drone outside. Debris drifted from the hull of the *Gerald R. Ford*: hangar bay three had widened into a gaping hole with sparking edges. Amid the wreckage of drop crafts floated lifeless, charred jumpsuits.

I quickly double-checked our duty roster. The MOTHs were distributed in Delivery Vehicles throughout hangar bays seven and eight. None had been in hangar bay three.

I exhaled, relieved. It was selfish I know, because other men had died before they'd even had a chance to fight. But none of my MOTH brothers had perished, and that's all I cared about right then.

Still, I knew that any one of us could be next.

The view returned to the CDC as Lieutenant Commander Braggs switched back.

"We're in drop range, sir," the Tactical Officer said over the comm.

"About damn time," Commodore Hanson replied. "Open hangar bays and prepare Delivery Vehicles for drop. I want them out before we take any more damage."

I felt the hull shake again.

"Taking Gat and rail gun fire from enemy fighters," Tactical Officer Miko said. "We've lost turrets three and four."

So much for our vaunted point defense.

"Fire a broadside of mortars," Commodore Hanson said from the bridge. "I want those fighters kept away."

"Firing," Miko said. A moment later: "Commodore, wouldn't momentum carry the Phant pilots to our ship, regardless of whether or not we destroyed the fighters that contained them?"

Silence. Then:

"Hard dive," the Commodore said calmly.

"Sir, that will take us dangerously close to the moon," Miko said.

"Hard dive," the Commodore repeated.

"Initiating hard dive," the astrogator answered.

"Hangar bays are open, sir," came another voice on the bridge.

"Extend the Delivery Vehicles," Commodore Hanson intoned. His voice had remained incredibly calm throughout all this.

"Extending Delivery Vehicles."

The audio and video feed from the CDC abruptly cut out.

"All right men, time to concentrate on the drop." It was the Chief, speaking over the Alfa platoon comm.

Not yet! I thought. I truly wanted to know how the battle would end. I supposed I'd find out on the surface, one way or another.

If I survived the drop.

A Marine was seated directly opposite me in the Delivery Vehicle. Above his head was a portal, and through it I saw the far bulkhead shift to the left, and rotate.

"What happens if one of those enemy Gats hits us on the way down?" a Marine said. The question made me wonder how many other commanding officers had let their men watch the battle.

"If that happens, you'll be having a private conversation with your creator," Tahoe told him.

The Delivery Vehicle jerked and stopped rotating. The gravity field cut out, replaced by the weightlessness of space.

Through the portal I could see ten other Delivery Vehicles, held aloft by rails as they slid from the hangar bay. Beyond them, I watched DVs dropping from other hangars on the *Gerald R. Ford*, and the hangars of our escort ships in the distance. I saw the flashes of explosions everywhere.

The moon Tau Ceti II-c floated below, while the blue clouds of the gas giant provided an ever-present backdrop above. The moon's atmosphere was strangely devoid of weather patterns—terraformed colony worlds, including moons, usually had at least some cloud cover.

The DV dropped.

Through the portal, the *Gerald R. Ford* vanished. I could see one of the other Delivery Vehicles falling ten meters to our right. A few seconds later, that DV disintegrated under a white hail of incoming fire.

I worriedly glanced at the MOTH roster on my HUD.

No casualties in my platoon. Yet.

At first I thought we'd been hit as well when flames filled the portals and tinted the cabin orange. But then I realized it was just atmospheric entry.

Once through, the pilot steered us toward the insert site. I saw other surviving Delivery Vehicles thrusting alongside our craft, plus a couple of the larger payload shuttles in the distance.

As we neared the surface, the pilot applied air brakes, followed by reverse thrust.

We touched down.

I glanced at my companions, the sixteen individuals—brothers—who had survived the drop with me.

I almost expected to see vomit smears on a few of the face masks. Hell, I'd felt like throwing up during the drop myself, especially when the other Delivery Vehicle had disintegrated. But a quick glance around the compartment told me there were clean masks throughout the group. MOTHs and Marines were tough bastards.

The back ramp lowered.

"All right, men," Facehopper said. "Deploy and proceed to amtracs." That was the somewhat archaic nickname for the armored transport tanks that would carry us across the moon.

The clamps that held me in place folded open, and I piled out of the DV along with the others. An all-too-familiar landscape came into view. Black shale stretched to the horizon, like the rocks I had seen on Geronimo. It was like I was reliving a nightmare. I looked to my side, but Alejandro wasn't there.

Not a nightmare then, but harsh reality.

Facehopper led us toward our designated amtrac at a trot. The slight bounce to our step wasn't due to any cheer on our part, but rather the 0.92 G gravity.

DVs touched down all around us, unloading more men. The Marines raced toward the amtracs in controlled, purposeful units.

None of the enemy Avengers had followed us down—the fighters weren't built for atmospheric entry.

Two square-cargoed Builder shuttles landed to my left. Once we secured the designated spot outside Shangde City, the Builders would deploy and construct a forward operating base.

Skullcracker held out a gloved hand as he jogged. "Rad levels are fairly high. Probably have to juice up when we get back."

If we got back.

"Please tell me this place looked like this two months ago," Bender said.

"It didn't," Facehopper said from his position at point. "The moon used to be called 'Fragrant Meadow.'"

The bleak, shale-covered landscape was the furthest thing from a fragrant meadow you could get. Above, the sky was dim, just as if it were the onset of twilight on Earth, though the pinprick dot of the sun was high in the sky. Tau Ceti had a G-class star, just like Sol, but because of its lower mass, size, and surface temperature, it had roughly half the illumination. The off-color rays cast everything in a pale hue, giving the planet's surface the look of a graveyard of crushed and blackened bone.

In the distance, the immense Skull Ship ate up the sky like some ominous cloud, sheathing the landscape from the bottom of the horizon to the utmost heavens.

Around it, the gas giant consumed the rest of the sky. The planet, which dwarfed even the Skull Ship, made me feel quite insignificant. Those swirling swaths of blue and white were very much like the strokes of a paintbrush, and offered a smooth, natural beauty that was in sharp contrast to the ugly, alien design of the Skull Ship.

Nowhere up there could I discern the shapes of the battling fleet in orbit. They would be too far, and too small, to be visible. I did see closer objects streaking through the sky however, and I knew

those were the ATLAS 5s and the booster rocket p
needed to return.

A quick glance at the HUD map told r
ground assets and troops were SK. All our equipmeı..
reprogrammed to tag them as friendlies: green dots, not red. I diu..
trust them, but their ships had fought alongside our own in orbit so
I guess they were on our side.

For now.

The remaining ground assets were FI and UC. Humanity's finest specimens, as far as I was concerned. Especially after surviving a
harrowing drop like that.

Robot support troops fanned out ahead of us, including the
humanoid Centurions and their Praetor leaders, the Equestrian
automated tanks, and the flying Raptor drones. There were also
countless Hover Squad Support System (HS3) drones. The metallic, basketball-sized spheres hovered among the units in such perverse quantities that everywhere I looked I saw one.

"It's like a city of robots," Tahoe complained. "Am I the only
one who has a bad feeling about this?"

"Command believes the benefits of the robots far outweigh the
potential harm, mate," Facehopper said.

"And what do you believe?"

Facehopper glanced at him over his shoulder. "If they'd asked
me, which they didn't, I'd have told them to take their robots and
melt them down at the nearest ammunitions plant. We could always
use the spare ammo. What we can't use is robots turning on us in
the middle of battle."

Objects smashed into the ground some distance from the rest
of the convoy, sending up plumes of black dust. From the plumes
walked the massive forms of ATLAS 5s. There were roughly ten of
us for every one of them. Normally I'd be feeling pretty invincible
with them at my side, but today I felt only dread.

So far, there was no sign of enemy air support. Intel had told us o expect some possessed Raptors, which was why our own air support fanned ahead at this very moment.

Facehopper halted beside the open ramp of our designated amtrac and motioned the rest of us inside. The tall treads reached just over my head, but the remainder of the vehicle wasn't much taller. There were turrets on top for two gunners, shielded by black-tinted TAGS (Transparent Armor Gun Shields).

I rushed inside and sat down, closing the buckle, which had big grips to make for easier handling via jumpsuit gloves.

"The order is coming down the line," Facehopper said over the comm. "Open up your masks and don your aReal visors. Air's still breathable. No indication of viral toxins or other bioweapons."

"Still breathable?" Bender said. The robot support troops he operated would be on autopilot right now, moving into position on their own. "What are you talking about? I thought the probes detected elevated levels of carbon monoxide and chlorine? No indications of toxins my ass."

"There are only trace amounts present here," Facehopper said. "Save your oxygen until you really need it."

I opened my face mask. The polycarbonate and aluminum oxynitride lens wouldn't provide much protection against modern armor-piercers anyway.

I lowered my aReal visor. With my Implant offline, I couldn't uptick the power of my exoskeleton. Even so, before I'd deactivated the Implant I'd boosted the output of my suit to the max. That meant while I now had the strength of three men, the drain on my jumpsuit battery was also three times as great. Forget about saving oxygen—I would run out of suit power long before I ran out of oxygen.

The amtrac started up and proceeded across the black rock with the rest of the convoy. On my HUD map, I could see the ATLAS mechs interspersed among the vehicles, along with the Centurions,

Equestrians, and HS3s. Several remote-controlled
tanks brought up the rear.

Sitting there, waiting for the true battle to be _
but ponder the fate of the fleet in orbit. If all the allied ˅ ˍ
disabled or destroyed, there was no going home, not for any of us.

"Don't know why they made us open up our face masks,"
Bender said, drawing me out of my ruminations. He wrinkled his
nose in disgust. "Smells like FAN in here." Feet, Ass, and Nuts.

"You think this is bad?" one of the Marines said. "You Meat
Eaters should try rooming in the barracks with us sometime. Brings
new meaning to the phrase shit hits the FAN."

I leaned back, resting my head against the bulkhead.

"Stop that," Tahoe said, looking right at me. He was clearly
annoyed.

"What?" The moment I opened my mouth I knew exactly what
he was talking about. My foot was fidgeting.

With effort I stilled the muscles.

I glanced at the faces of the men who sat in the amtrac with
me. My brothers.

Would all of these men survive this day?

Would I?

I listened to the relentless hum of the engine, and the milling
sound as the heavy treads of the vehicle ground across the black
rock. The terrain was getting bumpier, I thought. I glanced at the
map. The city wasn't far ahead. Maybe ten klicks.

"Holy shit, man," one of the Marines said into the tense silence.
"Just received word, we've lost contact with the fleet."

"You shouldn't be broadcasting that information, private," Facehopper said. "We have a mission to perform. We don't need unnecessary distractions."

"*Unnecessary* distractions?" the Marine said. "I'd say it's necessary, man. Without the fleet, there's no going home."

Tahoe spoke up. "They've probably simply moved out of comm distance. The Skull Ship messes with the range of our InterPlaNet nodes."

I hoped he was right, because the alternative was the destruction or capture of the fleet. But I couldn't think about that now, because like Facehopper had said, I had a mission to focus on.

"Hang tight!" came the frantic voice of the driver.

The amtrac slammed to a halt, swinging sideways.

On the HUD map, I saw the vehicles around us swerving wildly. They were struggling to slow down and avoid hitting each other—indeed, the trailing amtrac almost smashed into us.

"What's going on?" one of the Marines said when all the vehicles had stopped. "We're still three klicks from the city."

Facehopper held up a hand, calling for silence. When he looked up, his expression was dark. "A sinkhole has opened up at the front. We've lost three amtracs."

I glanced at my HUD map. At the head of the bunched convoy, red dots started to appear in a circular pattern. First only a few. Then tens. Hundreds.

"Uh, Facehopper?" Skullcracker said.

"Form a defensive front on the amtrac." Facehopper flipped the vehicle's manual release latch, and the back ramp fell open. "Deploy!"

I followed Facehopper and Bender outside. We formed up in front of the amtrac along with the rest of the MOTHs and the Marines. Tahoe was right beside me.

Ahead, past the jumble of vehicles, ATLAS-sized crabs were assaulting the front of the convoy. I lifted my rifle and was about to engage, when from behind the crabs a huge tower of flesh launched heavenward.

It was a slug. One of the superbehemoths. The size of a dreadnought starship. Its skin was white hot, and steam rose from its flanks. "Burrowing" mode, as I called it.

The wall of flesh just kept coming and coming, with no end in sight. It was like a skyscraper rising from the depths of hell. The crabs were drawn upward with it, dragged along by the umbilicals that connected them to the slug.

Some of the troops and tanks were firing at the massive slug, launching missiles and grenades, to no apparent effect.

Higher and higher the behemoth rose until its form blotted out the sun and cast a shadow over the entire convoy.

Its upward motion finally ceased. The massive slug hung ponderously for a few moments as gravity nullified its momentum.

Instinctively, all weapons fire from the convoy ceased, as if we were all holding our collective breaths. Even the robots stopped firing.

Gravity kicked in, and the behemoth started to fall.

Sideways.

Toward the convoy.

Some of the amtracs in its path steered away frantically, slamming through the maze of halted vehicles. Other drivers and occupants wisely abandoned their amtracs and used their jetpacks to get the hell out of the way as that tower of flesh came tumbling down.

"Move, move, move!" Facehopper said.

I activated my jumpjets in a series of evasive bursts.

I was roughly thirty meters to the right when the superbehemoth collided with the surface. The shockwave from the impact literally knocked me to the ground.

I clambered upright and glanced over my shoulder, looking for Tahoe, my "buddy" for the mission. He'd landed just a few meters to my left.

The massive slug had crashed right down the middle of the convoy, separating us from the SK units on the opposite side and taking out a good portion of the amtracs in the process. Most of the ATLAS mechs and other jetpack-enabled ground units, robots and humans alike, on our side seemed to have emerged unscathed.

The alien behemoth lifted its head and swung it ponderously from side to side, howling. The shriek was earsplitting, and I found myself flinching.

I wasn't the only one.

"Damn," Bender said. "Someone's got PMS this morning."

The crabs launched from its white-hot skin, leaping like parachutists as the thin cords that connected them to the host unwound. The black, multiheaded beasts were as big as ATLAS 5s, and their bodies were translucent so that I could see their hell-black hearts beating within.

I set my rifle to full automatic mode, and fired at the cords, which were quite thick on these crabs—sometimes the size of tree trunks. It took a few bursts to cut each one, but it was worth it because every severed cord killed a crab. The alternative was to fire at the crabs themselves, in the spot where the eyestalks joined the carapaces, which was tricky given the speed and size of the creatures.

"Get back, people!" Facehopper roared. "Air strike!"

Hellfires slammed into the slug from above as the Raptors homed in.

None of us had time to clear out, and the shockwave from the blast threw us far back.

A shuttle roared past, dropping a load of Napalm D along the slug's entire upper surface. The adhesive flames coated the behemoth's skin, burning intensely, but the thing seemed unconcerned. The Napalm would have been far more effective against the crabs, but the shuttle couldn't drop it on them, not while the creatures swarmed our ranks.

Of course, others around me had no reason not to release their own local incendiaries against the crabs. Unfortunately, the things merely became frantic when the sticky flames engulfed them, and in their rampaging ended up rubbing the jellied gasoline onto amtracs and even mechs, spreading the flames and basically using our own incendiaries against us. Luckily, severing the cord would instantly drop a thusly afflicted crab, putting it out of its misery.

A bunch of human-controlled M1A5 Abrams tanks, UC and Franco-Italian models, rolled past me. The tanks formed a defensive half circle around the behemoth's right flank and unleashed hell, aiming into the wounds caused by the hellfires. The gunners assigned to the turrets of the surviving amtracs joined in, concentrating fire on the smaller crabs, protecting the tanks.

From where I stood with my unit on the far flank of the slug, I could see huge black spots marring the previously unspoiled white skin. Those spots gushed a thick, dark blood. On the upper flanks, the Napalm still burned brightly.

"Bender, Equestrians are requested in a support capacity," Facehopper said.

"On it."

The Equestrians, the AI-driven tanks drone operators like Bender babysat, came forward and joined the Abrams, firing in unison at the superbehemoth. Normally the robot support troops would have been sent ahead first, but because of the unexpected nature of the attack, the convoy hadn't been properly deployed. If I was in charge of the convoy, I would have sent the Equestrians to scout far ahead of us. But what did I know? I was just a grunt.

I glanced at Bender. I knew he was observing the battlefield on a higher plane beneath that visor of his, directing the robots under his command like the pieces of a life-or-death gameboard. He probably had at least three of the twenty Equestrians with us under his direct control, not to mention numerous Centurions and Praetors.

"Forward, people!" Facehopper said. "Protect the tanks from the Worker crabs. Aim for the cords."

My platoon mates and I rushed forward with the Marines, taking cover behind one of the amtracs about three ranks from the front. The vehicle was Franco-Italian, judging from the paint.

I fired above the horde of swinging mandibles and pincers with my rifle, aiming once again at the tree-trunk-sized cords.

Tahoe had great success beside me with his heavy gun, and he mowed down those cords just as well as the gunners in the turrets and the ATLAS mechs. All that gunfire going off around me sounded like fireworks.

The massive slug was taking a battering from the tanks, and started to phase out from existence—one of its defense mechanisms. The tanks had to stop firing, lest they take out some of the SK friendlies on the other side in the crossfire. Indeed, some of the units on both sides took shelling before the allied parties realized what was happening.

The crabs connected to the main body didn't phase out with the host slug, and kept up their relentless assault.

Most of the tanks focused their attention on the crabs now, switching to Gatlings.

I threw a grenade, and got a crab, sending its pieces flying in three directions. Then I mowed down a cord.

A crab came up behind our amtrac, but Tahoe was there, drilling its underside with his heavy gun. The thing backed away, and I fired at its cord. The stringy organic umbilical split open, spewing black blood over the amtrac, and the crab keeled over.

The superslug began to fade back in. It had slithered forward during its absence from this universe, and it reappeared now over some of the Abrams and amtracs, consuming said vehicles. That was good, I thought, remembering when I myself had plunged inside one of the smaller slugs while it was still fading into existence—I'd tunneled my way out in a stream of gore, killing it.

Except this time all that happened was we lost several of our Abrams, Equestrians, and amtracs. The creature was too huge for the engulfed tanks to make much of a difference.

The flanks of the behemoth towered roughly ten meters above me. Thanks to the interdimensional shift, the Napalm D flames on the creature's upper flank had gone out entirely, when the fire should have lasted at least another ten minutes.

The men around me unleashed rockets and launched grenades. I decided now was as good a time as any to put the Carl Gustav I'd brought along to use. Officially known as the M7 Multi-Role Anti-armor Anti-tank Weapon System, those recoilless rifles packed a mighty powerful punch.

I swung the recoilless rifle down and fired it. I manually loaded the next two rounds, firing them off in succession.

The behemoth was almost completely black now, from all the wounds. Yet it fought on.

I almost respected the thing for its fighting spirit, its refusal to give up.

Almost.

Bullets started to come in at me from the far right, closer to the sinkhole. At first I thought the attack was accidental cross fire, because when I glanced that way, I saw a bunch of ATLAS 5s and Centurions outlined in friendly green. But when those units kept advancing and firing into our ranks, I realized the truth.

They were possessed.

"Take cover!" Facehopper said.

I sheltered on the far side of the amtrac, away from the incoming bullets, along with the rest of the unit. I quickly scanned the black surface around me, searching for any Phants in liquid form, but I didn't see any.

For the most part I'd mentally blocked out the firework-like noises of the gunfire around me, but I knew something was wrong, sound-wise. I realized what it was: the gun turrets on the amtrac we sheltered behind weren't firing.

I glanced up.

The gunners lay slumped in the turrets, decapitated. Crabs were still assailing us on the other flank.

"Dyson, get up on that gun!" I said, then spun toward Tahoe. "Watch my back. I'm taking down some of those Centurions."

I leaned out from the cover afforded by the amtrac and scanned the rightmost flank through my scope, looking for a Centurion or Praetor to target. There, between two upturned tanks, I saw a Praetor command unit advancing with seven Centurions at its back. Wedge formation. The robots were waling into our ranks with heavy machine guns.

I aimed at the Praetor's chest, which housed the brain case, and saw several droplets of glowing blue condensation.

Definitely possessed.

I fired.

The Praetor toppled over.

Five of the seven Centurions with it continued their charge unabated, while the other two broke off to attack the crabs. Centurions were usually linked to Praetors and would revert to previous pro-gramming if the link was severed. This meant the unaffected five were possessed, too.

I started terminating the remaining Centurions, one by one. I got three of them before the gunfire from the remaining two homed in on me. I ducked behind the amtrac, and heard the hail-on-a-tin-roof sound of ricocheting bullets.

"Facehopper!" Bender said. "I've lost most of my robots."

"What do you mean you've 'lost' them, mate?" Facehopper said, bringing his rifle down, and ducking behind the amtrac. "Clarify. Have they been disabled, or possessed?"

"Possessed, man!"

Facehopper didn't look too happy. "Why didn't you pull them back when you saw the Phants?"

"That's the thing!" Bender said. "I didn't *see* any, dude!"

"They're on the ground around us!" I said. "Somewhere . . ."

"Well I figured that," Bender said. "But I still didn't see 'em!"

A rocket blast shook the amtrac.

I peered past the edge.

More possessed Equestrians, ATLAS 5s, and Abrams tanks were bearing down on our position. Any assets containing AIs were vulnerable to possession, regardless of whether humans could pilot them or not; Abrams (and ATLAS 5s) were no exception. Compounding the problem was the fact that our aReals didn't mark the possessed units as enemies—I saw green across the board.

About a quarter of the convoy had redirected its fire toward the turned units, while the rest concentrated on the superbehemoth. Shuttles and gunships swooped in, unleashing more hellfires at the slug, which had just returned from another hiatus to its hidden dimension.

The gunships aimed high, but my unit and others were still fairly close to the slug, and sometimes the shockwaves from the air strikes hurled us to the ground. We certainly got splattered with our fair share of gore. A huge chunk of flesh struck Tahoe after a particularly intense air strike. I knelt beside him.

"Tahoe," I said, flinging the slippery, pliant mass aside. "You all right?"

"Never better." Tahoe's jumpsuit was covered in black ink. His face, too. He wiped some of the liquid away, and the skin seemed fine underneath—at least the ink wasn't acid or something. Still, when we got back to the ship, the Infection Control Practitioners would probably make him spend a few hours in the detox wing before letting him mingle with the rest of the crew, regardless of whether he passed the bioscans or not. "Tastes like sperm soup."

I frowned. "And how would you know what sperm soup tastes like?"

"Uh, never mind."

The crazy things people joked about when fighting for their lives . . .

The two of us hugged the amtrac once more, pinned down by gunfire from the possessed units on our right flank.

Beside us, the slug finally went down in a vile display of exploding body parts and gore.

The last few living crabs turned over and crimped up, their dead bodies remaining behind while the superbehemoth vanished from existence.

What a damn pain.

Now that the slug was gone, I was able to see the SK ranks again, and they surged forward to join us, taking up positions throughout the convoy, helping us shoot down the possessed robots.

Dyson momentarily left cover. "Go away, we don't need your help!" Dyson shouted at the arriving SKs. "Go—"

Facehopper forcefully hurled him to the ground behind the amtrac and pinned his chest with his knee. "Stay behind cover, caterpillar. Do your job, and let the SKs do theirs."

Tahoe sat back against the amtrac and closed his eyes, obviously exhausted.

"It's not over yet, Tahoe," I said, reloading. I aimed out past the edge of the amtrac, at the robots. "We need your heavy gun!" I fired and took down a possessed Centurion. "Tahoe . . ."

"I know," Tahoe said. "Just need a minute, Rade."

I was worried he'd been shot or something, but his vitals seemed tolerable, and I didn't observe any punctures in his jumpsuit. The huge slab of meat that had struck him earlier might have crushed some of his internal organs though.

"You sure you're all right?"

He forced a grin. "Never better." He turned around and got back into the fight.

Another slug chose that moment to slam its body out of the distant sinkhole. It was pitch-black. Not in "burrowing" mode, then.

A second black slug slithered forth right after the first, coming out at a slightly different angle.

Then a third.

Each slug was just as big as the superbehemoth we'd just killed.

Two hundred ATLAS-sized crabs leaped down from each of the slugs, for a combined force of six hundred. As usual, the crabs immediately dispersed into our midst, making an air strike on them impossible.

"Uh, Facehopper, don't think this assault is going too well," I said, switching my aim to the crabs. "And we haven't even reached the city yet. This is ridiculous."

Facehopper flashed me a wicked grin between his own rifle bursts. "Guess we won't be setting up a forward operating base anytime soon, mate."

One of the crabs landed beside the amtrac, right on top of an unlucky UC mech. The unpossessed ATLAS 5 toppled backward, and one of the crab's razor-like pincers sliced clean through the cockpit.

I unleashed hell from my rifle, cutting away the trunk-sized cord, which snapped backward.

The dead crab tumbled aside.

I checked the vitals of the ATLAS 5 pilot on my HUD. Pitch-black: dead.

"Well Tahoe, it's time for me to make a difference," I said, already running toward the mech at full speed.

"Got you covered, Rade," Tahoe sent over the comm.

I saw the callsign overlaid in green above the ATLAS 5.

Dragonfly.

Before the battle, all qualified spec-ops men had been provisioned to pilot the ATLAS 5s. This meant, in a pinch, we MOTHs could operate any UC mech that became available.

The brain case of the ATLAS 5 was unharmed, and except for the slit in the cockpit, the mech seemed otherwise undamaged. Since the Marine pilot was no longer alive, Dragonfly's AI took over, and it stood up, turning toward the nearest crabs to "defend," which was its default mode. Bullets from possessed robots on the far right ricocheted past it—the ATLAS 5 would treat those robots as friendlies, at least until one of them threatened a green human target.

I reached the mech and activated my jumpjets, simultaneously transmitting a verbal signal directly to its callsign.

"Dragonfly unlock!" I shouted.

The mech turned toward me while I was still in midair, and its damaged cockpit fell open. The dead pilot slumped forward onto the open hatch, and when I landed, I unceremoniously dumped him to the ground, saying a silent prayer for forgiveness. I knew if his spirit was watching he'd understand why I treated his body so poorly. I had to get that mech moving. And *now*.

I threw aside my rifle, and other extraneous gear that would get in the way of the inner cockpit, and then I stepped into the compartment, hoping none of those incoming bullets found its target, and that none of the crabs would take the opportunity to pounce. The hatch sealed and an elastic cocoon pressed into my jumpsuit. Dragonfly routed its vision feed to my aReal visor.

Control of the mech switched over to me.

I stood at the heart of a war machine that contained over a thousand hydraulically actuated joints. It had onboard hydraulic pump and thermal management. Crash protection. Jumpjets. A head-mounted sensor package with built-in LIDAR, night vision, flash vision, zoom, and other augmented reality perception boosts that smoothly integrated with my helmet aReal. The mounts on either forearm could hold up to three weapons each. The typical loadout was Gatling, serpent, and incendiary thrower for both arms, with the addition of a hot-deployable ballistic shield on the left arm for protection against armor-piercing rounds.

The Gatling gun was already loaded into the right hand, and the ballistic shield the left. I swung the large shield toward the incoming gunfire on my right flank, and I told Dragonfly, "Override friendly fire protection."

I loosed several threads of high-energy bullets from my Gat, terminating three Centurions. Then I sprinted away from the possessed robots, heading toward the three freshly emerged slugs.

Without my Implant, control of the mech was via the pressure sensors lining the inner material, rather than by thought, and it felt a little like wading neck-deep through a morass. I knew I'd quickly get used to it, especially with the strength-enhancement provided by my jumpsuit.

I wove between the friendly amtracs and tanks, and the ATLAS-sized crabs. The same size as me, now. I shot my Gatling at the cords of the crabs as I ran, easily severing them. I avoided confronting any crabs head-on, because I knew they were too big to simply bash aside. Not like the smaller crabs I'd faced on Geronimo. That battle seemed like the good old days compared to this.

I was no longer taking incoming fire, so I swung the shield back to my left, keeping it at the ready.

The gunships and Raptors were raining hell on the slugs, but I knew it was only a matter of time before they ran out of explosive ordnance. My intention was to let off some serpent rockets at one of the existing wounds in a slug, and assess the damage capability. I didn't want to get too close, however, not while those air strikes were in progress.

Seemed I approached too close after all though, because just then one of those hellfires landed slightly off target.

As in, a few paces behind me.

The explosion sent my mech hurtling forward.

I collided with one of the crabs, and the two of us pummeled into the enormous flank of the slug. I landed in the small gap between the convoy and the behemoth. I got up and tore open the crab's umbilical with my Gat before it could recover.

I ran along the rightmost flank of the superslug, firing my Gatling at close range into its meaty side, tearing it a few new mouths. I didn't dare launch a serpent rocket, not at this close range. I'd been tossed around enough today by explosive ordnance.

All of the crabs were engaged farther away from the slug, amid the convoy, so I faced no resistance. I kept on running and firing until I reached the rear of the slug.

The sinkhole lay directly ahead.

It was relatively quiet out here, so I decided to have a look inside. A quick recon could only help us, after all.

I sprinted toward the opening, keeping a watchful eye on the battlefield behind me.

I reached the sinkhole.

Below, a tunnel ramped downward at roughly forty-five degrees.

It wasn't the tunnel that caught my eye, however, but rather what occupied it.

"Uh, Facehopper," I sent over the comm. I was stunned. I couldn't believe what I was seeing.

"What is it, mate?" Facehopper returned.

"We got a problem."

"Why? What do you see?" Facehopper would have known I was standing next to the sinkhole, thanks to his HUD.

"Things are going to be getting real nasty, real quick," I said.

"Say again, Rage?" Facehopper sent.

Along the bottom of the tunnel, a long, glowing, liquid mass leisurely rippled upward, reminding me of a waterfall flowing in reverse.

"An army of Phants is coming out of the sinkhole."

CHAPTER FOUR

Shaw

I was running. Queequeg kept up alongside me.

A pack of eight hybears was in hot pursuit.

Apparently this pack had discovered the cairn I'd made from my earlier kill, and they'd tracked my scent all the way to the Forma pipe. I guessed as much, anyway, because it was either that or blind luck that they found me. Luckily, Queequeg had spotted them when they were far away on the western horizon, giving me time to flee.

I'd been running ever since.

I was using up my freshly charged battery at a horrendous rate, and though I had reached my top speed, the pack was still gaining.

Queequeg purposely kept pace with me, though he was capable of greater speeds. I kept telling him to run ahead, and that I was dead either way, but he wouldn't listen.

Anyway, my problem was that there was nowhere to hide, not out here. No trees. No buildings. Just endless dunes of shale. There were some defiles in the cliff walls at the far edge of the valley, but they were too far away to reach in time.

I didn't have a jetpack. Or a proper weapon. All I had was an alien mandible superglued to a rifle. Plus a knife.

In previous encounters, I'd faced more hybears than this of course, but that was when I had a fully loaded rifle. Ever since I'd run out of ammo, the most hybears I'd faced was two at a time, with Queequeg at my side.

Not eight.

I'd just have to wing it. Which was basically what I've been doing since I crash-landed on this planet.

I could hear the whoops growing closer behind me, sounding with greater frequency and enthusiasm.

I glanced at my oxygen levels, and despair washed over me.

What was the point of even trying?

It was over.

I had only an hour of oxygen left.

Why bother to fight?

I should just face the facts.

I was dead.

Might as well just give up.

I'd given it the good fight.

Tried my hardest.

It was pointless to resist further.

Still, it made me a little sad, knowing that I'd come all this way only to die in the end.

What a waste. Not just of my own limited time in the universe, but the time of all those who'd invested in me. Who'd seen the potential I had. The instructors. The officers. Captain Drake.

Rade.

He wouldn't have given up.

He wouldn't have given in.

He told me of the trials he'd endured during MOTH training. How people had quit around him left and right, but he had stayed firm through it all. He'd stayed the course. He told me he had resolved early on that he would become a MOTH, or die trying.

If you're going through hell . . .

I was going to fight for every last ounce of life.

I was going to fight to the bitter end.

Believe in yourself, Shaw.

Because no one else is going to do it.

I chose the site where I would make my last stand. It was a rise, about thirty paces ahead and to the right, higher than the surrounding ground. A good spot to defend.

I swore that the price for my life wouldn't be cheap. I planned to take down at least three of them before the end came. No matter what.

I swung down my rifle with its razor-sharp mandible attachment, and, as I crested the rise, I turned around to meet my foes. Queequeg continued on ahead, probably not even aware I'd stopped.

It was better this way. I didn't want him to die, too.

Whooping with bloodlust, the pack didn't slow. None of them were deterred in the least by the fur of their brethren glued all over my jumpsuit.

I swung my rifle-scythe down and got the leader of the pack as it came in.

The momentum of the blow left me vulnerable to the next two. The animals vaulted forward—

I sidestepped—

One hybear struck me.

The force of the blow sent me skidding backward across the shale, and the weapon flew from my grasp.

I landed on my side, with the hybear on top of me.

Those ferocious jaws bit at my face mask. Teeth raked scratches across the glass. One of the bear-like claws punctured my jumpsuit, tearing into the flesh of my upper arm. I grimaced in pain.

A breach alarm sounded in my helmet.

"Warning, suit integrity compromised. Warning . . ."

I lay on my side, and my back was shielded thanks to the rucksack, so I felt nothing as the animal's other forelimb raked the area. I was never so glad for the extra burden of the sack as right then. My only worry was that the hybear would sever one of my backward-facing life-support lines.

The animal withdrew its claw from my upper arm. I winced in pain as the skin and muscle of my wounded shoulder bulged outward to seal the tiny suit punctures.

Before the hybear could strike again, I wrapped my hand around the knife at my utility belt and shifted sideways, pushing the animal off me with my strength-enhanced exoskeleton. I drew the knife and sliced the surprised hybear's belly clean open in one smooth motion.

I scrambled to my feet as it rolled around in pain beside me. I was at a loss as to why the others hadn't attacked yet.

Then I saw Queequeg.

Two dead hybears lay at his feet, and he was backing away from the remaining four, growling, his teeth misting with the green blood of his kills. He had a steaming wound just above his right shoulder blade.

Those four hybears had their backs toward me.

I sheathed my knife. Stepping forward, I scooped up my rifle-scythe and with it took the hind leg clean off one of the beasts that antagonized Queequeg.

The other three hybears swung around to look—

Queequeg launched forward, plunging into the rightmost hybear, and the two of them rolled down the rise.

The three-legged hybear struggled away.

That left me facing two.

I swung and jabbed at them with the rifle-scythe.

They backed away warily, snarling, flattening their manes.

I drew my knife, aimed, and threw.

The animal I'd targeted dodged, and as it did so I swung my rifle-scythe into its side.

The sharp blade passed clean through the lung cavity and emerged from the front part of the hybear's chest, pinning the animal to the shale. Green steam gusted from the wound.

The other hybear came at me before I could withdraw the weapon.

Not letting go of the stock of my rifle-scythe, I vaulted to the other side of the injured animal, twisting the blade in its flesh.

I wrenched the weapon free, and used my momentum to swing at the remaining hybear as it leaped at me. I took its head clean off.

I turned toward the other writhing beast, and mercifully ended its life.

I dashed down the rise to find Queequeg finishing off the last one. He held the animal firmly to the ground, his jaws wrapped around its neck in his favorite killing posture. The legs of the pinned animal convulsed three times before it finally died.

Queequeg released the animal, glanced up at me to make sure I was uninjured, in his opinion, then nonchalantly started eating. A slight mist rose from different scratches all over his body, but otherwise he seemed fine.

I glanced toward the top of the rise, confirming that no more attacks were coming from that quarter, and then I collapsed to the shale.

I'd actually won. Incredible.

Of course it was entirely thanks to Queequeg, who continued munching away on his kill.

I'd let him feast, all right. For as long as he wanted.

I won . . . but that didn't change the fact I still had less than an hour of O_2.

Was this really how it was going to end? Asphyxiated on my own toxic air, on a planet eight thousand lightyears from home?

Probably. But I was going to fight to the end. I'd promised myself that. For the whole hour, if that's all I had.

My upper arm started to throb with renewed pain now that the threat of the moment had passed. I became aware of the breach alarm once more, which had continued to sound in my helmet all this time, unheeded, unnoticed.

I glanced at my arm: blood steamed from the small punctures where the skin and muscle underneath had swollen outward to seal the suit. The red steam came in pulses timed to my heartbeat.

According to the readout on my HUD, my hybear attacker had cut no major arteries or veins. Essentially a flesh wound. That meant I wouldn't have to open up the suit with a SealWrap to apply a bandage underneath.

Still, the whole area underneath was swelling (and bruising) because of the pressure differential, and it would only worsen if I didn't patch the suit.

I resignedly retrieved the suitrep kit from my cargo pocket and proceeded to patch the puncture. When I was done, the breach alarm ended.

The oxygen warning light didn't go out, however. Less than forty-five minutes left before I died of hypoxia.

Hypoxia. I remembered training for it back in flight school. Well, training to recognize the symptoms, anyway. There was a certain qualification where they took a group of us up in the unoxygenated cabin of a jetliner. We took turns taking off our breathers, and were given a simple set of instructions to follow involving a deck of cards. We'd pick a card from the deck, identify it, put it back, and repeat until hypoxic symptoms occurred, then put the breather back on. For the first minute or so, most recruits completed the instructions well. After that, things quickly went downhill. Our minds started operating mostly on automatic. I don't remember my own session, as the formation of new memories was one of the first things to go when the brain was deprived of oxygen, but apparently I failed the first time. I kept showing the card I'd been previously ordered to pick from the deck, and I kept saying it was the ace of spades, even though I was repeatedly told to reattach my breather by that point. Finally my training buddy had to put my breathing mask on for me.

Who knows, maybe the oxygen indicator in my suit was wrong, and I'd already run out of O_2. Maybe my mind was operating on automatic right now.

Though if that were the case, I doubted I'd have the ability for such a lucid internal debate . . .

Queequeg, who had been busy eating, suddenly raised his head and started growling.

That was one of Queequeg's faults. Though he was usually always on the alert, sometimes, when dining on a fresh kill, he could become oblivious to his surroundings. Twice before he'd let a hybear sneak right up to us unawares.

He'd done so a third time, apparently.

I noticed a darkness stretching across the shale beside me, originating from behind.

A rather tall shadow for a hybear . . .

I slowly reached for my rifle-scythe as Queequeg continued to growl.

The shadow shifted—

I made an all-out lunge for the weapon and spun around—

Meeting the eyes of a man in a black jumpsuit.

He held an automatic rifle of some kind, aimed right at me.

I heard Queequeg repositioning behind me.

"You tell your pet to stay back," the man said in the thick accent of someone who spoke native Korean-Chinese. I couldn't tell if he was military or civilian.

"Easy, Queequeg," I said. "Easy. This is a friend. *Friend.*"

The growl Queequeg gave told me he knew this wasn't a friend, but he remained still, thankfully. I didn't want the animal to get shot.

"The two of you killed eight of them without a gun," the SK said. "Very impressive. For a white devil."

"You just stood by the whole time and watched?" I said incredulously.

He shrugged.

I glanced at the rifle. "It's not even loaded, is it?"

He lifted the barrel toward my face mask. "Do you care to find out?"

I stared at him for a long moment. He was too far away to hit with my rifle-scythe, and by the time I retrieved and threw my dagger, he would've shot me in the face. No, this guy had me at his mercy.

As I continued to look at him, I realized his suit wasn't just black, but he actually had shards of Geronium glued to it. All the better to blend into the landscape, I supposed. Using the aReal in my helmet glass, I tried to pull up the public profile associated with his embedded ID, but all I got was his ID number. He'd blanked his profile, then.

Queequeg continued growling.

"Queequeg," I said warningly, glancing over my shoulder.

The hybear sat back. His ears were flattened, and his tail remained stiff. He definitely knew we were in trouble.

"You must teach me how to tame them, sometime," the SK said. "I could use a *Chéngdān* pet."

"What do you want?" I said.

The SK ignored my question. "You wear a nice suit. Very becoming. With all that fur, you could almost pass for one of the Chéngdān. Almost."

I smiled sarcastically. "Yours is pretty sick too. Must have taken you a long time to glue all those rocks onto it. Can't be good for your health, though. All the radiation, I mean."

He grinned toothily, keeping his automatic rifle trained on me. "Radiation does not affect me."

"You never said what you wanted."

The grin faded, and he seemed angry. "Does everyone always have to *want* something? Maybe I am merely a Good Samaritan."

That gave me a chuckle. "When you're the only person on a planet eight thousand lightyears from Earth, and you suddenly meet another person and he's pointing a rifle at you, the Good Samaritan postulate kind of goes out the window. So I ask again, what do you want?"

He smiled. It didn't touch his eyes. "Yes. I have a rifle pointed at you. Do you know why? Because I am not sure I can trust you. And as for what I want . . . maybe . . . maybe all I want is companionship."

Companionship. It was a nice thought, if he could be believed. Still, I had more important needs at the moment than companionship. "Do you have any oxygen you can spare?"

"Mm? Oxygen. It is a precious commodity on *Hēi Sö*." That seemed to be his name for the planet, and according to my helmet aReal it meant "Black Death." "Perhaps if you would be willing to do certain things for me, I could give you some oxygen, yes."

I scowled. "What kinds of things?"

"Oh, I am easy to please, no worry, no worry. Do not look at me that way! It is not what you were thinking. Not at all. There is no way we can do *cào* in these jumpsuits anyway! Ha!" According to my aReal, cào meant sexual intercourse. "I can't even visit Miss Five!" He made a masturbatory gesture.

I felt my brow furrow. "You stay away from me."

"I am joking," he said, emphatically. "Joking."

I just shook my head. He sure had a strange sense of humor . . .

"My name is Fan," he said, edging closer. I saw now that he had a grizzled beard, and weathered lines around much of his face. Must have been in his mid-fifties at least.

"Fan?" I hesitated. "You can call me Shaw, I suppose."

"Shaw." Fan scrunched up his face inside his helmet. "Like George Bernard?"

"Never heard of him."

"Shaw Chopra," he said, obviously accessing the public profile of my embedded ID. I wished I'd blanked it, like he had. "UC Navy Astrogator." Gotta love Radio Frequency Identification.

"Yup. Tell me, are you alone, Fan? Are there others?"

"Except for two support robots, no others. And you?"

"I am alone." I glanced at his rifle. "Maybe we can come to some sort of arrangement. Are you thinking what I'm thinking?"

"The enemy of my enemy is my friend?" Fan said.

"Not really what I was thinking, but sure," I said.

Fan seemed confused. "I do not understand. What is your arrangement?"

"All I meant was, maybe you're right. You're alone, I'm alone, we should team up."

For a second I thought Fan was going to agree. Then his face darkened. "Do you really want to team up?"

I gave him my most winning smile. "I really do."

Fan kept me in the sight line of his weapon a moment longer, then he lowered the rifle slightly. "Well!" He broke into a grin. "We should prepare these carcasses. Food does not grow on trees around here. Ha! It can be the first shared act of our new friendship! You start with this Chéngdàn." He beckoned toward the animal Queequeg had been eating. "And I will choose one of the others."

I shrugged, then retrieved my knife and knelt beside the carcass. I started skinning it.

Satisfied that I was working, Fan climbed the small rise, keeping his eyes on me and Queequeg the whole time. When he reached the top, he knelt beside the closest hybear body and set the rifle down.

Got ya.

I looked over my shoulder.

Queequeg took that as his cue. The animal bounded up the short rise with lightning speed.

Before the SK could reach his rifle, he found himself pinned to the ground under Queequeg's weight, with a nice set of claws pressing into the fabric just beneath his helmet, threatening to puncture the suit.

Queequeg knew not to kill him. Not right away, at least. Because Fan was a human, like me.

"Call it off!" Fan said frantically. If he was a civilian, his suit probably wouldn't be strength-enhanced. And even if it was, whether he could shove Queequeg away before having his throat ripped open was questionable. Queequeg was the fastest hybear I'd ever seen.

I casually approached, and snatched the rifle from where Fan had dropped it. "Not bad for a 'pet,' wouldn't you say?"

"Yes. Beautiful animal." To Queequeg: "There, there, nice Chéngdān."

Queequeg snarled in return.

I aimed the rifle squarely at his face mask. "How's it feel to have a barrel poking you in the face?"

"Uh, good?" Fan said. "If it pleases you, call the nice Chéngdān off."

"If it pleases me?" I cocked my head. I considered prolonging his torture, but decided he'd had enough. "It does please me. All right, that's enough Queequeg. You can let him go. Queequeg!"

He released Fan, but not before snapping at the air in front of the captive's face mask, making Fan wince. Queequeg returned to my side.

Fan clambered to his knees and kept his hands in the air.

"Remove your bailout oxygen canister, and toss it over to me," I said.

He didn't move.

I swung the firearm toward the ground and squeezed the trigger.

The loud boom and the explosion of black shale beside Fan confirmed the weapon was loaded after all.

Queequeg started slightly, but remained in place. The animal had heard me fire a rifle before, when I still had ammo, so he was used to the sound by now.

Fan, on the other hand, leaped right into the air. He hastily unbuckled his life-support system and disconnected the bailout cylinder. He threw the cylinder my way, re-securing the system to his back.

"You never had any intention of teaming up, did you?" Fan said.

"I'm a bit of a lone wolf, but depending on what you have to offer me, I may just stick around. However, I'm the one who gets the rifle." I retrieved the bailout canister, then moved several paces away so I could swap mine out for his. I was just glad the UC and SKs had the same supplier for their jumpsuits, which ensured universal connectors. "Queequeg, watch him."

Queequeg snarled, voicing such intimidating growls that Fan actually retreated a step.

"You're the one who drained the oxygen from the Forma pipe back there, didn't you?" I unbuckled my life support. I'd be breathing surplus suit oxygen until I reattached it.

Fan kept his eyes on Queequeg. "If it pleases you, yes. I am a terraforming engineer. A civilian contractor. I used to live inside that chimney. Until the Yaoguai demons came and destroyed the generator."

I nodded. "So how long have you been watching me?"

"I did not watch you long. I was returning to get some parts from the chimney . . . I saw you emerge. I hid, and followed you. Then the pack came."

"I see. You said the demons came and destroyed your machinery. You mean the crabs?" I remembered the sinkhole inside the Forma pipe, and the beasts inside it.

Fan shook his head. "Crabs? I do not know this word."

"They have claws, like this." I pantomimed a snapping claw with my glove. "And a few heads. A hard carapace." I knocked on my chest piece with a fist.

"You speak of the *Mara*?" Fan said. "The creatures with many heads, and three hearts? Connected by cord to—"

"Yes, that's them."

He frowned at my interruption. "Well, the mist of the Yaoguai came, and I fled. When I returned, the Yaoguai were gone, but my equipment was sabotaged. Unfixable. The tanks still had oxygen so I chose to stay for a little while and work on a small project of mine. One night, a few Standays later, the floor caved and the Mara came. I held them back with my rifle. Then I used a grenade to seal the hole, severing the cords of the Mara. They died. No others came."

I finished securing his bailout canister to my life-support system, then I swiveled the entire apparatus around so that it rested beneath my rucksack. It locked into place. I glanced at the O_2 readout: eight hours now remained. What a relief to see the oxygen bar back in the positive.

I retrieved the rifle. "For a civilian, you've quite the fighting spirit, if you really took down those crabs on your own."

"Civilian contractors who work with the military are trained to fight," he said, puzzled. "Is it not the same with your UC?"

"Probably. Either way, you got lucky as far as I'm concerned. If those crabs were determined, they could've gotten to you. A couple more sinkholes and you wouldn't be here."

He scowled like I'd just given him the gravest of insults. "It was *skill*, not luck."

"Sure. Anyway, what have you been doing for oxygen? You've

obviously long since depleted the Forma tanks back there. You should be well on your way to the next pipe by now. Unless you have another source."

He seemed reluctant to tell me. I gave my hybear friend a look. Queequeg advanced a pace, growling louder than he had yet.

Fan recoiled. "Okay, I speak. I speak!"

Queequeg glanced at me, and I nodded. The animal stood down.

"I have engineered a solution from the Forma equipment," Fan said resignedly. "I have created a small solar-powered extractor. It uses a heating unit to raise the temperature to 2,500 degrees Kelvin. I put rocks into the extractor, and the heat boils away the oxygen. Hydrogen from the atmosphere strains through a tungsten shield, combining with the oxygen to form water. The water pumps into an electrolyzer, and half of the water separates into hydrogen and oxygen. The hydrogen is returned to the atmosphere, the oxygen and leftover water are stored for my use. Simple as cake, as they say in the UC."

I felt my lips quirk. "Inventive. I want to see this extractor of yours. Lead me to it."

"You want oxygen, I understand, I do," Fan said. "But there is a problem. It will not extract enough for the two of us. We can share for now, but in the long run we will use up oxygen faster than we can replenish it."

"How much can you make?"

"I can make one canister in a week," he said. "But I just refilled my canister this morning."

If that were true, then it really would only work for one person. Advances in rebreather and canister technology had boosted the oxygen capacity to ten days, but if it took seven days to refill a canister, and Fan and I kept distributing the oxygen equally between ourselves, eventually we'd run out of O_2.

"One canister's worth per week?" I told him, suspecting a lie somewhere. "Seems like a lot to me. I didn't think there was that much oxygen trapped in the surface rocks."

"You know how modern rebreather technology works, yes?" Fan said. "The canisters do not actually store ten *days* worth of oxygen. Most of the O_2 and CO_2 you exhale is recycled. Even in semiclosed mode. When you breathe out, the carbon dioxide is redirected to the internal CO_2 to O_2 converter, which changes—"

"Yes yes, I know all about the glow-discharge and permeation process that disassociates the CO_2 into carbon monoxide and oxygen. What, you think they don't educate us in the UC Navy?"

Fan shrugged. "So then you know an oxygen cylinder stores only a day of air, but lasts *ten* days in practice."

"Sure, but a day's worth of oxygen is still a lot of rocks to process with some jury-rigged extractor," I said.

"Did I mention I have two support robots helping me collect the rocks?"

"Well, I might have to borrow one of those robots when I get my own extractor."

Fan seemed confused. "Your own?"

"I'm going to take you to the next Forma pipe, and you're going to make me another oxygen extractor."

His confused expression deepened. "I am?"

"Yes. We'll go back to your camp first, that way you can fill me up with however much O_2 your extractor has produced. I take it the machine isn't portable?"

He shook his head.

"Didn't think so," I said. "I'll keep refilling at your campsite until I have enough oxygen to make the journey to the next Forma pipe, then." I assumed by the time I'd extracted enough oxygen to make the journey, Fan would still have sufficient O_2 to join me.

I prodded him forward with the barrel of the rifle. "Come on then, finish cleaning the meat from that carcass, then lead the way to this camp of yours."

He didn't move.

"Look, Fan—"

"If it pleases you," he interrupted. "There is another, closer source of oxygen. With it, we can make the journey to the next chimney sooner."

I felt my eyes narrow. I didn't know if it was my instincts, or my military training, but I suspected a trap. That, or he was just trying to keep me away from his camp for some reason. "Another source?"

"One of the ATLAS mechs your people brought to this planet. At least, I assume it was your people, because it is not one of ours."

I actually laughed. "There are no functional UC ATLAS mechs left on this planet."

Fan's expression soured. "George Bernard Shaw, who you claim to have never heard of, said, 'My way of joking is to tell the truth, because it is the funniest joke in the world.' I can prove I have seen a UC ATLAS mech."

"All right. I'll play your game. Prove it."

Fan spread his hands. "On this ATLAS mech there is a black cat spray painted on the front. With yellow eyes. Ah, you recognize what I say as the truth now, yes?"

A black panther was the symbol of Bravo platoon, MOTH Team Seven.

The question was, why was the mech so far south, when it had originally landed thousands of klicks to the north?

"Let me see a vid clip," I said.

He spread his hands in what seemed regret. "Unfortunately, I did not make one."

I frowned. "I'm assuming the mech isn't operational? Otherwise you wouldn't be alive right now."

"It is operational. But you are right, I *am* lucky to be alive. It shot at me when I approached."

"Possessed?"

Fan shrugged. "Maybe the Yaoguai inhabits it. Maybe not."

The AIs of the mechs had been programmed to tag SKs as hostiles before the drop, so it made some sense that the ATLAS would have fired on him, even if it wasn't possessed, especially with his blank public profile giving an inconclusive civilian status. Unfortunately, if it *was* possessed, the mech probably would have behaved the same way. And there was no way to determine if a Phant possessed a mech by mere sight alone, because the large size of the ATLAS occluded the alien vapor.

The only way I'd know for certain was by approaching the mech.

If it fired at me, then it was possessed. I died.

If it did not fire, then it wasn't possessed. I lived.

There were other benefits to having a working ATLAS 5 other than oxygen, so trying to obtain the mech would be worth it, despite the risk.

"How far?" I said.

"Six hours."

"Share the location marker with me."

When the sharing request came up, I accepted, and a new waypoint appeared on my HUD map along with fresh map data.

I plotted a course to the provided waypoint, and saw that Fan was right. Assuming the data he sent me was accurate, and not modified to deceive me, if we kept up a good pace we should reach the mech in six hours.

Still, I had only eight hours of oxygen left on the bailout cylinder. That would be cutting it mighty close. If the mech wasn't possessed, I should be able to enter the cockpit and link my life-support system to the ATLAS 5's, assuming it actually had any O_2 left. There was a chance the AI of the mech would refuse because I wasn't provisioned to operate it, but I figured the chance was small. Besides, there were certain directives all UC AIs had to follow in regards to the preservation of human life.

On the other hand, if the ATLAS 5 *was* possessed, then I had no chance whatsoever.

I tried not to think about that.

"Fine," I said. "We'll go to the ATLAS mech. But if we don't reach it after six hours, I'm taking your main cylinder. Seems like a fair trade to me."

If it came to it, I wouldn't actually take Fan's oxygen and let him die just so I could live. But I wanted him to think I would.

Fan pressed his lips together thoughtfully. "It is fair." A playful glint came to his eyes. "When we find the mech, we will have celebration sex?"

I rolled my eyes, and sat back as he finished carving the meat from the hybear. I kept the rifle trained on him at all times.

This was going to be a long day.

CHAPTER FIVE

Rade

The mass of glowing liquid continued to flow up the sinkhole, toward the surface. The alien entities were all the same blue color, and packed so close together I couldn't tell where one Phant ended and another began. That was good in a way, because by grouping together like that, the alien liquid made for an easy target. Not that it really mattered, because bullets and grenades didn't harm Phants.

Although, I hadn't tried flame yet . . .

I swapped my Gat for an incendiary thrower and loosed flaming streams of jellied gasoline into the glowing mass.

The stuff worked great, adhering to the entities and sheathing them in flames that burned all the fiercer thanks to the oxygen-rich atmosphere.

Unfortunately, all I did was convert the alien beings into mist form. Now instead of a river of Phants, I faced a living, gaseous wall of them.

Nicely done, Rade.

"Facehopper, did you hear what I said?" I sent over the comm. "There's an army of Phants coming out of the hole. We have to get out of here!"

"I'm on the horn with the Chief," Facehopper sent back. "Bourbonjack is trying to convince the Lieutenant Colonel to pull the battalion back. The Lieutenant Colonel's not listening, apparently."

"Wonderful."

A bunch of the newly vaporous Phants veered toward me. I wasn't planning on letting them possess my mech, so I spun around to make the return trek to my unit.

"Okay, looks like they're going to attempt to close the sinkhole with an air strike," Facehopper sent. "Rage, you better get out of there. As in, *now*!"

"I already tried incendiaries. I wouldn't recommend any further—" I was cut off by the abrupt roar of shuttles passing overhead.

"Uh . . ." I activated my horizontal jets at full burn as cluster bombs fell all around me. Some were aimed for the massive slugs, others for the sinkhole. Either way, this whole area was about to go to hell.

I couldn't get away fast enough. The explosion hurled me violently forward, and the temperature rose by at least thirty degrees in the cockpit. I felt the heat through my jumpsuit and the liquid-cooled undergarment I wore.

My mech rolled along the hard black surface, and I finally came to a halt when I smashed into an amtrac at the edge of the convoy.

I clambered groggily to my feet. My forehead was steeped in sweat, and perspiration oozed down my ribs.

The thick cord of a crab was tangled around my thigh. I must have collided with it at some point during my impromptu flight.

The crab connected to that cord got up beside me, and moved just as lethargically.

I aimed my Gatling at its cord and fired. The taut umbilical broke away like an elastic stretched beyond breaking, and the crab toppled over. I stepped free of the cord to grind one of the crab's many heads into the shale. It felt somehow satisfying watching that black brain tissue ooze from either side of my steel foot.

I surveyed the area, getting my bearings, assessing the impact of the latest air strike.

Two of the behemoths sustained massive hemorrhaging along their uppermost flanks; the skin was ragged and uneven there, and exposed muscle glistened with black, oozing blood. Even so, while the behemoths appeared momentarily stunned, I knew they were otherwise very much still in the fight.

The third slug, meanwhile, had faded out, and was only now returning to this world, having avoided the air strike entirely.

Roughly a hundred crabs were still connected to the three of them, and these rose too, shaking off the daze caused by the shockwave; they seemed ready to resume the attack.

Among the enemy, the possessed robots were the quickest to recover. Most were already back on their feet, shooting at whatever targets pleased them.

The soldiers and unpossessed support robots on our side had pulled back, maintaining fire the whole time.

As for the sinkhole, it remained open. Maybe it had collapsed deeper inside, but I wasn't about to go back and check. I didn't see any Phants, so maybe we got lucky and the sinkhole had indeed caved at some point along its length. Maybe the alien entities were trapped.

Except you couldn't trap a Phant. I'd seen those things seep right through metal. Something as simple as a collapse wasn't going to stop them.

And then a few seconds later I realized why I hadn't seen the Phants.

It was because they weren't in the sinkhole anymore.

All around me, right in the middle of the convoy, Phants began to descend from the sky, where the cluster bomb had apparently displaced them. Some reliquefied before reaching the surface, and a glowing rain descended in places, possessing any robots it struck and incinerating any men.

Other Phants reached the surface while still in vapor form, and became liquid shortly thereafter.

I was lucky, because none of them touched my mech.

So far.

Either way, it was just mayhem around me. Sheer mayhem. Marines were dying, robots turning, and all the while crabs and possessed robots cut a swathe of destruction through the ranks.

"Facehopper!" I said into the comm, weaving between the liquefying mists and allied vehicles, trying to reach my unit.

"Brings a whole new meaning to the phrase 'Charlie Foxtrot,' doesn't it, mate?" Facehopper sent, using the euphemism for cluster-fuck. He switched to the squad-level comm. "All units under my command, fall back to the insert site. Save as many of your brothers as you can. I repeat, fall back to the insert site and save as many as you can."

"No more air strikes," someone shrieked over the global comm. "I repeat, no more air strikes!" A name at the bottom of my HUD indicated the speaker as Lieutenant Colonel Trowell.

"Uh, sir, you're broadcasting battalion-wide," someone else transmitted.

I shook my head. Another battalion led by an idiot.

Around me, more ATLAS mechs and robot support troops began turning against us. Gunfire went off on all sides.

The convoy was in full retreat, otherwise known as a "tactical retrograde," because the military never retreats. Those amtracs still operational sped away. Gunners fired from the turrets. Soldiers in jumpsuits ran between them. I saw more than a few fleeing men fall from gunfire, or to a crab. I even saw two ATLAS 5s founder. I checked the vitals on each of the pilots with my aReal. Pitch black.

I spotted Facehopper on the HUD, and weaved through the wreckage toward him. As I ran, I did my best to take down any crabs that entered my sight line, and to shield my brothers from gunfire.

Facehopper was on his feet, as was Tahoe beside him. Tahoe glanced my way and let off a quick burst of machine-gun fire at something just behind me.

I continued running, trusting Tahoe's accuracy completely, knowing that if it was something he couldn't handle, he'd let me know.

"Thanks, Tahoe," I sent him.

"Pick up the pace, Rade," he transmitted. "Some nasty things behind you."

A missile alarm went off in my cockpit.

I activated my Trench Coat and immediately dropped. Seventeen pieces of metal burst from Dragonfly's upper back and prematurely detonated the two missiles aimed at me. After the shockwave passed, I crawled to one knee, pivoting around.

An ATLAS 6 was bearing down on me from thirty meters away. It was clearly an SK variant, judging from the Chinese characters spray painted on the chest piece: 死亡, which meant Death, according to my aReal.

The ATLAS 6 model was so new that the UC was still evaluating it. The SKs were rumored to have made ATLAS 6 purchases already, and I guessed I was witnessing proof of those purchases. I recognized the expanded weapon and ammunition slots from pictures leaked on the Net. Disposable ballistic shielding covered the chest piece. On the shoulders, mini-rotors provided extra lift during jumps. It stood roughly twice as tall as the model 5, and loomed over my mech.

Retail price was thirty billion bitcoins, or ten times the cost of the previous model.

Never thought I'd feel outmanned, outgunned, and outclassed while riding an ATLAS 5, but there it was.

I made a mental note to have a little talk with the Chief when we got back. I wanted to know why the hell Big Navy hadn't purchased us ATLAS 6s yet. Those models would've come in quite handy against the bigger crabs and slugs.

The ATLAS 6 opened fire at me with its Gatling gun.

I swung up my ballistic shield and hurried over to the abandoned remains of an upturned amtrac, taking cover.

In addition to the ATLAS 6, Phants homed in on my position. As did more robots. And crabs. And slugs.

I loaded the serpent launcher into my right hand and peered past the edge of the amtrac.

The ATLAS 6 wasn't there.

Where—

A shadow blocked out the sun.

I instinctively launched my front-facing jets, hurtling Dragonfly backward.

That action saved me, because bright threads of Gatling fire rained down on my previous position from the sky. Those threads would have torn into Dragonfly's head, and taken out my vision sensors. The high-energy bullets likely would've continued right on downward, drilling straight through my unshielded cockpit and into my own head.

The ATLAS 6 slammed onto the edge of the upturned amtrac, landing on one knee.

Jets still firing, I was about ten meters away now, and fired off three serpents.

The possessed ATLAS 6 responded with its own Trench Coat

and dove behind the amtrac. Two of my missiles flew wide, the third was destroyed by a fragment from the Trench Coat.

This Phant knew what it was doing.

I was still thrusting backward courtesy of my front-facing jets. I hadn't been paying attention to my HUD map, and rammed into an out-of-commission amtrac.

I shut off my forward jets and dropped the short distance to the ground. I was on the outer perimeter of the area formerly occupied by the convoy. Out of range of the Phants, but not the guns.

I hurried around to the other side of the amtrac, taking cover. I peered past the edge.

I'd lost sight of the damned ATLAS 6 again. It couldn't have been part of the original convoy, because I would have seen its location on my HUD map, marked out as a "friendly." It must have been on the moon before we got here. That meant it may have been possessed weeks ago, which would explain the skill of its Phant pilot.

I glanced skyward. Nope, the ATLAS 6 wasn't coming at me from that vector again. It could be anywhere then.

Behind me, the battered remnants of the convoy were in full flight, the amtracs, tanks, soldiers, and mechs well on their way down the plain. The trailing units were about twenty meters away from me, according to my HUD. That was a gap I could readily close. Assuming, of course, I wasn't mistaken for an enemy unit by my own guys.

Holding my ballistic shield behind me, I got up and sprinted like hell toward the retreating convoy.

Tahoe and Facehopper were there, thirty meters ahead, laying down suppressive fire.

They'd waited for me.

The shale exploded as gunfire from the enemy line struck all around. Rockets went off.

Tahoe was down on one knee, and he fired a Carl Gustav at a target behind me.

Facehopper helped him reload, and Tahoe fired again.

I started to slow down. I wanted to help them.

"Keep going, Rage!" Facehopper said, as he and Tahoe continued to lay down suppression.

I obeyed his orders, though my instincts cried out for me to stop. I wanted to stay behind and ensure they made it. I didn't want to lose them, like I'd lost Alejandro.

But I knew they'd be right behind me.

They had to be.

I checked my HUD map. Sure enough, Tahoe and Facehopper were sprinting after me, a ways to my left. They made smaller targets, and in theory were safer if they stayed away from me, because I'd draw the majority of the enemy fire.

As I neared the convoy, I started taking fire from the good guys, too.

"Facehopper! Taking friendly fire! Relay my coordinates to the troops!"

"Relaying . . ."

The incoming fire became so bad I had to drop. The good guys proved better shots than the enemy, and threads of Gatling fire erupted into me. I propped up my ballistic shield in front of me. It was fairly beat up by now, and I knew it couldn't take much more of this abuse.

The gunfire abruptly let up.

"You're good to go," Facehopper sent.

He and Tahoe sprinted past the periphery of my vision.

I got up to follow them.

My missile alarm went off.

I launched the Trench Coat and dodged to the left, throwing myself once more to the ground.

The missiles detonated behind me, and the shockwave roared over Dragonfly.

I crawled to my knees and spun around.

Ten meters ahead of me, a towering form stomped forward, pulverizing the shale beneath its feet with every step.

The ATLAS 6.

Its Gatling guns swiveled into place—

I swung my ballistic shield up just in time. At this range, the Gats were just brutal. Dents appeared all over the shield, and the whole thing warped and bent. It sounded similar to the kind of hail you'd get in a tornado.

The shield was going to fail any second.

There was nowhere to go. Nowhere to run.

Except perhaps one place . . .

I got up and broke into a sprint, running straight at the possessed ATLAS 6, using its latest position on my HUD map for guidance. I fired off my rear jets for an extra horizontal kick, and I smashed into the mech, hitting the taller enemy in the waist. I must have been going at least fifty kilometers an hour. I was an ATLAS wrecking ball. Still, I knew I wouldn't make more than a dent in the ballistic outer layer of its hull.

On impact, the two of us tumbled onto the hard rocky surface. I ended up on top of the oversized ATLAS.

I immediately slid off, avoiding a crushing blow from one of its fists.

I held up my shield as it let loose another stream of Gatling fire from where it lay on the shale.

I maneuvered around the fallen mech, deftly positioning myself out of the line of fire, but staying close.

The ATLAS 6 started to rise—

I hurled myself onto its back.

The ATLAS 6 fell forward.

I fired my Gatling into its upper back at point-blank range, but the bullets merely ricocheted like the sparks from a welder's torch, leaving behind large dents.

The mech shifted beneath me.

I didn't have much more time. If I wanted to cause damage while outside the sight lines of its weapons, I had to do it now.

I ignored most of the external tubes and servomotor feeds, most of which had backup systems, and instead reached down between the jetpack and tore out the fuel line. I was just glad Nova Dynamics conveniently designed their fuel intakes the same way as on the older models, for easy laceration.

With fuel spraying all over the place, the ATLAS 6 crawled to one knee and pivoted its torso, slamming its heavy elbow into my chest piece. I hurtled backward and landed sprawling.

I swapped out my own Gatling for the incendiary thrower and fired a stream of jellied gasoline.

The ATLAS 6 had turned around, and the sticky, flaming substance coated the entire front side of the mech. I ran sideways toward it, trying to ignite the fuel spraying from its jetpacks, but the ATLAS 6 jettisoned its pack.

Smart.

The mech came at me, ignoring the fact its entire front side was on fire. ATLAS mechs were rated to operate in incredibly hot environments. You could place a mech on Venus or even the light side of Mercury, and the ATLAS would endure for at least two hours before experiencing any sort of failure. Of course, this assumed a mech operating in AI mode, because the cockpit temperature would be oven-like. The Phant inside the ATLAS 6 may have been converted to vapor form by the heat, but that didn't seem to affect its control of the ATLAS 6 whatsoever.

I was expecting the Gatling guns to unload on me again, but the fiery mech swapped them out. Maybe it was out of ammo.

I thought it was going to load its incendiary thrower like I had, but the actual weapon the ATLAS 6 mounted surprised me.

An energy ax.

That was new.

It was the biggest, baddest ax I'd ever seen. White bolts sparked up and down the metallic surface. The blade itself was made of rediscovered wootz steel, whose sheets of microcarbides and graphene were tempered within a pearlite matrix, creating the sharpest and hardest substance known to man.

I switched the Gat back into my right hand, and took several steps back.

The flaming ATLAS 6 gripped the hilt of the energy-laden weapon with one hand, then rushed forward and swung it down on me.

I rolled to the left, loosing a thread of Gatling fire at the area just below the cockpit hatch, toward the brain case. The ballistic shielding built into the mech's skin held up well. I figured at this range my Gats would penetrate in about ten seconds.

Unfortunately I didn't have ten seconds.

The energy blade came down again.

I twisted to the right, then ducked, swinging my leg around—

The loud *clang* of metal on metal filled the air as my foot made contact with the ankle of the ATLAS 6. I got lucky, because its weight was unbalanced, and I managed to trip it.

The fiery mech landed with a resounding thud.

I fired again at its shielded backside, and managed to destroy a servomotor feed tube. There was no immediate effect because the ATLAS 6 was already getting up.

Three crabs suddenly surrounded me.

I'd taken too long.

I leaped backward, mowing through their cords.

More crabs stalked in.

Small-arms fire swept past from behind me, lacerating the umbilicals before I could get to them. The attached crabs fell down, dead.

On my HUD map I saw two nearby green dots.

Tahoe and Facehopper.

They'd dug in not far to my left, Tahoe with his heavy gun, Facehopper with his standard-issue rifle. They were probably out of rockets and grenades by now.

The ATLAS 6 had taken advantage of my distraction to close—I saw the energy blade swinging down on me nearly too late.

I managed to sidestep.

Not soon enough.

The blade passed through Dragonfly's right arm, cleanly severing it.

My own arm was fine, secured inside the cockpit with the rest of my body. Still, it came as somewhat of a shock, because now when I moved the arm it was like moving a ghost limb.

Tahoe and Facehopper continued to keep the crabs off me, letting me focus on the more immediate threat of the ATLAS 6.

The fiery mech lifted its blade to strike again.

I swung my entire body forward. I wanted to get inside the range of the weapon. My head only reached the middle of the taller mech's waist, and I ended up colliding with its upper thighs. The flames around its torso had mostly gone out by now, so there wasn't much of the fiery substance left to rub onto Dragonfly.

I pushed with the shield on my remaining arm, putting the full weight of my three-tonne body behind it. I activated my horizontal jets for an added boost.

The arms of the ATLAS 6 clanged loudly against my shoulders, but its energy blade cut harmlessly into the air behind my body.

I continued shoving. The ATLAS 6 finally gave some ground, stumbling backward. The possessed mech started slamming its elbows into the top of Dragonfly's head.

The inner cocoon of the cockpit translated the impacts to my own head, which was forced to the left and right. The hull shuddered, and I knew if I didn't do something soon, the ATLAS 6 would bash Dragonfly's head right off.

I pushed backward, firing reverse thrusters, and broke away. The energy ax swept downward, nearly striking me during my retreat.

I landed a good ten paces from the enemy.

The possessed ATLAS 6 was already running toward me. Behind it, I could see one of the massive slugs not too far back, along with several more possessed mechs and robots. And of course the ever-present crabs.

I had to end this. And now. If not for myself, then for Tahoe and Facehopper, who were still valiantly firing away, defending me as best they could. All of us would soon be overwhelmed.

I clambered upright, and swapped out the ballistic shield on my left hand for the serpent launcher. At this range, there was a good chance I'd damage myself as well as the ATLAS 6.

It was either me and the mech, or Tahoe and Facehopper.

But before I could fire, the ATLAS 6 surprised me.

It unmounted its ax and threw the weapon toward my cockpit.

Instinctively, I raised my arm to block the blow, while dodging to the right at the same time.

I deflected the ax, but ended up slicing the tube of the serpent launcher in half.

Wonderful.

I released the useless rocket launcher, letting it fall away. I scooped the energy blade off the shale beside me.

I never got a chance to use it.

The taller mech leaped forward, colliding with me.

It wrapped its arms around me from behind as we rolled to the ground.

It tried to stand, and lift me from the ground, but I could hear its servomotors struggling with Dragonfly's weight.

The ATLAS 6 elected to remain on its knees, and squeezed its arms tighter, slowly crushing me against its chest.

I heard the protest of metal as my cockpit buckled slightly.

I couldn't lift my remaining arm, which was pinned to my torso, rendering the energy ax I held completely useless.

I rocked violently, trying to break the death grip. I managed to topple the two of us to the shale, but the ATLAS 6 didn't relent.

"Dragonfly, launch Trench Coat," I said.

"At this range," Dragonfly's AI intoned, "there will be significant damage to—"

"Override safety protocols! Zulu Alpha One!"

"Safety protocols deactivated."

"Launch Trench Coat."

Those seventeen pieces of metal launched from my upper back, spraying the potentially heat-weakened hull of the ATLAS 6.

The enemy's hold on me weakened.

I flung my arm outward, breaking the ATLAS 6's grasp.

I pivoted to find several Trench Coat pieces embedded within the brain case of the ATLAS 6, just beneath its cockpit area.

I got lucky. The enemy had been in the perfect position.

I rammed the energy ax into its brain case, finishing the job, then I gave the charred and smoking ATLAS 6 a good kick. It fell away lifelessly.

"That was for Alejandro, motherfucker."

My Trench Coat system was permanently damaged now. I hoped no other missiles homed in on me.

A possessed ATLAS 5 landed in front of me, ahead of a fresh onslaught of crabs. Obviously it was less experienced than the last one, because it was only now loading its Gatlings into the "on-hand" position.

"Damn it."

I withdrew the energy ax from the fallen mech and threw it.

The blade embedded deep in the ATLAS 5's brain case, and the mech fell.

I turned around and ran.

Facehopper and Tahoe joined me, running alongside about ten meters to my left.

"How come you always get to have all the fun?" Tahoe said over the comm.

The rear guard of the routed convoy lay about one hundred meters ahead of us.

I took long strides, basically leaping from one foot to the other while loosing repeated horizontal bursts from my jumpjets. I was careful not to travel more than a half meter from the ground lest I become an even easier target.

Facehopper and Tahoe did the same in their powered exoskeletons beside me, using their jetpacks to add to their forward momentum.

A thread of Gatling bullets tore past from behind, from either an Equestrian or a mech, and I was forced to run at an angle. I positioned myself behind Tahoe and Facehopper, covering them with Dragonfly's beat-up body. I loaded the ballistic shield into my hand and held it behind me. I hoped no further missiles locked on to my mech.

A stream of return fire erupted from our convoy, silencing the enemy guns.

The three of us closed the gap with the laggards in the convoy, and I felt relieved to finally lose myself in the protection of that rag-tag mass. If any missiles came now, I had plenty of other targets in the way. It was perhaps a deplorable thing to feel, but it was true.

Weaving through the convoy, I followed Facehopper toward our assigned amtrac. A flash drew my eye skyward.

The Raptors overhead had taken hits, and both of them were on decaying flight paths, smoke streaming behind. It wouldn't have been hard for the enemy ATLAS mechs or Equestrians to take out those airborne units, because the targeting processors on the serpent missiles did most of the work. All the possessing Phants had to do was point and shoot, and launch enough missiles to overwhelm the countermeasures of the Raptors.

Our side still had gunships and other airborne support crafts, which were wisely keeping out of range. Apparently the order to withhold air strikes was still standing. Probably a good idea.

We finally reached our assigned amtrac, and Facehopper and Tahoe hopped up to join the gunners in the turrets.

I glanced back, gauging the enemy's progress. I didn't think we were going to outdistance them any time soon. The possessed ATLAS mechs and robot support troops could easily match our speed, and had broken away from the slower crabs and slugs— which still moved along with surprising swiftness behind them.

I noticed most of the crabs had returned to the "sheathed" positions on the slugs, while the superbehemoths themselves moved in a way I hadn't seen before, which reminded me of the lateral undulations of a snake—their bodies alternately flexed left and then right. Transversal muscular waves added to the forward motion, passing from head to tail with creepy regularity, at turns expanding and compressing their bodies.

"Got some good news," Facehopper said over the comm. "Three parts. First, contact with the fleet has been restored. Second, the Chief reports the *Gerald R. Ford* is intact, and has taken out the enemy flotilla in its entirety. Third, all drop ships are cleared for return."

"We're going to evac *already*?" Dyson transmitted. "Sir?"

"We are," Facehopper said. "We need to regroup, and rethink our strategy for another day. We're losing too many assets."

"So I got something on my mind," Bender sent. I noticed he wasn't in the amtrac, according to the HUD, but rather keeping pace some ways to the right. Dyson wasn't aboard either, for that matter. "The *Gerald R. Ford* defeated the small flotilla you say? Wahoo baby and all that. But what happened to the rest of our fleet? The carriers sent against the Big Bad mofo?"

I glanced at the horizon behind me. The Skull Ship remained in place, hovering against the twilit sky. It was hard to imagine anything sent against that ship had succeeded in any way.

"No news on the remainder of the fleet," Facehopper replied, rather curtly.

We reached the insert site and the amtracs started unloading. The Marines hurried to the drop ships in orderly groups. The crafts assigned to the units were marked out on each member's aReal, so everyone knew exactly where to go. The robot support troops still on our side went off to their own drop vehicles. I remembered how many HS3 scouts had been present when we'd first landed. I only spotted maybe five of the basketball-sized HS3s in total now.

The remaining Abrams and Equestrians dispersed at maximum speed onto the plains behind us, because, like the ATLAS mechs, they utilized booster rockets for the return trip.

None of the ATLAS 5s themselves were yet retreating to those boosters, I noted.

"The order is coming in," Facehopper said over the comm as he and Tahoe jumped down from the amtrac. "ATLAS 5s are to remain behind until all drop assets have lifted off. If you are in an ATLAS mech, do not proceed to the booster rockets. Protect the drop vehicles." He glanced significantly at me.

"I'll give them hell, sir," I said.

Facehopper's gaze lingered on Dragonfly's sparking, severed limb. "Are you sure, mate?"

"I'm not out of the fight. Not by a long shot."

"I'm staying with Rade." Tahoe took a step toward me.

Facehopper extended a blocking arm. "No. You're not."

Tahoe maneuvered past Facehopper and continued toward me.

Facehopper jumped him from behind. The two scuffled in their strength-enhanced exoskeletons and in moments Facehopper had Tahoe restrained and weaponless on the ground.

"You insubordinate little shit," Facehopper said. "Ever heard the expression, don't bring a knife to a gunfight? If you don't have a mech, you don't stay, mate. It's as simple as that. Now move before I have your dumb ass court-martialed."

Tahoe got up, abandoning his heavy gun on the ground.

"Take your weapon, Mr. Eaglehide," Facehopper told him.

Chastened, Tahoe retrieved the weapon.

"Now get to the DV."

Tahoe jogged toward the assigned Delivery Vehicle with hunched shoulders.

"Sorry about that, mate," Facehopper said to me over the comm after a moment. "Someday Tahoe will understand why I did that."

"Yeah." I felt bad for Tahoe. He just wanted to stay and help me. I would've wanted to do the same for him.

"Now listen: Most of the ATLAS 5 booster payloads landed to the northwest. Do you see them on your map?"

I zoomed out on my map, and saw the flashing blue dots that indicated the payloads. "I see them. I can make it."

Facehopper's eyes dropped to Dragonfly's sparking limb once more. A bit doubtfully, I thought.

"See you topside, sir," I said before he could add anything further, or change his mind. "You owe me a beer next liberty."

"I owe you more than a beer." He gazed past me, at the growing group of ATLAS 5s forming a perimeter beyond the amtracs and DVs. "There are a couple of other MOTHs out there. You're not alone. You're never alone. Stick together. Watch each other's backs. And always remember: you've had it worse. This is damn well luxurious compared to some of the crap we've been in." With that, Facehopper cut communications and ran after Tahoe toward the designated DV.

I approached the line of ATLAS 5s that had taken up defensive positions along the edge of the insert site. The mechs were distributed in a zigzag pattern, about ten meters apart. Each one had burrowed into the shale, and lay prostrate, with the ballistic shield held out in front at a downward angle. The position of those shields ensured only a small portion of each mech was exposed, namely the barrel of the weapon held by the other hand. The video feed from the scopes of either the Gats or the serpents could be fed directly to the cockpit, so the pilots wouldn't even have to peer around the edges of the shields to aim. The angle of the shields also encouraged the upward deflection of incoming bullets, away from the mechs.

Basically we were forming a line of one-man, mobile machine gun bunkers.

It was a good thing the enemy didn't have air-strike capability. If they'd dropped some Napalm D, they would've easily routed us from our makeshift dugouts. It was what we would have done when faced with a similar situation.

At a glance, most of the mechs in the defensive line seemed just as battered as my own. Some had arms and other pieces missing. One ATLAS 5 had half its head blown off. And judging from the vitals I saw next to each mech on my aReal, more than a few of the pilots inside were wounded. Some seriously.

Yet they all fought on.

I marched toward a mech labeled "Bender-Rocketman" on my aReal.

"Hey, Rocketman," I sent him over the comm. "I'd quote a line from the song here, but you know, copyright issues."

"You don't even *know* any lines from the song," Bender retorted.

"And you do?"

No answer.

I nodded at his mech. "Hope the owner gave it to you willingly."

"Hey, what are you trying to say, bitch? The dude was dead." Bender's face appeared in the upper left of my aReal courtesy of a vidlink overlay. "What happened to your arm?"

"Had a little tangle with an ATLAS 6," I told him.

"You serious?" Bender said. "I didn't think the SK bitches brought any with them."

"They didn't."

"Daaamn. Who won?"

"Since I'm still standing, I think it's pretty obvious."

Bender chuckled. "Yeah man, but with one arm, that only counts as half a win."

"A win's a win, whether your mech comes out of it with one arm or two."

"If you say so," Bender answered.

I started digging in behind him. "You get to be my shield today." Since I had only one arm, I couldn't have a weapon and shield active at the same time. I'd have to choose one or the other, and to be effective I'd chosen the Gatling gun, which meant my ATLAS 5 remained unshielded. I didn't think I'd be able to burrow deep enough into the shale to protect my whole body. Hence, I'd have to share Bender's ballistic shield.

"Hell no!" Bender said. "I ain't being no one's goddamn human shield! Find someone else to make a bigger target with."

I knew him well enough by now to realize that was his way of agreeing, albeit grudgingly, so I ignored him and continued digging in.

168

"Bitch," he sent.

"Hey," I transmitted. "You're the one who's my bitch. I'm in back, after all."

Though his vid feed had cut out, I could imagine his disgusted expression. "Don't go all gay on me."

After I'd settled in, I aimed my weapon over Bender's shield, and transferred the vid feed from my Gatling to the cockpit and surveyed the battle space from the weapon's point of view.

The line of possessed mechs and robots had halted a short distance beyond weapons range. The enemy front appeared to be waiting for the slugs to catch up. That they even knew about weapons range was telling. I had a feeling more than a few of those Phants had possessed human-designed robots before.

"Hold your fire," came a voice over the comm channel we'd put together for the ATLAS units. I saw the speaker's name at the bottom of my HUD: Sergeant Crabbuster.

Nice.

"We're going to bust some crabs for you, sir!" someone joked over the comm.

When the three superslugs reached the ranks of the possessed robots, the enemy line moved forward in a coordinated advance.

None of the targets were in range. Not yet.

I switched to Dragonfly's POV and glanced up and down our lines. I viewed the name and rank of each pilot on my aReal. Privates, sergeants, and corporals from across the three allied nations. Brave, brave men. Thirty-three of us in total.

The enemy meanwhile had at least a hundred robots, half of them ATLAS 5s. They also had the superslugs and their attached crabs.

We were vastly outnumbered.

But what the enemy had in numbers, we made up for in heart. Not to mention skill. We'd invested countless hours over the past few years training inside these mechs. The possessed ATLAS 5s? The most time any of the Phants had had to practice was two months. We outclassed them.

At least, that's what I believed.

Hoped.

"Dammit," someone said over the comm. "Those drop ships are sure taking their time."

I swiveled to look. The drop ships had been arrayed in a rough circle, and the closer crafts had already departed. Marines were still loading into the remaining drop vehicles, and some of the soldiers on foot still had a ways to go.

Apparently the order to withhold air strikes had lifted, because just then two gunships swept overhead. I switched my view back to my Gatling, and watched the gunships strafe targets.

The enemy line easily shot down both gunships. One of the pilots managed to steer his rapidly descending craft into the possessed ranks, taking out two enemy ATLAS 5s in the crash.

I checked the vital signs of the gunships' occupants: dead. It was horrible to think it, but it was almost better that way, because we wouldn't have to worry about mounting a risky rescue.

A shuttle darted in from the side and loosed a few hellfires at the enemy ranks, and as it passed high overhead it dropped a couple of cluster bombs, one of them incendiary.

The ground shook as the shockwave passed over my position, and a massive fireball plumed from the enemy front, covering the skies.

I saw the glowing liquid of Phants spew out from that plume and splash the no-man's land between our opposing sides. That none of it reached our ranks was sheer luck.

Then a voice came over the comm. "I've lost control!"

So much for sheer luck.

On the far right flank, Gatling fire erupted.

"Eject, Marley!" someone said. "Eject!"

More Gatling fire. One of the green dots on my HUD turned black.

"Target eliminated," a grieved voice came over the comm.

"Rightmost units, reposition," Sergeant Crabbuster transmitted. "Move away from the liquid seeping from that mech on the double!"

Overhead, the shuttle pulled away. Either the pilots had seen the unintended side effects of their bombing run, or someone had told them to get the hell away.

The enemy front was well within range now.

"Engage!" Sergeant Crabbuster sent over the comm.

I started picking off the weaker Praetors and Centurions with my Gatling. Some of them were on fire from the jellied gasoline splashed by the incendiary bomb, and I could see the glowing mist of Phants around the brain cases of the smaller units as the heat converted the alien entities to vapor.

Other defenders along the line were opening fire as well. Gatlings unleashed. Serpents launched.

Many of the possessed ATLAS 5s knew how to use their ballistic shields, and they provided cover to the weaker units beside them. Some of the possessed mechs fired off Trench Coats in response to the incoming rockets. Most of the enemy combatants simply returned fire. They were spread out in a wide line. All the better to outflank us.

Up and down our zigzagging ranks, defenders launched Trench Coats in response to incoming missiles.

The superslugs surged forward, through the enemy front, drawing fire away from the robot units. Connected by their "ripcords," crabs started plunging from the slugs. Most of the crabs touched down in the battlefield in front of us, but some managed to land right in our midst.

I covered Bender, protecting him from crabs while he concentrated on the more dangerous robots. We made a surprisingly good team.

"Sinkhole on our six!" someone said over the comm. Directly behind us.

I swiveled around, switching my vision to Dragonfly's perspective.

Another sinkhole had indeed opened up in the middle of the insertion site. Two slugs and their respective crabs had emerged, and were harassing the drop ships we were assigned to protect. These slugs were smaller, roughly half as big as the behemoths, and their crabs were a quarter the size of my mech. Still, they wreaked havoc upon the Delivery Vehicles, despite the Gatling guns those crafts employed in defense. There were just too many of them.

As I watched, a slug plowed into two DVs, knocking them over. The crabs from it swarmed the vehicles. Claws ripped into the fuselage, mandibles tore out squirming human bodies and promptly ripped them apart.

"Marines, hold the line!" I sent over the comm. "MOTHs, on me!"

I clambered to my feet. Along our ranks, five ATLAS mechs, including Bender's, rose from the shale and joined me. I had hoped for more, but five MOTHs were the equivalent of ten ordinary men as far as I was concerned. Dyson, surprisingly enough, was the other MOTH from Alfa; the remaining three were from Bravo platoon.

"Dyson, what the hell are you doing in an ATLAS?" Bender sent. "Actually never mind. Just watch where you put your unskilled ass. I ain't coming back for you if you go down."

"Nice to see you too, Bender," Dyson returned.

Together we sprinted toward the new sinkhole as Delivery Vehicles launched frantically around us.

The smaller crabs had thinner cords, but because I was running low on ammo I chose my shots selectively, issuing very short bursts, taking care not to fire unless I had a clean target. I did a lot of bashing and stomping as well.

Wading through the upturned, twitching alien carapaces, I fought my way to the side of the slug closest to the drop vehicles and unleashed Gatling fire all along its flank, just above the skin, aiming to cut away as many of the umbilicals as I could. Like a barber shaving hair.

My MOTH brothers were beside me, doing the same thing. In moments we'd severed roughly three-fourths of the crabs connected to that side.

Then we turned our attention on the slug itself.

The thing was white hot, and steaming, which meant it had freshly burrowed through the surface. It was, thankfully, one of the smaller ones, so our Gatling bullets actually had some effect on it.

"Yo!" I could hear Bender yelling over the comm. "You like that, bitch? You like that?"

I switched to my incendiary weapon and vomited a swathe of adhesive flame onto the slug's skin.

"Let's move back for some serpents, boys!" I said.

We retreated to a safe distance, fighting off a few more crabs along the way, then unleashed our serpent rockets into the slug. Explosions rocked its body.

The thing seizured, its body alternately rounding then inverting, like a larva thrown onto a heating element. In its frantic death throes, it ended up coming right at us. I moved too slowly, and took a meaty hit in the chest, sending me flying backward several paces.

Before I could do anything, I found myself surrounded by a half-dozen crabs, and the second slug was fast bearing down on me.

Time to start bashing.

I splattered three of the small crabs with every thrust of my lone arm. I crunched two underfoot with each tread of my feet.

But for every one killed, three more replaced it. I couldn't move my lone arm fast enough.

Pincers clanged against external tubing and servomotors. Mandibles chewed at exposed wiring. Warning indicators went off inside the cockpit.

I loaded my incendiary thrower.

Turning, I unleashed a stream of flame and ignited an entire row of the things. The fire just consumed the alien entities. They screamed and flailed about, trying to rub the flaming adhesive from their carapaces. I sprayed fire for a few more seconds, but was forced to back off because the heat from the conflagration became too intense.

Something bashed into me from the side and I was sent sprawling.

Three crabs were instantly on top of me.

I couldn't use the incendiary thrower at this close range, because some of the fiery substance might splash my mech. If Dragonfly caught fire, there'd be no dousing it and my cockpit would quickly become an oven.

I was able to bash one of the crabs aside, but two more immediately replaced it. I struggled to stand up, but the crabs kept coming, beating me down. I attempted to swap out my incendiary thrower for the Gat, but the swiveling weapon mount got jammed on the legs of a crab.

So now I had no weapons.

Threads of Gatling fire abruptly came in above me, severing the crabs at the umbilicals.

I was finally able to stand.

I bashed the dead crab from my hand, freeing up my weapon mount. The Gatling finally swiveled into place.

I turned toward my rescuer.

Bender.

"Thanks for coming to my rescue," I said into the comm.

"Who says I was coming to your rescue?" Bender was just waling on those crabs. "Maybe I just wanted to steal your kills."

"Steal away, brother."

"I ain't your brother!" Bender slammed his huge metallic fist down and split a carapace in two.

Behind me, the other slug had died and faded from existence. So at least I didn't have to worry about an attack from that vector. Unless something else emerged from the sinkhole.

"All drop ships are away!" Sergeant Crabbuster announced on the comm. "To the booster payloads, people!"

"Man," Bender said. "Just when I was starting to have fun."

Four crabs came from nowhere and jumped Bender, pinning him.

I aimed at the connecting cords, but something shoved me forcefully from behind, hurling me to the shale.

More crabs.

What—

Another slug had come out of the sinkhole behind us.

The clatter of mandibles on steel filled my cockpit. I lifted my Gat and let off some rounds into a crab's soft underside.

Gatling fire from my right flank mowed down the remainder.

I clambered to my feet in time to witness threads of Gatling fire clear the area around Bender, too.

"I didn't need your help!" Bender sent me as he got up.

"Wasn't me."

I looked to my right. My aReal identified the ATLAS 5 standing there as "Dyson-Pitchfork."

"Dammit, caterpillar," Bender transmitted. "I had the situation well under control."

A bunch of crabs jumped Bender once again from behind.

"I can see that," Dyson transmitted.

Dyson and I helped Bender beat the crabs off.

"Let's go!" I said, advancing through the mob. "Stay close!"

The three of us fought our way through the horde as yet another slug emerged from the sinkhole.

An ATLAS mech appeared on my nine o'clock. Then two more. The MOTHs of Bravo platoon.

Brothers to the end.

Now that the drop ships had all launched, the defending ATLAS 5s piloted by the Marines had fallen back. The mechs were moving in a wedge formation, cutting a path through the horde of fresh crabs. Only fifteen mechs remained.

We joined their line. MOTHs and Marines continued forward in a unified front of atomic-powered steel.

We broke free of the swarm and sprinted across the vast Geronium plain at full speed, traveling in the direction of the payload elements.

Behind us, the possessed mechs, robots, liquid Phants, and superslugs overran the now undefended insertion site, joining the newer slugs and crabs.

But we were far ahead of them.

According to my HUD map, the booster rockets were distributed across a quarter klick of land. The ATLAS mechs in our wedge formation separated into smaller groups, heading toward the different clusters of blinking dots on the map.

Whoever reached a booster first took it. That was the unwritten rule, and no one seemed to mind, because in theory there were more boosters available than mechs, given the losses we'd incurred.

My group had whittled down to five ATLAS mechs by the time I'd come close enough to take a booster.

Dragonfly decided to turn on me in that moment, as the ATLAS 5 fired its Gatling into the booster rocket as I approached.

The fuel canisters found on the jetpacks of mechs and jump-suits were designed not to explode when struck by bullets. The tanks found on booster rockets, however, offered no such guarantee.

Thus, when the stream of Gatling fire from my mech struck, the booster's large fuel tanks ignited. Spectacularly so.

All five mechs nearby, including my own, were sent hurtling backward by the ensuing fireball.

"Just what the hell are you doing?" Bender sent.

"I'm not in control."

Somewhere along the way, one of the Phants had entered my ATLAS 5 without my knowledge, biding its time. I don't know why it waited. Maybe at first it had wanted to board our ship via the mech—a Phant had attempted something similar back on Geronimo. But then with all of us close to the booster just now, maybe it thought it wouldn't ever get a better opportunity to take down so many mechs at once, and it decided instead to attack. Who knows? This was an alien entity, and its thinking was completely alien to our own.

Dragonfly started to rise from where it had fallen.

I had to stop it.

I activated the cockpit release, and the inner shell folded away as the hatch fell open. I drew the pistol from my belt, and aimed into the small crack beneath the cockpit, between the hatch and chest piece. In my gun sights I could discern the mech's brain case. It was slathered in glowing condensation.

Before I could fire, Dragonfly reached inside and wrapped its fingers around my arm. My jumpsuit was useless—those colos-sal digits easily crushed the exoskeleton, not to mention my mus-cle and bone underneath. I felt tendons rip and fasciae tear and bones splinter. The whole arm felt like it had been caught in a meat grinder, and pain worse than any I had ever felt before flashed through my being.

Dragonfly tore me out of the cockpit and flung me aside like a rag doll.

I landed several meters away, and blacked out.

I must have been under only a few seconds, because when I came to, the battle space hadn't changed all that much around me, according to my HUD.

I started to sit up.

That's when I realized I couldn't use my right arm.

The whole limb was a mangled mess, barely connected to my shoulder socket via a piece of skin and loose jumpsuit. Blood poured out of the empty shoulder joint like a geyser, in bursts timed to my beating heart.

I vomited. Twice.

Feeling incredibly nauseated, I reached into the left cargo pocket of my jumpsuit leg assembly with my good hand, and retrieved the suitrep kit. I was vaguely aware of Gatling fire erupting close by as blood slowly pumped from my wound.

I fumbled three skin seals out of the kit. I shoved my arm back into its socket and braced the glove against the ground, so that the torn limb stayed in place. Since the jumpsuit was ripped open, I was able to numbly slide the skin seals over the exposed flesh of my shoulder area, one by one. The seals activated, instantly suturing the wound and halting the blood loss. I tentatively sat back, lifting the near-severed limb from the ground. My arm remained in place, thanks to the sutures. Couldn't move it though.

I didn't feel any pain, surprisingly. Just an incredible lethargy.

I was in shock.

I tried to stand.

Unfortunately, I'd lost a lot of blood. Stars filled my vision. Hydrostatic pressure was at an all-time low in my veins, and I nearly blacked out again.

Plunking myself back down, I retched.

I blinked the stars away, trying to get my wits about me.

All suitrep kits came standard with one IV, filled with a plasma volume expander. Using my teeth to hold the IV tube, I managed to hook the tube into the injection slot of the glove on my good hand. Then I connected the bag of plasma volume expander to the tube.

Inside my glove, a needle extended directly into the dorsal venous network of my hand, and started pumping the much-needed volume expander into my body.

Still using just the one hand, I secured the fluid bag to my belt with tape. The pain started to come then, so I quickly slotted some morphine into the glove, and let it inject.

I felt better immediately.

I stared at my mangled arm. I felt distant, almost disconnected from myself. There was no vomit this time. Just . . . curiosity.

First I'd lost the arm of my ATLAS mech.

Now I'd gone and basically lost my arm for real.

I almost couldn't believe it.

A part of me noticed that the nearby Gatling fire had ceased.

Two mechs rushed toward me. Bender's and Dyson's. From the stooped posture of Dyson's ATLAS, I thought he was injured somehow. Might've been mere external damage, though.

"Wait while I load Rage," Bender said to Dyson. "Then I'll take you to the next booster."

"I'm fine." Dyson sounded winded. "Don't need an escort."

"You're not fine."

"See you in orbit." Dyson sprinted off in his ATLAS 5.

"Wait! Bitch."

Bender's mech, "Rocketman," carefully plucked me from the shale and lowered me behind its head, just above the jetpack, into the seat specifically provided for a passenger. I sat back, facing Bender's six, and weakly buckled the seat belt with one hand.

"Rage, you gotta patch your suit before we launch," Bender said. "Rage?"

"I'm on it."

Bender hurried after Dyson, but the other ATLAS already had a good lead on him. "Dumb ass thinks he doesn't need my help."

As Bender ran, I groggily worked on repairing the huge gap that had been torn into the shoulder area of the jumpsuit. Like Bender said, I had to do it before we launched, because otherwise I'd be pinned by G forces and before I knew it I'd be surrounded by the void of space.

Fighting the drowsiness caused by the blood loss and morphine, I ended up wrapping all four suit seals around the shoulder area. The suit was only slightly damaged below that point, as far as I could tell.

To confirm that I hadn't missed a spot, I shut my face mask and initiated internal pressurization and oxygenation.

"Suit integrity one hundred percent," the friendly female voice intoned from the speakers in my helmet.

I still couldn't use my mangled arm, but at least I was space-ready.

In theory I needed to wait an hour before entering a zero-g environment to prevent risk of decompression sickness, but obviously I had more important things to worry about.

In the distance behind us, I watched the possessed Equestrians and ATLAS mechs break away from the enemy front; they were trying to hunt down the laggards among us before we all escaped.

"And there he goes," Bender said. "Guess the bitch is fine after all."

On the HUD map I saw Dyson's dot blink repeatedly, indicating liftoff.

Soon Bender reached a booster, and began the hook up.

"You ready Rage?" Bender said.

"Yes."

"How's your suit integrity?"

"One hundred percent," I said.

He paused, and I knew he was confirming my status on his aReal.

Incoming gunfire started to come in on us.

"Damn it. Piss off!" Bender initiated liftoff.

I watched the landscape fall away below, along with the half circle of possessed ATLAS 5s and Equestrians, and the robots, crabs, and slugs beyond them. It was a good thing we'd retreated when we had, because the numbers were just insane down there.

I felt the Gs then. I was positioned so that most of the force bore down on my lower back, but I hardly felt a thing.

Gotta love morphine.

In fact, I was barely awake by that point.

"How are you back there, Rage?" Bender said.

"Heavenly," I murmured. I had a sudden, urgent thought. "Check the brain case. Gotta check the brain case." I wanted to make sure no Phants sneaked on board via the ATLAS 5s or any other machines after we docked.

"Sure thing, Rage," Bender said.

I don't think Bender understood me, but I didn't have the energy or clearheadedness to explain it to him.

I must have passed out, because the next thing I knew, we were floating in high orbit above the curved horizon of the moon. The beautiful blue clouds of the gas giant swallowed the heavens beyond. Everything was dead quiet.

My suit integrity remained stable at one hundred percent.

The rockets let off one final burn, and then the boosters broke away from the mech.

Bender fired the ATLAS 5's jetpack in controlled bursts.

On my HUD map, I observed a distant green dot ahead of our position, labeled *Gerald R. Ford*.

I shifted slightly, feeling a different kind of nausea now, caused by the disorientation of space, where there was no up and no down, no left and no right.

"Rage, you okay back there?" Bender said.

"Never better, bro." To the AI in my helmet, I added softly, "Deploy barf bag."

I threw up into the flutter valve of the bag.

CHAPTER SIX

Shaw

At my request, Fan carried my rifle-scythe slung over his back. I kept his loaded weapon to myself, along with his last three cartridges. I was a little surprised his ammunition had held out for as long as it did. Either he had a brilliant danger sense or he had a huge stock of supplies at his camp.

I had let Fan clean one carcass before we left the fallen pack. There wasn't really time to carve up any more of the things, not unless we wanted to fight off other hybear scavengers.

I brought up the rear, while Queequeg trailed Fan, nipping at the heels of the SK. They made an odd pair. Queequeg, a cross between a hyena and a bear, and Fan, a human in a jumpsuit with black shale glued all over it.

We'd been marching for almost five and a half hours, and Fan had barely said a word. I seemed to recall a certain SK notion regarding good manners, where custom dictated that the guest remain silent until the host initiated conversation. I supposed I was the host in this case, and I could certainly use some conversation right about now. Light, superficial conversation—I didn't want to get to know Fan overly well. I didn't want to get attached to him, not on this planet where it was so easy to die. Especially when he was basically the enemy.

"How in the world is the radiation not affecting you?" I said. That was relatively superficial.

"Mmm?" Fan glanced over his shoulder, slowing. Queequeg gave him a good nip and he increased his pace again.

"You have Geronium rocks plastered to your suit. And you've been walking on a planet made of it every day. You should be dead."

"If it pleases you, I have subdermal medications for that."

I nodded. "But how long is your medication supposed to last?"

He laughed. "All right, I admit it. The medications have expired. I have had radiation sickness for months. It gets worse every day."

"Oh."

"What about you, Shaw Chopra? You are protected?"

"I have subdermals, yes. And they're still active." I wasn't about to tell him my own were nearly exhausted. Another reason I wanted to find the ATLAS 5: better rad shielding. "What happened to the other Forma techs? You weren't the only one, were you?"

"Oh no, no, no. There were five others. I was out surveying when the recall shuttle came. They were in a hurry. They did not wait for me."

"Nice of them."

"Yes."

"You know, where I come from, we have a slogan. *No one is left behind.*" I didn't know why I was telling him that. I wanted to show him how much better the people of the UC treated each other, I supposed.

"Good slogan. But then, why are you here Shaw Chopra?"

I chuckled. "Touché."

We were in the equatorial valley I had nicknamed the Main Rift, a large canyon that ran halfway across the planet and put the Grand Canyon of Earth to shame. I scanned the edge of the gorge, searching for the series of defiles where the ATLAS 5 apparently resided. I double-checked my map. We would be reaching the area soon.

"You speak unusually good English for an SK," I said.

"If it pleases you, I grew up in the United Countries."

I noticed he was using the polite "if it pleases you" a lot more now. Speakers of Korean-Chinese prefixed it to the front of their sentences when addressing someone considered a superior, and since I was the one with the rifle . . .

"You're a defector, then."

"If it pleases you, no. I am but a poor immigrant who moved away before reaching the age of mandatory enlistment. I did not want to fight. If it pleases you—"

"Stop saying that!"

He seemed confused. "What?"

"*If it pleases you.*"

He hesitated, glancing back at my rifle. "If it ple—" He stopped, licking his lips. "Tell me, Shaw Chopra of the UC Navy, you have fought many of the Yaoguai?"

I increased my pace, walking forward so that I was by his side, two meters to his right. "You mean the crabs and slugs?"

"No. The Yaoguai. The mist demons."

Yaoguai. That literally meant monster, in Korean-Chinese. "You believe they are demons?"

"Why else would they possess our robots? The bad spirit, taking over the good?"

I regarded him curiously. "You said you had two robots helping you, back at your camp. How many did you have to start with, before you were stranded?"

"Eight. The Yaoguai took the other six. It is lucky the robots were unarmed, or I would not be here now. So you have fought them? The Yaoguai?"

"I wouldn't say *fought* is the operative word. Ran, more correctly. Why, you've found a way to beat them?"

He snickered. "No, no. But I had hoped you had. The only way to beat a Yaoguai that I know of is to run, as you say. If you do not, you lose."

"Yup," I said. "You definitely lose. Being burned to a crisp isn't something I'd call winning."

"It is a fate worse than death. I have seen the Yaoguai take the Chéngdān—the hybears. It is hideous. To have your body disintegrated, then your being, your essence, transported to a hell beyond imagining, where every day is an endless trial of tortures . . . it is unimaginable."

"We all have our own versions of hell I suppose. But dead is dead." I thought of Big Dog and Alejandro, who had died at the hands of the Phants. Rade had shown me the vid logs of their deaths. It wasn't a very good way to go.

I think Fan sensed I didn't want to talk more on the matter, because he changed the subject.

"When we find this ATLAS mech, you will give me my rifle back?" he said.

"I'll consider it."

"We will stay together?"

I pursed my lips. "We will. Until we get to the next Forma pipe and you make me another oxygen extractor, at least." The O2 tanks on the mech wouldn't last forever, after all.

"You like to be alone, Shaw Chopra?"

I had to smile at that. "I told you, I'm a lone wolf."

"I do not understand," Fan said. "What does being alone have to do with being a wolf?"

"Well, wolves usually travel in packs, right? So, I'm not like the other wolves. I don't travel in a pack."

Fan grinned widely in understanding. "Ah. So you are not like an ordinary wolf. You travel alone."

"Yup. Just said that."

"I am the same. Or have been. These past fifteen Stanmonths, I've—"

"Fifteen Stanmonths?" Standard Earth Months. "Is that how long you've been here?" I almost couldn't believe it, but I supposed it made sense. The SKs had fled this system roughly fifteen to sixteen months ago. And I thought being here *eight* months alone was bad. I could only imagine what it must have been like to endure this world for double that time. And without a companion like Queequeg.

"You are the first human face I have seen since I was abandoned," he said. "Other than my own. And yours is far prettier."

I grinned. "Flattery will get you everywhere."

"I hope so. Though I am not certain how we will consummate our relationship while trapped inside these cumbersome jumpsuits."

I rolled my eyes. "Please. Not the sex thing again. If you ever bring up consummating again, I might have to get rough with you."

"Maybe I like rough?"

I swung the rifle barrel slightly toward him. "You wouldn't like my kind of rough."

He blinked rapidly. "My apologies. As I said, I have been alone for more than a Stanyear. I have lost a few of my, how do you say . . . social niceties. Not that I had very many in the first place. Ha! It was only a joke, little one. A joke."

"Don't call me little one."

He sighed profusely. "But you are little compared to me, at least in age, Shaw Chopra." He said my name slowly, dragging out every syllable. "Shaw. An odd name for a woman. You really do not know who George Bernard Shaw is?"

"Nope."

"He was a twentieth-century playwright and novelist. I remember his work from primary school, in the UC. Did you ever read 'Androcles and the Lion' in class?"

"I was homeschooled in France. Lived on a cider farm. Didn't do any George Bernard Shaw."

"Ah." Fan clasped his gloved fingers. "Well, it is the story of Androcles, a Christian on his way to the great Colosseum of ancient Rome, where he was to be executed by a lion."

I snickered. "Sounds like a wonderful story to teach children."

"Yes. The lion spared him."

I thoughtfully tapped the glass of my face mask with one hand. If I didn't have a helmet, I'd be tapping my chin. "So let me guess. I'm the big, bad lion, and you're the kind, gentle Androcles, and you're hoping I'll spare you."

"No," Fan said. It was his turn to snicker. "The ATLAS mech is the lion, and you, my dear, are Androcles."

Well, that was a rather disturbing thought.

We headed toward the layered rock that bordered this section of the Main Rift. I could see a series of defiles eroded into the rock. The map on my HUD indicated the promised ATLAS 5 was just ahead.

"Would you like to see one of the aliens?" Fan said.

"What? No. I've seen enough of them to last a lifetime."

He raised an eyebrow. "Even the bipedal ones?"

That got my attention. "What are you talking about?"

"You did not know? So much for the great knowledge and prowess of the UC Navy. Yes, there are humanoids among the demons. Not human, but alien. Follow me, it is but a short way. Follow."

He turned down a smaller defile eroded into the canyon wall.

I hesitated, suspecting a trap. The position of the mech on my map was clearly indicated in the *neighboring* defile, not this one.

I pointed my rifle at him. "If you try anything—"

He glanced askance and raised his arms. "There will be no trying of anything . . ."

I followed him into the defile. Not for the first time I wondered if this planet had ever had an Earth-like weather system, one that could've sent floodwaters rushing down the surface to carve out this valley and its network of gorges.

Queequeg's body language changed when he entered the defile. His ears flattened, and his long tail curled tightly over his back—the posture a hybear assumed when preparing to fight.

After a few moments I spotted a gray jumpsuit lying spread-eagled on the ground ahead. I thought the suit belonged to an SK at first, but as I got closer, I realized the jumpsuit was far too large to house an ordinary human being.

Queequeg froze, growling deep in his throat. I rested a hand on his head, and in his tense state, the animal snapped at me. If I hadn't withdrawn my hand in time he would've given me a good suit puncture.

I didn't blame him for being distracted and high-strung.

I felt that way too.

"Fan. Stand against the wall over there, where I can see you."

Fan bowed. "As you wish." He moved to the edge of the defile.

I approached the motionless jumpsuit, while Queequeg and Fan stayed back. My heart beat faster with each step.

Relax, Shaw. It's obviously dead.

But I couldn't relax.

The jumpsuit lay prostrate, but I couldn't tell if I was looking at the front or the back, or if it was even intended to have a front or back. I'd never seen a jumpsuit design like this before. It was all gray tubes and spheres and servomotors. Three legs. Seven arms—four in front, three in back. Well, I don't know if you could exactly call those arms, *tentacles* might be a better word. I saw no elbow joints or fingers of any kind, just long tubes that ended in stumps. From the way the material crinkled in the middle, I thought the appendages might be able to grasp things in a manner similar to an elephant's trunk.

I knelt, and gazed warily at the translucent dome that capped the jumpsuit. It seemed completely intact, and without a scratch anywhere on it. I leaned forward slowly, peering over the rim bit by bit, half expecting some small, skittering alien to burst forth at any moment and attach itself to my face.

And then I was staring fully into the dome, right down into the suit. Inside was . . .

Absolutely nothing.

I sat back on my haunches.

"It's empty," I said, unsure whether to feel disappointed or elated.

"It is," Fan agreed.

"You could've told me that in the first place."

"I could have, yes. But why spoil the surprise?" He smiled widely.

I shook my head, standing. "Idiot." I brushed bits of shale away from my knees, then I gave the empty suit a good kick. The torso shifted slightly before slumping back into place.

"I found it a few months ago, just like this," Fan said, glancing upward. "Perhaps the humanoid fell from the cliff top and died in the fall. Or perhaps it exhausted the necessary gaseous or liquid atmospheric elements necessary for its survival."

"Or it died of radiation poisoning." I stared at the empty dome, considering the possibilities. So many ways to die out here . . .

A surge of anger filled me, and I rounded on Fan. "Are there any other aliens or alien objects around here I should know about? Don't hold stuff like this back, you hear me? If you want to live, you have to keep me in the loop. I'm the one in the military. I'm the one with the training and survival skills to see us through this. You're a mere civilian. *Comprenez-vous?*"

Fan lifted his hands nervously, but when he spoke, he seemed slightly affronted. "This mere civilian has survived fifteen Stanmonths quite well without you, Shaw Chopra of the UC Navy. But I am not holding back. This is the only alien I have seen, other than the Yaoguai and the Mara of course. I promise you. I did not say anything about it before because I assumed you had seen one."

I kept the rifle trained on him a moment longer, then lowered it. "All right. I believe you. Now let's get out of here, if you don't mind?"

I kept glancing back at the jumpsuit as Fan led me out of the defile. It made me nervous, and I was just glad when we reached the opening and left the alien behind.

We walked along the edge of the valley, beneath the towering cliff of black rock, toward the next defile, where the ATLAS 5 awaited. It was still some distance away, but my nerves were starting to act up again.

I was glad when Fan spoke.

"Do you think we will ever see Earth again?" he said.

I sighed, wishing he'd chosen a different topic.

"We will." I didn't look at him, didn't want him to see the lie in my eyes.

"You do not sound too convinced."

I couldn't hide the lie from my voice, could I? I decided not to say anything further.

"Tell me, Shaw Chopra," Fan said. "You must have taken a Gate to come here. Was it the same Gate we built? Or did the UC build its own? Either way, it is obvious you came here in secret, because my people would never willingly share this place with you."

"Good guess," I said. "We built our own Gate in secret."

"Ah, so that means we have two Gates leading back."

"No," I said. "Your SK friends dismantled theirs when they left."

"Oh." He seemed perplexed. "But the UC Gate is still intact, yes? The road home is still open to us?"

I wanted to tell him the truth, but I couldn't. "Yup. The UC Gate is still there."

If he knew there was no hope for us, no way we'd ever leave this star system, he might just give up right there. I still needed him, for a while anyway, either to make me another oxygen extractor, or to give me his own. It was a selfish reason for lying to him, but it had to be done. Because I wasn't going to give up, even if there was no obvious way home. I'd find one, someday. I'd sworn I would.

He was all smiles. "That is excellent news! All we have to do is find a ship. A shuttle with stasis pods will do. You have one, I assume? Unless you made some sort of jumpsuit drop to arrive here?"

"I had a shuttle," I said, unable to keep the regret from my voice.

Fan studied me. "Had? What happened to it? Any chance we could repair it?"

I felt I was revealing too much, and was treading in dangerous waters. Well, might as well tell him the rest. It wouldn't reveal that I'd destroyed the return Gate. "The AI decided to land while I was in stasis. Wasn't a soft touchdown: sheared the left wing right off."

Fan exhaled in disappointment, and his breath fogged the lower portion of his face mask. "A bit too much damage for even my superior repair abilities. Without the parts, or a 3D printer, there is nothing we can do. Why would you let the AI land?"

"Wasn't my choice. As I said, the AI landed while I was in stasis."

Fan cocked his head in commiseration. "There is an old saying where I am from: Never let the autopilot land the airplane."

I smiled wistfully. "Wish we had that saying."

Fan compressed his lips. "And I wish more of my people heeded its warning." He paused, as if hesitant to tell me more. Then: "I lost a daughter in a spaceline crash. The AI malfunctioned during reentry."

"I'm sorry to hear that."

"Yes. She was . . . the light of my life. My everything. But, that is not fair to the rest of my family. I have a wife and four other daughters. A family of women. One woman is a handful, but a family of them? Unmanageable!" He smiled sadly. "My oldest was named Lìxúe. It meant 'Beautiful Snow.' We called her that because her complexion was perfect, not a single blemish. It was smooth white, like snow. And she had such long, silky black hair. She was seventeen when she died. She was returning to Earth after a lunar beauty pageant.

"She was so shy, she would have never entered on her own. But we goaded and convinced her. We helped her practice, too, for the posing, and the onstage interview. So it was our fault, really. Mine." His chin quivered beneath his face mask. "I deserve this punishment. I deserve to be marooned on this hell for the rest of my days. That is why I know I will survive the radiation poisoning. I am meant to suffer. I deserve it. I hope for it."

I didn't know what to say. To be honest, I just wanted him to stop.

"I remember watching the pseudo-live feed of her performance as it streamed from the moon. She was spectacular. Never again would I witness such a beauty as she. Never again. She was just *glowing*. All the training and drilling we did with her paid off. She performed the poses perfectly. Her pageant catwalk was impeccable. She wore the different outfits like a queen. Even the swimsuit, can you imagine? A queen in a swimsuit! For the onstage interview, she was asked the question, 'How can we solve the war over Geronium in Mongolia?' She won the pageant because of her answer. Do you want to know what that answer was?"

"Just stop it, okay?" I said.

"What?" He seemed genuinely stunned. And hurt.

"Look, I don't want to know anything about you or your dead daughter." I know it was cold, but it had to be said. "I don't want to get attached to you. Keep the conversation light."

"Why?" Fan was blinking rapidly. "So it will be easier to kill me?"

I shot him a look. "That's not what I meant."

"Then what did you mean?"

"You know as well as I do how harsh and deadly this environment is. Humanity wasn't meant to live here. Either of us could die at any moment. All it takes is a puncture or gash in our suits, something too big to patch, and we're gone. Look at our boots. Yours have just as much tape as mine. They're not going to last forever. What happens when we run out of tape?

"The number of ways to die out here is endless. Don't even get me talking about the hybears, and the alien beasts. But as I told you before, I'm military, and I'm trained for scenarios like this. Sort of. Anyway, I'm the one most likely to survive, got it? I don't care if you've lasted out here fifteen Stanmonths. You've already admitted you've exhausted your anti-rad medication. You think you're meant to live, and to suffer? I have news for you: you could die any day. So I'd rather not get attached. And besides, you're basically my enemy. Your men shot up some good friends of mine on this world. I shouldn't even be talking to you. The only reason I'm with you, for now, is because I need you. Is that understood?"

He didn't reply. I hated speaking so coldly, but everything I said was true. He might not have been responsible for the men who fired at Rade and his platoon, but he likely had similar orders. I had to be careful around Fan. Still, he *had* lowered his rifle when we first met. I had to give him credit for that. But it could have been a ruse. Maybe he had intended to reach my shuttle, then shoot me when we got there. And now that I'd revealed I didn't even have a working shuttle, maybe I was of no use to him anymore, and he might kill me the first chance he got. He might be lying about being a civilian, too.

Yes, I had to be very careful around this man.

"I said, is that—"

He raised a hand. "Yes, yes. I understand."

"Good. Now let's move."

He remained still.

"What is it now?" I said. My patience was wearing thin. And I was normally a patient person. I had to be, given my situation these past eight months.

"My daughter's answer was, if we want to solve the war in Mongolia, we should get to know the people of the UC. We should invite their citizens to billet with our own in a cultural exchange. The war will end if we work together, side by side, toward the common goal of peace."

It was a good answer, I had to admit. But I forced myself not to care. We were as far away from Mongolia and the social issues of Earth as we could get. "The two of us, working here and now, will have no affect on the relations of our countries back home."

"But it is a start, you have to admit," Fan said. "Even if we are working together for all the wrong reasons. Because we face a common enemy."

"That sounds like the right reason, to me."

"As I said, it is a start." He pointed toward a defile cut into the rock face five meters ahead. "Your mech is in there."

I stared at the narrow gorge, this ominous crack of darkness in the valley wall.

So it was time to face death.

I'd enter that defile, and either I'd never return, or I'd come out piloting an ATLAS mech.

I wanted to turn back. I wanted to flee. But I couldn't. Every moment was precious. My oxygen reserves were running out. Live or die, I had to go in.

"Right, then," I told him. "Wish me luck."

He did no such thing.

I approached the entrance. This defile appeared way tighter than the last one. The flashing dot on my HUD map promised that the mech awaited around a bend some twenty meters inside.

"Queequeg, stay," I said. "Watch him."

I steeled myself, and then, rifle at the ready, I entered the defile.

Queequeg followed me.

I turned on the animal. "I said stay!"

Queequeg sat down and whined softly.

I advanced cautiously into the gloom. I heard soft footfalls behind me, and glanced back.

Queequeg had resumed his accompaniment.

I almost got mad at him but I realized there was no point. Nothing I could say or do would make him remain behind.

He wasn't going to let me face death alone.

That was loyalty for you. Something you couldn't buy. Something you had to earn.

In the Navy, I had taken loyalty for granted, because the people I had served with, the people I had trained with, were all innately loyal. It was the nature of the service. We had shared something with each other that we'd shared with no one else. That we *could not* share with anyone else. Living together. Training together. Fighting together. You couldn't get more intimate than that. And it was that intimacy, that sense of sisterhood and brotherhood, of belonging to something bigger than yourself, that bred loyalty in the Navy.

Just as the experiences Queequeg and I had shared bred loyalty. I'd saved his life on more than a few occasions, and he'd saved mine. I didn't take for granted the loyalty he showed me, not at all. I had earned every iota of it. As he had earned mine.

Good old Queequeg. Loyal to the end.

The farther we traveled into the tight defile, the darker it became, the high black walls denying the sunlight.

Queequeg started to chatter and low nervously beside me.

"Quiet, Queequeg," I hissed.

For once, the hybear obeyed without question.

I reached the bend indicated on my map. I saw telltale scuff marks on either rock face, which could have been made by something large and mechanical as it squeezed past the tight turn. Whether or not an ATLAS mech had made them was another story, however.

The flashing waypoint on my map beckoned to me.

Well, here goes.

I held my rifle at the ready. My index finger trembled uncontrollably against the outer edge of the trigger guard.

Slowly, warily, I stepped around the bend.

Nothing shot at me.

I crept forward. Around me, the defile widened slightly.

After only three paces I froze.

Fan had told the truth after all.

Ahead, thirty meters away, an ATLAS 5 loomed in the dim light.

The mech stood roughly three times the height of an ordinary man, a giant robot soldier with arms, legs, and a pinched head. Its outer surface was hued differing shades of black to match its surroundings. The black panther spray painted onto the chest piece stood out almost in relief. Numerous dents and scratches covered the metal.

I realized the ATLAS 5 wasn't active because the vision sensors on its forehead were dark. Maybe it was in some sort of standby mode. That, or the reactor core had failed.

Or perhaps it was just possessed.

I took another tentative step, vaguely wondering if it was a good idea to keep my rifle aimed at the steel giant. Especially when that rifle was of SK make.

Step by slow step I approached, leaving the safety of the bend behind me. I was risking everything by doing this. I should've stayed back and thrown a rock or something.

I was about to retreat and do just that, but my motion must have triggered a wake-up signal because a yellow glow abruptly flooded the ATLAS 5's vision sensors.

The mech swiveled its twin Gatling guns straight toward me and opened fire.

CHAPTER SEVEN

Rade

I fell asleep (or blacked out) shortly before Bender's mech docked with the *Gerald R. Ford*, and when I came to, I was on a bed in the Convalescence Ward. I heard the *beep, beep* of multiple wireless EKGs from other beds around me.

The place was packed. Wounded personnel occupied every bed. I didn't recognize anyone from Alfa or Bravo platoons, so I assumed most of the men were Marines. My Implant was still offline, so I couldn't just pull up the profile associated with each man and check.

I flexed my fists, or tried to. Only the left one responded. The right limb wouldn't move at all.

I studied the arm. It wasn't bandaged, like I would have expected. It did have a needle jabbed into the dorsal venous network of the hand, with a tube leading to an IV drip, but otherwise there was no sign the limb had ever been mangled in the crushing grip of an ATLAS 5. It did appear paler than my left arm, and far less muscled. When I spotted the thin, circular scar around the shoulder area, I had a sudden sinking feeling in my stomach.

Hesitantly, I touched the limb with the fingers of my other hand, confirming what I feared: my old arm had been unceremoniously chopped off and replaced with a bio-printed graft.

I knew this because the texture of the skin was slightly off, somewhat similar to corrugated cardboard. It felt the same as Chief Bourbonjack's bio-printed hand, which I shook when Facehopper had first introduced me to Alfa platoon. I still remembered Facehopper's words at the time: *The Chief's got more body parts shot off than anyone I've ever met.*

I was well on my way down that path.

Wonderful.

Disturbed by the texture, I continued running my hand up and down the arm. The nerve endings seemed to be functional in the limb at least, because I felt the pressure of my fingertips, and when I gave the forearm a good pinch, I cringed at the pain. So it was partially working.

Now I just had to figure out how to move it.

"Welcome back, Mr. Galaal," someone said nearby.

I glanced to my left. "You again."

"Me again." Doctor Banye had been the GMO (General Medical Officer) of the *Royal Fortune*, and he must have transferred to the *Gerald R. Ford* along with Alfa platoon. Still, I hadn't expected to have him attending me—maybe the ward was just short-staffed, given the number of wounded from the last battle. Robots performed all the surgeries anyway these days. Doctors merely gave the approval.

The dark-skinned man was dressed in blue scrubs, and he still hadn't learned how to properly comb his hair, instead leaving it in a wild, disheveled mess. Just like his scraggly beard. That ingratiating smile made him look like a cross between a Fakir and the Cheshire cat.

"What's the deal with my arm?" I tried to move the bio-printed limb again. Still nothing.

"The skin tone will even out with exposure to UV rays," Banye said. "And obviously it's going to take some time before the muscle mass is restored. But given the ample PT you MOTHs perform, the arm should be looking much the same as the other soon enough."

"I'm not so concerned with how it *looks*, doc," I said. "I can't move the thing."

"Ah!" Banye steepled his fingers, and tapped them together repeatedly. "How can I explain this? You have a completely different arm now, one that just so happens to reside in the same place as the amputated one."

"Yeah, doc, I kind of figured that," I said.

"You must understand, when you move your hand, you're actually moving the old, nonexistent ghost hand. Obviously that won't work. Instead you have to learn to activate the muscles of the new hand, using an entirely different part of your brain. It can take some minds a very long time to reorient to the new neural pathways, though MOTHs usually adapt quicker, because of your innate competitive drive, I suppose. You MOTHs don't like to be out of action very long."

"No we don't." I tried moving my fingers again. Still nothing. "Any suggestions to hurry the process along?"

"It helps to activate the pain pathways. Take a stun pen, set it to maximum voltage, and apply it to the part of the arm you wish to train. Here, let me show you."

He retrieved a metallic stun pen, turned the dial to the max, and held it to the bio-printed limb. "I am now activating the thermal nociceptors at the tip of your thumb."

I felt an intense burning sensation in my thumb.

"Ouch!" I said.

He withdrew the pen.

"Now move the thumb."

I tried. Nothing.

He applied the pen again, and while the rest of my body flinched at the pain, the arm did nothing.

"Move the thumb," he said.

Couldn't do it.

He repeated the painful process ten times in total, and the last three times I managed to twitch my thumb after he withdrew the stimulus.

He tossed me the stun pen and I caught it with my good hand. "Practice."

"Great. I get to inflict pain on myself all day."

Banye's tone took on a cynical edge. "Not so different from what you MOTHs do all day anyway, is it?"

"Good point. Is it dangerous at all?"

Banye shook his head. "The device doesn't actually harm tissue. It's a *stun* pen. Stimulates the nerve endings via harmless jolts of electricity."

"Sure doesn't feel harmless," I said. "I don't remember Lui having to do any of this when you replaced his leg below the knee."

"Oh he did, believe me. You just didn't see it. A lower leg replacement is actually far easier to adapt to, because the human body learns to walk on something like a stump fairly quickly, and of course a bio-limb is far more than an ordinary stump. Plus, during locomotion, the toes aren't really put to use, at least not with the same level of motor coordination expected of the arms and fingers, so someone with a replaced lower leg can usually be up and about by the next day."

It made some sense, I had to admit.

Then I had a sudden thought, and narrowed my eyes. "So tell me. What other body parts did you decide to replace without my permission this time?"

Banye blinked rapidly, but the smile never left his face. "I don't know what you mean."

"You know exactly what I mean."

"Oh." Banye's smile edged toward the sheepish. "I suppose I do. You are speaking of a body part other than your arm?"

I smiled obligingly. "Yes."

He backed away, saying nothing.

I shook my head. "Be straight up with me, doc. Tell me what you did."

"Well, I noticed in your record that you are genetically pre-disposed to retinitis pigmentosa, which means you had a sixty percent chance of total blindness by age forty. Also, your eyesight wasn't twenty-twenty. So, I took the liberty—"

"Ahh no," I said. "Hell no. You didn't. You couldn't have."

His grin wavered. "Err, well, I thought—"

I struggled to get up.

Banye wasn't smiling anymore. He retreated to his office in a hurry and barricaded the door.

I lowered the safety rail, swung my legs off the bed, and got up. I wheeled my IV over to the nearest mirror. My eyes looked fine as far as I could tell. Even so, I pulled down the skin beneath my left eye, and rolled the eye upward. Stamped onto the sclera of the underside I saw the tiny letters ANDERSON INC.

"You bastard." I performed a similar inspection on my right eye. Same stamp.

I glared at Banye through the window of his office. "You replaced my eyes!"

I went back to my bed, and glowered at the Marines around me, most of whom seemed amused.

"Wipe those smirks off your faces," I said. "He's your doc, too. Probably a good idea to confirm he hasn't bio-substituted your testicles."

That stopped the smiles.

A couple of men actually checked.

The doctor tentatively emerged from his office when I slid the safety rails of the bed back into place.

"Hey, doc, can you triple the size of my dick?" one of the Marines said.

"Now now," Banye answered. "Essential procedures only."

"That *is* essential," another Marine said. "Jack's got a dick so small his wife confuses it for his pubes."

"Please, I'm dealing with a patient now." Banye approached my side.

I considered making a lunge at him, but thought better of it. Instead, I said, "Why the whole eyes? Couldn't you just replace my lenses or something?"

"Well, yes, but that would have done nothing for your genetic predisposition. I thought you would be pleased. You now have no chance of blindness, and you have better than twenty-twenty vision. Verily eagle-eyed! Perfect for a spec-ops man." Banye sounded excited as he latched onto that latter point, and he became all smiles once more. "Can you imagine that? You no longer have to rely on your rifle scope to correct your vision, or your aReal visor!"

"I don't want eagle-eye vision!" Again I had to suppress the urge to throttle him.

"Can he see in the dark?" a Marine asked. "Or through women's clothing?"

"Quiet, please!" Banye scolded the man. "And no, he can't."

"Then what's the point?" the Marine said.

I closed my eyes, letting my lungs deflate, promising myself I wasn't going to hurt the doctor.

What did it matter? As long as I could see. And looked normal.

"Don't worry," Banye said. "You won't have to undergo the same neural adaption period as a new limb. Once grafted, ocular tissue is essentially part of the brain, and as far as your mind is concerned your new eyes are exactly the same as the old ones. It is similar to replacement organs running on the autonomic nervous system—the intestines, the lungs, and so forth—none of which require retraining."

"Don't talk to me," I said, turning away from him.

Banye sighed, but he left me alone to harass another patient.

I closed my eyes, just wanting to shut out the world for a while.

The bastard replaced my eyes!

"Is that you, Rage?" a weak voice came from the far side of the room.

"Dyson?" I sat up, but it was a big ward and I couldn't see where he resided.

"Yes, sir!"

You'd think he'd be the last one I'd want to meet right now. But he was a member of my platoon, a familiar voice among a group of strangers. Someone who reminded me of who I was and the people I fought with. A brother, who had been injured with me. Maybe not the most beloved brother, but a brother nonetheless.

I had to go to him.

I got up and wheeled my IV toward the side of the room where I'd heard his voice. I spotted him in one of the beds near the corner.

He looked a little pale to me. I could see the square-shaped impression of a bandage wrapped around his chest, beneath the patient gown.

"What happened to you?" I said.

"Took a good hit in the stomach is what happened," Dyson said. "Next time, try to give a little warning before you decide to sic your ATLAS 5 on us."

I glanced at his chest. "Your stomach was punctured?"

"I'll say. Thanks to shrapnel from the exploding booster rocket. I tell ya, it's painful as hell when your stomach acids spill out and start dissolving your guts."

I raised a halting hand. "Too much detail."

"Sorry. Anyway, I made it all the way into orbit, but passed out before I docked with the *Gerald R. Ford*. Pyro from Bravo platoon had to bring me in. When I came to, I discovered the doc had replaced my stomach, my duodenum, and the lower half of my esophagus. Don't know if all that was warranted or not. But he says I'll be able to smell a match burning from a klick away."

"Is that what he said?"

"Strangely enough. And I know he's right, because my sense of smell has already improved. Take this room. I've been in wards before, you know, from training injuries. But I've never really noticed the smell. The disinfectant, the sweat, just this overall odor of human suffering. Did you know, I can pick out the individual smells of each man around me? I even smell *you*, Rage."

"Yeah, but don't tell me what I smell like. So the doc replaced the olfactory receptors in your nose then."

He nodded slowly. "Probably. Though I have no idea why. I broke my nose when I was a teenager, but I can't see that necessitating an olfactory operation."

"Yeah well, he decided to swap out the lower three inches of my friend's intestine during a lung operation, simply because my friend had had a prolapsed rectum at one point in the past. The doc called the operation a 'preventative' measure. And you just heard what Banye did to my eyes, right? It's ridiculous. Just because I didn't have twenty-twenty vision. I was only half joking when I told the Marines to check their testicles. The guy's a bit whacked."

"I'll say." Dyson rubbed his own eyes, apparently mortified at the thought. "This friend of yours whose lower intestine was replaced, he's on the Teams?"

I nodded warily. "Was."

"What happened to him? He quit?"

I stared at Dyson for a moment. Then I turned away, because I was close to punching him. "He'd never quit. And he didn't. He gave the ultimate sacrifice for his Team. He saved my life."

"I'm sorry," Dyson said.

"Forget it."

"He's the one I was sent to replace, wasn't he?" Dyson pressed.

"Leave it alone, Dyson."

I heard him swallow behind me. "I'd do the same, you know. Give my life for the Team."

"We all would," I said. "I need some rest. Take care."

I moved off, not so much because I needed rest, but because I was worried he'd say something to set me off.

I reached my bed and lay down.

That's when Tahoe and Facehopper showed up.

"Look who's gone and gotten his arm replaced," Facehopper said. "How's it feel?"

"What, to lose my arm?"

"No, mate." Facehopper poked my bio-printed limb. "To lose your leg. Of course your arm!"

I sat up. "Well, it's like I've had one too many beers and slept on my arm all night, and only now woken up."

"So not too different than usual," Facehopper joked.

"Pretty much. Except the symptoms are reversed. Instead of the arm being numb but fully movable, I feel everything but can't move it."

"Sounds like a new type of drug."

"Yeah. The Banye Bio-Printed Specialty. So how'd you guys know I was up?"

"We told the doc to ping us as soon as you were awake. We were in the middle of PT, so I had to order everyone to stay behind. You can expect more visitors to trickle in later. Tahoe should've stayed behind too, but the disobedient little bastard wouldn't take no for an answer."

"Hey," Tahoe said. "There are some orders that can't be followed. Like abandoning one's friends."

Abandoning one's friends.

Like I'd done to Shaw.

Tahoe abruptly fell to his knees and teared up. "Rade." He clasped my good arm to the elbow. It was the clasp of brothers. "I'm sorry I wasn't there, brother. I should've stayed behind with you. I should've disobeyed orders. I . . . I just . . ."

"No, Cyclone," Facehopper said. "If this is anyone's fault, it's mine. I should have been the one who stayed behind. I should have ordered Rage to eject from his mech, and taken the ATLAS from him. Instead I returned to the DV with you like a coward."

"There was no cowardice in what either of you did," I said. "Like you said at the time, Facehopper, don't bring a knife to a gunfight. I was in a mech. You weren't. And if you'd ordered me to eject, I probably would've told you to take your command and shove it up your ass. Sir."

Facehopper laughed. "I thought as much. Which is partly why I didn't give the order in the first place. Didn't want to have to court-martial you and ruin your career when I got back."

"Yeah, well, it truly isn't the fault of either one of you," I continued. "By the way, Facehopper, this is exactly why I never want a position like yours. The burden of command. I couldn't take it. Leading Petty Officer. It's not for me."

Facehopper smiled. "Burden? Hardly. It does have its perks, mate. It's kind of fun having people obey your every word. As long as you can get over the guilt when someone under you gets hurt. Besides, given a changing battle space and outdated orders, every MOTH is supposed to take the initiative and lead his brothers, completing the mission however he can. I've seen you do the same."

"Not like what you did back there," I said. "Honestly, making the decision you made? Calling Tahoe back? I don't think I could have done it. I would've let him stay. I would've let every MOTH stay. To protect one man. And I would have put everyone at risk by doing so. What kind of a leader is that, Facehopper? No, I can't make the decisions you do. You're the leader, not me. And I respect the burden you carry, I really do."

"Thank you," Facehopper said. "I think. By the way, if you ever do become LPO, here's a tip for dealing with the guilt: beer. Drink it in vast quantities. Speaking of which, I owe you a drink." He glanced over his shoulder at the Marines, all clandestine-like, then lowered his voice. "The guys jury-rigged a distillery down in engineering. Been brewing up some fine rotgut. Unofficially, of course. As soon as you're declared fit for duty, I want you to unofficially march your pretty arse down there."

"Will do," I said.

"Cheer up, mate." Facehopper punched my grafted shoulder. "You'll be out of here in no time."

"Hey, don't be attacking a defenseless man in a hospital bed," I said.

"You're hardly defenseless!"

He came in at me again, forcing me to knock the blow aside with my good arm. After some playful tussling with him and Tahoe, which resulted in the unintended, painful extraction of the IV tube from my hand, requiring the doc's intervention, my friends pulled up chairs.

"For an injured man, you sure fight well," Facehopper said, panting.

I was breathing harder than the both of them, and I knew Facehopper was just stroking my ego. He wanted to encourage me to heal up and get the hell out of the ward.

I had an urgent thought. "Did anyone check the brain cases of the ATLAS 5s after our return? If any of the Phants—"

"We checked all ATLAS units. And the tanks. And the Centurions. Basically anything with an AI. We found nothing. But you do know the hangar scanners fleet-wide were modified to warn of condensation buildup anywhere inside the bays, right? Months ago."

"Oh yeah." I'd forgotten about that. Technology always moved fast, and if you didn't pay attention you were left behind. "We really need to build that tech into the ATLAS units."

"We do indeed."

Dyson wheeled his IV over to join our little group.

Facehopper gave him a curious look. "Shouldn't you be in bed?"

"No, sir," Dyson said. "Just getting in my daily PT, sir."

Facehopper laughed. "If you call that PT, you've got some serious injuries, mate. That or you've grown soft."

"The latter, sir. I'm a big softie."

Facehopper chuckled again. "Ever the comedian."

Dyson took another step, then flinched, grabbing at his chest.

Tahoe slid forward to help, but Dyson waved him off.

"Sir," Dyson said to Facehopper. "May I ask the sit-rep?" Situational report.

Facehopper frowned. "You may not. You don't have to worry about anything except healing up right now, mate."

"You don't understand," Dyson said. "Not knowing is worse than anything else. I can't heal, not when my mind is preoccupied with what happened down there. I have to know: How many men did we lose? And did any MOTHs die?"

Facehopper shot another surreptitious glance at the Marines, who feigned sleep and disinterest but likely were listening attentively. He spoke quietly. "Hope we get clearance to turn on our Implants soon. Voice communication is so . . . insecure, despite what the Chief believes. You want the sit-rep? Fine. The gist of it is, we lost half the battalion. That's right. Two hundred fifty men dead. And more than half of the robot support troops were captured. ATLAS 5s, Centurions, Equestrians. Raptors. You name it. Wasn't pretty.

"There were no casualties to report in Alfa or Bravo platoon, thankfully. You two were the only MOTHs seriously injured. Tahoe had some minor internal bleeding, and Chief Bourbonjack, Snakeoil, and Meyers had a few flesh wounds, but the Weavers fixed them up hours ago.

"As for the situation in orbit, the *Gerald R. Ford* and escorts managed to disable the entire SK flotilla that attacked during the drop. I don't know how the *Ford* kept from being boarded, given how hot things were out there before we left. But the supercarrier pulled through.

"The rest of the fleet wasn't so lucky. The remaining allied carriers tasked with engaging the Skull Ship were destroyed. To the last vessel. Some were boarded by Phants, but the crews valiantly refused to allow their ships to be taken, and chose instead to detonate their reactor cores."

"They're all dead?" Dyson said in stunned disbelief. "No survivors? But some of them were supercarriers like our own. With over five-thousand crew each."

"Keep it down," Facehopper hissed. "We need you to be strong now, caterpillar, of all times. It's what we trained you for. You thought Trial Week was hard? Real life, real missions, losing real friends, losing real ships. That's hard. That's a true test of your mettle. You think you can handle the real world? Do you, mate?"

Dyson's features hardened. "Yes, sir. I can, sir."

Dyson glanced at me and I put on a brave face, but the truth was, I was stunned too. Twenty carriers wiped out, just like that. The losses were staggering. I wasn't naive enough to believe the vessels we'd sent against the Skull Ship had succeeded, but I'd hoped most of them had escaped. The defeat was a crushing blow, one that only further hammered home the point: How could we hope to take down or capture an alien starship that was a quarter the size of a moon?

"I think it's time for Dyson's naming," Tahoe said.

Facehopper grinned, though it seemed a bit forced. "Why yes. I believe you're right, mate." He glanced at Dyson. "You've been properly blooded. Are you ready for your callsign?"

I felt a wave of resignation for some reason, but I managed to stifle it. I told myself Dyson was a good man. That he deserved a callsign. But a part of me couldn't let go of the fact I resented his being here.

Alejandro should be the one standing beside me. Not this impostor.

I shut my eyes. It wasn't Dyson's fault. None of this was.

It was mine.

All mine.

I opened my eyes, sighing internally.

Dyson seemed appropriately unhappy by Facehopper's statement, and that lessened my resentment toward him.

"I don't know, sir," Dyson said. "I thought I'd be thrilled when my naming day came. Instead, I feel . . . I don't know, like this is wrong somehow. Why should I be rewarded a callsign when so many good men died out there? I don't deserve this."

"That you feel this way is exactly why you deserve it," Facehopper said. "You're one of us now."

Dyson looked down, and I thought he was going to refuse again. "I have a request, sir," he said instead.

Facehopper lifted an eyebrow.

"May I specify my own callsign?"

"No," Facehopper answered immediately. I had the impression he planned to answer in the negative no matter what Dyson asked.

"But I've had a name in mind for the past six months, sir. And when you hear it, I think you'll agree that it has to be my callsign."

"This is highly unusual," Facehopper said. "A caterpillar choosing his own callsign? It's just not done. But I'll humor you. What name do you want?"

"I'm the kind of guy who embraces whatever situation he finds himself in, sir. You throw me in a sewer pipe, I'll swim through the feces to complete the mission. You throw me in a vat of piss, I'll dive to the bottom to plant the explosive. You—"

"Okay, enough examples," Facehopper said, wrinkling his nose. "That's pushing the limits of my patience, not to mention good taste. Get to the point."

"Well, my point is, when someone gives me a name, *any* name, I'll embrace it, just like I would any other situation, and wrap it around myself, and make it my own. That way no one can harm me with that name, because it has no power over me whatsoever."

"I'm not really sure what the bloody hell you're getting at, mate, but please enlighten me, and quickly. What name do you want?"

"Caterpillar, sir," Dyson said.

Facehopper stared at him incredulously, then erupted in uproarious laughter. "Caterpillar!" He fell to his knees, just cracking up. "He wants to be called Caterpillar!"

Dyson laughed along with us.

Facehopper finally recovered, and pulled himself upright. "That was classic. You're a regular comedian, Dyson. I almost want to do it—name you Caterpillar—just to make fun of you for the rest of your days. But I can't bring myself. We're not like some other military branches, where the callsign is a mockery of the individual in question. For us, it's always been an honor. I have a better name in mind for you. Much more appropriate to your personality. What do you think of *Hijak*?"

Dyson's face screwed up. "Hijak? Why Hijak?"

"I heard about how you hijacked the Marine's ATLAS 5, mate."

Dyson raised his palms defensively. "Hey, I really thought the Phant had gone inside."

"Wait," I said. "What happened?"

Facehopper glanced at me. "During the battle, when those Phants were possessing mechs left and right, Dyson here tells an ATLAS pilot that he swears he saw a Phant drift inside. The Marine ejects, and Dyson goes up to the abandoned mech and hoists himself inside, taking over."

"Hey." Dyson shook his head. "Like I said, I really thought a Phant entered his mech. But when I checked the brain case through the crack between the cockpit hatch and hull, I saw nothing. So of course I took the mech."

Facehopper chuckled. "Of course. So there's that, and I also heard about the kills you hijacked from Bender. So there we have it. Hijak: if you don't watch yourself around him, he'll hijack your kills, and your mech."

"Hijak." Tahoe nodded, pursing his lips. "I kind of like it."

Facehopper glanced at me. "Rage?"

I smiled and ruffled Dyson's hair, which he obviously hated, judging from the glare. "Hijak it is."

Alfa platoon assembled in the briefing room one week later.

A week of waiting, for most of us. A week of recuperating, for others.

An air of excitement suffused our ranks. We were finally going to *do* something.

Namely, our jobs.

I flexed my replaced hand. I'd been practicing almost all day, every day, with the stun pen. I could move most of the arm through the expected range of motions, though mobility wasn't entirely restored to all my fingers yet. I could bend my trigger finger precisely, however, and that's all I really needed to do to be operational.

The entry door irised open and Lieutenant Commander Braggs marched inside. All chatter faded away. As usual, I felt instantly intimidated by his sheer towering size. His hard features seemed even harder today, if that was possible, and I saw deep lines marking out the angular planes of his face.

"Alfa platoon," Lieutenant Commander Braggs said. "Lieutenant Colonel Trowell sends his regards for the help you gave during Operation Crimson Pipeline. Especially those of you who bought time for the drop ships." He gazed in turn at Dyson, Bender, and me. "News from above has trickled to my ears. There's the possibility a few of you may be getting medals, and I hope—"

"You can take the medals and shove 'em up the Brass's ass," Bender said. "I don't need to be no political pawn. Sir."

The Lieutenant Commander grinned politely. "Interrupt me again, Bender. Please."

Bender shifted uncomfortably.

"Yes," Lieutenant Commander Braggs continued. "I know very well how much you all love your medals. I'll be sure to relay your opinion, Bender, up the chain of command. Word for word."

Bender gulped audibly. I was glad I'd kept my mouth shut, though I felt the same way about medals as Bender.

"Anyway," Braggs continued, "the gesture from Command is appreciated, from my standpoint. The number of medals awarded a platoon can only increase its prestige, regardless of whether the actual platoon members decide to wear them or not. Though to be brutally honest, prestige isn't going to matter all that much now. We're at war, people, against an alien race none of us understands, facing technology far superior to our own. And so far, we're losing.

"But I didn't call you here to debate the merits of medals in times of war, or to bemoan our technological inferiority. I have a new direct action deployment for you. A mission that could lead to some critical intel.

"During Operation Crimson Pipeline, a small convoy of SKs from the battalion actually managed to penetrate the enemy line and reach the city. At least, that's the official story. We believe the SKs landed another convoy on the far side of Shangde City, unbeknownst to the allies, but that's beside the point. In any case, this second group didn't do much better than the first, but they did reach the city proper. After a pitched battle, they fled, but not before making an interesting discovery.

"Distributed throughout the city, among the resin structures erected by the Burrowers and Workers, are robots and ATLAS mechs on patrol, kindly donated by the previous inhabitants. I'm sure some of our own units are joining them at this very moment. But there are also possessed Artificials, and a certain Artificial in particular."

A retinal vid feed filled my vision, taken from the point of view of one of the SK soldiers. I saw a humanoid figure in the distance, moving amid a sea of crabs. Gunfire came in from the left. The distant figure glanced toward the source of the gunfire, and the crabs immediately surged that way, followed by the host slug.

The vid zoomed in. The figure was an Artificial, its face the spitting image of the SK President Guoping Qiu, the so-called "Paramount Leader." Droplets of glowing purple condensation covered the base of its neck, above the camos. It was one of the more common models of Artificials manufactured by the SKs, because the actual Paramount Leader liked to make it easier for the population to adulate him. I think he'd issued an actual decree to the robot manufacturers stating that half the models sold to the distributers had to have his face on them.

The vid feed cut away.

"That Artificial is your High-Value Target," the Lieutenant Commander said. "The intelligence boys at the Special Collection

Service believe if we secure this Artificial, we can use it to communicate with the possessing Phant."

"Once we retrieve the High-Value, what's to stop the Phant from escaping?" Trace said. "I assume we'll be given some sort of containment device?"

"You will indeed." A three-dimensional, box-like schematic overlaid my vision. "Our SK allies have been in contact with the alien race for a little longer than we have, and they've come up with a glass cage equipped with an electromagnetic core specifically designed to bottle up Phants. They've used it to capture two of the entities so far. The design can be expanded to encompass larger subjects, specifically Artificials possessed by Phants."

"Wait a second," Ghost said. "If the SKs have captured Phants already, why not simply put an Artificial inside one of these existing holding cells, let the Phant possess it, and then interrogate the bastard?"

"The SKs tried that. Once possessed, the Artificial didn't say a word. But the SKs have only captured blue Phants so far. You may have noticed in the vid, the High-Value Target is possessed by a purple one. The faster, quicker variety, which are far rarer."

"Quicker and rarer doesn't mean more intelligent," Lui said. "What makes the Special Collection Service so certain a purple one will be more talkative than a blue one?"

The vid feed of the city returned, this time from another point of view. I thought it was from an HS3 drone.

The Artificial followed three meters behind an injured SK soldier. The man was on the ground, pulling himself forward with his arms alone, struggling to get away.

Crabs surrounded the two of them, but kept their distance.

The Artificial said in Korean-Chinese, "Do not fear, you are safe now. Join us." He extended a hand as the SK soldier looked back. "Join us."

The soldier glanced from side to side; his gaze was met by crabs wherever he looked. The SK reached toward his belt, pulled the pin on a grenade, and blew himself up.

The unharmed Artificial turned aside, shaking its head in disgust, and the crabs dispersed.

The vid feed terminated.

"Alfa platoon won't be alone on this mission," the Lieutenant Commander said. I thought he was going to reveal that Bravo platoon would be joining us, but instead he said, "You'll be teaming up with an SK platoon—"

The groans cut him off.

He looked around incredulously. "Am I talking to a group of highly trained spec-op assets? Or a roomful of children? Show some discipline here."

"The SKs will shoot us in the back!" Manic said. "Look what they did on the last operation: leaving us behind as bait while they dispatched a second convoy to the city."

"If it makes you feel any better," Braggs said, "they left their own boys behind as bait too, fighting at our side down there." He pressed his lips together. "Access to the containment blueprint is contingent upon an SK presence. We need that blueprint. So put aside all feelings of hatred and mistrust, because the orders are clear. If you're done whining . . ."

He ran his gaze across the room. "Your two platoons will be dropping separately. Once in position, you will provide bounding overwatch of one another. You'll be going in light. No ATLAS mechs. No robot support troops. You'll only get HS3s, and a very few at that. For one thing, we don't want to make too great a show of force and scare the Artificial into hiding. For another, we don't want to risk donating any more of our expensive technology to the enemy than we have to. Also, by sending in only one SK and one UC platoon, the theory is we'll attract less attention.

"The SKs have agreed that our platoon will bring the High-Value back into orbit. The captured target will be transferred to the *Cinquecento*, a Franco-Italian frigate that survived Operation Crimson Pipeline. The FIs have always been a neutral party, and by giving the High-Value to them, we ensure all sides have equal access."

"One thing," Fret said. "How are we supposed to find the Artificial? It's a big city."

"I'll let you in on a little secret, Fret. The High-Value has chosen to inhabit a piece of human technology. And human technology is trackable. That's why we're giving you HS3 scouts."

"What about the EM interference from the Phants and the Skull Ship?"

"Not a concern. Sure, because of the signal degradation you won't learn the High-Value's location until the HS3s return from their citywide sweep. But once you have the position, it becomes a quick grab-and-go operation. I'll delve into more detail on the technical aspects during the prelaunch briefing."

"This glass containment device we're stowing the High-Value in," I said. "I'm assuming it's heavy? How are we planning to haul it through the city without support robots?"

"Two of you will have to be porters. Facehopper, I think you've found a volunteer." Lieutenant Commander Braggs gave me a devious grin. Me and my big mouth. I'd gone against one of my old tenets from training: never attract instructor attention. And Braggs was the closest thing to an instructor as I could get out here in the real world. "It'll be almost like ATLAS PT back in training, except now you'll get to port your load with a strength-enhanced jumpsuit and a jetpack."

He always makes it sound so easy, Trace transmitted subvocally, thanks to our temporarily reactivated Implants. He used the Platoon line, which excluded Braggs.

I'm just waiting for the kicker, Lui sent. *It's coming. I can feel it.*

"After you acquire the target," Lieutenant Command Braggs said, "you will return to the secure extract location on the northeast edge of the city."

Facehopper frowned. "By the time we capture the target, things could be fairly hot down there. Couldn't we move the extract location closer to the High-Value Target once we make a positive ID? Otherwise we'll have to fight our way tooth and nail back across the city."

And here we have the kicker! Lui sent.

Braggs shook his head. "We can't risk deploying a shuttle any closer. Too easy to get shot down by the city's automated defenses or by possessed ATLAS mechs. Once you have the target, you'll have to make a return trip across the city to the extract location. As for fighting your way out, after you have the target in your possession, you'll have full authorization to call in air strikes. Two MQ-91 Raptors will be standing by in the vicinity."

"Assuming the Raptors themselves don't get shot down," Lui said. "And that our commos"—communications officers—"can break through the EM interference to relay proper air-strike coordinates."

The Lieutenant Commander nodded gravely. "No one ever said it was going to be easy."

At least he finally admits it, Lui sent. *A simple grab-and-go operation, huh?*

Quit whining, Facehopper transmitted. *You didn't sign up for easy. None of us did.*

Damn straight, Skullcracker sent.

"Well if there are no more questions, rest up," Lieutenant Commander Braggs said. "The prelaunch briefing is at 1100. The drop is at 1200. Dismissed."

It was nice knowing you, people, Fret sent.

Positivity, mate, Facehopper transmitted. *Positivity.*

Fret shook his head. *You're far too upbeat for a MOTH, Facehopper. Pessimism saves lives. As a soldier, you can never have too much of it. Positivity, on the other hand, even in small doses, is lethal. Especially to spec-op units.*

Facehopper grinned. *At least I'll die with a smile on my face.*

CHAPTER EIGHT

Shaw

As the ATLAS 5 opened fire, I dropped, more out of reflex than anything else, because hitting the ground wouldn't save me. There was nothing to hide behind: no rocks, no hollows. Maybe if I'd turned back instead, I might've made the bend in time. Fan had survived his encounter with the mech, after all. Still, I'd made the mistake of letting my guard down, and traveling too far from the bend.

There was no turning back.

I lay there, and accepted death in that moment.

But it did not come.

The bullets apparently weren't meant for me.

I opened my eyes. I didn't dare move my head, but I swiveled my eyes as far up as they would go, and I saw the stream of Gatling fire tear past, above, and to my left, aimed at something behind me.

There was only one other thing that could be behind me . . . a certain loyal companion who wouldn't stay back when I told him to.

Queequeg!

The Gatling fire ceased.

Dreading what I would find, I glanced over my shoulder.

To my relief, Queequeg was not there.

I stood up cautiously, and backed away from the ATLAS 5, my hands raised in a gesture of surrender, though whether or not the mech would interpret the action as such was questionable. I felt, maybe unjustifiably, that any attempt to withdraw would attract more Gatling fire.

But I had to check on Queequeg.

Step by slow step I retreated. I kept my rifle aimed skyward, and considered tossing it away entirely, all too aware it was an SK model. In the end, I kept it, because I still had to deal with Fan out there.

After what seemed an eternity, I slipped past the bend into the outer section of the defile, only to find Queequeg long gone.

"Queequeg!" I turned the audio amplification on my external speakers up to full. "Queequeg!"

The animal peered apprehensively past the far edge of the defile. I felt relieved that he hadn't run off. But of course Queequeg wouldn't. The bonds of loyalty between us were too strong.

I glanced at the bend behind me, and when I was satisfied that the ATLAS 5 wasn't going to pursue, I jogged toward Queequeg. I had to check on him and make sure he wasn't injured.

"Queequeg! Come!" I beckoned as I ran, but he didn't move. "Queequeg. It's okay. Come!"

Queequeg reluctantly approached. His ears and tail were pointed straight up, a sign he was yet on high alert.

As I neared, his gait switched to a lope, then an all-out sprint.

He leaped into my arms, bowling me over.

I landed flat on my back. If I hadn't been wearing a jumpsuit, his weight would've crushed me. I found myself staring into this gaping maw as Queequeg licked my face mask, leaving steaming lines of saliva on the glass.

"Queequeg. Good to see you too, boy." With some effort, I slid him off me. "Are you hurt?"

I performed a thorough check, but he seemed fine. No green, misting wounds. He must have run away the instant those Gatlings turned on him.

I petted him between the shoulders. "Queequeg. You scared me."

He lowed in response.

"I take it things did not go well in there?" Fan walked down the defile toward us from the entrance.

"I'm alive," I said. "So things went extremely well. I don't think the ATLAS is possessed."

"Are you so sure? Maybe it wishes to talk with you."

"Maybe. Though it didn't really respond too well to Queequeg."

Fan scoffed, grimacing at the animal. "That is entirely under-standable."

Queequeg bared his long, sharp canines in a rictus and growled at him.

"That's right, Queequeg," I said. "He's an asshole."

Fan seemed taken aback. "What did I ever do to you other than help?"

I steered the rifle barrel toward him. "Whether you end up help-ing or hindering when all is said and done is the question, isn't it?"

He eyed the weapon uneasily. "When are you going to trust me?"

"Trust an SK? The only SK I'd trust is a little girl or boy. Too young for the indoctrinations to have taken full effect. I've read some of the propaganda your Paramount Leader feeds the population. How the UC is a land of homeless people, jobless because of the robot revo-lution. How our nations are always cold and covered in meters of snow. How we line up to receive food stamps, and riot when it comes time to fetch the actual food. Oh, and my favorite, how some of us are reduced to catching songbirds from the trees and eating them. *Yummy!*"

"Not all of us believe the propaganda, you know," Fan said. "You would be surprised at how many people use the Undernet, and the Tor2 anonymity network, to bypass the state-owned websites and media. Sure, we have to be careful what we say in public, but we know the truth. And I told you, I grew up in the UC. I know from personal experience it is not all bad."

"Sure, but you've been hearing how bad we are your entire adult life. Some of that ill will has got to stick."

He sighed.

"Look," I said. "I'll trust you when you've earned that trust."

"I led you to the ATLAS mech, did I not?"

"You did," I said. "But whether or not you guided me here because you hoped the mech would kill me remains to be seen."

Fan threw up his arms. "So this is how it is going to be. Go to your ATLAS mech, then. I am but an evil, indoctrinated SK."

I gave him a long, hard look, then I turned toward Queequeg. "Guard him, boy. Stay."

I backed away. Queequeg seemed happy to remain behind this time. Queequeg, who had faced down packs of hybears and gatherings of beasts at my side, was deathly afraid of the ATLAS mech.

I didn't blame him.

I was scared of the iron giant too.

I approached the bend once more, and felt the rising trepidation all over again.

I strapped the rifle over my shoulder—probably best not to approach the mech in any manner that could be construed as aggressive.

I stepped into the bend and emerged past the threshold.

The ATLAS 5 remained right where I left it, looming a good thirty meters away.

Its Gatlings were pointed right at me.

I remained motionless for a long moment, waiting for those Gats to open fire. Expecting them to.

Nothing happened.

I took a step forward. Another.

I became more confident, and increased my pace, though my approach was still one of utmost caution. I was ready to hit the deck at a moment's notice, though doing so wouldn't save me. I was so close now I wouldn't even realize the mech had fired, not until my body was pinwheeling backward from the impacts of hundreds of bullets, each one ripping a fist-sized hole into my flesh.

Actually scratch that. I'd never know.

At a fire rate of one hundred rounds per second, I'd be dead instantly.

The aReal built into my faceplate automatically outlined the mech in green, which was supposed to mean "friendly." The aReal also placed a generic *ATLAS 5* label above it.

"ATLAS, stand down," I said, shakily.

Nothing.

The metallic monster wouldn't be provisioned to respond to my vocal pattern, but perhaps I could reason with the AI within. In emergency situations, all robot support troops, including mechs, were programmed to protect UC Navy personnel. The trick was to convince the mech that this was an emergency.

I stepped forward three paces.

"ATLAS, stand down."

Still nothing. I suddenly felt extremely conscious of the hybear fur I'd plastered all over my jumpsuit. What if the fur confused the artificial intelligence of the mech? No. The ATLAS 5 would rely on the radio frequency signal from my embedded ID. All robots did.

I advanced two more steps. I was now five meters from the mech. That iron tower of weapons and servomotors stood roughly three times my height.

"ATLAS, stand down."

No response.

"ATLAS 5. Friendly is present. I repeat, friendly is present. Stand down."

Those glowing visual sensors stared emotionlessly at me from the red strip that visored the top of its face.

I began to fear the mech was possessed after all.

"ATLAS 5," I said again. "Friendly is present. I repeat, friendly—"

I heard the servomotors buzz to life, and those twin Gatlings lowered. The suddenness of the movement actually made me jump.

I closed my eyes in relief, and exhaled.

The mech had stood down.

When I looked at it again, I was ready to take charge.

"ATLAS 5, identify," I said forcefully.

The ATLAS stood to its full height.

I no longer felt very confident. I was so small and vulnerable, cowering there beneath the mech. If there was one thing that was intimidating, it was three tonnes of metal gazing down on you while you were dressed in nothing but a furry jumpsuit.

The ATLAS didn't respond.

"ATLAS 5, identify?" My voice sounded soft, squeaky to my ears.

Yup, I'd definitely lost all my confidence.

The mighty mech finally deigned to answer.

"ATLAS Generation 5," a deep, authoritative, almost rude voice blared down from above.

I winced, turning my internal speaker volume way down. It sounded like I was standing in front of a megaphone.

"Serial number 5010452," the ATLAS continued. "Mac address 01:53:65:53:21:cf. Callsign, Battlehawk."

Okay. Now we were getting somewhere.

"Battlehawk, open," I said.

The ATLAS remained motionless. "You are not provisioned for that command."

Well, it was worth a try.

"Battlehawk, follow tight," I said.

"You are not provisioned for that command."

Hmm. This wasn't going to work.

"Battlehawk," I said, in a tone reserved for a misbehaving child. "Repeat to me the first order of the Machine Constitution."

"The preservation of civilian human life in all its forms overrides every other directive, except mission critical," the mech intoned.

Ah yes, I had forgotten the military modification. For normal robots, the first order of the Machine Constitution was *the preservation of human life in all its forms overrides all other directives.*

The inclusion of the word "civilian" was a subtle distinction, but since the AI within the mech would follow the Constitution to the letter, and I wasn't a civilian, the ATLAS wouldn't help me if I pursued that angle.

However, there was another military modification I touched upon earlier, one I might be able to use. "You are programmed to protect all UC Navy personnel in emergency situations, are you not?"

"That is correct," Battlehawk answered in its deep voice.

"What if I told you that this was an emergency situation? And that to protect me, you must obey my every command?"

"Demonstrate proof of emergency," Battlehawk said.

"Battlehawk, my oxygen canisters are running low. I have maybe an hour left in the bailout canister. Do you confirm?"

The mech remained motionless. After a moment: "I confirm."

"Battlehawk, open," I said.

"You are not provisioned for that command."

I exhaled in exasperation.

"Battlehawk, you just agreed that my oxygen supply was critical.

If you do not open, if you do let me interface with your oxygen tanks, I cannot recharge my own supply. I will perish. At your hands. You will have allowed a member of the UC Navy to die. *This is an emergency situation.*"

Battlehawk's cockpit hatch still did not open. "You are not a qualified ATLAS pilot."

That's right, the military AI's could read *private* profiles from embedded IDs. Battlehawk had seen my ATLAS qualification score, or rather, my lack thereof.

"Battlehawk, listen to me. I've spent numerous hours in the simulator. I've passed the qualifications. I know my way around an ATLAS 5. I'm an astrogator. If I can handle something as complex as a starship, I think I can handle a little old ATLAS mech."

Of course a starship or even a shuttle operated very differently from a mech, but I wasn't going to mention that to Battlehawk's AI.

The ATLAS 5 swiveled its head slightly, almost like it was cocking its head in amusement. "The simulator does not reproduce the actual ATLAS pilot experience," Battlehawk said. "The simulator does not move with the pilot." I'd heard about that—apparently moving around for the first time was very disorienting to most beginning ATLAS pilots. "The simulator uses an approximation of the actual physics found in reality, especially on worlds with differing atmospheric pressure and gravity, such as this one. The simulator assumes optimal interface conditions, which includes a fully operational Implant. Your Implant is currently offline." I'd heard about that too. Reputedly, operating a mech without an Implant was the same thing as trying to wade across a swamp: slow and difficult. At least at first.

"I understand all of that," I said. "But it doesn't change the fact that if you don't open your cockpit and let me inside, I'll die of hypoxia within the hour."

The mech didn't move.

I met those glowing yellow eyes defiantly and I didn't back down. It felt almost like we were locked in some sort of staring match. But of course that couldn't be possible, not with a machine.

I should have never come here. I should have told Fan to take me directly to that oxygen extractor of his. Then at least I would have had a chance. But now, faced with this stubborn mech, I was going to die.

It was time to pull out all the stops. "Battlehawk. This entire situation is an emergency. For the both of us. Look, when was the last time you were in contact with your platoon, or the ship? That's right, more than eight months ago. I'm trapped on this planet. As are you. My ship, *our* ship, abandoned this system. I'm the only member of the UC Navy left on this world. And I'm surrounded by hostiles.

"Bioengineered animal packs manufactured by the SKs roam the plains. And below the surface lurk the beasts, the alien lifeforms I'm certain you've encountered. So I have no doubt this qualifies as an emergency situation. To protect me, you have to let me inside your cockpit. You have to let me pilot you. I'm vulnerable out here. Dying. Don't you detect the radiation in the air? There's better rad shielding inside your cockpit. Battlehawk? My oxygen is running out. You have to let me in. You have to open up."

I sat down, lowered my head, and rested my helmet on my knees. Stupid, stubborn mechs with their stupid, stubborn AIs.

I heard an unexpected click come from the direction of the ATLAS 5, followed by the clang of a metallic door falling open.

I looked up.

The central hatch of the mech had fallen open, and the cockpit beckoned within.

"Thank you," I said, climbing to my feet.

"Stow your weapon in the provided storage rack before you enter," Battlehawk said.

That's right. Because an internal cocoon would wrap my body when I went into the cockpit, the only weapon I could really carry was a pistol at my belt. The rifle would just get pushed into my jumpsuit, and might even puncture it.

"I don't see the rack. Where—"

A sound came from behind the mech, like metal shuddering aside. I supposed another compartment had just opened up.

I went to the back of the mech and sure enough discovered a recess behind its leg. Within, an empty rack awaited my weapon. I stowed the SK rifle in the rack, placing all the ammunition I'd taken from Fan on the provided shelf. There were already some grenades and ammunition rounds on the shelf, I noted.

"Weapon stowed." I stepped back.

A panel irised closed, concealing the recess.

I went to the front of the mech, climbed the leg rungs, stepped onto the open hatch, and swung myself inside the cockpit. I oriented my body so that I faced outward. I glanced into the crack between the hatch and the hull, peering at the brain case and confirming that it wasn't surrounded by the glowing vapor of a Phant.

The hatch closed.

The inner shell of the cockpit pressed into me from all sides. I couldn't see anything except the mech's dark interior. Despite all my simulator hours, I was entirely unprepared for the sudden feeling of claustrophobia.

I tried to pretend I was somewhere else. Astrogating a starship in the vast openness of space, maybe. Yes. I was in space now, not buried under three tonnes of metal.

It didn't work.

I started hyperventilating.

Battlehawk's sensor arrays routed their audio and video feeds to my helmet, so that I viewed the world from the mech's perspective.

It didn't help.

"Switch me over to your internal O_2 tanks, Battlehawk," I gasped. Maybe I was running out of oxygen. That must be the problem.

I heard a series of metallic clanks behind me as the feed valves of my oxygen canisters connected to the recharge lines of the mech; the ATLAS 5's main O_2 lines now fed directly into my jumpsuit's life-support system.

"Oxygen recharge initiated," Battlehawk said.

I was still hyperventilating.

I had the presence of mind to check the O_2 levels of Battlehawk's tanks. They were nearly full. So oxygen wasn't the problem.

I had to stop breathing this way. Every moment of hyperventilation was a moment of wasted air. Besides, I couldn't pilot the mech, not like this.

I shouldn't have felt this way. Life aboard a cramped starship certainly wasn't for those who feared confined places. But this was different somehow. At least on a starship, I actually had room to move. Here, I was clamped in *on all sides.*

You can get through this, Shaw. You have to.

I closed my eyes and thought back to my days as a child on the farm. Picking apples, bringing them to the grinder, bottling the cider. The work was done entirely by hand, without robots. There was something soothing about leaving out the machine element and interacting directly with nature. You knew your own hands would never break down, or turn on you.

In my mind's eye, the farmland stretched to the horizon on all sides. Unhindered. No walls. No cocoons.

My breathing stabilized.

I opened my eyes.

I pretended what I saw was the view from my own body. That I wasn't trapped inside three tonnes of metal. It wasn't so different from my own consciousness, I supposed, trapped within the flesh and blood of my body. Not so different at all.

I waited a moment, taking long breaths. I could do this.

I took a tentative step. It felt like I was moving my leg through deep water. I sensed the mech shift, and I knew the matching steel foot had moved with me. I glanced downward, and took another step, watching Battlehawk's leg travel in sync with my own.

But looking down was a mistake, because I nearly lost my balance.

I flung out my arms to stabilize myself, and the mech's arms moved in concert with my own. I managed to remain upright by having the mech grip the rock face beside me.

I kept Battlehawk's steel hand braced against the rock and took a few more exploratory steps. I proceeded forward slowly and carefully, and grew more confident with each step. The sensation of trudging through deep water subsided, and I removed Battlehawk's hand from the wall.

I was actually getting the hang of it. It was like I merely resided within an extra-large jumpsuit. Piloting three tonnes of metal wasn't so bad, not at all. And I rather enjoyed it. I felt powerful. Invincible. Ready to take on an army of beasts. I probably could, now.

I remembered all the stories Rade had told me; how he'd faced countless hordes of those crabs and slugs and just mowed them down. I'd thought he was exaggerating at the time, but I realized, inside a mech like this, I could probably kill a crab simply by stepping on it. The smaller ones, anyway.

The endless, repetitive whir of servomotors reflected from the walls around me. Below, shards sometimes flew upward as my massive feet crunched into the shale underfoot. That's right, I finally no longer thought of those feet as Battlehawk's, but *mine*.

I was Battlehawk, now. An ATLAS 5 mech. Designed for combat. Bred for dealing death. I was reborn as a being of steel, servomotors, rockets, and bullets. No one, not man, not hybear, not even beast, could defy me. I almost wished a sinkhole would open up right here, so I could prove myself.

Then again, that probably wasn't a good idea . . .

Don't fall for your own bull, Shaw.

There was one thing I had to do before passing the bend and rejoining my companions.

"Battlehawk, a few moments ago you fired on one of the non-native lifeforms of this planet," I said.

"SK bioweapon, class B, hyena-bear recombinant," Battlehawk said. "Hostile."

"Well yes, I suppose they are, in general. But this lifeform is nonhostile. You are not, I repeat, not to fire upon him. His name is Queequeg, and he is my friend."

Battlehawk did not answer.

"Battlehawk, give me your assurance that you won't fire on Queequeg. He's saved my life more times than I can remember. Battlehawk?"

No answer.

Sometimes it was a matter of wording the request the right way, because apparently certain keywords influenced the AI's decision tree algorithm more than others. How did I do it in the simulator again? "Battlehawk, tag the previously encountered lifeform as nonhostile."

"Tagging previous lifeform as nonhostile," the AI said.

So that was it. "Thank you."

The bend proved a tight fit, and only with effort did I jam my new, larger body past the cramped walls. I inflicted several more dents in the arms, legs, and chest piece.

Queequeg waited precisely where I'd left him, guarding Fan. The animal was looking right at me, his eyes big as saucers.

Queequeg turned around and hightailed it out of the defile.

"Queequeg, wait!" I said. "Battlehawk, broadcast my—"

But Battlehawk was already loading the Gatlings into my hands.

"Battlehawk, stand down, what are you doing? Battlehawk, I'm in control now! We agreed, remember?"

Apparently I wasn't, and we hadn't.

As Queequeg vanished beyond the entrance to the defile, Battlehawk trained its twin Gatling guns on Fan.

Oh.

The SK raised his palms in surrender, and backed away.

"Target acquired," Battlehawk said in its authoritative male voice. "Preparing to terminate."

"Stand down!" I said. "He is a friendly."

Battlehawk did not stand down.

Knowing he could never reach the defile's entrance in time, Fan fell to his knees and put his hands behind his head.

Battlehawk, not me, *never* me, took a massive step forward.

"Battlehawk!" I said. "He is unarmed. He is a friendly. A civilian! Stand down!"

I frantically resisted the movements of the cocoon that wrapped me, but I was pinned, locked inside this steel body, just an observer, powerless to do anything. I would watch helplessly as Fan was gunned down.

"Embedded ID profile inconclusive," Battlehawk said.

That's right, Fan had wiped his public profile, and because he was SK, the mech couldn't access Fan's private profile. Assuming he even had one.

"Facial recognition in progress," Battlehawk continued. "Sino-Korean feature match. Correlating with NGI biometric database."

Military-grade UC AIs stored a local, apparently secure copy of the Next Generation Identification database, which contained the biometrics—facial features, fingerprints, retinal scans—of all UC citizens. "Target is not a UC citizen. Target queued for termination."

"Yes he's SK, but he's a *civilian*," I pleaded.

"Target queued for termination," Battlehawk persisted.

"No," I said. "He's a civilian. And he's helping me. Battlehawk, if you kill him, you disobey your own programming to protect me. Because if he dies, I die. Battlehawk, do you understand? You can't kill him. Battlehawk?" Then I remembered the magic words. "Battlehawk, tag the target as civilian."

A moment passed.

"Tagging target as civilian." The Gatlings folded away.

I'd been pressing so hard against the inner cocoon that when the mech suddenly ceded control back to me, my arms almost slammed together.

Fan slumped. He held his gloves to his face mask, and I thought he was trying to hide tears of relief.

Honestly, I felt like crying too.

But there was still the matter of Queequeg.

"Queequeg?" I shouted.

No response came from the edge of the defile.

I didn't want to approach and scare him further. I knew he was waiting out there somewhere beyond the defile. At least, I hoped he was.

I was loath to leave the cockpit to retrieve Queequeg, not after all the work it had taken to convince Battlehawk to let me inside in the first place. Who knows? If I went out maybe Battlehawk would decide my updated O_2 situation no longer warranted an emergency situation.

I'd just have to find a way to convince Queequeg to obey me while I was still inside the mech.

"Battlehawk, voice amplification, maximum."

"Voice amplification maximum," Battlehawk repeated.

"Queequeg?" I said.

I winced as the close walls deflected the amplified syllables back at me.

Fan slid his hands over his helmet, where his ears would have been were he not wearing a jumpsuit.

I turned the voice amplification down a notch. "Queequeg?"

Still no response.

I supposed I'd have to risk leaving the mech after all, because I wasn't going to continue without Queequeg. But if I ejected, and went to the animal, there was still the problem of introducing him to the ATLAS. This wouldn't work if Queequeg ran away every time I boarded Battlehawk . . .

I decided to try one last thing before I left the cockpit: a lullaby I sang to Queequeg shortly after I'd found him, when he was still an abandoned babe swathed in his mother's umbilical. It was a lullaby my own mother had sung to me.

"Tender one, sleep tonight. Sleep, because though the dark is near, the stars will always guide you."

Queequeg timidly poked his head around the far end of the defile.

I continued the song. When I beckoned with one hand, the movement caused him to duck beyond the rim of the defile once more.

I sang away.

Queequeg's head eventually appeared again.

I beckoned—I had to get him used to seeing the mech move.

Queequeg didn't shirk this time. He just remained still, his eyes saucer-shaped, his ears and mane folded flat.

I stopped singing for a moment and said, "Battlehawk, tag target as nonhostile." Just in case.

"Target already tagged as nonhostile."

I resumed the lullaby.

Queequeg apparently screwed up his courage, because the animal finally approached. Very cautiously.

I continued to beckon, but not too quickly. I didn't want to make any sudden movements. I was humming the song now, letting Queequeg come near.

Fan watched dumbfounded. I supposed all of this would appear somewhat ludicrous to a bystander. It wasn't every day you saw an ATLAS mech humming a lullaby to a bioengineered bear-hyena hybrid. But hey, this was my pet we were talking about here, and I didn't care if I embarrassed myself in front of Fan.

Queequeg halted twenty paces from Battlehawk. He seemed like a small rabbit to me from up here.

I ended the song.

Queequeg abruptly crouched, baring his teeth and growling.

I wondered if he thought I'd been devoured by the mech or something.

"Queequeg, it's me," I said.

The animal perked up immediately when he heard my voice, and his ears pricked. But then he growled again.

"It's all right Queequeg," I said soothingly. "It's me. Shaw." I pointed slowly at myself. "Shaw." I'd done this before when I'd first trained the animal all those months ago. He had to recognize the word and the gesture. He had to.

Either Queequeg had indeed understood me, or he was too confused to do anything other than cock his head and stare at the ATLAS 5.

I slowly knelt to one knee, and held out an open palm.

"Come," I said, gently. "Come."

Queequeg approached warily. When he reached my hand, he tentatively licked the outer edge of my giant finger.

"That's a good boy." I carefully reached behind his neck, and scratched him with said finger.

"So you have obtained your mech," Fan said from where I'd left him beside the wall.

Queequeg swung toward Fan and growled.

The SK frowned, but I could see the alarm in his eyes. He actually feared the hybear more than the ATLAS. Amazing.

"I got my mech." I agreed, slowly pulling my hand away from Queequeg.

"Do you trust me now?" Fan said.

I glanced at the SK. He seemed so small and insignificant beside me. Less than a child. "Not really. But it looks like you get to keep your main cylinder after all."

He smiled sardonically. "Why, thank you, oh great mech pilot. But what about my rifle?"

"What about it?"

Fan crossed his arms. "You said you would give it back. When we reached the ATLAS."

"No I didn't. Don't put words in my mouth. The deal was, you'd get to keep your main oxygen cylinder."

Fan sighed profusely. "You are a crafty one, Shaw Chopra of the UC Navy. Let us return to my oxygen extractor, then. With your mech, we can move the device easily. We can take it with us to the next Forma chimney, where I will start work on your extractor."

I regarded him crossly, though of course he couldn't see my expression. "So you're dictating my actions now? You realize I'm the one up in the ATLAS 5, don't you?" Though what he said wasn't a bad idea. Taking his extractor to the next Forma pipe would save us a lot of time.

"I only speak the truth, Shaw Chopra. We must do this. The oxygen tanks in your ATLAS will not last forever."

"They won't," I conceded.

"See? You need me. Without me, no extractor. No extractor, no oxygen. Not in the long run."

I wondered once again how much I could truly trust him. I considered abandoning him right there. That was probably the best move. But my conscience wouldn't let me.

Besides, he was right. If I wanted to survive on this world in the long run, I still needed him to build me an oxygen extractor.

He had wanted to stick together before. And I could see why he might want that even more now. With a mech at his side, he'd never have to fear the hybears or beasts of this world ever again.

Maybe he planned to steal my ATLAS mech somehow. I wished him luck on that front, given how hard it had been for me to take control of Battlehawk in the first place, and I was actually UC.

I stood to my full height, which had the unintended side effect of frightening Queequeg—my pet quickly moved to the defile wall, behind Fan, like he was using the SK as a shield.

I edged past the two of them and continued forward at a comfortable pace, heading to the defile entrance. In moments I emerged into the valley beyond.

I turned around.

Fan was right behind me, but Queequeg kept his distance.

"Come on, Queequeg," I said.

Queequeg approached to within five meters, but refused to come any closer. That was probably for the best, because I didn't want to accidentally step on him—as an animal, Queequeg didn't have any means of transmitting his position to my helmet aReal, so I had to keep track of him by sight.

"How fast can you travel in that?" Fan said.

"Fast. You won't be able to match my speed. But here, let me show you a little UC innovation. Something we add to all our mechs."

I scooped him up.

"Put me down!" Fan protested.

I set him on my back, just behind my head, in the provided passenger seat.

"Impressive." Fan sounded sarcastic. "But I believe the Sino-Koreans employ this so-called innovation in our mechs as well."

"Buckle up and enjoy the ride." I moved forward, feeling confident enough to switch to a moderate lope. My balance remained stable. So far so good.

Queequeg easily kept pace, though he gave me a wide berth, staying twenty meters to my right.

"Well, Queequeg?" I said. "Think you can keep up?"

I upticked my speed, broke into an all-out sprint—

And promptly fell flat on my face. I skidded across the surface, plowing a long furrow into the shale.

Fan swore in Korean-Chinese behind me.

I supposed I had some more practicing to do.

CHAPTER NINE

Rade

The MOTH Delivery Vehicle rendezvoused with the SK shuttle about twenty klicks northeast of the city, and together the two vessels approached the distant skyscrapers. We were two platoons from disparate space-faring nations of Earth. Nations ofttimes enemies, brought together by a common threat.

This should prove interesting.

The drop had been easy this time, compared to the first. The *Gerald R. Ford* had been well out of range of the point defense of the Skull Ship, and we faced no opposition from any other vessels, thanks in part to the valiant captains and crews who had refused to allow their starships to be taken, choosing to detonate their reactor cores over capture. Heroes. All of them.

The drop vehicles hugged the surface of the moon on approach, because Shangde City was defended by possessed ATLAS mechs and automated air defense weapons. The SK convoy that had breached the city during Operation Crimson Pipeline had managed to cripple the air defenses along the northeasternmost extremities, and it was from that vector we approached.

Clamped in against the bulkheads of the delivery vehicle, the members of Alfa platoon sat opposite and facing one another.

"I don't trust them," Hijak said. The MOTH formerly known as Dyson was seated beside me. I decided to start referring to him by his callsign in my head, otherwise a world of confusion awaited me. Tahoe was the only one I continued to call by his real name. He'd gone through MOTH training with me, and he deserved that honor.

Hijak was staring opposite him at the portal above Bender's head. I followed his gaze, and saw the SK shuttle outside, which shadowed our movements some distance starboard.

"None of us trust them," Facehopper said. "But we have a job to do. And we're going to do it."

"For once I have to agree with Hijak," Lui said. "I don't like this. It stinks of subterfuge. The SKs are going to betray us the first chance they get."

Skullcracker flashed a big grin, and the skull tattooed into his face matched the fierce smile. "If they betray us, I'll be introducing the SK platoon to a little friend of mine." He patted the barrel of his heavy gun.

"I like my friend better," Fret said, shifting the Carl Gustav on his shoulder.

Ghost chuckled. "True artists don't rely on recoilless rifles or heavy guns. That's like throwing a bucket of paint on a blank canvas. Sure, sometimes you'll create something half-resembling art, but for the most part, all you'll get is a mess of collateral damage." The albino warrior hefted his sniper rifle. "Now this, on the other hand, is the round brush of the true artist. With it, I can paint the battle space with utmost precision and care, taking out a target five klicks away without harming a hair on the civilians beside him."

Fret smirked. "What about the civilian standing behind the target who gets battered by the somersaulting body?"

"Never happen," Trace interceded. "Nine times out of ten, anyone lounging near a target is a target themselves."

"And nine times out of ten, statistics are made up on the spot," Fret said.

"Okay, enough already," Bender said. "I get the point, bitches."

"Who are you calling a bitch, bitch?" Trace said.

"Sniping sucks," Fret said. "When I have fifty targets all bunched up and running toward me, I'll take a recoilless launcher over a peashooter any day."

"I'll take an ATLAS," Bomb said. He'd shaved off his mohawk and was now completely bald, but he'd grown his beard out so that it was the scraggliest of all. He looked like a black Santa Claus, minus the paunch. Not that I could see much of the beard beneath his jumpsuit helmet.

"An ATLAS would be good, too," Fret agreed.

"The suits we're wearing now are almost ATLAS mechs," Tahoe said. "The ATLAS 1s were body-hugging, strength-enhancing exoskeletons with face masks. No weapon attachments. No jetpacks. Basically jumpsuits. The ATLAS 2s were a streamlined, slim-downed version of the same, with jetpack attachments. Jumpsuit design branched off from the twos, and it was only when the ATLAS 3s came out that the modern mecha design emerged. The ATLAS 3 was no longer body hugging. The user resided in a cockpit at the heart of the mech, and his movements controlled the arms and legs and weapons systems."

"Well, it's good to know someone else took the ATLAS history class," Facehopper said. I couldn't tell if he was being sarcastic or not, since that was an actual course.

"They make you take it in Fourth Phase, now," Hijak said.

"You don't say?" Bomb wore a thoughtful expression. "I seem to recall taking that course. Forgot everything I learned, though. Too many shots to the head, if you know what I mean."

"You ain't never been shot in the head, bro," Bender said. "Me and Fret, well, that's a different story."

"Me, too." Snakeoil raised his hand sheepishly.

"Sure, Snakeoil," Bender said. "But you ain't suffered brain damage. Me and Fret, now . . ."

"You have brain damage?" Hijak said. "Well, that explains a lot."

Bender's eyes flared like embers. "You better shut it, caterpillar, because I'm this close to ripping your head off and shoving it down your throat." He pinched his gloved thumb and forefinger so the two digits almost touched.

Hijak didn't back down. "I'm not a caterpillar anymore, bitch."

"That's it." Bender reached for the manual clamp release.

"Hold," Chief Bourbonjack said. "Don't you get up, Bender. Goddammit, we're on an operation here. We don't have time for preschool antics. You're spec-ops. A team." He stared at Bender a moment. "Tell me that you can work together. Tell me that you'll be there for him. That you'll take a bullet for him. Tell me."

Bender gazed back defiantly, then lowered his gaze. "I'll be there for him," he said quietly.

"What's that?" Chief Bourbonjack said. "Speak up, Bender."

"I'll be there for him," Bender said.

"For who?"

Bender glanced at the Chief. "For Hijak."

"Tell it to his face," the Chief said.

Bender bit his lip, then looked at Hijak. "I'll be there for you."

"Tell him you'll take a bullet for him," the Chief said.

Now that he'd said the first part, Bender's resolve seemed to strengthen. "I'll take a bullet for you, Hijak."

I could hear the conviction in his voice, and I knew he would.

"Your turn," the Chief instructed Hijak.

"I'll be there for you, Bender," Hijak said. "I'll take a bullet for you."

"Now shake on it. Do it!"

Hijak extended a hand. Bender lifted his, too, from where he sat on the opposite side of the MDV. The two of them strained against their clamps and shook.

"Good," the Chief said. "We go into battle as a team, we fight as a team, and we go home as a team. That's what makes us MOTHs. When you're out there, getting shot at from all sides, nothing matters except your team. Not your country. Not your mission. But the man beside you. Save his life, and you save your own. Remember that."

The compartment fell into reflective silence.

"Mauler?" Facehopper said.

"Yes, sir?" Mauler was the new callsign of the other former caterpillar, Meyers, who replaced Big Dog as heavy gunner. He was a bona fide native of the UC, not an immigrant. One of those very few who actually volunteered to join the service, not because he had to, like the rest of us, but because he *wanted* to.

"Tell us why the Chief gave you that name," Facehopper said.

Mauler glanced in the Chief's direction, and Chief Bourbonjack inclined his head in consent.

"During the firefight," Mauler said, "one of the enemy Centurions came at me from behind. It had no weapon, so it knocked me down. Tried to pin me with its weight. I'd dropped my rifle, so I started punching it. Again and again. Busted its head. Broke its vision sensors."

"You should have seen the dents in the Centurion's head." The Chief chuckled. "When Mauler took off his gloves later, his knuckles were soaked in blood. He broke half the bones in his hands."

"Nasty." Skullcracker shook his head.

Facehopper grinned. "If you can get that reaction from Skull-cracker, you know you're doing something right."

"Mauler displayed true MOTH spirit that day," Chief Bourbonjack said. "He didn't give up. We do what we have to do to save our lives, and the lives of our teammates."

The lives of our teammates . . .

I wondered again, as I had so many times before, whether there was something I could have done to save Alejandro. I would've gladly broken my hand, or every bone in my body, to save him.

"Got anyone back home?" I asked Hijak, trying to distract myself. I was making an effort at putting the resentment I felt toward him behind me.

He looked at me. "No. Well, unless you count family."

"Of course I count family."

"I thought you meant like a girlfriend or something." Hijak said. "Which I don't have. But I got my parents. What about you? Girl back home?"

I smiled wanly. "No. Not anymore."

"Broke up, huh? The service is tough. Especially for spec-ops people."

"It is." I glanced at Tahoe, looking to change the subject, or at least get the attention off me. "Tah— Cyclone here, has a wife and two kids back home."

"That true?" Hijak said, turning to Tahoe. "You must seriously miss them."

Tahoe closed his eyes, obviously annoyed. He didn't answer.

"What did I do?" Hijak glanced at the other members of the platoon, but most of them studiously avoided his eyes.

Bender, however, was staring right at him. "You're an insensitive, morale-leeching bitch, is what."

"Bender . . ." Chief said.

Bender shrugged, and looked away.

"So how'd you end up in the UC?" I said to Hijak.

"Me? Parents emigrated a few months before I was born. They were too old for the draft. But they had the money to buy their way into citizenship. Did you know it only costs 500,000 bitcoins? Pony up the funds, invest in a municipal bond or UC company, create ten UC jobs, and the government assigns your family permanent residence status. Funny thing is, for all the money they had, my parents couldn't buy me out of the draft."

"Bet they tried, though," I said.

"They did. First they had my records hacked. But the anti-tampering system put everything back the next day. Then they tried to bribe the local politicians and military officials. That didn't work either. Finally they wanted to switch out my embedded ID. By that point I'd had enough. I told them to stop, because of course it wasn't going to work. Too many checks and balances in the enlistment process, otherwise the SKs would've installed sleepers in our ranks years ago."

"Who says they haven't?" Bender joked, glancing at Lui.

"Hey, if I was an SK sleeper, I would have terminated your ass years ago," Lui retorted.

"So what happened?" I asked Hijak.

"Well, I took my parents out to the most expensive restaurant in town and broke the news: I'd enlisted in the Navy and was shipping out to New Great Lakes the next day."

"And you chose the spec-ops rating," I said.

"I did. Like all of you, I chose this." He regarded me thoughtfully. "I heard you immigrated, not because you wanted to someday become a citizen, but because you specifically wanted to join up?"

"I did."

"Do you ever regret it?" Hijak said.

I answered without hesitation, giving him the answer that was expected of me, though inside I was full of regret. "Not for a minute. You asked me if I had anyone back home. I don't. But the truth is, I don't need anyone. These are my brothers now. This is the only family I'll ever need. Right here. Right now."

"Wooyah," Skullcracker said.

Yeah. Wooyah.

Chief Bourbonjack gave me a searching look. Had he heard the grief in my voice? He was the only one who knew of my transfer request; was he regretting not fulfilling that request now? Was he worried I'd let him or my platoon brothers down during the mission?

I promised myself right then that I wouldn't fail my brothers, nor allow anyone to die on this mission.

Because if I lost anyone else, it would kill me.

I forced myself to focus on the mission. The past was over and done. It wasn't going to help the present.

I stared at the glass container roped to the deck in the middle of the MDV. Engineering had received the blueprints only hours ago and had rushed the construction. I hoped the design was up to par. Capable of holding a seven-foot-tall man, it was a rectangular, box-shaped contraption with glass making up its six faces. Steel braces reinforced the eight corners, while handholds and clip-in carabiner loops for the actual portage rounded out the container. The bulletproof glass was composed of a combination of various plies of polycarbonate, PVB (polyvinyl butyral), glass, and thermoplastic urethane. Only the most powerful armor-piercing rounds could penetrate it. Still, the glass by itself wouldn't hold a Phant—the metallic circles embedded in the floor and ceiling of the container performed the actual containment, via some sort of electromagnetic beam. At least, that's what the SKs claimed.

Assuming we could get the High-Value within the metal circles before the Phant seeped out.

Glancing toward the cockpit area, past the seated outlines of the pilot and copilot, I was able to discern a portion of the city through the main window. The outermost buildings loomed about two klicks away, and were coming on fast. The place looked like a forest whose trees of steel and glass struggled to grow out of the black, bulbous disease that encased them.

It was a city that once teemed with life. A city where people had laughed and cried and walked the streets in safety, where children had played, adults had shopped, and robots had fulfilled human-kind's every need.

A city that was now a war zone, reduced to a shadow of what it once was by an alien invader.

One million people lost.

This had been humanity's moon.

Humanity's colony.

And the invaders had come and blatantly taken it from us.

Humanity wouldn't stand for it.

We couldn't.

We'd blast this alien invader from our side of the galaxy and send it back to where it belonged.

Someday.

Maybe today was the first step in achieving that goal.

Maybe today would change everything.

I sincerely hoped so.

"Launch HS3s," Chief Bourbonjack said. "And moderate speed." "Launching HS3s and moderating speed," Mordecai, our pilot, answered.

I heard the swoosh as rockets discharged from underneath the fuselage, and I saw the twin streaks of booster rockets pull ahead, carrying the drone payload to the city.

I quickly lost sight of both objects, but I knew six HS3 scouts would eject from each rocket a short way from the city, leaving the spent shells to fall harmlessly to the ground.

"This is a hot drop, people," Chief Bourbonjack said. "I don't care how many LIDAR obfuscators and background rad maskers this puppy is throwing out. There are goddamn alien beings out there, using our own goddamn tech against us, and I want you on the highest goddamn possible state of goddamn alert. Understood?"

"Understood, sir!"

"Good," he said grimly. He glanced down the line. "TJ, anything to report from the HS3s yet?"

"HS3s have separated from the boosters," TJ, our lead drone operator, said. The tanned Italian must have been feeling a bit handicapped without his usual complement of support robots. All they'd given him this time around were a dozen HS3s. Though I guess he was lucky, because our other drone operator, Bender, didn't get any. "The insert site at the northeastern edge of the city seems clear. Should I initiate stage two?"

"That's a negative," the Chief said. "I want the drones to take up an overwatch position on the insert site. First sign of trouble, we turn back. If things turn sour during the insert, and the SKs want to stay and get themselves blown out of the sky, that's up to them."

"Moving HS3s into 360-degree overwatch position," TJ said.

Still flying low, the MDV throttled down. Through the portal opposite me I watched the SK shuttle match our speed.

"TJ?" the Chief said. "Update me."

"All clear," TJ answered. "So far."

A three-story building filled the portal, blotting out my view. The MDV's right wing hovered in line with the second-story windows.

The craft slowed further, and started to descend.

"Prepare to deploy," Chief Bourbonjack said. "I want a defensive perimeter. Cigar shape. Rage and Cyclone, stay aboard until I give the order."

The compartment shook as the MDV touched down.

The down ramp folded open.

My shoulder and waist latches clicked aside.

"Deploy, deploy, deploy!" Chief Bourbonjack said.

Tahoe and I watched as the platoon moved out at a crouch, each man staying close to his assigned "buddy."

Tense moments ticked past. On my helmet HUD, the green dots of the platoon assumed a cigar shape around the MDV. There were no other targets, and everything seemed good. Even so, Tahoe and I exchanged a worried glance. The waiting was always agonizingly long when you stayed behind.

I fingered the three-meter-long cord slung to the shoulder opposite my rifle strap. When it came time for jetpack portage, I'd use that cord to secure myself to the glass container. Tahoe carried a similar cord. For now though, we'd just use our gloves.

"Rage and Cyclone, bring the package."

I looped my gloved fingers around a lower handhold on the left side of the glass container, while Tahoe took the right. We lifted in unison. As usual, we'd upticked the muscular strength of our suits to the max before turning off our Implants, so porting the half-tonne container was really no worse than ATLAS PT in training. Though it was still heavy, and without Tahoe's aid I would've never hoisted it from the ground.

We hurried down the ramp at a crouch, and as soon as we stepped onto the black rock that coated the streets, we lowered the container.

I dropped to one knee and slid the strap of the sniper rifle from my shoulder. My jumpsuit, like everyone else's, had darkened to match the black surface below. Through the sniper scope, I scanned the streets and alleyways for any sign of movement.

Beside me, Tahoe did the same thing. He carried a standard-issue rifle—his porter role denied him the usual bulky heavy gun.

Shangde City reminded me a little of my home country, because the buildings weren't overly tall, and there was only one level of road system, unlike, say, New Chicago, where the multilevel roadways used the heaven-reaching skyscrapers as supports. I guessed with so much room to spare, the city planners didn't have any real need to build upward, and outward worked just fine. Unfortunately, that only increased the level of urban sprawl we'd have to navigate on the way to the High-Value.

One thing kind of ruined the whole "home country" reminiscence for me, and that was the bulbous black shells that encased the lower halves of most buildings. Those shells had an uncanny resemblance to anthills caking the bases of trees, replete with multiple access holes. The only thing missing were the ants. Giant-sized.

There was no sign of alien life. Or any life at all, for that matter. The only noise was the hum of the MDV behind us, waiting for liftoff confirmation.

The SK platoon was deployed behind the opposite building, according to the blue dots on the HUD map.

Blue was an interesting choice of color for them. Normally friendlies were green, enemies red, and things like waypoints and payloads blue. In the previous battle, the SKs had been tagged as green, but this time we'd labeled them as payloads: not enemies, but not entirely friendlies, either. By tagging them blue, we'd left open the ability to fire on them without having to issue a "disable friendly fire" command. This would spare us precious seconds, potentially saving our lives if the SKs reneged on their part of the bargain.

Of course, both platoons had tagged the ATLAS mechs and other war machines to automatically appear as enemy combatants, regardless of whether those machines were of SK, UC, or FI make.

Any robot other than the High-Value Target and our own HS3s was considered fair game.

"Waypoint Boston achieved," Chief Bourbonjack said over the comm. "We have ourselves a successful insert. Golden Arrow, you are cleared for takeoff."

The MDV launched, and I cringed at the engine roar. I glanced at the black bulbs caking the buildings, waiting for the crab hordes to erupt from the many holes.

But none came.

Returning the same way it had come, the MDV passed low overhead, flying out onto the plains where it would wait for our return signal. The Lieutenant Commander had decided against leaving the insert crafts in the city proper, in case a roving band of ATLAS mechs or Centurions stumbled on it. Or in case the aforementioned crab hordes decided to emerge while we were gone.

The SK shuttle left the cover of the three-story apartment building beside us and joined our MDV in retreat.

"Status, Snakeoil?" the Chief said.

"Golden Arrow is making toward the safe harbor site one klick away," Snakeoil said. "Signal reception is extremely poor. We'll probably lose contact as soon as we leave this spot. Meaning we'll have to return to this exact location if we want to call for extract. That or distribute some HS3s behind us as we go, to function as network repeaters, extending the range."

The Chief pursed his lips. "Once we move out, I'd rather keep the HS3s deployed ahead of us in a scouting role."

Snakeoil nodded. "Then better get any last-minute requests to the LC in now, sir."

"Fair enough," the Chief said. He glanced at TJ. "Raptor status?"

TJ shrugged. "Not reading a thing from them. They're flying too high . . . too much interference."

The Chief frowned. "I'll ask the LC to lower them." To Snakeoil: "What's the air like?"

"Breathable, sir," Snakeoil said. "Minimal toxins."

"Then open up your face masks."

We did, then lowered the aReal visors built into our helmets.

"Smells like balls out here," Bender said.

I put in the obligatory jibe. "Your favorite smell."

Bender shot me a sarcastic grin. "Only yours, baby."

"The LC has refused my request to reposition the Raptors," Chief Bourbonjack said. "Any lower, and they'll be within range of the air defenses. Looks like we're on our own for now, boys. Maybe we'll have better reception when we get airborne."

It didn't really matter all that much as far as I was concerned, because as mentioned in the briefing, we weren't authorized to call in any air strikes right now anyway—the Brass didn't want to risk damage to the Artificial.

"Facehopper, get us in sight of Dragon," Chief Bourbonjack said. That was the callsign of the SK platoon deployed with us.

"On my order, people, take the side street indicated on your six and rendezvous at the waypoint," Facehopper said.

I zoomed in on my overhead map and saw the flashing blue dot of the waypoint Facehopper had just added.

"On me." Facehopper dashed into the side street. The rest of the platoon followed at a crouch.

Tahoe and I hoisted the glass chamber by the handles and set off. The two of us had to run in unison, but that was something we had trained at. The long, looping nylon cords slung over our shoulders swayed with each step.

I turned onto the designated side street. The black, bloated substance plastering the walls of the buildings on either flank made it feel like we were traveling deeper into some sort of alien nest.

Which we were, of course.

The platoon halted at the far end of the street, and we crouched against the black gum caking the building.

Tahoe and I set down our load.

"Dragon in sight," Facehopper said.

I checked the map. The blue dots indicated that Dragon platoon resided across the street in an alleyway, but I didn't actually see any of them with my own eyes.

"TJ, bring the HS3s around and sweep the area," Chief Bourbonjack said.

"Bringing HS3s around and sweeping the area," TJ repeated.

One of the drones flew past and proceeded down the lane. Across from us, the SK equivalent of an HS3 drone emerged from an alleyway and followed a similar path.

I zoomed in on my aReal. Yes, now I saw the SK platoon. They were huddled against the black plaster in the alleyway opposite ours. Their jumpsuits had changed coloration to match the surface, making them difficult to discern.

I zoomed in closer, and realized the foremost soldiers were kneeling, and had their sniper rifles trained on us.

Fret had apparently made the same realization as I had, because he said, "Uh, their rifles are aimed at us, you know that, right?"

"I have them in my scope too, don't you worry," Trace said. Peering into his rifle sight, he was crouched on one knee near the edge of our alley.

"As do I," Ghost said.

I lifted my own sniper rifle, and positioned myself so that I got a bead on one of the SK snipers. "Me too."

The unpleasant memory of my last encounter with a company of SKs surfaced, as I'm sure it did in the minds of my platoon brothers, and the tension in the air became almost palpable.

It felt like an SK bullet might come in any second and tear right through my scope, into my eye.

"Who aimed first?" Bender said.

"They did," Trace said.

"It doesn't matter who aimed first," Chief Bourbonjack said. "Stand down."

Trace and Ghost hesitated, as did I.

"Stand down," the Chief repeated. "Don't make me say it a third time."

Still we hesitated. Trace finally lowered his rifle, followed by Ghost and me. I was convinced we were going to be riddled with armor-piercing rounds any second.

No bullets came.

I zoomed in on my aReal and watched the SK snipers lower their weapons.

The tension in the air eased somewhat.

"That was close," Fret said.

"Stay on your toes, boys," Chief Bourbonjack said, his voice dark. "It's not over yet."

"HS3s report all clear," TJ said. "Other than Dragon, we're all alone out here."

Chief Bourbonjack nodded. "Initiate stage two."

"Initiating stage two. Deploying HS3s for High-Value Target sweep."

I watched the green dots of the drones fan out across the HUD map. The SKs presumably had their own HS3 drones sweeping the area, but none of theirs showed up on the map.

The HS3s started winking out as they traveled beyond the reduced signal range imposed by the EM interference of the alien race. Even so, I knew the drones would continue to fly down the streets, searching for the signature of our target: the possessed SK Artificial.

All Artificials and robots contained a built-in wireless adhoc network node and a unique MAC address associated with that node. Because of the aforementioned interference, the already weak range of the node would be reduced to around thirty meters. So, assuming the Artificial hadn't turned off its network node, and hadn't spoofed the address to create a decoy, eventually the HS3s would find a match.

Eventually was the key word.

All we could really do now was settle in and wait.

Our specialty.

"Feels almost like we should cross the street and introduce ourselves to the SKs or something," Bomb said.

We wouldn't, of course. According to the briefing, our platoons were to provide bounding overwatch for one another. We would remain separate the entire mission, even once the High-Value Target was captured.

"Bounding overwatch," Bomb muttered, obviously thinking about the mission, too. "You think they even know what that *is*?"

"Of course they do," Lui said. "Just because they're Sino-Korean doesn't mean they don't grasp basic small unit tactics. You think it was coincidence they kept trying to overwhelm our flanks during the Geronimo ambush?"

"Those were crack units," Bomb said. "They sent their best out to that planet. Wouldn't you if you planned a mission eight thousand lightyears away? But these guys? Come on."

"They're good enough, don't you worry," Chief Bourbonjack said. "The SK brass knew we'd send MOTHs. That means they sent their best, too. The SKs don't want to look bad. And neither do we, coincidentally. This is an important mission, boys. Don't go messing it up on account of your mistrust of the SKs."

I sat back against the bulbous black rock that encased the building beside me and prepared myself for the long wait.

Some hours later, a green dot abruptly appeared on my HUD map, to the west.

Then another.

A third.

My platoon brothers stirred.

"See that?" Trace said.

The HS3s were returning.

Red dots started to appear, too, clustered at various points throughout Shangde City: the last known recorded positions of enemy units.

A flashing blue dot appeared as well, this one inside a warehouse-like building near the center of the city.

The High-Value Target.

The entire region around it swarmed with red.

"Doesn't look good," Fret said.

"Chief," TJ said. "I'm only reading six HS3s. Looks like we lost the others."

The Chief nodded slowly. Then he glanced at me and said, "Rage, Cyclone: prepare the package for jetpack portage."

I slid the nylon cord from my shoulder and secured the locking carabiner on one end to my utility belt, then fastened the opposite carabiner to the container's handle. Tahoe did the same on his side. This way, if either one of us dropped the container while we jetted from building to building, the three-meter-long cord ensured it wouldn't fall too far. Assuming the cord didn't drag down whoever had dropped the container, too.

I exchanged a glance with Tahoe through the two plates of glass that separated us. He looked determined. We were going to port this container through hell if we had to. And with all those red dots swarming the HUD map, it looked like that was precisely what we were about to do.

"TJ," Chief Bourbonjack said. "Did we get visual confirmation on the target?"

"I'm reviewing the vid feed as we speak," TJ said. After a moment, he shook his head. "No, Chief. The HS3s couldn't get close enough. All we have to go on is the MAC ID. Which can be spoofed."

"Do you think it's spoofed, TJ? Your gut instinct."

"My gut instinct?" TJ tightened his lips. "It's real. There wouldn't be so much red around the target, otherwise."

The Chief nodded. "That's good enough for me. Facehopper, take the platoon out."

"Got it, Chief." Facehopper turned toward us. "Bender, compute a trajectory to our target. I want the path with the least amount of horde activity. Mark out overwatch spots for Dragon and Alfa."

A few seconds later a blue trajectory appeared on my HUD map. The curving lines passed between the buildings, with flashing overwatch waypoints positioned along the way.

"Done," Bender said.

"Relay the trajectory to Dragon," Facehopper said. "Ghost, Trace, and Skullcracker, provide moving overwatch of the advance. You choose the hides. We'll be playing leapfrog with Dragon as we advance, and if possible I want you to cover their positions, too. We meet at Waypoint Chicago, across the street from the warehouse containing the High-Value Target. Understood?"

"Yes, sir!"

Ghost, Trace, and Skullcracker activated their jumpjets and vanished onto the rooftop of the building beside us.

"Trajectory relayed to Dragon," TJ said.

Across the street, the entire platoon of SKs abruptly launched skyward and moved out.

"What in the *hell*?" Chief Bourbonjack said. "We were supposed to go first."

Dragon platoon crested the rooftop of their own building, then leaped onto the next building. I noticed the latter members among them ported a glass container similar to our own. It seemed they intended to capture the High-Value Target before us. If that happened, we'd be forced to listen to a secondhand, filtered version of the interrogation.

"Should we provide overwatch, Chief?" Facehopper said.

Chief Bourbonjack frowned. "They're still in range of the comms, but they're not answering. So that's a negative on the overwatch. I believe we have a race on our hands. We move, and we move now! Take us out!"

"Understood." Facehopper turned toward the rest of us. "Follow tight!"

"Damn SK traitors." Hijak wore an I-told-you-so expression on his face.

Facehopper launched skyward, leaping onto the rooftop of the building beside me. One by one, the rest of the platoon followed. Everyone wore extra fuel canisters this mission. It increased our individual weight, but it was necessary if the platoon wanted to stay off the ground and avoid the alien hordes.

I wrapped my gloved fingers around the handhold on my side of the container, waiting for the others to complete their jumps. Because of our portage duties, Tahoe and I had the most fuel of anyone on the mission, topping out at five canisters each.

When everyone else had jumped, I glanced at Tahoe through the glass container. Like me, he was kneeling, with one hand wrapped around the handhold on his side.

He nodded.

The two of us leaped, firing our jets in sync.

Once Tahoe and I reached the rooftop, we proceeded after the platoon, bringing up the rear.

To conserve fuel, none of my platoon brothers fired their jets continuously. Instead, we used the strength-enhanced jumpsuits to increase the range of each jump. We'd leap off the side or rooftop of a building with the suits, and then let off a quick jumpjet burst, adding to our existing momentum. That small tactic alone tripled the jumpjet range.

I was the one in charge of calling out the jumping cadence for Tahoe and me. I'd also set up my aReal to transmit a visual cadence to Tahoe, sending a green light the moment I shoved off a building, and a violet light when I fired my jetpack.

"Contact," I said as I reached the side of a building.

"Jump." I pushed off.

"Thrust." I fired a jet burst.

"Contact," I said as my boot touched the ledge of the opposite building. "Jump. Thrust."

"Contact . . ."

We had to compensate at times as one or the other of us got out of sync, but it was a simple matter of firing a stabilizing burst. In any case, Tahoe and I easily kept up with the rest of the platoon, and we made good progress toward Waypoint Chicago.

Motion drew my gaze to the left in midjump. I saw Trace, Ghost, and Skullcracker jetting between rooftops, shadowing us on overwatch. Good men.

TJ had sent the HS3 drones ahead of us to act as scouts, and according to them, Dragon platoon was still a half klick in the lead.

I kept to the trajectory Bender had drawn on the HUD map. It was actually a three-dimensional route, which my aReal overlaid onto my vision as a series of blue rectangles, creating a sort of wire-frame tunnel for the platoon to follow.

According to my HUD map, the first horde of enemy units was quickly approaching. I kept glancing at the map, watching those closely packed red dots grow near . . .

One moment the platoon was leaping over the black-caked buildings of a quiet, empty street, and the next the ground veritably seethed with activity. Alien crabs and slugs crawled everywhere below, competing for space among the smashed vehicles and other former accoutrements of urban living.

I suddenly wished the buildings were higher, because the aliens became utterly berserk below—they were acting in what I had heard described as "hive defense" mode. Their mandibles chopped frenetically at the air, and their whole bodies gyrated as if in time to some hidden song. Fresh slugs poured from the holes in the black substance coating the lower halves of the buildings. Crabs leaped upward en masse as we passed, trying to pluck members of the platoon from the sky. Launching from the backside of a very big slug, a couple of crabs nearly succeeded.

Our stealth was now gone, but that didn't necessarily mean that we couldn't complete the mission. The HS3s were still flying ahead, ready to provide us with the latest updates on the High-Value Target's position once we were in range.

More than one slug launched its ponderous body skyward in an attempt to bash us from the air. We had to alter our flight path, expending precious fuel to avoid them.

"Uh," Manic sent over the comm. "I thought this was supposed to be the path of least resistance?"

"Blimey!" Facehopper sent. "The battle space changes in real-time, you know that, mate. Dragon stirred them up bloody good when it passed."

"Speaking of our SK friends," Manic transmitted. "It would appear they've found themselves in a bit of a pinch."

On the HUD map I saw the green dots of the HS3s strung out ahead of us. The drones indicated Dragon platoon was roughly thirty meters from the warehouse, where the High-Value resided. And judging from the red amassing around them, the SKs were pinned pretty good.

"We'll come to their aid," Facehopper answered. "After we reach Waypoint Chicago as planned. We should be within sight of Dragon once there."

The blue trajectory I was following abruptly updated as Facehopper made adjustments.

"Note course changes," Facehopper sent over the comm.

Continuing to vault from building to building, my platoon brothers and I made the necessary course corrections, and we ended up in a side street that had much less horde activity.

Waypoint Chicago was just ahead, on the rooftop of a twenty-story building, one of the tallest we'd come across so far. I thought it was an office building of some kind, judging from all the glass windows. The warehouse holding the High-Value Target was just beyond it, though hidden from view.

One by one my platoon members pushed off from a smaller apartment complex. Each man landed on the upper portion of the office tower, using the concrete ledges spaced every three stories to make their way toward the rooftop in jumpjet spurts.

Tahoe and I brought up the rear, jumping the ten-meter gap between ledges like pros. We landed on each ledge at the same time, then jumped and thrusted simultaneously. Our stabilizing jets countered the buffeting winds, which were quite strong at this height.

The rest of the platoon vanished from view on the rooftop above.

Tahoe and I were almost there. Only three more ledges between us and the rooftop . . .

Just as we landed on the third ledge from the top, the weight of the container abruptly shifted.

Tahoe had dropped his end.

In that moment, time seemed to slow, and through the glass I saw the stunned expression he gave me.

Blood dripped from his hand, and I realized he'd been shot.

The container moved downward, pivoting around my lone grip.

The three-meter cord that secured Tahoe to the container had somehow become tangled around his jetpack, and as his side descended, the carbon-fiber cord sheered right through his fuel canisters.

The cord reached its three-meter limit, and hauled Tahoe over the ledge.

The bottom of the container smashed into the side of the building.

I was dragged over the ledge, too.

I lost my grip on the handle, and the three-meter-long cord connecting my belt to the container stretched out.

I activated my jumpjet in an attempt to slow my descent. The cord grew taut, making a sound like a whip. My belt strained against the jumpsuit, wrenching me downward.

I managed to land on a lower ledge. Balancing there precariously, I went down on one knee, and flattened myself against the window.

The winds slammed me, combining with the drag from the container to nearly tear me from the ledge.

The cord turned, and the glass container scraped against the window three meters below me. Tahoe in turn dangled three meters underneath that, at the end of his own cord. The wind tossed him about, and he kept spinning around. Blood dripped from his wounded hand. The next ledge looked to be about five meters below him.

Much too far.

I tried reeling in the cord. However, even with the enhanced strength of my jumpsuit, I couldn't pull both Tahoe and the container up against the force of gravity.

I glanced down at the dizzying heights, steeling myself against the vertigo, wanting to fully gauge the situation. The crabs were swarming below, sensing an easy kill. Some of them had already started climbing the bulbous black substance affixed to the lower half of the office building. The substance ended about twenty meters below Tahoe.

I didn't think the crabs could scale smooth glass. Still, with only a small ledge holding me up, and limited fuel in my jetpack, and a cord pulling down on me with the combined weight of Tahoe and a half-tonne container, I didn't find that fact all too reassuring.

"Chief," I transmitted. "We've hit a bit of snag. Could use some help here."

"I'm sending Bender and Hijak to get you," the Chief returned.

Tahoe and I started taking incoming fire from the fourth or fifth floor of the adjacent building. I couldn't pinpoint exactly where—my aReal didn't have enough data to trace the route back to potential sources, which would've helped the rest of the platoon snipe them.

"Chief, taking fire!" I sent.

"Doing what we can," the Chief answered.

Below me, Tahoe had finally managed to stabilize himself against the glass, despite the buffeting winds.

But Tahoe's next words hit me like a gunshot.

"I'm going to cut away," Tahoe announced, reaching for the knife in his utility belt. "There's no time for anything else. It's the only way to save you and the package."

If he did that, he'd never survive. A fall from this height without a working jetpack? The exoskeleton wouldn't save him. He'd break every bone and pulp every organ in his body.

"Tahoe, hold!"

But he didn't listen to me.

The fingers of his good hand wrapped around the knife hilt.

I'd already watched one friend die saving me.

And now I was about to watch another.

CHAPTER TEN

Shaw

After several more spectacular falls I finally got to the point where I could sprint relatively smoothly in the ATLAS 5. I ran in a practice circle, and when I hadn't stumbled for a whole twenty minutes, Fan allowed me to carry him via the designated seat again. Maybe it wasn't entirely trust that compelled him to sit there, because I also told him if he didn't ride with me, I'd leave him behind. He'd already sent the location of his oxygen extractor to my aReal, so in theory I could run ahead and take it for myself, using the strength of my mech to haul it away. He'd have to trek to the next Forma pipe on his own and build himself another. Assuming his oxygen didn't run out before then.

Of course, I wouldn't have *really* ditched him like that. Just wasn't my nature. Besides, I didn't know if the extractor coordinates he'd given me were real or fake, so I couldn't abandon him even if I wanted to.

Queequeg shadowed Battlehawk ten meters to my left, clipping along beside me. He loved it when I let him run like that. I didn't blame him. There was something special about propelling yourself forward under the power of your own muscles, feeling the air burning in your lungs and the wind running through your hair. Okay, I supposed I myself wasn't *really* operating under the power of my own muscles, not completely, and I didn't *actually* feel the wind in my hair, but I certainly felt the burning in my lungs. I was working hard inside the inner cocoon of the mech, sprinting in place, suspended in the cockpit. The ATLAS 5 probably had an auto-run capability, but I preferred being in control.

Now that I had a mech, some new options for leaving the planet had opened up. The first involved tracking down the booster-rocket payloads that would have come down with the mechs. The payloads would be near the original landing site far to the north, and might take a week to reach at this speed. Since I had enough O_2 now, instead of making my way toward Fan's oxygen extractor, I could go north, retrieve the boosters, and launch myself into space.

Though there wasn't much point in doing that, as Battlehawk didn't have enough jumpjet fuel to actually go anywhere once I attained orbit. And where would I go anyway? There was no Gate, not anymore.

Unless . . . what if I waited until the Skull Ship made a reappearance? It had returned once before, since I'd crash-landed. The sky had filled with clouds that towered all the way to the heavens. A terrible storm had ensued and since I had been caught away from the shuttle, which still had power at the time, I was forced to take shelter in a sinkhole. An unpleasant encounter with the beasts had followed.

In any case, I had a theory that a Skull Ship appeared every four Stanmonths or so to refuel.

And it had been about four months since the last appearance.

But how would I get on board without being blasted from the sky?

That was a problem for another day.

But right now, there was something I needed to check. Something only Battlehawk could reveal to me.

"Voice projection off." I didn't want Fan to hear my next commands.

Battlehawk's AI answered from somewhere deep within the cockpit. "Voice projection disabled."

"Battlehawk, replay your archived audio and vid feeds for me, starting from the moment you landed on this planet."

"Initiating video replay."

The playback speed was 4x. I shrunk the video to one-fifth its original size, and moved it to the upper right of my Heads-Up Display as I ran.

On the video, I saw the members of Bravo platoon enter the excavation site and approach an ominous-looking shaft drilled into the darkness. The ATLAS 5s were too big for the shaft, so the pilots ejected and deployed the four mechs in a guard capacity.

The sixteen members of the platoon rappelled down the shaft.

Battlehawk scanned the now-empty excavation site. I saw giant dump trucks, monster mining shovels on treads, and the ever-present walls of Geronium, enclosing everything like a prison. The view kept returning to the shaft. Everything seemed calm. Lifeless.

Sometime later, two MOTHs emerged from the shaft—only *two*, out of the original sixteen. Kasper and Pyro. The spec-ops men hurried into the other mechs, and ordered Battlehawk and the remaining ATLAS to follow tight.

Crabs flowed out of the shaft as if from a disturbed hornet's nest. The survivors fought them for a few minutes, but when it became clear the odds were overwhelming, the MOTHs fled toward the MDV.

A sinkhole opened up behind one of the dump trucks, and a white-hot slug barreled out, launching fresh crabs. More and more slugs emerged, carrying with them two hundred crabs each.

Man and machine fought side by side, MOTH and ATLAS versus crab and slug. But the enemy proved inexorable. For every two crabs that fell, five more appeared. Worse, blue Phants drifted en masse from the sinkhole, forming a deadly, impassable wall of vapor. While the crabs and slugs slowly closed on both flanks like a noose, the Phants approached head-on, immune to all the weaponry the ATLAS 5s threw at them.

Seeing them made me wonder why the Phants didn't fight entirely on their own. They couldn't be hurt, they killed all life and controlled all robots . . . maybe there weren't enough of them. Or maybe the appearance of the slugs and crabs was some kind of swarm response built into the biological aliens.

Whatever the case, the way to the MDV was blocked.

The MOTHs fled.

The beasts harried and pursued them for the next few hours. At some point, a wave of dormant Phants arose in ambush from the landscape ahead, directly in front of the group. The two leading mechs made it through, but Battlehawk and the other ATLAS 5 became possessed.

The video feed became tinted blue. I paused the playback, and rewound, because I thought I noticed something odd about the possession incident. I resumed playback at normal speed.

What I saw was decidedly odd, but maybe not entirely unexpected. Shortly after possession, the two mechs looked down at their hands and body, as if they were experiencing what it was like to have arms and legs for the first time. Battlehawk took a tentative step, and nearly fell, just as I had foundered my first time. The mech took another wobbly step, and another. The possessed ATLAS 5 seemed like a baby struggling to walk for the first time.

Crabs and slugs tore past Battlehawk and the other mech, giving the pair a wide berth, apparently sensing the Phants within. When the alien horde was gone, Battlehawk and the other mech resumed exploring their new bodies.

I set the playback speed to 4x once again, and watched as the mechs advanced from wobbly steps all the way up to full-blown sprints. Battlehawk's owner soon became proficient in using its jumpjets and full complement of weapons. The Phant nearly blew its own mech up when it stupidly pointed a rocket launcher at its vision sensors—I was reminded of a child who had discovered a pistol in his father's dresser. Peering down the gun barrel was always the best thing for the child to do, right? Luckily, the Phant steered the weapon aside right before pulling the trigger, and the rocket streaked harmlessly past. However, the discharge obviously frightened the possessing Phant, because it threw the mech's arm outward as if trying to rid itself of serpent launcher and arm alike.

Eventually, Battlehawk returned to the excavation site with the other mech. Crouching near the rim, the two mechs secretly observed a new party of men loitering within the site.

It was the MOTHs of Alfa platoon, returned from their failed mission to find Bravo.

Near them, where the shaft used to be, remained only a collapsed crater. All the MOTH weaponry was pointed at that crater, waiting for something to emerge. Expecting something to.

The video feed began to wobble slightly, and I thought the ground was shaking.

The platoon ran toward the opposite rim of the excavation site, weaving between the giant trucks.

The sole mech with Alfa platoon remained behind, buying the others time.

It was Hornet.

Rade's ATLAS 5.

I stumbled and fell.

"*Chòu sān bā*!" Fan said. The crash hurled him some meters ahead of me. He hadn't buckled up again, despite my insistence. "Again you fall!"

I ignored him. My attention was focused entirely on the vid. I enlarged it to take up the full screen, and slowed the playback to 1x.

Battlehawk and the other possessed mech assumed a position behind one of the dump trucks, and eventually engaged Hornet. I cheered for Rade the whole time, entranced. I was cheering against myself, because I felt like I was actually there, fighting him. It wasn't a good feeling.

Go, Rade!

I knew he would win in the end, but still, not knowing *how* he would win, and watching how close to demise he came each time, was extremely nerve-wracking.

When a dump truck backed over Battlehawk, I exhaled in relief.

I never thought I'd feel so glad to be run over in my life.

The vision feed blinked out, and when it cut in again, Battlehawk was no longer at the excavation site. The mech had been dragged inside a hangar bay of some kind. I could see the dome-shaped buildings of an SK outpost beyond the bay doors.

Battlehawk's vision was no longer blue-tinged and had returned to normal.

Rade's mech was gone. Well, I already knew what happened next. Alejandro would be dead by now. And with him, a part of Rade.

I closed my eyes, remembering the shared grief, and the days spent comforting Rade when he returned. Well, those days were long gone now. I had to focus on the here and now, on outcomes I could affect, rather than those I could not.

I concentrated on the vid feed. Around Battlehawk, Weaver-like robots worked, fixing the damaged mech. The robots weren't possessed as far as I could tell. I didn't see any of the characteristic vapors that would've betrayed the presence of Phants in the smaller robots.

I increased the playback speed to 8x. The repair robots eventually moved away, clearing the way for the approach of a Phant. Battlehawk's self-defense algorithms activated. It loaded its Gatling guns and attempted to fire at the glowing blue mist, to no avail.

The ATLAS 5 became possessed once again.

The mech moved south along the rocky plains, sprinting at near its maximum speed. I switched the playback to 32x, and watched the time indicator scroll past. A few days of constant running later, Battlehawk reached the Main Rift. At least I thought it was the Rift, given the sprawling canyons and towering rock formations.

I slowed the playback speed to 8x as Battlehawk approached a very large sinkhole, the largest I'd ever seen, about as wide and long as a football stadium. Despite the vast size of the hole, none of the alien beasts were present.

The possessed mech went inside, lighting the way with its headlamps.

Navigating the circular tunnels and jagged caves, the mech reached a small natural cavern of sorts. An odd-looking metallic disc was embedded in the cave floor. Fibonacci spirals etched the surface.

Battlehawk stepped over the disc.

Suddenly the mech was no longer in the cavern, but in a corridor, standing over a similar disc. The bulkheads, deck, and overhead of a ship surrounded Battlehawk now. The surfaces were made of lattices of closely set pipes and rods positioned at different angles at various planar depths. The different planes overlapped so many times that they created the illusion of a solid surface.

The mech walked along a dense gangway formed from the confluence of those lattices. A large robot stepped aside to let Battlehawk pass. No, it wasn't a robot, but an alien wearing a jumpsuit of some kind, a translucent glass dome sitting atop the suit. Inside, a dark head regarded the mech with two lizard-like eyes.

I switched the playback speed to 1x.

Battlehawk entered a passageway. There was a broad window on one side, revealing stars and a planet. Not Geronimo, but a gas giant of some kind.

Where the heck *was* Battlehawk?

The mech entered an expansive room. Various glass holding tanks lined the bulkheads. Inside each tank, robotic, spider-ish arms—I'll call them Alien Weavers—hung from the ceiling. Some of the tanks were filled with liquid, others air. I realized I was looking at a multitude of different life-supporting environments, because within those tanks I saw beings like nothing I had ever seen before.

There were creatures from fairy tales and creatures from nightmares. In one tank, a jellyfish-like entity replete with a circle of razor-sharp teeth floated in a vaporous environment. In another resided some kind of plant being, resembling a giant lizard with pine needles bristling from the bark of its body. In a third tank a tentacled, squid-like creature with two heads drifted to and fro.

This was, for all intents and purposes, an alien menagerie.

The Alien Weavers operated on roughly half those creatures. Metal parts were drilled and grafted into restrained bodies. Tiny microchips were jabbed into unconscious brains.

The Alien Weavers were making cyborgs of some sort.

Battlehawk walked into one of the empty tanks, and the entrance sealed shut behind it.

The mech's vision returned to a normal hue as the possessing Phant vacated its brain case.

Another Phant vented into the tank, moving very fast. A purple one.

I had the impression the blue entity was leaving so that the purple Phant could take over.

But Battlehawk was the quicker. Now that the internal AI was back in control, the mech activated its defensive subroutines.

It turned toward the nearest glass wall, firing its twin Gatlings while initiating a horizontal burst from its jetpack.

The ATLAS 5 collided with the weakened glass and burst right through.

Battlehawk retreated at full sprint the way it had come, evading gaseous Phants and shooting down two humanoid aliens in jumpsuits along the way.

It arrived at the chamber with the metallic disc on the floor. Stepping over the disc, the mech instantly appeared in the cavern on Geronimo once more. I had a feeling the disc could be tuned to different destinations, and that it was sheer luck the destination still pointed to Geronimo. But this was alien technology, and whatever human intuition I might have was likely to be way off the mark.

Battlehawk sprinted through the underground tunnel system, emerging from the sinkhole with its jetpacks firing at full burn. When it landed, the mech kept on running, and proceeded down the middle of the Main Rift.

The ATLAS 5 constantly swiveled its head around to scan its six, but there were no pursuers.

I increased the playback speed and watched the time indicator count off the hours as the mech continued to flee.

Finally Battlehawk swerved into a defile cut into the Main Rift, and squeezed past a tight bend. Then it turned around, aimed its guns down the path, and waited.

Time elapsed.

Nothing appeared.

Battlehawk had escaped.

The mech initiated its "call home" beacon, as per standard recall protocol, and entered hibernation mode.

The vision feed jumped.

A figure in a black jumpsuit peered past the defile's bend.

A human. Text overlaid the identity scan: *Embedded ID profile inconclusive.*

A square appeared around the helmet, with the words: *Facial recognition in progress. Sino-Korean feature match.*

Target.

The latter word appeared in big, flashing red.

Battlehawk opened fire.

The SK vanished, and Battlehawk entered hibernation mode once more.

The vision feed jumped.

I watched myself approach in my hybear-fur jumpsuit.

I shut the video down, and my view of the outside world returned.

"Shaw Chopra, are you all right?" Fan was saying. "Shaw Chopra?"

Queequeg was jumping around and howling in concern beside me.

"I'm fine, Queequeg," I said, ignoring Fan. "Queequeg, I'm okay."

I stood up, and the mech hummed to life, rising with me.

Queequeg hastily put some distance between us.

"What happened to you?" Fan said.

I glanced down at him. I couldn't get over how small human beings appeared when viewed from the heights of an ATLAS mech.

"We have to make a slight detour," I told him, resisting the urge to call him "little man."

"That is a terrible plan," Fan said.

"I think it's a very good plan," I countered.

"The Mara will kill you before you cause any damage."

"They won't," I told him.

"What do you have against them, anyway?" Fan said. "They have not invaded human space. Why the grudge? We are the ones who invaded *their* space."

"They've killed some good people. That's a good enough reason for me to stage an attack. They're not friendly."

Fan studied me beneath the endless daylight. "You know nothing about their intentions! They are an alien race, with an alien consciousness! If you found yourself in a beehive, surrounded by worker bees, would you think they were unfriendly simply because they followed their biological imperative and attacked you for invading their hive?"

"What are you trying to say, that these aliens are big, lovable honeybees protecting their hive?"

"That is exactly what I am trying to say. Except they are more than simple bees. You risk your life to stage an attack against a superior alien race, who—"

"They're not superior," I said.

"Let me correct myself: a *technologically* superior alien race," Fan said. "Whose only crime was the defense of their colony."

"We have to do this. *I* have to do this." For Alejandro, Big Dog, and all the dead of Alfa platoon. "If you don't want to join me, then don't. I've already set a waypoint to that oxygen extractor of yours. I'll meet you there in a few days. If I don't return, things will go right back to the way they were before. For you at least."

"No," Fan said, quietly. "I will come. I cannot allow you to go alone. Still, that does not mean I approve."

"Well, I was actually going to insist that you stay behind," I said. He started to protest but I cut him off. "Look, I don't really need you. You'll probably just get in the way. You're in a jumpsuit. I'm in an ATLAS 5. Slight mismatch there in terms of armor and firepower."

"I am coming, Shaw Chopra of the UC Navy. I cannot go back to the way things were before, as you say. To being eternally alone. But you must promise me, at the first sign of trouble, we leave. If we arrive and the sinkhole is surrounded by Mara, we go."

I nodded. "If there are beasts patrolling the whole area, obviously we're not going in."

Fan nodded. "Then let us go and get this done with."

I had the ATLAS set the necessary waypoint, and I followed the contours of the wide valley at a run. Fan sat in his usual position on my back, while Queequeg loped along to my right.

Time passed very slowly for me. It felt like I was running toward my doom. I kept telling myself I didn't have to do this. That Fan was right. *We* were the invaders. *We* were in the wrong.

Yet all I had to do was remember the agony on Rade's face after Alejandro's funeral. Or my own pain upon hearing the news of Alejandro's death. Pain commingled with guilt: I'd lost a good friend, and yet I was relieved Rade had been one of those who'd lived.

I hoped that by doing this, I'd rid myself of that pain and guilt once and for all.

It took about four hours to reach the sinkhole I'd seen in Battlehawk's vid archives. The size of the hole was indeed immense. The vast entrance sloped down into the darkness at a gradual angle of around thirty degrees, almost like the outgoing ramp of a drop ship. Because of that angle, the sunlight only traveled a few meters inside, and darkness quickly shrouded the view. It looked evil somehow.

I wanted to turn back. But I couldn't. Not now.

"To quote a UC expression," Fan said from behind me. "I will be damned if I am going in there."

I actually laughed. It was a bitter, forced laugh. "Bit late for second thoughts now, isn't it? Because I'm certainly not taking you back. You better start walking."

"Let me down," Fan said.

I did.

Fan walked to the edge of the sinkhole. "Give me my rifle."

"No."

He glanced over his shoulder at me in exaggerated disgust. "You are up there in an ATLAS 5 with Gatlings and jumpjets and rockets. What do I have? A jumpsuit superglued with pieces of rock. Shaw Chopra, you must give me my rifle."

"Not yet. Besides, all the firepower in the world won't do a thing against the alien mists, if we encounter them."

Fan grimaced. "Very true. Yet another reason for us to avoid this place. The Yaoguai will have our souls."

"All right. Stay here then. What about you, Queequeg? Are you coming?"

The animal halted a firm distance away from the sinkhole, and refused to advance any farther.

"I guess I'm doing this alone, then." I switched on Battlehawk's headlamps and started down into the darkness.

A few paces in I heard muted howling behind me. I glanced back.

Queequeg leaped to and fro near the entrance, like he wanted to advance but some invisible barrier kept him from doing so.

Fear. It was a powerful obstacle.

"You don't have to come, Queequeg," I said. "You're free now. I release you. I don't . . . I don't know when I'm coming out again." Maybe I'd never see the light of day again.

I wanted to linger, but I knew if I did that I might very well change my mind.

If I was doing this, I had to do it now.

I turned around and plunged into the darkness.

I didn't look back.

I never imagined the farewell between Queequeg and I would be so abrupt, but it was what it was. Let's just say I wasn't a big fan of good-byes. The hardest good-bye of my life had been when I'd abandoned Rade. I hoped he found it in his heart to forgive me for what I did. I knew he would have come with me. But I couldn't allow it. One of us had to make it back. One of us had to return to Earth. To humanity.

At this very moment Rade was probably doing PT on a white sandy beach somewhere, or hitting the pubs in New Coronado with Tahoe and the rest of his platoon. Training and living his life under the open air, without the constant threat of death hanging over his head.

I'd join him, someday. I'd reach Earth. I had to. I had made a promise to myself. It's what kept me going each day.

I wasn't a quitter.

The Navy had taught me that.

My training had repeatedly drilled the core values of honor, courage, and commitment into my head. That, and the fact you never gave up. Not ever.

What was the quote Rade had told me once? The one by Winston Churchill? Yes:

Never give in—never, never, never, never. If you're going through hell, keep going.

I wasn't going to die down here. I wouldn't allow myself. I *would* see the sky once again.

I would.

And one day I would even make it back to Earth.

Just not today.

I had toyed with the possibility of using the disc device to teleport my mech to the alien ship. But that would be like transferring from house arrest to a maximum-security prison. I'd be on a vessel run entirely by aliens, with no idea how their systems worked. Even if I somehow managed to capture a key individual, assuming there was such a concept in the alien race, I wouldn't be able to communicate with them to negotiate any terms for my hostage. Plus, I'd stand out like a sore thumb the moment I arrived.

Unless I could disguise myself somehow . . .

"Battlehawk," I said, hit by a sudden inspiration. "Are you equipped with any electromagnetic pulse weapons?"

"I am equipped with limited EM capabilities. No actual weapons-grade emitters are installed by default."

"So there's no way you could mimic the EM signature of a Phant?" I said. "Make the beasts think you're possessed? You have the alien EM signature on file, right?"

"I have stored the alien EM signature, but I cannot mimic it," Battlehawk said. "I am equipped with limited EM capabilities."

Well, it was a nice thought.

I marched resignedly into the darkness. Around me, the walls, floor, and ceiling formed a perfectly continuous circle.

Battlehawk had already mapped out the cave system for me, all the way to the transportation device. Unexplored side passageways and tunnels appeared as black sections on the HUD map, in what was commonly referred to as the "Fog of War."

I had no intention of exploring those side passageways. I would head for my objective and nothing else. Get in, do what I came to do, get out. I wanted to be *alive* when this day was done, after all.

There was no sign of beast activity. It seemed almost a little too quiet.

And then I heard a scuffing behind me.

I turned around to illuminate the area with my headlamp.

Queequeg lowed softly. He'd joined me once more, loyal to the end. Still, his body language was all fear: mane flattened, ears folded back, tail curled below the belly. It took a great deal of courage for him to be here.

"I won't forget this, Queequeg."

I spotted a light coming from the tunnel behind him.

"And then there were three," Fan said, his silhouette emerging from the darkness. He beckoned into the depths. "Should we . . . *roll*, as they say in the UC?"

The three of us proceeded into the dark.

Battlehawk's footfalls sounded disturbingly loud to my ears as they echoed down the tunnel. I tried to tread as gently as possible, but it didn't really help. The thud of a three-tonne weight repeatedly striking solid rock wasn't going to come across as soft.

I turned into a side tunnel, as indicated by my HUD map. Like the main tunnel, it was perfectly circular, but only four meters in diameter. That still gave me a meter to spare on all sides, though the concave floor forced my ankles inward slightly, requiring some extra balance on my part.

"Battlehawk," I said. "Isn't there some kind of support probe you can launch? An HS3 or something? It would be good to have an early warning on any hostiles."

"Affirmative," the mech's AI answered. "There is the ASS."

"The *ASS*?"

"The ATLAS Support System."

I rolled my eyes at the acronym. Leave it up to the military to come up with something so crude and smart-alecky. "I see. Launch it. Destination: Waypoint Alpha."

A compartment opened on Battlehawk's shoulder and the ATLAS Support System drone floated down the tunnel. A revolving cone of light illuminated the rock around it in a corkscrew fashion.

On my HUD, I viewed the vid feed from the ASS in the upper right. The signal pixelated and froze every few seconds, but otherwise the tunnel ahead looked exactly the same as where I currently walked.

The vid feed progressively worsened the deeper the probe traveled, until the pixelization became so bad I couldn't discern a thing. I had Battlehawk recall the probe before I lost contact entirely, then

I instructed the ASS to maintain a scouting position a steady twenty meters ahead.

We proceeded forward, and the tunnel opened into a vast cavern. The black walls yielded to crystal structures that could best be described as yellow quartz. The crystals were beautiful I supposed, but I had trouble appreciating them. Firstly, there was the sense of impending doom I always felt when entering a sinkhole, the feeling that a horde of beasts could come piling out at me any moment, which wasn't entirely unfounded. Secondly, I'd made the mistake of glancing at the telemetry report on my HUD. We were about fifty meters underground. *Fifty meters.* The knowledge triggered my claustrophobia. In space I usually dealt with any claustrophobia by spending long hours looking through the portal at the vastness outside.

But I had no portal here. Just thousands of tonnes of rock over my head, fifty meters thick. Not to mention the three tonnes of metal encasing me.

It's not far now, Shaw. Soon enough you'll be done. Then you can go back, take a nice warm bath and soak for a while.

None of it was true, of course. But it helped take my mind off the claustrophobia. I had to remain strong now, if not for myself, then for Queequeg and Fan, who were relying on me to get them through this. They were here because of me, and I wasn't about to let them down.

I took a deep breath, and proceeded.

The probe led the way to the next four-meter diameter tunnel. I dreaded leaving the cavern behind for the smaller tunnel, but I pretended I was entering the sinkhole for the first time again, and that there was hardly any rock above me.

Somehow it worked.

Finally, two more caverns and one fork later, I reached a natural cavern, the smallest yet. A metallic disc was set into the rock in the middle of the floor. I recognized the disc from Battlehawk's vid archives—Fibonacci swirls engraved the surface, those "golden" spirals that occurred everywhere in nature, from the shells of snails to the spiral arms of galaxies.

"All right," I said. "This is it."

I sent the support probe into the next tunnel to make sure no beasts were waiting to ambush us. Everything seemed clear.

"I'll set the timer for fifteen seconds." I input the desired countdown into the warhead. The IED (Improvised Explosive Device) was comprised of three serpent rockets bundled together, with the payload element of one serpent exposed. I'd convinced Battlehawk to reveal the necessary access passwords earlier.

With luck, the IED would teleport to the alien ship and cause some major damage. And if the IED didn't teleport, then hopefully it would put the disc out of commission. Either way, *something* would be damaged. Maybe us. If the IED didn't teleport, I wasn't sure we'd be able to escape the blast wave in time. Explosive force was always magnified in confined spaces after all.

I activated the IED and positioned it on the disc, using the blue indicators Battlehawk overlaid onto my vision as guides. Those indicators told me exactly where the mech had stood during its own teleportation.

I pulled my arms back, but the IED didn't vanish.

I adjusted the position slightly, jerking my hand away because I was worried I'd be teleported along with the device.

But still the IED remained.

The timer was down to eleven seconds.

"Looks like it's not going to teleport!"

I hurried out of the small cavern and into the previous tunnel, then dropped to the floor.

Fan jammed himself under me, while Queequeg, somewhat confused, ran on. The animal paused some distance in front of me.

"Keep running, Queequeg!"

The IED detonated.

The blast wave passed over Battlehawk.

The cockpit temperature momentarily spiked, but otherwise the mech incurred no damage, at least according to the indicators on my HUD.

And just like that, it was over.

There was some dust in the air now, but it wasn't enough to obscure my vision. My headlamp penetrated nearly as far into the dark as before, and I could discern the nearby tunnel walls almost perfectly ahead of me.

What I couldn't see, however, was Queequeg.

"Queequeg?"

I stood, and peered both ways down the tunnel. "Queequeg?"

Still nothing. I was getting worried now.

"I'm fine, in case you care," Fan said from below me.

I ignored him.

I was about to go looking for Queequeg when at last he appeared from down the tunnel, stepping into the light. While he seemed unharmed, he was definitely not happy, judging from the low whine he issued from his throat.

"Don't worry, we're almost done, boy." I turned around. "Time to check on our handiwork."

"Is that wise?" Fan said. "We should be running. Very fast."

He was right. But I had to know.

I hurried back into the small cavern.

There were a few scuff marks, and some charred areas on the metal, but otherwise the disc seemed entirely undamaged.

What a waste.

"I don't understand," I said.

"And that is the crux of it," Fan said. "We are dealing with an alien species a thousand times more advanced than our own. Of course we do not understand their technology. You thought you could use their teleporter, did you? And then you thought you could blow that teleporter up? Ha! We are like cavemen compared with them. I do not know why I even listen to you. *Da nao jin shui.* You have water leaking in your brain."

A proximity alarm sounded in my cockpit. Red dots appeared some fifteen meters ahead of where I'd placed the support probe, forward of our position. Those dots were bound together in a tight column by the confines of the tunnel.

"Time to run," I said.

I was about to do just that, when beside me Queequeg issued a deep growl from far back in his throat.

"Easy, boy," I said.

He continued to growl. He was staring back the way we'd come.

It was possible that crabs were approaching from behind, too, via one of the unexplored side passageways.

If so, then we were trapped.

"Battlehawk, recall the probe."

That was the funny thing about animals. They had this sixth, danger sense. Humanity had the same intuition buried deep inside, but our intellect blinded us to it. Whenever we had a bad feeling about something, we ignored it, rationalized it away, compartmentalized it to the furthest recesses of the mind, when, more often than not, we were right to have that feeling.

Queequeg had issued a warning, and I wasn't about to ignore it. I was inside an ATLAS mech, but I didn't feel safe.

The support probe arrived, and I immediately sent it down the retreat tunnel, where Queequeg still gazed. The red dots from the forward tunnel had frozen now that the probe was no longer there to update the enemy targets. The closest dot was twenty meters away when it last updated.

I instructed Battlehawk to unlock the storage compartment.

"Fan, go to the storage compartment and take your rifle. Grab any other weapons you find there. Including the grenades."

He did as instructed. "What is happening?"

I heard a distant chittering sound then, amplified by the internal speakers in my cockpit. I couldn't place the direction of the noise.

Beside me, Queequeg had stopped growling. He remained stock-still, with his head held high, his ears cocked, and his mane erect.

The hybear was readying himself for a pitched battle.

"You hear it?" Fan said.

"I do."

On my HUD map, the support probe reported more red dots arrayed in a column, these ones covering our retreat vector.

Queequeg was right: we were indeed trapped.

The chittering sound grew louder.

"Gatling guns in hand, Battlehawk."

CHAPTER ELEVEN

Rade

D angling from the office building high above the street, I watched as Tahoe wrenched the knife from his utility belt. He planned to cut the cord that bound his body to the glass container. His jetpack was no longer operational. Once he severed his lifeline, he would plunge four-teen stories to the asphalt, colliding multiple times on the way down with the black substance that caked the lower half of the building.

He would die.

I wasn't going to let him sacrifice himself for me.

I'd stop him.

Like I should have stopped Alejandro.

"Don't you dare cut that cord, Tahoe," I said as the bullets came in from the building across from us. "I appreciate what you're trying to do, but I won't be able to lift the container on my own anyway. Subtracting eighty kilos from something that weighs half a tonne isn't going to make a whole lot of difference. Do you understand me? Tahoe, put the knife away."

Tahoe hesitated, his knife a fingerbreadth from the cord. Blood dripped from the gunshot wound in his other hand, oozing from the tiny perforation in his glove. Bullets slammed into the glass windows of the office building around him, threatening to inflict more such wounds.

"Tahoe! Sheath the knife! If you cut that cord, I'm cutting mine too. To hell with the mission—I'm going to let the package drop, and I'm going to jet down and rescue you. So if you want to mess everything up, go ahead and slice the rope."

Tahoe looked up, and I saw the agony of indecision on his face. Finally he cursed in Navajo and withdrew the blade.

"Then what do we do?" he said.

It was hard to think with bullets smashing into the building on all sides. One shot created a circular hole in the glass window right beside my head.

I crouched lower on the ledge.

A marksman could use those glass impacts to home in on me. It's what I would have been doing.

I'd probably be hit any second now.

"This is what we'll do," I said, ignoring the vertigo as I gazed down at Tahoe from the dizzying heights. "I'm going to step off, fire my jets, and lower you to the next ledge. Once you're in place I'll land beside you. Then we'll reel in the package together."

Tahoe shook his head. "Bad idea! We'll be exposed the whole time!" Glass shards continued to explode around him. "And what will you do after that? Carry me to the top?"

I couldn't do it on my own and he knew it. Without his jetpack helping out, I'd never get enough acceleration to make the roof. The load was just too heavy.

I ducked as the glass window cratered beside me. "Bender and Hijak are coming! They'll help!" Though so far, there was no sign of either of them.

Tahoe shook his head. "We don't have time to wait for them. I have a better plan."

He sheathed the knife and then, ignoring the wound in his hand, he climbed the cord unsteadily, crimping the loose segments in his gloves as he went. When he had clambered a meter upward, he began pounding the glass with the glove of his strength-enhanced free hand. The first three blows spidered and cratered the surface, while the fourth shattered it entirely.

Clearing the leftover glass shards from the frame with his boots, he thrust his feet inside, ostensibly standing on the floor. He grabbed the inside of the window frame with his free hand, releasing his hold on the crimped cord and hauling himself inside.

Nicely done, Tahoe, I thought. *But now what?*

I'd have to go inside with him.

I dropped from the ledge, using a few bursts of my jetpack to slow my descent. Below me, I saw Tahoe's cord vanish within, and I knew he was reeling it in. For a second I thought he would manage to maneuver the entire container inside, but then the cord slackened and the container descended past the broken window. He hadn't been able to grab the handholds.

When I neared the shattered window, I thrusted inside with my jets and landed prostrate on the floor beside Tahoe.

I fought against the drag of the glass container, which was transmitted through the cord clamped to my waist. I couldn't get a grip on the floor—too many loose shards of glass covered the area.

I slid backward . . .

Tahoe caught me, and the two of us slid toward the opening together.

My mind had blanked. It was one of those times in battle when the stress of it all simply overwhelmed me. I was like a zombie, and I just stared at the gap behind us, where the window had shattered from floor to ceiling, and I watched our cords inexorably slide over the edge, drawing us to our doom.

I was vaguely aware as bullets ricocheted from the rug around us.

"Rade!"

Tahoe's sharp tone brought me back.

I fired my jetpack. The engine strained, carrying the two of us inside in ragged spurts.

Behind us, the edge of the container abruptly snagged on the opening, and I couldn't advance farther. At this point, I was just wasting fuel.

I braced myself against a nearby office desk, and deactivated my jetpack.

The desk pivoted under the combined weight of my jumpsuit and the container, and I was pulled toward the gaping hole in the window once more, towing the desk along with me.

Tahoe and I hauled on our cords, trying in vain to draw the container inside. We succeeded only in dragging ourselves closer to the window.

The gunfire continued around us.

A bullet struck the edge of my cord, and it frayed slightly.

Tahoe glanced at me urgently. "Hang on!"

He unlatched the cord from his belt and, straining under the weight, passed it to me. I was pulled even harder toward the window.

Tahoe dove toward the opening. He braced his lower body against an adjacent metal beam, and then plunged his torso outside. He was trying to grab the glass container, and physically haul it inside.

The desk continued to pivot, crushing a garbage can in its path.

Gunfire sprayed the air above me, battering the metal sides of the desk.

I tugged on the cords, keeping my eyes fixed on the frayed section, which held for the time being. I activated my jetpack, moving backward slightly, wanting to aid Tahoe.

Abruptly I felt the weight shift.

Tahoe's torso reemerged, and I realized he'd managed to grip the container.

He backed away from the window, grunting, slipping on broken glass. I tugged harder on the cords, and applied my jetpack.

I saw a sudden spurt of blood erupt from Tahoe, and I knew he'd just been shot. *Again.*

He didn't waver. He kept on pulling.

I didn't dare let up on the cords, not at this critical juncture. Instead I did what I could to help him, straining against the weight, reeling in the cords bit by bit.

Finally we had the container completely inside, settled squarely on the floor.

I rushed forward and grabbed a free handhold, and together Tahoe and I dragged the container away from the opening, using the container's bulletproof glass as a shield.

The shots from outside hadn't ceased. In fact, machine gun fire now joined it.

Impact craters appeared on the far surface of the container, but so far none of the bullets penetrated.

We dragged the container behind the desk. It was only half-protected there, because bullets continued to pound the container's upper half.

We hauled another desk in front of it, and with our combined strength, Tahoe and I managed to hoist the second desk on top of the first, successfully shielding the precious cargo.

When it was done, we plunked down behind the container. We needed a moment to gather our strength.

"You okay?" I said.

He grunted some noncommittal response. In training I often asked him the same thing, sort of mockingly, whenever he breathed harder than me.

I wasn't mocking him now though.

The gunfire waned, erupting in sporadic bursts.

"Chief, we're inside the building," I said over the comm. "Chief?"

Static.

I regarded Tahoe. He had his suitrep kit open on his knee, and he was sprinkling topical hemostatic powder, commonly known as Mister Clot, into the fresh puncture in the mid-ulna region of his suit's forearm.

"You look like shit, bro," I said, panting slightly.

Tahoe gave me a strained chuckle. "Does that turn you on?" He mimicked my ragged breathing, though I could tell his good humor was forced. He'd been shot twice, after all. "You know, it's a good thing they shoot us in training. Otherwise I don't think I could take this crap."

"You've been shot since training. Back on Pontus, if I recall. In the shoulder."

"Don't remind me of that pompous place," Tahoe said, breathless. "Pontus."

"Same difference." He closed his eyes, wincing as the last of the powder flowed from his palm and into the suit puncture. "Never get . . . used to it. Even though the suit absorbs some of the impact, when you're hit, it's not pleasant. My wife's going to kill me when she finds out."

"She will." I studied his arm assembly. "That powder won't last. Your wounds are going to break open as soon as we start moving. We have to apply the skin seals."

"It's good enough for now," Tahoe insisted, closing the suitrep kit.

"Show me."

He held up his arm. His punctured glove had dripped blood earlier, but the flow seemed to have stopped. And no blood leaked from the forearm wound either. Maybe he was holding his arm at just the right angle though, so that the blood oozed down the inside of his suit rather than out the perforations.

I checked his vitals on my aReal. His diastolic and systolic pressures seemed stable.

Still, that could change at any moment.

I reached for his suitrep kit. "Gotta patch you up, bro."

He intercepted my hand, and returned the kit to his left cargo pocket. "No time. You'll have to shed my glove and arm assembly. Use up minutes we don't have. We're exposed here. The enemy could launch rockets at any time. You know that. Or maybe they're sending combat robots up the stairwells as we speak. We have to get to the platoon. Check your HUD. They're still on the roof. Probably pinned. They need us. The powder is doing its job. You can patch me up later. Let's go."

Against my better judgment, I acceded.

I took in our surroundings. The floor of the office building was basically an open space filled with cubicles, desks, and cabinets. It was lit by emergency lights.

The SKs had provided us with interior blueprints of all the buildings in Shangde City before we landed, and the map of this floor was visible on my HUD at this very moment, centered around my position.

I zoomed out on the map, and spotted the elevator and stairwell.

"Chief, we're making our way to the stairwell," I said over the comm.

The Chief didn't answer.

Tahoe had thought the platoon was pinned on the roof, but it was also possible our brothers weren't even there anymore. We'd lost contact, which meant the green dots representing their positions were outdated. Chief Bourbonjack had dispatched Bender and Hijak to help us, for example, but according to the HUD map they were still up on the rooftop with the rest of the platoon.

"Ready?" I asked Tahoe.

In answer, he took his cord from me and reattached it to his belt.

A rocket-propelled grenade passed through the window and detonated on the far side of the stacked desks.

"Go, go, go!"

I grabbed my handhold, Tahoe gripped his, and we hefted the glass container between us.

We weaved our way through the other desks positioned across the floor, making our way from the gaping window and its incoming fire.

More rockets went off behind us, upturning desks. Bullets ricocheted everywhere. Glass shattered as other windows broke away.

"*Fuck!*" Tahoe said.

The container shifted toward him as his grip momentarily weakened.

"Tahoe, you okay?"

The container straightened once more.

"Go!" he said.

I proceeded. On the other side of the container, Tahoe was limping.

He'd been shot.

Again.

We rounded a corner, finally leaving the line of fire.

"Where you hit?" I said, beginning to lower the container.

"Right foot!" Tahoe yelled, jerking the container upward. "Keep moving!"

I glanced at his feet and saw the crimson splatter at the base of his right boot.

We didn't have time to rest, because red dots from laser sights appeared on the walls and floors around us, coming from beyond the glass windows on *this* side of the office tower now.

The robot snipers had apparently relayed our coordinates to their friends in the opposite building.

Wonder-freaking-ful.

"Move!" I said.

"Already said that!" Tahoe retorted.

We broke into a sprint.

Beside us, the entire wall of windows basically exploded as a hail of laser-sighted sniper fire poured in.

Ahead, a sealed glass doorway blocked access to the elevator hallway.

With my free hand, I drew the 9-mil from the holster at my belt and let off several shots, shattering the glass. I truly loved my mini-armor piercers in that moment.

Precious cargo in hand, we ducked into the hallway.

At last we had a break from the gunfire—the walls of the hallway were mercifully made of concrete instead of glass. The emergency bulbs seemed dimmer here, probably because the hallway had less natural light flowing in from outside.

"Chief, do you read, over?" I sent on the comm.

Nothing.

We proceeded toward the nearest elevator.

I hit the "up" button with the grip of my 9-mil, just in case the emergency power actually supplied the elevators. The triangular button didn't light up, of course.

I turned toward the stairwell, but there was no way the glass container would fit through the slim doorway.

"We're going to have to port it up the elevator shaft," I said.

Two figures abruptly burst through the stairwell door. They had their pistols trained on our heads.

I almost shot them on reflex.

"Dammit." I lowered the 9-mil.

Bender and Hijak lowered their own weapons.

"There you freaknuts are!" Bender said.

Tahoe and I rested the container on the floor.

Bender glanced between the container, the stairwell, and the elevators, and apparently came to the same conclusion as I had because he waltzed right up to the elevator.

"Going up?" Bender jammed his gloved fingers into the gap between the twin doors, and pried the metal plates apart. It was a good thing these doors were of traditional design. The irising style of the newer models would've been a bitch to wrench open.

Hijak approached the elevator shaft. "Looks climbable." He pointed out the pipes running along the three walls—conduits containing electrical wiring, plumbing, and whatever else the robot engineers had decided to bake in. He glanced at me. "What do you think?"

I made a quick calculation with the help of my aReal. The quarters were too tight for jetpack use, but there was just enough room for all four of us to crawl along the walls of the shaft while porting the container.

"It's not going to be easy," I said.

"We didn't sign up for easy." Bender aimed his 9-mil into the shaft and with several quick shots he cut the six carbon-fiber cables.

I heard a screeching noise some distance below—probably the sound of the elevator cab's governor device engaging. It would clamp down along the vertical rails of the shaft and halt the cab.

With the cables now severed, Bender leaped inside, landing against the left wall. He wrapped his gloves around a pipe and turned toward me. "We're gonna rock this shaft, baby!"

Hijak jetted to the right side. "Let's do it."

Tahoe and I shoved the glass container into the opening. It was a tight fit. The far end started to dip, but Bender and Hijak flowed forward inside the shaft, stabilizing the container.

"Got it?" I said.

"Yeah!" Hijak grunted.

Bender laughed. "Suck it up, caterpillar."

"Name's Hijak, bro."

"Whatever, caterpillar."

The Chief might be making them work together, but that didn't mean Hijak and Bender actually liked each other.

Once the cargo was in place, I squeezed past the small gap between the container and the shaft, using the pipes and other small footholds for purchase, and joined Bender on the left wall. Tahoe did the same, positioning himself beside Hijak on the right.

We turned on our helmet lamps and proceeded up the shaft under exoskeleton-enhanced power.

I could hear Bender's ragged breathing beside me. He was a big man, with a lot of extra muscle weight to lug around. Still, he wasn't the only one who struggled, pressed up against the wall like that. The added weight of my jetpack fuel canisters certainly didn't help me, and my arms burned from the effort, despite the aid provided by my jumpsuit.

Since we could use only one hand to climb while gripping the container, the four of us had to devise a unified strategy. Before releasing my hold on the pipe in front of me, I set my boots at an angle to the shaft, and pressed my upper body against the container. Once I had purchase, I released the pipe and reached higher, shifting my weight away from the container and pulling myself upward.

I set up my aReal to transmit a visual cadence to the others; it sent a green light the exact moment I shoved against the container, and ensured all four of us performed the movement in unison—otherwise the container would've swayed back and forth as one side pressed into the other. I also voiced the cadence as we went: "Press. Heave! Press. Heave!"

We made good time, considering we had to climb five stories one-handed. Even so, it was a draining, personal struggle for us all.

Tahoe especially. Even though he had three gunshot wounds, he didn't flag, or voice one word of complaint.

Hijak worked in a marching song from Basic between my own vocal cadence.

"Everywhere we go-o," he said.

"Press. Heave!" I said.

"Don't be going and singing garbage from Basic," Bender said.

"Everywhere we go-o." Hijak tried again.

"Press. Heave!" I said.

Tahoe answered. "Everywhere we go-o."

"People wanna know-o."

"People wanna know-o."

"Who we are-r."

Bender shook his head with a grimace, but finally joined in. *"Who we are-r!"*

"So we tell them."

"So we tell them."

"We are the Navy!"

"We are the Navy!"

"Press. Heave!"

When we reached the top of the shaft, I maneuvered with difficulty to the ledge in front of the sealed doors. Both of my hands were fairly numb at this point from lack of circulation, and my arms burned from lactic acid buildup.

During the drop, I'd reviewed the designs of several Shangde City buildings. The SK engineers here had a preference for rooftop-opening elevators, and this one would likely prove to be no different. I wasn't sure if that was good or bad.

I heard the "rat-a-tat" of sporadic gunfire beyond the doors, and hesitated.

"Rage, what the hell, man?" Bender said. "Open the doors before our arms fall off."

I quashed my misgivings and forced myself to pry the twin plates of metal apart.

As expected, the elevator opened right onto the office tower's rooftop terrace.

I swept my eyes over the area, taking in the situation.

The entire platoon was still up here. Most of the men lay prostrate along the rooftop edge closest to the warehouse, where the High-Value Target resided. They peered into their weapon sights at targets I couldn't see from my current location. Rooftop superstructures provided various fallback positions. Skullcracker was one of those watching their backs, and he gave me a two-finger salute.

The Chief's voice came over the comm. "About time you boys showed up."

"Hey, Chief," I said.

I grabbed the foremost handhold on the container and helped slide it onto the rooftop. Above the container, some of the dangling elevator cables had curled up, but now they fell back into the shaft, making a sound like a whip. Had to be careful around those—errant, swinging carbon-fiber cables could cut off heads.

"You good?" Bender said, stepping past the container to take in Tahoe and me.

"Yeah, we're good," I answered.

Hijak and Bender rejoined the platoon.

I removed the cord that linked me to the package, and I went to Tahoe.

Exhausted, he was seated with his back to the container.

I unlatched his blood-splattered boot before he could stop me.

"No time," Tahoe started to protest. "Help the others."

I ignored him. "Your blood pressure is dropping."

I twisted his boot to the right. When I removed it, a gush of blood swilled from the rim.

I examined his foot.

His big toe was shot right off. Blood spurted from the wound in regular pulses.

"Well, guess I won't be joining the ballet anytime soon," Tahoe said.

"Why would you want to join the ballet?"

"What do you think? The chicks, of course."

I fetched his suitrep kit. "Don't worry, ballet's still open to you. The doc will print you a new toe."

"Just like he printed you a new arm?"

"Yeah. Just like that." I wrapped a tourniquet around the ankle to halt the blood flow, then I loosely wrapped a bandage around his severed toe. The inside of the bandage was coated with Mister Clot, which would impart quite the sting when I tightened it.

Tahoe winced in anticipation. "Wonder what other body part he'll swap out on me?"

"Your vagina, bro," I said.

He laughed, and I used the moment to tighten the bandage extra hard.

His laugh quickly turned into a howl of pain. Tahoe bit into his glove, muffling the sound.

I removed the tourniquet, and when I was satisfied that the toe bandage was holding, I twisted his boot back on, finished with the leg.

Ignoring his protests, next I unscrewed his glove and arm assemblies, then patched his secondary gunshot wounds.

When that was done, I replaced the assemblies, leaving his jumpsuit intact.

"You're good to go," I said. His blood pressure was markedly improved. He probably could've used a plasma volume expander IV, but he would live. "Need some morphine?"

Tahoe shook his head.

"All right, no morphine." I turned toward the platoon. "I'll be right back."

"You think you can convince someone else to lend me their jet-pack?" Tahoe said.

"And make them miss out on all the fun of porting the container? Don't think so, bro. Sorry."

"Damn."

It was just like Tahoe—even though he was shot multiple times, he still wanted to do his part to complete the mission.

I crouched between the rooftop superstructures, and when I neared the edge of the building, I dropped and low-crawled the rest of the way. I assumed a position beside Facehopper.

He didn't even spare me a glance: he was too busy aiming through his sights and firing.

I held my rifle to eye level. "Sit-rep?"

"Not good," Facehopper said. "We came to the aid of the pinned SKs. Now we're pinned, too."

Through my scope I gazed at the rooftop of the twelve-story warehouse across the street below. The elusive High-Value resided inside the tenth floor of that building, according to the last known position transmitted by the HS3s.

An empty shuttle pad dominated the middle of the warehouse's roof. Beside the pad was a sealed freight elevator, useless without power. Various superstructures ate up the remaining rooftop real estate, offering cover to Centurion snipers. There were twenty-four of those combat robots on the rooftop alone, according to the red dots on my HUD map. About a third of them seemed to be shooting at us, while the remainder were gathered on the leftmost side, aiming down at Dragon platoon, whose members were pinned on the fourth and fifth floors of the building adjacent to ours.

Unlike the office building I was on, the warehouse didn't have many windows. Maybe two or three per floor. Centurions fired from some of those windows, but the majority of the remaining combat robots were distributed throughout the glass-walled buildings around us. Roughly half of those combatants seemed to be firing up at us, while the rest focused on Dragon platoon.

On the street twenty stories below, Centurions and ATLAS mechs also fired at Dragon platoon, but not at us—we were out of range. I saw an alien slug down there, bashing Dragon's building so fervently I had the impression the behemoth was trying to mate with it. The building itself was curiously free of the black, caking substance that sheathed so many of the other structures.

Crabs launched from the backside of the slug in droves, and clambered up the building, but Dragon platoon mowed them down the moment they reached the fourth floor.

I briefly wondered why none of the street-level ATLAS 5s used their jetpacks to ascend the twenty floors to our rooftop, and I decided either the mechs realized they would be far too exposed during such a long jump, or they didn't have enough jumpjet fuel.

I did see one ATLAS 5 make a jetpack leap into the fourth floor of the adjacent building. Right into the heart of Dragon platoon.

I wouldn't want to be a member of that platoon right about now.

"Requesting permission to go in and help them, sir," Lui sent.

"Negative," Chief Bourbonjack said. "Protecting Dragon is secondary to our main objective. Besides, I'm sure the elite members of Dragon can handle one little ATLAS mech. We have our hands full up here as it is."

"What a mess," I said. "We should just call in an air strike. Orders be damned."

"Believe it or not we already tried," Facehopper said. "The interference is off the scale here. Despite our high elevation, we can't get through to the Raptors. Our comms aren't worth a bloody damn."

Tahoe unexpectedly low-crawled to my side. Somehow he managed to grip the stock of his weapon with his injured hand.

I could only shake my head at his courage as he peered into the rifle and let off a shot.

Beside him, a few paces to the left, I noticed portions of the rooftop had crumbled away entirely. We'd taken heavy rocket blows there.

"They stopped firing rockets?" I asked Facehopper.

"They tried serpents for a while," he answered. "Until they realized the rockets couldn't hit us, not while we're up here and they're down there."

I was still gazing at the crumbled portion of the rooftop. It was like a giant mouth had taken huge chunks out of the building. I could see twisted sections of rebar extending from the gaps like the spindly legs of a dead spider. The rebar tips were dissolved right off. "Looks like their rockets hit pretty hard to me."

"That's not rocket fire." He indicated one of the higher superstructures behind me, where the concrete was smashed near the top. The damage was moderate, but nowhere near the level of destruction at the edge of the rooftop. "*That's* rocket fire."

Confused, I returned my attention to the missing portions of the roof. "Then what the hell did that?"

"The alien."

"The alien?"

"Don't worry, he's focused on the SKs. Won't fire unless we piss him off." He let off a shot. "There he is. See him?"

On the warehouse rooftop a large form rose from cover. It wore a tall, black jumpsuit, and had multiple arms, or tentacles of some kind. Within a glass dome an octopus-like head looked out on the world. It carried some kind of rocket launcher in three of its tentacles.

Maybe I should have been floored with fear. Or gaping in amazement.

Another type of alien.

That was a momentous discovery wasn't it?

For me it just was another enemy target.

The alien aimed its weapon at the SKs in the opposite building, and let off a soundless, invisible round that caused an entire portion of the building to crumble away, leaving behind twisted rebar and jagged concrete. Just like our rooftop.

Moments later Dragon returned fire.

The alien jumpsuit twitched left and right as the bullets struck. The entity dropped, taking cover once more.

I scanned its jumpsuit in my scope, but couldn't see any signs of perforation.

Those armor-piercing rounds had bounced right off the jumpsuit.

Was it possible the fabric was made of something akin to the ballistic shield of an ATLAS mech?

I aimed my crosshairs directly at the glass dome of the crouched alien. Its suit might be impenetrable, but no glass in the known universe could stop a MOTH sniper bullet.

I fired.

The alien's body immediately slammed to the side, and it rolled some distance across the roof.

An instant later the thing stood up again. There wasn't a scratch on the "glass" dome.

It turned its launcher toward us.

"Uh, who fired at the badass alien?" Manic said.

The platoon retreated from the edge at a run. I followed close behind Facehopper.

He glanced over his shoulder at me. "What part about not pissing off the alien did you miss, mate?"

The entire border of the rooftop behind us, railing and all, crumbled away. I ducked behind a nearby superstructure, and watched more sections break off as the alien systematically collapsed the roof with its weapon. I was forced to retreat to a structure farther back as those impacts kept coming in.

For a while there, I thought we were going to have to dive into the elevator shaft to escape.

The attack finally ceased after one quarter of the roof had been dissolved.

The platoon slowly crept back toward the edge.

A gaping hole three stories deep had been carved into the top of the building. I wondered how long the rest of the damaged rooftop would hold.

"Nicely done, Rage," Facehopper said.

I gazed through my scope. The alien had returned behind cover, and was concentrating fire on Dragon platoon once again.

I didn't know quite what to make of the little bastard. But I *did* know that I wouldn't be firing at the thing again.

Movement drew my eyes to the shuttle pad on the warehouse. The doors of the freight elevator beside it were sliding open.

So much for the building not having power . . .

I stared at the opening doors, and as the metal shape within came into view, I had a sudden sinking feeling in my stomach.

It was an ATLAS 5.

The mech emerged from the elevator at a run, headed toward the rooftop edge closest to us. It took a running leap off and fired its jumpjets.

"ATLAS 5, incoming!" I switched my rifle to full automatic mode, releasing a stream of bullets at the mech as it roared in a parabolic path toward our rooftop.

The ATLAS 5 unfortunately decided to return the favor, and threads of Gatling fire erupted from it, chewing into our building.

One of my platoon brothers launched a rocket.

The ATLAS 5 responded by firing its Trench Coat. The metal shards detonated the rocket prematurely, and the mech continued toward our building unharmed.

My exposed brothers and I were forced to disperse beneath that incessant Gatling fire, taking cover behind the remaining super-structures.

I dove behind a rooftop exhaust port. Tahoe ended up beside me.

The enemy ATLAS landed, sending up a plume of cement dust. The roof shook precariously, and for a moment I thought the remainder of the terrace would collapse.

"If anyone has any rockets left, now's the time to use them, people," the Chief sent over the comm.

Grenades started going off around the ATLAS 5, but that served only to attract its attention. The mech stepped forward, unloading round after round at the source of the grenades—one of the massive rooftop aerials.

"Oh shit!" Lui retreated from the aerial as it tore apart, ducking behind the shack-like superstructure of the stairwell instead. The glass container wasn't far from him. No one had taken cover behind the container, I noted—none of us wanted to endanger the mission.

The mech tramped malevolently toward Lui's superstructure. Lui looked like a defenseless child beside that towering mass of servo-motors and armaments bearing down on him.

"Uh, guys," Lui transmitted. "Could use a little help here."

The ATLAS was about four meters from Lui, and closing. Its back was to me.

"I'm going in," I sent over the comm.

"Rade, wait—" Tahoe grabbed at me.

But I'd already left cover.

I vaulted toward the mech, combat knife in hand, and activated my jumpjets.

Like most MOTHs, I knew the ATLAS 5 like I knew my own body. And that included its weaknesses.

When I landed on its back, the mech swung around and bucked, trying to get me off. There was an electro-defense system that could be installed to prevent what I was about to do. It worked by electrifying the entire outer skin of the ATLAS, frying any jumpsuit interlopers. However, it wasn't a popular add-on, because it took up the Trench Coat slots.

And because I'd seen the Trench Coat fire, I knew the electro-defense wasn't installed.

As the mech bucked, I reached between the jumpjets and cut the fuel lines with my knife. Then I jabbed a gloved finger into the upper segment of the line, right into the main fuel tank itself.

"Laser pulse, 800t," I said. My helmet picked up the request, and the surgical laser in my finger, ordinarily reserved for slicing open a jumpsuit for medical purposes, activated.

It pulsed for eight hundred trillionths of a second, right into the heart of the fuel tank.

I'd already started shoving away as the fuel ignited.

The jetpack and its fuel canisters were designed not to explode under ordinary conditions. Even if a bullet pierced, the containment integrity of the canisters would persist, and the fuel would simply vent.

In that moment, the ever-expanding, igniting fuel had nowhere else to go but the nozzles of the jetpack, which activated all at once.

Some of those nozzles were bigger than others, and provided the easiest egress for the exploding fuel. The biggest nozzle was for upward thrust, so the ATLAS 5 went flying into the air.

I fell backward hard, hitting the rooftop, knocking the wind out of myself. But I got lucky, because other than some minor melt damage to the outer sections of my glove, I was mostly unscathed. The surgical laser port on my glove was now offline. Melted away.

"Thanks, bro," Lui sent. "I think you just used up one of your nine lives though."

"Still got lots of lives left, don't you worry, brother," I returned.

A possessed Centurion abruptly burst from the stairwell and opened fire.

"Ambush!"

My platoon mates eliminated it.

Another Centurion emerged.

When that one toppled, Fret and Skullcracker moved forward, and unleashed hell into the stairwell.

On my HUD map, the red dots of enemy combatants appeared inside the stairwell and vanished just as quickly as they came. My two brothers were just mowing them down.

"Guys, watch it!" Bender said.

Widening pools of glowing liquid emerged from the fallen robots near the entrance, and flowed toward Skullcracker and Fret.

Skullcracker tossed four grenades into the stairwell, then slammed the door shut. He and Fret danced over the glowing pools to rejoin the platoon.

I felt the roof vibrate as the grenades exploded, and a black plume erupted from the outline of the stairwell door.

Ghost, Trace, and Skullcracker kept their aim on the stairwell, while the rest of the platoon turned their weapons toward the edges of the building. I was almost expecting another ATLAS 5 to leap onto the rooftop with its Gatlings ablaze.

"All right," Chief Bourbonjack said. "I'd hoped to clear the warehouse rooftop, and take out that alien somehow, but it's obvious we can't hold this position much longer. Enemy robots in the stairwells. ATLAS 5s on our doorsteps. Liquid Phants closing in. We have to make a move. Stop pussyfooting around. Rage, do you have enough fuel to port the package across to the warehouse and back again? Assuming you and another platoon member took a direct path to the High-Value's floor from here?"

On my map I input a test trajectory, and ran a simulation of two platoon members jetting across with the container. The fuel costs were steep, but within my current levels. Though whether

I'd have sufficient fuel to return to the outskirts of the city for the extract afterward was questionable.

"I have more than enough to cross there and back, Chief," I said.

"Good. Hijak, you're going with Rage. The HS3 scouts have sent the updated location of the High-Value's floor. Aim for that location. Jet across with all you have, and get your asses inside there. The rest of the platoon will provide suppressive fire. We'll be coming in right behind you, situation permitting."

I confirmed Hijak's fuel levels via my aReal, then I glanced at Tahoe, looking for his blessing. The Chief had given an order, and I wouldn't disobey it, but I wanted to know that Tahoe was okay with this.

Tahoe knew what I wanted. He gave me a slow nod.

I hurried to the glass container. I felt bad about leaving Tahoe behind, but maybe it was better this way. What we were about to do was a last ditch, desperate effort. Jetting across like the Chief wanted would expose Hijak and me to intense—and I mean *intense*—gunfire from all sides. Sure, the platoon would provide suppressive fire, but I didn't think the possessed Centurions really understood the point of suppression. They'd keep firing on us regardless.

By now, most of the platoon had low-crawled back to the damaged edge that overlooked the warehouse. Manic, Bomb, and Lui watched the three remaining edges of the building, respectively, while Skullcracker stayed where he was, heavy gun guarding the stairwell door and elevator shaft.

"Wait here," I told Hijak, crouching forward.

I reached the damaged rooftop edge with its tendrils of twisted rebar, and peered over.

The warehouse across from us had very few windows. There were only three, spaced far apart, on the floor where the High-Value Target currently resided.

I aimed at the middle window.

Bullets started to ping the edge below me as Centurion snipers homed in on my, and the platoon's, position.

I marked the destination window, programmed my planned trajectory into the jetpack interface, and dispatched the route to Hijak's aReal.

"Accept the trajectory, Hijak," I sent over the comm.

He did.

I rejoined Hijak at the container and attached the leftmost cord to my belt. Hijak had already secured himself to the rightmost.

"You think you can handle this, Hijak?" I said. "It's going to get pretty intense out there."

"The more intense the better, sir!"

I almost chuckled. Caterpillar bravado.

But he wasn't a caterpillar anymore, I had to remind myself.

I stared for a moment at the gaping hole beyond the rooftop edge, and at my platoon brothers stationed there, firing down at the enemy and taking fire in return.

"You see that ahead of us, Hijak? That's fate."

Hijak seemed puzzled. "What are you saying, we're doomed?"

"No, only that, every action we've ever done in our lives, every decision, every choice we've ever made has brought us here, to this mission, to this moment. Right here, right now, is what we've prepared for our entire lives."

Hijak appeared surprisingly calm. "I'm ready for this moment, sir. I've been waiting for it since I was born. Let it come. For good or for bad."

I nodded slowly.

We knelt, wrapping our gloves around the handholds of our respective sides. Together we lifted the container, feeling the weight of destiny in our hands.

We approached our brothers, halting three paces from the edge, just out of the line of fire from below.

"Sync to my jetpack, Hijak," I said.

Hijak nodded. "Synced."

I drew my pistol and tightened my grip on the container's handhold with my other glove. "Ready, Chief."

"Suppressive fire, boys!" the Chief announced.

The platoon opened fire all at once.

I glanced at Hijak: "On three.

"One . . .

"Two . . .

"Three!"

I took a run at the gaping edge, and vaulted into empty space, trying to get as much momentum as I could from my strength-enhanced jumpsuit. Hijak did the same beside me. The container seemed heavier than ever.

I switched to autopilot and my jetpack took over. It fired bursts at full power, following the preprogrammed trajectory I'd input. The container twisted and jerked beside me, threatening to wrench free of my grip. Somehow I held on to the damn thing. In that moment I promised myself that if I ever got out of this alive, I'd invent some kind of attachable jetpacks for containers like this. I'd become a billionaire.

As we traversed the chasm between the two buildings, Hijak's jetpack thrust in sync with my own, automatically accounting for any discrepancies in the flight path to ensure he followed the exact same trajectory.

To compensate for the height difference between ourselves and the destination, we fell ten stories in four seconds.

Those were the longest four seconds of my life.

Not just because of the drop, which was terrifying in and of itself.

But the gunfire.

In training, the instructors hammered into our heads that jetting in full sight of the enemy left you completely exposed.

They were right.

It was a good thing our possessed robot friends weren't especially good shots. Even so, if any among the enemy had launched a serpent missile while we were in transit, they would have taken us down. The missile targeting systems alone would have guaranteed it, considering how exposed we were.

But the enemy didn't launch any missiles.

The destination window neared fast. Because it wasn't all that wide, we'd have to traverse it in single file: me, followed by the container, then Hijak. I'd programmed that configuration into our trajectories already, so as we closed, Hijak veered off to the side, positioning himself and the container to my rear. My arm swung around as the handhold pivoted behind me.

Now came the moment of truth.

If the glass was bulletproof, then Hijak and I were screwed.

With my 9-mil, I shot at the window several times before impact.

The glass broke away in big pieces.

What a relief.

The jetpack cut out as I passed inside.

I collided heavily with the smooth floor and slid forward, my momentum draining away.

Behind me I heard the woosh of a rocket as it passed near the window outside. One of the ATLAS 5s on the street had launched a serpent after all. Too late. The rocket wouldn't be able to track us now.

My mental gloating was interrupted as the glass container abruptly plowed into me from behind. Quite forcefully.

I'd forgotten that heavy objects have greater momentum than lighter ones. I should have dodged the impact.

I slipped sideways as the container shoved me onward, and I ended up gliding alongside it. The cord that bound me to the container grew taut, and I was dragged for a few seconds until the object slid to a halt.

According to the HUD map, the High-Value Target lay directly ahead, along the far wall.

I unlocked the cord from my belt and rose to one knee. I held my 9-mil to eye level and scanned the room.

The entire area was basically one big room, similar to the floor plan of the office building, but instead of cubicles and desks partitioning the area, the space was divided into a lattice of brick pillars arranged in rows and columns. Crates and empty pallets were stacked between some of the pillars, blocking the view to the far wall (and the target). Overhead, bright, working LEDs lit the area. No emergency lamps here.

I didn't see any immediate threats.

"Chief," I sent into the comm. "We're in."

Static answered me.

I heard the clang of metallic footsteps.

I hurried behind a pillar, and Hijak ducked against the one beside me.

I holstered my pistol, silently sliding the rifle down from my shoulder.

I gazed through the scope, scanning from left to right. Still didn't see any threats . . .

Wait.

There.

A Praetor, near the center of the room. Advancing toward me and Hijak. I hadn't seen it before because the long row of pillars had obscured my view.

I aimed for the brain case in the chest and fired.

I got it. The Praetor vanished from sight, tumbling behind one of the pillars.

Normally when you found a Praetor, a squad of Centurions was close behind. But these Phants could possess Praetors and Centurions alike, and once possessed, there was no guarantee the Centurions would continue to obey the commands of the Praetor.

The robot may have been acting alone, but I wasn't going to take the chance.

I gave Hijak the "advance" hand signal, and I moved forward at a crouch, rifle at the ready. I ducked behind every third pillar, scanning the room each time. Nothing.

When I neared the fallen Praetor, I gave it a wide berth. The glowing blue liquid of the Phant had spilled out, and it edged toward me (a little indignantly, I thought) as I hurried past. It moved far too slowly to reach me, however.

Nine pillars later, I spotted the High-Value.

The Artificial stood in the exact spot indicated by the HUD map. It just waited there, facing me, motionless on the far side of the room. Through my scope, I confirmed it was the spitting image of the Paramount Leader. Its eyes were closed, and it was smiling as if privy to some inside joke.

"Chief," I sent into the comm. "High-Value Target spotted."

As usual, static.

The Artificial, or the Praetor, before I terminated it, must have called in support units, because the clank of metallic footsteps echoed across the room, heralding the arrival of more robots.

Remaining behind the pillar, I scanned the forward area, identifying the stairwells at the far corners of the room where the Centurions were piling inside.

I glanced at the HUD map for any sign of my platoon mates. Seeing nothing, I double-checked over my shoulder.

No one had come.

"Chief?" I sent into the comm. "What happened to coming in right behind us?"

No answer.

"He did say, *situation permitting*," Hijak piped up.

I could only shake my head.

I returned my attention to my rifle sights. The Centurions had fanned out across the floor, but hadn't spotted me or Hijak yet.

My scope passed the motionless Artificial again, and I paused. Something seemed off about this whole situation, somehow. My danger sense was firing, and I sensed a trap.

Well, we'd come this far. Couldn't really turn back now. We'd just have to proceed slowly, and carefully, sticking to everything we'd learned and practiced in training.

First order of business: ensure the High-Value didn't flee.

"Hijak," I transmitted. "How's your sniping?"

He tapped the barrel of his sniper rifle. "They don't give us these babies unless we've earned them, sir."

Maybe, but my first instinct was that he sucked. I didn't want to believe anyone else could ever be as good a shot as Alejandro.

I suppressed the thought.

"All right," I said. "Take out the High-Value's right foot. I'll get the left. On three. We have to get both at the same time. I don't want the High-Value limping off on one foot."

"Wait a second. Is that a good idea? Sir?"

"I don't have time to argue with you, Hijak. Rules of Engagement say we're fine. We're supposed to capture the High-Value. Whether we bring it in with or without feet is irrelevant. It's a robot. It's not going to feel any pain."

"But how do you know the Phant won't abandon the body if we shoot its feet?"

"Would you prefer the alternative? Losing the High-Value because it decides to run? No, we'll just have to take the risk. While we still have time."

"What if it just drags itself away with its arms?" Hijak insisted.

"We'll reach it before then. Look, can I count on you or not?"

Hijak hesitated only an instant. "You can count on me, sir."

"Good. On three." I aimed past the pillar, exposing as little of myself as possible.

"One."

Brick shards exploded against my face as bullets ricocheted from the pillar. I'd been spotted.

"Two."

More shards. I knew I might receive a fatal head wound any second. But I didn't flinch. Just a little longer . . .

"Three."

I pulled the trigger.

The Artificial's upper body swung forward as both its legs pinwheeled backward from the force of the impact, and it flopped to the floor.

I ducked behind cover.

So Hijak was as good a shot as he said he was, after all.

Then something exploded from the direction of the High-Value.

I crawled to the opposite side of the pillar and looked out.

Beyond the line of Centurions, the floor had collapsed in a circular pattern where the Artificial had fallen, and the High-Value was now gone.

A blur of motion to my left caught my eye: a Dragon HS3 drone hovered past.

Likely the SKs had sent in their own porters by now, and they'd taken up a position on the level just below. They had set explosive microcharges and stolen the High-Value right out from under us.

Damn it.

They were good, I'd give them that.

I shot the HS3.

The damaged drone spiraled across the line of Centurions and swooped into the circular pit. I heard a distant crash.

"We have to get down there!" I wasn't about to let the SKs seize the High-Value Target. Not after all this work.

I unhitched a grenade from my belt, let it cook for three seconds, then launched it toward a group of two Centurions. I cooked two more grenades in turn, releasing them shortly thereafter.

The explosions went off one after another.

I peered through my scope and started terminating the remaining Centurions, aiming at the brain cases. Hijak did the same on his side. Our ammo was running low.

Ahead, to the right and left, more Centurions piled down the stairs. The alien in the jumpsuit decided to join them, carrying that huge, nasty particle weapon with three of its tentacles.

I'd just about had enough of this.

"Mark the pit on your HUD," I told Hijak.

Then I threw a smoke grenade.

"Run!"

The grenade exploded, and I dashed into the smoke screen. I heard the whiz of bullets as the Centurions fired at us anyway.

Though I couldn't see a thing in the smoke, my HUD indicated the pillars around me as blue wire frames, and the circular pit in the floor appeared as a two-dimensional outline.

I leaped into the pit, plunging from the smoke to the level below, not knowing whether I'd land in a roomful of possessed robots or something worse.

I crashed to the floor and rolled aside. I got up on one knee and scanned the room, aiming my rifle from quadrant to quadrant.

No robots.

The level appeared almost identical to the one above, replete with equidistant pillars.

As Hijak landed beside me, I spotted the two SK porters, sheathed in gray jumpsuits, not far ahead. They were placing fresh microexplosives, this time to blow the outer wall, probably because there weren't any obvious windows nearby. They had the footless High-Value Target secured inside their own glass container.

Though trapped, the Artificial wasn't properly positioned inside the container—the Artificial sat on the edge of the metallic circle etched into the glass floor. That meant the electromagnetic containment beam was inactive. Yet the possessing Phant hadn't fled—drops of purple condensation still covered the base of the High-Value's neck, reaching up from underneath its camos.

Odd.

I dashed toward the SKs. "Wait!"

The two porters turned back.

They were women.

Hijak and I halted two paces from them. We kept our weapons raised.

"Disarm the microexplosives," I said.

"You are MOTHs?" the nearest woman said in heavily accented English.

"I said disarm the microexplosives!" I waved the barrel threateningly.

The two women exchanged a glance, then raised their hands in surrender. That seemed kind of easy, considering they were supposed to be elite commandos.

"Give me the detonation device." I glanced at the remote in the closest SK's hand.

In response, she pressed the detonator and activated her horizontal jumpjets, hurtling right past me. She must have dialed up the blast intensity of the microcharges beforehand, because the explosion threw me to the floor.

I heard a high-pitched keening in my ears, and bright stars filled my vision.

I drunkenly blinked the points of light away, but before I could recover, a heavy boot pressed into my chest. Groggily, I tried activating my jetpack, but it malfunctioned.

The woman disarmed me, then unbuckled my jetpack, rolling me to the side. As the pack fell away, I saw why the controls hadn't responded: I'd landed atop the glowing liquid of a Phant, and it was flowing into the jetpack. On the floor nearby lay the crumpled shell of the HS3 I'd shot down. I hadn't realized the drone was possessed.

Jetpacks had limited AIs, but the nozzles began to fire out of sequence as the Phant took control.

This was all very odd. The Phant could have killed me. I had seen the alien entities incinerate entire jumpsuits while the human occupants were still inside. It was how Alejandro had died. But instead, this one chose to spare me and possess my jetpack.

Why? I was starting to suspect that given the choice between AI and flesh, they would choose the AI first.

I tried to resist as the woman plasticuffed me, but my mind was still foggy, my body slow. The high-pitched keening in my ears had faded to a distant buzz, but all sound still seemed muffled.

The woman hauled me toward the glass container. In front of it, a wide, gaping hole had been blown into the warehouse wall, nine stories above street level.

The woman secured the plasticuffs to the loop built into the lower left corner of the container.

Inside the glass, the Artificial watched me with an empty expression, the stumps of its feet occasionally sparking.

"You should really turn on the EM containment field," I said to the woman. My voice sounded distant.

The SK woman gave me a mocking smile.

The second woman secured Hijak to the other side of the container in the same way. Hijak had his head bowed, and he bore a nasty cut along his temple. He kept blinking the blood from his eyes. His jetpack was also gone.

"Chief, we've been captured," I sent over the comm. Weakly.

Static.

Metallic clangs issued from behind me.

The Centurions from the floor above were leaping through the hole in the ceiling.

"Uh," I said.

The clangs continued as more robots landed, punctuated by a single loud thump as the alien in the jumpsuit plunged down.

The women quickly hoisted the glass container between them, with help from Hijak and me, since we wanted to get the hell out of there. Then the SKs vaulted outside and activated their jumpjets at full burn.

What happened next was a blur of adrenalin-fueled helplessness. My life was in someone else's hands and there was nothing I could do about it.

Hijak and I were dragged through the air by the plasticuffs while the women steered the container. The cuffs dug into the wrist area of my suit, threatening to puncture it. The street flowed by, nine stories below.

We smashed through a window on the building across from the warehouse, and landed roughly. Other SKs in gray jumpsuits unhooked Hijak and me from the glass container, then deactivated our PASS (Personal Alert Safety System) devices, which could be used to track us—though probably not very far in the alien-induced interference.

Two of the SKs tied us to their backs, just above their jump-jets, then they carried us through the city, leaping from building to building, following the rest of the SK platoon over the swarming crabs and slugs. The glass container was ported along through it all.

Oddly enough, none of the enemy robots on the streets fired at us. Maybe it was an illusion. Maybe they *were* firing, but their aim was so bad I just didn't notice. Or maybe they didn't want to harm our precious cargo.

Eventually we emerged from the southwest corner of the city, precisely opposite the original waypoint we had used for the insert.

I tried reaching the Chief several times over the comm, but I never got through. It was pointless to keep trying, because he couldn't come for us now.

No one could.

The SKs unceremoniously strapped Hijak and me to the floor of a drop shuttle, alongside the caged Artificial. The SKs never once activated the EM field inside the glass container. I kept expecting the Phant to flow free, but it didn't.

Instead, the host Artificial merely smiled at me.

The SK soldiers clamped into their respective seats, and the drop shuttle sped away.

CHAPTER TWELVE

Shaw

Queequeg moved deftly among the ranks, dodging claws, evading mandibles, just tearing a path through the cords and severing the crabs from their host slug. It was a trick I'd taught him in earlier fights, and it was the fastest way to dispatch the smaller beasts.

I followed in his wake, piloting Battlehawk, shooting any crabs that Queequeg had missed or that came at him from the sides.

Fan guarded the rear from his perch behind my head. He was using the rifle, ammo packs, and grenades he'd retrieved from my mech's storage compartment. He targeted the cords of the crabs too, and was doing an admirable job of protecting my back. I was fairly certain he was military by now, judging from some of the kills he'd made. I supposed that was a plus. I needed someone who could fight along with me.

We had held out for a surprisingly long time, mostly because of the tight nature of the tunnel, which siphoned the enemy toward us in manageable quantities, so that the most we faced at any one time were two or three.

Even so, I knew it was only a matter of time before our ammo ran out. When Fan exhausted his, I'd be forced to watch our back more often, leaving Queequeg exposed. Soon thereafter my Gatlings would empty, then my serpents, and finally my incendiaries.

Not good. Not at all.

We were trying to reach the surface, shooting and hacking our way back through the rearmost tunnel. It seemed hopeless. But I'd faced countless hopeless situations before. I'd always gotten through. Always.

Now wouldn't be any different. It couldn't.

We reached the slug that was the source of the current batch of crabs. Queequeg pulled back, allowing me to whale on the beast with my Gatlings until the alien phased out.

Queequeg, Fan, and I rushed through the temporary gap left by the evanesced slug, and we ran right into the next opposing group of crabs.

The slug meanwhile rematerialized behind us, blocking our retreat vector, but also cutting off attacks from crabs in that direction.

"Let me know if the situation changes behind us," I said, wishing I still had the second pair of eyes afforded by the ASS drone, which we'd lost to a crab.

"The situation changes!" Fan said. "The big one disappears again to allow the other Mara to pass!"

The slug had realized its mistake, then.

"Well don't just sit there," I said. "Fight!"

I felt the pressure of a medium blast wave behind me.

"That was my last grenade!" Fan said.

"Do what you can!"

I'd been careful to use my Gatling guns in controlled bursts to conserve ammo, but my left one clicked now when I fired it.

Empty.

I cycled in a serpent launcher instead. According to the supply indicator on my HUD, this was the final rocket. Battlehawk had already exhausted most of the serpent inventory during its tenure with Bravo platoon, and I'd already emptied the last three from the right-side launcher when I'd made the Improvised Explosive Device.

So, one rocket left.

Had to make it count.

I aimed the launcher down the tunnel, and though I couldn't see the slug through the darkness, I knew it was down there somewhere.

I fired.

The warhead detonated roughly thirty paces ahead, and the flash illuminated a tsunami of crab body parts.

I hadn't hit the slug then, but I *had* inflicted damage on its minions.

The blast wave sent crabs in the immediate area flailing into the floor and walls.

Queequeg was knocked off his feet.

Battlehawk held its ground, although the cockpit shuddered around me.

One crab recovered right away, and tried to get Queequeg while he was down.

I split the crab in two with a Gatling burst from my right arm.

No one hits my friends while they're down.

Another crab got up in front of me.

I depressed the weapon trigger—

My right Gatling clicked.

Out of bullets entirely now.

The doomsday scenario I had rehearsed in my head so many times before was finally upon me. Trapped in a cave, surrounded by beasts, slowly running out of ammo. It didn't matter if I was in a mech or a jumpsuit, the final outcome was the same.

Don't give up! Don't give up! Don't give up!

I cycled the incendiary throwers into both hands. These weapons fired some kind of oxidant and combustive together, allowing me to throw flames even in zero oxygen. I turned toward the rear, away from Queequeg, and activated the incendiaries. The crabs behind me were roasted, yes, but as soon as the creatures left weapons range the fires immediately flickered out.

The crabs devised a strategy: they would dive in and get struck by the jellied gasoline, then they'd retreat, the flames would quench, and then they'd dive right back in again.

I decided it was best to save the incendiary throwers for the slug, so I turned back toward Queequeg and began using Battlehawk's body as my main weapon.

This involved a lot of bashing and stomping.

"Stay still!" Fan said. "I hit nothing when you move like that!"

"Do your best!" I said. "Stay alive!"

I wasn't an infantryman. I had no training in small-unit tactics. I didn't know the proper strategies for close-quarter combat situations, nor did I even know the full capabilities of the mech. I considered telling Battlehawk to fight the battle for me, but I remembered all too well what an AI had done to my shuttle, crash-landing it while I slept.

No. I fought my own battles. And if that meant I had to take a brute force approach, and smash whatever came my way, then so be it. The crabs were relentless, but I wasn't going to back down. I'd force my way out or die trying.

Still, if Battlehawk knew something that could save my life . . .

"Battlehawk, any ideas?"

"Keep doing what you are doing," the AI intoned.

Very helpful.

I waded through the living and the dead, striking with my fists, tromping with my feet, making my way toward the next slug, which

I couldn't yet see. I had refused to let Battlehawk fight on auto-pilot for me, and yet I was doing that very thing myself. My mind operated on automatic, blatantly killing everything around me, so that when I came across Queequeg's snarling face in the mayhem, I nearly smashed it in.

I truly was a killer now. Worse than Rade ever had been.

Stunned and ashamed by what I had become, I didn't move.

Queequeg leaped past and bit into the umbilical of the crab beside me, which had taken advantage of my inaction to attack my mech.

Other crabs surged forward to assume its place, and in moments they were literally all over me. Mandibles chewed at external pistons and compressor joints. Pincers clattered against exposed tubing and wiring.

It sounded like I was inside a flimsy tin shed covered in insects. Warning indicators blared all over the place, though I had no idea what most meant. I knew my right elbow joint was damaged, because I couldn't bend the arm all the way. My left arm was slug-gish. My right eye camera winked out intermittently.

I discovered flamethrowers worked wonders in close quarters. Fire at a crab clinging to your chest piece, and the thing instantly released you, howling in pain.

I flung a bunch of the creatures from my body in this way, and then cut a swathe in front of me, using the intense heat to send the crabs leaping back in waves. It didn't last, of course. They resorted to their dive in/dive out tactics again.

I'd lost sight of Queequeg. My loyal friend was probably dead. Buried under one of those carapaces because I'd let myself become overwhelmed. I hadn't been able to defend him, like a proper mas-ter should.

Still, a part of me hoped he was alive.

A weak, dying part.

I released another long scythe of flame, and then launched a horizontal burst from my jetpack, wanting to quickly claim the space I'd cleared with my incendiaries. I must have thrusted at the wrong angle though because I found myself traveling both forward *and* upward.

My head crashed into the ceiling at a forty-five-degree angle. I fell to the ground, landing in a prostrate position.

Mental note: jetpacks and enclosed spaces don't mix.

"*Get up!*" Fan said, the urgency very clear in his voice.

I'd forgotten about him, and to be honest, I was a little surprised he was still alive.

But he was right.

I had to get up. Crabs were already all over me.

I used my incendiaries to send those crabs skittering away. Some of the jellied gasoline dripped onto my chest piece, but it instantly flickered out due to lack of oxygen. I sat up and tried to fire off more rounds, but both incendiary launchers clicked.

So that was it. I had nothing left to attack with now, save Battlehawk's body.

When I rose, I saw the alien slug waiting just ahead, at the edge of the light cone cast by my headlamp. Its girth filled nearly the entire tunnel. Several crabs lurked between us.

I instantly regretted expending my incendiary throwers. Without weapons of any kind, there was no way I was taking down that slug.

But I wasn't going to quit.

I'd fight to the very end.

Then I saw the Phants.

The evil, malicious mist edged along the tunnel wall, seeping past the slug.

The sight made me shrivel inside.

So much for not quitting.

There was nothing we could do now.

We were, essentially, doomed.

"I'm out of ammo!" Fan said.

Like I said . . .

A heavy blow from behind sent my mech stumbling forward, toward the Phants.

The blow came again, and I collapsed entirely.

I tried to move, but couldn't.

Multiple crabs had my ATLAS pinned.

Ahead, the remaining crabs parted to allow the Phants through . . .

I heard two thuds, and the weight shifted above me so that I was free.

"Fan?" I said, starting to rise. Crabs still clung to Battlehawk, but there were too few to pin down the mech.

"That was not me," Fan answered.

An inhuman cackle echoed above my head, then Queequeg landed in front of me, green steam rising from multiple wounds in his matted fur. His teeth were bared, and he growled defiantly as two crabs flowed off my mech and backed him toward the others. One of the Phants veered toward him.

Feeling a sudden rage, I grabbed the closest crab and dragged it toward me as I rose to my full height. I crushed it underfoot, splattering its innards across the floor. I turned toward the other crab that threatened Queequeg, and bashed it against the wall with my fist. Its carapace burst into a meaty mess.

No one touches my hybear.

Queequeg leaped away from the Phant and ducked underneath the carapace of a crab as its pincers moved in to grab him. He deftly maneuvered to the other side of the crab and leaped up, clasping its umbilical cord between his jaws and biting down, severing it.

The crab collapsed.

Queequeg sidestepped another blow from behind, tearing off one of the heads of a third crab before leaping away.

I bashed my way to his side, then Queequeg and I slowly retreated from the Phants, fighting our way back.

"The Yaoguai. They come!"

Fan was right.

The mists were gaining.

We weren't going to make it.

No.

We *were* going to do this. We were going to win. I didn't know how, but we would. I had to believe that. Otherwise I'd just give up right there.

Then a crab got Queequeg.

Right in the belly.

Tore his body in half.

He looked at me as he fell.

One last time.

His eyes pleading.

Master.

Help me.

But I couldn't.

It was too late.

There was nothing I could do for him.

Queequeg put his head down and closed his eyes for the last time.

I watched as my valiant friend, my heroic companion for these past eight months, died hideously, having laid down his life for me.

A blind rage filled me, and I fought, fueled by hatred and revenge. I killed the crab that got him, and I tore a path through the remainder. Just killing, killing everything.

I turned around and approached the slug, and the Phants. I wanted to face them. Wanted so badly.

Kill Queequeg, would you? Kill my best friend, my only *friend, in the world?*

They were going to pay.

I was going to slaughter every last one of the things.

The glowing mists closed on me from both flanks, but I dove past them, aiming straight for the slug.

I activated my jumpjets in a full-bore horizontal blast. I leaned forward and slapped my hands together in front of me, forming a pointed wedge with my fingers, effectively converting Battlehawk into a big torpedo.

I was going to tear a path into the slug and rend its body to shreds from the inside out. I was going to hack through its heart, carve up its lungs, rip open its entrails.

I was going to show them what happened when you messed with my friends.

But when I collided with the slug, my metallic body crumpled against the tough skin, and then I was flung backward.

I hadn't penetrated.

Hadn't harmed the thing in the least.

I lay prone, stunned and disappointed, on the ground.

The Phants closed. The slug remained motionless—I had the impression it was holding back, saving me for the alien mists.

I forced myself to rise, feeling beaten.

But I wasn't going to quit. Not yet. Though I sorely wanted to.

I couldn't, or Queequeg had died for nothing.

I activated my jetpack, zooming away from the Phants, and the slug.

I landed amid the crab horde, and I started slogging my way through the morass of mandibles and pincers. I felt like a helpless larva hurled into the center of an anthill, trying to make my way off the hill while the swarming ants relentlessly attacked.

All my limbs felt extremely heavy now. I don't know if it was because of the crabs hanging from my body, or the consecutive damage inflicted by them. One of my headlamps winked out.

I just kept swinging my arms and lifting my legs, plowing onward.

I saw another slug at the periphery of my reduced light cone, blocking the rearward path, too.

More Phants edged past it.

So this was it.

My last stand.

I was hemmed in on all sides.

My only regret was that another human being would have to die with me. If there was a way I could've saved Fan, I would have gladly chosen that path. But there wasn't.

Unless . . .

"Fan, are you still there?"

"Yes."

A crab leaped at my face. I grabbed two of its legs, and pulled crosswise, tearing the limbs clean away. Then I gave the carapace a good kick, sending it tumbling into the next wave.

"How have you survived so long?" I said into the comm.

Fan chuckled. "I wedged myself between the jetpack and upper back of your mech. They do not realize I am here."

"Way to fight like a man," I said.

"I am an engineer, not a warrior."

"Whatever. You're military. I know that now."

Another crab bit into my right arm. A big one.

I slammed it into the cave wall twice, cracking its carapace open. "Fan, I'm letting the mists take Battlehawk. The Yaoguai."

"*What?*" The terror was evident in his voice.

I bashed a third crab aside. "It's what they want. It's the only way out. For you, anyway. I'm not sure if I'll make it. Stay alive if you can."

"They are demons. You will die. I will die. Hideous deaths."

A fourth crab bit into my thigh.

"We're dead anyway," I told him. "Stay hidden, and you might live."

I bashed the crab aside, and then I turned toward the closest Phant.

"Wait, Shaw Chopra!" Fan exclaimed. "You cannot do this! Just because you have lost your pet—"

I barreled through the crabs and leaped into the alien vapor.

CHAPTER THIRTEEN

Rade

The universe had changed.

Humanity, once considered the dominant species in the galaxy, had abdicated its throne.

The galaxy, once our playground, was ruled by a technologically superior race, leaving us confined to the sandbox of our homeworld.

Subservience was not in our nature. Not in *my* nature.

But here I was, trapped on Earth, living a life that was not my own. A victim of circumstance.

"You're a bit introspective tonight, Rade," Shaw said.

"Introspective?" I dug into a piece of venison. "No. I'm downright pensive."

"What's on your mind?" she said.

"Ah, nothing."

"Still miss the Navy, don't you?" she said.

I was a hunter now. I caught and cleaned my own food. I lived a simple life. The only concern I had was feeding myself and my wife with what the woods provided. Gone were the days when I piloted steel monsters into battle against creatures from nightmare, fighting side by side with men closer to me than brothers. Gone were the days of endless drills and PT and carbohydrate-dense food. Gone was the camaraderie. The warrior spirit.

I'd given it all up. Asked the Chief to transfer me to a different Team, and shortly after that I'd quit. I was deported at the end of my deployment, and the war ended without me. Not in humanity's favor.

As for Shaw, she had been a prisoner of war, but was returned by the enemy as a token of goodwill. We were together again, and living out our lives in peace.

I was happy.

At least, that's what I told myself.

Shaw got up and went to the window of the log house to stare at the countryside beyond. The setting sun tinted her face a winsome orange. She looked so beautiful standing there in the waning light.

I couldn't believe I was contemplating leaving her.

She rested a hand on her belly, which swelled with the pleasant hump of pregnancy. "We moved out here to get away from it all, but you have too much time on your hands now, and all you do is sit and think about the past. Maybe we should go back to the city? Get a serving robot. Get food vouchers. Live the way everybody else lives."

I shot her a look. "You know very well why we don't live in the city. We're safer out here."

"The war is over, Rade. Humanity surrendered. We gave up our ships and agreed to reside on Earth. The cities are safe now. Humanity won't be attacked again."

I set down my fork. Maybe a little too hard. "There's no way I'm moving out to the city, not with all those Burrowers under the surface. You know they're attracted to populated areas. Sure, they've left humanity alone. For now. But as far as I'm concerned they could emerge again at any time. So no, we can't go back." I paused. "Not you and the baby, anyway."

Shaw lifted her hand from her belly and turned from the window so that half her face was cast in shadow. "What are you saying?"

I couldn't hold her gaze. "Nothing."

I concentrated on the deer meat. Sliced a piece. Ate it. Methodically cut off another piece. I felt Shaw's piercing eyes on me the whole time.

"If you want to go, then go," she said, her voice barely above a whisper. "I've never held you back. And I won't do it now. But believe me when I say this: there's nothing for you out there."

I slowly met her eyes. "Maybe you're right."

She opened and closed her mouth, like she wanted to tell me something, then she looked back out the window. "Such a beautiful evening. How warm do you think it is tonight?"

I sliced off another slab of meat. "I don't know."

"Check your Implant."

"Fine."

HUD on, I thought.

The aReal built into my head, otherwise known as my Implant, overlaid a log-on window across my vision. A typical log-on session lasted two weeks, and it must have just expired, requiring me to reenter my access credentials.

Automatically, I started thinking my password.

Alejandro—

Something stopped me. I'm not sure what.

"No," I said.

Shaw smiled patiently. "No?"

"Check the weather with your own Implant," I said defiantly.

She came forward, and rested a tender hand on my cheek. "I had my Implant permanently removed. Don't you remember, honey?"

"Well, I'm sure we have another aReal around here somewhere." I don't know why I was being so uncooperative. She just wanted me to check the weather after all.

"Sweetie, we gave all that stuff away before we left the city. The only way we keep in touch with the world and our friends is through your Implant. Speaking of which, I want to send Lindsay an e-mail. Would you mind?"

I sighed. "Fine."

I started thinking my password again.

Alejandro has—

Again something stopped me.

I glanced at her. "Who's Lindsay?"

She furrowed her brow. "Don't play this game. Lindsay, my friend from bootcamp."

"You're talking Navy bootcamp? As in Basic?"

Shaw rolled her eyes. "What other bootcamp would I be talking about?"

I thought back. Shaw and I took Basic together. We were in the same recruit division. "I don't remember anyone named Lindsay from Basic," I said slowly.

"You don't?" Shaw said mockingly. "Are you telling me you knew the name of everyone in Basic? That's what I thought. E-mail please."

"Why don't I remember you ever sending an e-mail to Lindsay before?"

Shaw frowned. "You've been having a lot of trouble with your memory lately. Tell me, what were you doing one week ago? A month? You don't know, do you?"

"Of course I know," I said. "Last week, I—" She was right, actually. "That's strange, but I can't recall . . ."

"It's the accident," Shaw said.

"The accident?"

"Look, do we have to do this now?" Shaw said. "I just want to send an e-mail."

I crossed my arms. "Not until you tell me what's going on."

Her face darkened and she turned away.

A deep rumbling came from outside, like the beginning of a long earthquake.

I heard branches and twigs breaking in the distance, followed by a familiar clattering.

"Get to the cellar," I told Shaw.

My old-school rifle lay against the wall by the door. I grabbed it and hurried outside.

By the light of dusk, an alien crab approached the log house from the woods. It was a smaller one, about as big as my body.

I lifted my rifle, aimed at the place where an eyestalk joined one of its multiple heads, and fired. The thing splattered.

Another crab came. Another. I shot them too. Methodically, just as methodically as I had eaten dinner.

As more of them appeared, I began targeting the cords, which, when severed, killed them just the same.

But the things kept coming.

Shoot a crab. Aim at the next. Shoot. Aim. Shoot. Aim.

There were too many of them.

It was hard to see in the dim light. If I logged on to my Implant, I might be able to target them faster, because then the crabs and their cords would be outlined in red.

For some reason, I resisted that idea.

I was forced to retreat inside the house; mandibles and claws snatched at the air behind my back.

I slammed the door.

Shaw hadn't gone to the cellar like I'd told her to.

Well, too late for that now. She was always headstrong.

"Barricade the door!" I said.

With Shaw's help, I upturned the table and rammed it against the door.

A claw smashed through the nearby window, and I shot it. Another claw appeared. Then the window on the opposite wall shattered. Mandibles poked through.

The house was surrounded by the things.

"Rade, use your Implant!" Shaw said. "Call for help."

I pulled up the log-on screen.

Alejandro has his—

I froze. I glanced at her. There was an eager sheen in her eyes.

"HUD off," I said aloud, and the log-on screen vanished.

"What have you done?" Shaw said.

Abruptly the entire roof sheared off.

Above us, a giant slug slammed its body downward like a bludgeon.

I knew none of my bullets would ever pierce it, but I fired anyway.

That ponderous body continued downward unhindered—

I woke, drenched in a cold sweat.

A dream.

I sighed in the darkness, then I blinked away the mist from my eyes, trying to get my bearings.

I was in a bed. It felt frigid, though I was covered in multiple sheets.

The bed shifted as someone moved on the mattress beside me.

That same someone rested a hand on my forehead.

"The dreams again?" A woman's voice.

Shaw?

Momentarily confused, I stared at her outline in the dark.

"I thought they'd stopped," the woman said, sitting up. The room brightened slightly.

Yes, it was Shaw. She reached toward the nightstand beside her.

I rubbed my eyes, and accepted the glass of water she offered me.

I staggered sleepily from the bed and went to the bathroom. The lamps detected my movement and the light level subtly increased along my route, providing barely enough illumination to see by.

I washed my hands in the sink and splashed my face in cold water. I slapped my cheeks. Not a dream.

"What's going on, Rade?" I said to my reflection.

I returned to the bedroom, and went to one of the windows. I stared at the darkened countryside outside; the house was surrounded by pines, willows, and other forest trees. My eyes drifted upward, to the starry sky.

Shaw came up from behind and embraced me. I could feel her baby bump press into my side.

"Shaw, tell me something," I said. "Do you ever get the feeling humanity was meant for more than this?"

"Than what?"

"We're restricted to our homeworld, yet we have the technology to travel to the stars. We should be up there, not trapped down here."

"But this is where we belong," Shaw said.

I didn't answer.

"Do you love me?" she said.

"I do."

"Would you do anything for me?"

"I would."

"Then come back to bed. You have a family now. A wife who loves you. An unborn child who needs you. Humanity doesn't want you to fight anymore."

"You're right," I said. "But something just seems . . . I don't know, off, somehow. Why is my memory so fragmented?"

Shaw's face became grave. "You know you've suffered selective amnesia since the accident. Your memories will return someday. The doctor promised they would. Do we need to see him? Am I losing you again?" A slight air of hysteria crept into her voice.

I pursed my lips. "No, honey."

She appeared relieved. "Good. Now come back to bed."

She led me back, and I closed my eyes.

Shaw fell asleep first. I knew because of the shift in her breathing.

Except, it wasn't *her* breathing.

I'd slept with Shaw countless times on the *Royal Fortune*. Heard her breathing beside me as she napped in the dark. Always her breath came in smooth, continuous patterns.

But there was nothing smooth and continuous about her breathing tonight: she paused briefly between each breath, like someone with a strange form of sleep apnea.

I dismissed it as a figment of my imagination. My memory wasn't right. We'd just discussed that. Maybe her sleeping and breathing patterns had changed after the ordeals she'd experienced as a prisoner of war.

Still, before I drifted off, I couldn't shake the uncanny sensation that the woman lying beside me looked like Shaw, sounded like Shaw, acted like Shaw . . .

Yet was *not* Shaw.

The next day I got up early and bid her a silent farewell as she slept. I noticed the apneic pauses again. Without sleep fogging my mind, those pauses seemed even more pronounced to me, and I convinced myself it wasn't really Shaw.

I abandoned her and the house because I wanted answers. I didn't really know where I'd go. In the dream, I'd told Shaw the cities were unsafe. Except that wasn't me talking, but rather the voice of my nightmares.

So the city, then.

I'd find my answers there.

I trekked through the woods to the nearest highway. I followed the deserted road for at least two hours, and finally arrived at a small French town. I asked for directions to the military entrance processing station. No one had a clue what I was talking about.

"There is no military, *mon ami*," one of the locals explained to me. "Not anymore. It has been outlawed for years, no? There are no wars anymore, no killing. We do not need a military. That is one thing you can't deny, about the Invaders. Despite everything, they've brought peace to the world."

"But at what price?" I said.

The local lowered his eyes. He didn't have anything to say to that, because he knew the price. Of course he knew. We all did.

Our humanity.

After a few hours of trudging unsuccessfully about the small town, I found myself at the bus station. I planned to secure a ride to a bigger city, but as I explored the station I realized all the platforms were empty. No buses. It seemed our humanity wasn't the only thing the Invaders had stripped away: they'd taken our transportation infrastructure, too. Though that was intrinsically linked to our humanity, wasn't it?

As I left the bus station behind, who should approach from down the street but Shaw, gripping the underside of her pregnancy hump as if her unborn baby were the most incredible of burdens.

"There you are!" she said. "I was worried sick. Are you happy now? Are you done? Can we go home?"

I banished the guilt I felt. "This isn't real. You're not Shaw, and I don't know who or what you are." I said those words as much for myself as for her. She couldn't be real. None of this could.

Yet a part of me knew that it was.

The world had fallen.

Humanity was a slave species.

What I once was—a MOTH, a member of the most elite spec-ops units in the galaxy—I could never be again.

No one could.

"Why do you say such things?" Shaw said. "You promised me you were well. That things would go back to the way they were before."

I touched my temples, searching for the unseen aReal that covered my eyes, but there wasn't one. "Whatever you're trying to do to me, it won't work."

"I'm not trying to do anything!" Shaw said, close to tears. "When are you going to understand that? Just stop this lunacy and come back home. Please, Rade, as your wife, I'm asking you. Begging you. Come home. For me. For your unborn son."

"I'm not going back with you. You're not my wife." I turned around, and started walking toward the center of town. The streets were oddly empty around me, as if the residents had shut themselves away in anticipation of some coming storm.

"Please don't do this, Rade," Shaw said behind me.

I didn't stop. I didn't look back.

The ground began to rumble. Around me, buildings collapsed inward.

The alien crabs from my nightmares emerged from multiple sinkholes. I backed away, but they came at me from all directions.

If I was going to die, I would do it fighting.

I raised my fists. "Come on, you pieces of—"

But the crabs weren't concerned with me. They passed right by. Their long cords trailed behind them, connected to a slow-moving slug. If they didn't want me, then what—

Shaw.

They wanted Shaw.

"Shaw, run!" I said.

But she didn't move.

For some reason I was frozen too.

The crabs halted, forming a circle around Shaw roughly a pace in diameter. Their mandibles clattered at the air and their claws snapped, but they made no further movements toward her. It was as if she was protected by some invisible barrier the alien entities could not penetrate.

The crabs on one side parted, making way for a blue Phant. It floated, in gaseous form. The Phant should have appeared as a liquid under Earth temperature and pressure. Yet there it was.

The glowing vapor drifted closer to Shaw. There was nowhere she could run. She was going to suffer the same fate as Big Dog and Alejandro, incinerated at the hands of a malevolent alien species whose motives I did not understand. Could never understand.

"Good-bye, Rade," Shaw said, reaching toward the glowing vapor.

"Shaw, no!" I still couldn't move. "Shaw!"

The Implant log-on window overlaid my vision.

Somehow I knew if I thought my password she would be all right.

Everything would. We'd go back to our home in the woods and live out our lives in peace, left alone.

Our home in the woods . . .

We didn't *have* a home in the woods.

"It's not real," I said.

The vapor touched her.

The scream I heard was very real.

———

Darkness.

I was naked, cold.

I felt a throbbing pain at the back of my head. I touched it, expecting to find a warm, wet wound surrounded by matted hair, but instead my fingers contacted a cold, metallic knob. About the size of a bottle cap, it was grafted right into my skull. I tried to rip it off, and gritted my teeth at the pain, but it would not budge. I stopped, worried that if I succeeded I'd pull out a chunk of brain tissue in the process.

I clambered to my feet. The floor, or deck, or whatever it was, felt frigid. Not a metal kind of cold. But stone.

I took a tentative step forward and bumped my knee against a hard surface in the darkness. A wall, also made of smooth stone.

I wasn't on a ship, then.

"Hello?" I said. "Somebody? Anybody?"

I held my breath and listened for long moments. I heard nothing. Absolute silence.

My first instinct was to check my Implant to see if I could bring up a map of my surroundings.

HUD on, I thought.

I was presented with the log-on screen to my embedded ID.

Wait a second. The device should still be deactivated, guarding against the mind-numbing flood of garbage data from the Phants.

And yet, someone had rebooted it.

Was I still in the dream? And if so, where did the dream end and reality begin?

Again I felt the urge to log on, but I resisted because I knew that's what my captors wanted. There were devices out there that could monitor the neural clusters that fired when a man thought the words and characters of his password. Devices like the metallic knob attached to my skull at this very moment.

Why would anyone want access to my embedded ID? For one thing, courtesy of the Implant, it contained a log of everything I'd seen and heard since implantation. The data was encrypted and inaccessible without the password. The encryption could be cracked via a brute-force attack, but it took a very long time.

HUD off.

They had tried to get to me using Shaw.

Damn it. She was the one person more precious to me than anyone else. What they had done in my dream somehow cheapened what we had together. They had invented a fiction, and made her my pregnant wife. What a gross perversion of her memory.

She was dead.

She'd never be my wife.

Shaw. My Shaw.

I could hear her voice in my head even now.

"Remember me in the deepest, darkest hours, when you think you can't go on. Remember me in the storm."

The first time she'd told me those words was after Basic, as her way of helping me through MOTH training. The second time was before the *Royal Fortune* Gated back to Tau Ceti, leaving her behind in the Geronimo star system, eight thousand lightyears away.

It was the last thing she ever said to me.

They'd constructed a false world in my head to trick me into revealing my password. With the proper tech, reading random memories to use as building blocks for that false world was relatively easy, but extracting something as specific as an embedded ID password . . . well, if you didn't know the engrams to target, that could take years. There were over one hundred billion neurons in the brain, with an exponential amount of neural connections and pathways between them.

I probed the darkness with my bare fingers. As I did so, I wondered if the chamber really *was* dark, or whether my bio-printed eyes had simply failed on me. Damn that Dr. Banye.

It didn't take long to map out my surroundings. I was confined to a square compartment cut into the stone. I could barely touch the ceiling if I jumped with my fingers outstretched, and when I held my arms out in front of me, I could only walk a pace in any direction before running into stone.

There was a metallic ring embedded in one wall, with a rope secured to it. Following the rope with my hands, I discovered it looped over an old-style pulley system in the ceiling. The free end of the rope dangled down into the center of the room, capped by a harness of some sort that hung just above my head.

I sat on the floor, knowing the pulley and harness couldn't be used for anything good.

A narrow slot abruptly opened in the base of the wall across from me, and a blinding ray of light shone inside.

"Hello?" I said, hurrying toward the light, shielding my eyes with one hand. "Hello!"

A bowl slid through the opening, and the slot promptly slammed shut.

"Wait! Where am I?" I felt around in the dark. The afterimage of the light was burned into my retinas. At least my eyes were working, then.

I discovered the featureless metal panel where the light had come in, a panel about the size of my forearm in length and width. I had missed it in my initial probings, due to its proximity to the floor.

I tried digging my fingertips into the edges, but couldn't find purchase.

I pounded at the panel three times. "I have to use the head! The washroom!"

I hammered it again. "I have to—"

The slot opened a crack.

"Defecate in the bowl when you are finished eating," a robotic voice said in perfect English.

"Where—"

The panel slammed shut, and I knew only darkness once more.

I groped blindly until I found the bowl, led as much by my sense of smell as anything else. I held it to my lips and slurped the thick contents. Bland, tasteless, watered-down gruel. But it was food.

When I was done, I set the bowl on the stone floor and carried out my other bodily functions. It was true what they say about your other senses being enhanced when you lose sight—never had my fecal matter smelled so bad. I had nothing to wipe with except the edge of the bowl, which wasn't very effective. I did my best to ignore the itching. I tried to pretend I was back in MOTH training, where the constant itch of sand down my pants from doing the Gingerbread Man felt way worse than this. I could almost hear the voices of the instructors:

Get wet and roll in the dunes! Roll, you dumbasses!

Believe it or not, I actually missed those days.

I relocated the panel in the dark, and set the stinking bowl in front of it. I waited, ready to grab the hand of whoever—or whatever—reached inside to retrieve it.

The slot eventually opened.

Ready to pounce, I squinted in the light.

No hand appeared.

Instead, the bowl simply slid through the slot of its own accord. Magnetized, apparently.

I considered shoving my arm through the slot after it, but I didn't like the idea of amputation.

The panel sealed, leaving me in a world of darkness once more.

I huddled against the stone wall with my legs bent, arms wrapped around my thighs, head resting atop my knees. I don't know how much time passed. An hour, maybe two.

And then . . .

The stone walls flared a blinding white, and I was forced to shield my eyes with one hand. I retreated to the far corner, cowering like a caged dog.

I heard the sound of stone grating on stone, like the lid of a sarcophagus sliding open. I squinted, peering through the cracks in my fingers, and I saw a figure calmly waltz into the room. The light from the walls was too blinding for me to perceive anything more than a silhouette. I thought the figure was a woman, though.

"What is your embedded ID password?" she said in the accent of a Sino-Korean.

I didn't answer.

Before I knew what had happened, I found myself quivering against the far wall, with waves of pain passing up and down my body. I was certain I'd been shot in the belly with an illegal helo-round, a bullet that sprouted six blades and rotated lengthwise after embedding, literally chewing up my insides.

Amazingly, the pain receded.

Without looking, I reached down and touched my abdomen. I felt no entry wound of any kind. I was uninjured.

"This is the Snake," the woman said.

I squinted at her in the bright light, and realized she held a rod of some kind.

"All I have to do is point it at your body, and squeeze. Then you feel its bite." She paced in a half circle before me. "Perhaps you have noticed the knob attached to the back of your head? In addition to monitoring your thoughts by piggybacking atop the existing web of carbon nanotubes you call an 'Implant,' the knob links the Snake to your brain, giving me direct access to the pain receptors of your thalamus via transcranial magnetic stimulation. Science is such a wonderful thing. With it, one can cure the most horrible of diseases. Or inflict the most horrible of pains. Can you imagine, a device that lets me induce currents in a select mass of neurons via a rapidly changing magnetic field? I'm so glad I was born in this day and age, in this time of wonders. Because the Snake is indeed a wonder. To be respected. Feared.

"Traditional pain is so inefficient. When one cuts into flesh, or burns it, eventually the neurons that signal pain to the brain are severed and numbed. Or the body part bleeds out, resulting in the same thing. But with direct access to the brain, none of that happens. Ever. I can inflict the worst kind of torment imaginable, without damaging the body. Of course, there is a chance the heart could stop, as the sheer agony causes the brain to amp the adrenals sky-high, but that is completely treatable. The best part? The pain receptors in your thalamus never dull. Meaning I can apply the Snake again. And again. *And again.*"

She tossed me a dirty, used rag. "The first sting was a light one. To introduce the two of you. I would like to demonstrate the full power of the Snake. I suggest you bite down on the cloth. If you value your tongue, that is. Of course, we can forego all of this if you reveal the password to your embedded ID."

I balled up the rag and stuffed it into my mouth defiantly. It tasted of iron. Blood from the previous victims.

The woman's silhouette pointed the Snake at my groin.

Agony exploded inside me. It was like I'd dipped my gonads into a nest of bullet ants, whose bite constituted the most excruciating venom in the world. Imagine fire-walking on coals embedded with rusty nails. Now do it again, dragging a certain sensitive area between your legs across those coals and nails.

Baring my teeth, I clamped down on the cloth. Didn't help. One of my molars, a rotten one that I should've had fixed months ago, shattered from the pressure. Because of the wide, rictus shape of my mouth, the tooth passed outward, slitting my lip. I hardly noticed. How could I? Not when the bullets of a Gatling gun tore into my nether regions, unwinding tubules, dissecting vesicles. The pain resonated upward, into my gut, and aggravated the whole area. My heart pounded against my chest so hard I thought it was going to burst any second. At least if that happened, I would find release. Until she revived me.

The whole time I was vaguely aware of a bunch of loud clicks, like the hum of a 60 Hz transformer, coming from the knob behind my head.

The sound of my brain frying.

I wanted to fall down. I wanted to shield myself. But the pain was too much, and all I could do was convulse in place, like a rag doll struck by twelve thousand volts, kicking and thrashing. I couldn't breathe. My eyes were shut tight, but my vision was tinted blood red from the glaring light that so easily penetrated my eyelids.

All I could think again and again in my mind was, *Morphine! Morphine! Morphine!*

Consciousness started to ebb away, but then, as quickly as it had come, the agony ceased.

I doubled over and spat out the cloth, inhaling violently. When I exhaled, a long stream of blood and drool trickled downward, connecting me to the floor. I felt secondary waves of ghost pain, which soon subsided, until the only hurt I felt was from my cut lip and burst molar.

"There, there," the woman said, patting me on the head like an owner who felt guilty after punishing her dog. "It's over now. You're going to be okay."

Panting raggedly, I clung to her leg, struggling to keep myself upright. When I had recovered somewhat, I pushed away, wanting to put some distance between myself and this evil woman.

"I am Jiāndāo," the woman said. "Your Keeper."

"Jiāndāo," I repeated weakly.

"Yes. The name means 'dagger' in your tongue."

"Dagger."

"Yes," she purred. "Dagger. And your name is Floor."

"Where am I?"

"It does not matter, Floor," she said matter-of-factly.

"What happened to the man captured with me?" Hijak.

"It does not matter. All that matters is you reveal the password to your embedded ID. Do so, and all of this ends."

She waited.

Squinting, I regarded her silhouette in the brightness. I knew I'd never be able to wrench the rod from her hands in time. Not before she inflicted the pain again.

Still, I had to try.

I lunged.

Too slow, of course.

It was like I was back in MOTH training all over again, except the pain was no longer self-inflicted, and hurt so terribly more than anything in training ever had. I don't need to describe it again. We are all human beings. We have all experienced pain. It comes with the territory. You cannot be human, and not know pain.

And as with all moments of agony, it passed.

When she released me, I lay there, cowering in the corner, panting, covered in my own vomit. Somehow I'd avoided biting off my own tongue.

I dearly hoped, with all my being, that she wouldn't apply the Snake again. I was almost ready to tell her anything.

Except the password to my embedded ID.

"Floor, are you listening?" the Keeper was saying. "Floor?"

I nodded slowly.

"I want to tell you a story," she said. Her tone was mockingly sweet. "The story of us. When you first came here, we sent you to the Weavers. You refused to give up your password, so the Weavers administered scopolamine. As you may or may not know, the substance renders its victims extremely susceptible to suggestion. But the drug had little effect on you. Maybe because of your training, which graduates only the strongest men, or maybe because of some innate resistance, but whatever the case it did not work, other than to promote memory loss.

"Next we tried the Simulation. Again, you resisted. Your mind kept throwing up barriers to protect you, drawing upon the horrors of your past to prove your present wasn't real.

"Finally, they sent you to me." Her silhouette tapped the rod against her thigh. Slowly. Methodically.

"Your will is strong," she continued. "I admit this. But I relish a challenge, and in the end I will break you, even if I have to resort to more traditional techniques. There is no need to continue resisting. No need to draw out the agony. You have proven your point. You are strong. A fierce, fierce man. But why prolong the inevitable? End it now. Find peace. Live a life free of pain. There is no dishonor in that, is there?

"So I ask again, what is the password to your embedded ID?"

Somehow I held out. Somehow I resisted.

I said aloud Shaw's words. "Remember me in the deepest, darkest hours, when you think you can't go on. Remember me in the storm."

The Keeper unleashed the Snake once again.

The interrogation continued like this for some time. It was getting harder and harder to refuse her after each bout of pain. To end it, all I had to do was log on to my Implant. Think my password. It was so tempting. Maybe if I was quick I could log on without the brain sensor picking up my password. Then I could message Hijak, if he was in range, and we could coordinate our escape. We could—

No. No matter how fast I was, the brain sensor would read my password.

There was no way out of this except to endure.

As I had endured in training.

The session ended, in time. The Keeper tied my wrists to the harness at the end of the rope above me, and left my limp body hanging like a piece of meat in the abattoir.

There I remained in the bright light, arms hoisted above my head, leather harness digging into my wrists. Ghost pain from the Snake lingered throughout my body. My broken molar throbbed.

What the hell had happened to me?

I was a MOTH, once.

More than a man.

I had piloted ATLAS mechs.

And now I'd been reduced to this.

Less than a worm. The plaything of a cruel mistress.

My name was "Floor." Something to be stepped on. Trodden over.

No.

I was still a MOTH. And always would be.

She was trying to break me. I couldn't let that happen.

Yet if that pain kept up . . .

Pain.

I'd grown soft since training. If I had been interrogated by her right after graduation, I wouldn't be having these thoughts. Hell, if this had *been* training, I wouldn't have even doubted my ability to resist. Because in training, I was ready to become a MOTH or die trying.

But the problem was, during training there was a light at the end of the tunnel. I knew that eventually it all had to end. But here, there was no such end.

I refused to die here, in some stone cell countless lightyears from Earth, as something less than a man. And that was how I *would* die, if I ceded to her will.

No, if I had to die, it was going to be as a MOTH.

I would resist. To the death if it came to it.

I wouldn't talk. I wouldn't reveal my password.

I wouldn't break.

My MOTH brothers were coming for me. I knew they were. That was going to be my light at the end of the tunnel. That was going to be the hope that got me through this. It would have to be.

Yet a seed of doubt took hold the moment I had that thought.

What if no one came?

What if my platoon brothers couldn't find me?

What if they didn't care?

I refused to believe that.

My platoon *would* come for me. Chief Bourbonjack, Facehopper, and the rest of my brothers wouldn't abandon me. No one was ever left behind.

But what about Shaw, came a dissenting voice from the recesses of my mind. *You saw how Big Navy abandoned her.*

I silenced that voice. I had to.

The Teams are different, I told myself. *We're not like Big Navy.*

Because if I believed for a moment that my platoon wouldn't come, I didn't think I could go on. Didn't think I could survive the humiliation, the torture. I'd just give up and die right here, rather than enduring what was to come.

I thought of what the Keeper had said about having direct access to the pain receptors in my brain. That was very illegal, and went against the tenets of the Fourth Geneva Convention. You didn't treat prisoners of war like this. No one did.

But since when did the SKs obey international rules? They'd actively encouraged privateering against UC ships for years, after all.

I wasn't sure how I was going to resist, not without losing my sanity. I thought back to the Code of Conduct all military personnel were to follow when captured. The code taught us how to conduct ourselves "honorably," as if there were such a thing when you were being tortured to death.

It went something like this: Never surrender. Make every effort to escape. When questioned, give only name, rank, and embedded ID number.

Easy, right?

That code seemed downright laughable to me about now.

The bright light was starting to get to me. There was no escaping it, not with my hands secured above my head. The rays penetrated straight through my scrunched eyelids, painting my vision a painful white-red, and causing my bio-printed eyes to itch and water. Snot streamed from my nostrils, and I was developing quite the migraine.

Just when I thought things couldn't get any worse, the braying music of some SK pop song blasted into the chamber. The thumping bass line rattled my ears and throbbed my chest. The high-pitched Korean-Chinese warbling of the "singer" didn't help matters, and grated on my nerves. Did I say music? I meant trash.

I couldn't even think anymore, not with that noise.

I was helpless. I simply hung there, my senses on overload, my body dangling above the stone floor, the harness digging into my wrists.

We MOTHs took pride in our ability to fall asleep on a whim, because there was no certainty when the opportunity might arise again.

But there was no way I could sleep now, not like this.

So I just hung there.

For how long, I don't know.

Hours.

Maybe a day.

Seemed like forever.

I kept telling myself my platoon brothers were coming. That they'd rescue me.

Yep.

Any time now.

The music shut off and the lights dimmed.

I tentatively opened my eyes, but the bright afterimage persisted, a chrome spot that blotted everything out. It was like I'd been hit with a flash grenade or a laser dazzler. My hearing was muted, too, and the approaching footsteps seemed muffled.

Someone unhitched the rope from the wall and lowered my body via the pulley, allowing me to rest on my knees. My arms still hung in the harness above me, supporting my upper body.

Vision slowly returned as my oversaturated retinal pigments normalized. I glanced upward, at my throbbing wrists. Bad move.

The movement made me dizzy, and I nearly blacked out. When the stars cleared, I saw my hands: swollen, purple messes.

I let my head sag back down.

"Are you comfortable, Floor?" Jiāndāo said, mockingly. "Are you pleased with your accommodations? If you have any requests, don't hesitate to contact the concierge."

I didn't look at her. Why would I? It would only egg her on. Besides, exhaustion filled me. That blinding light, that blaring music, my bindings, all of it had drained me to the core. The lack of sleep only compounded matters.

"You know," the Keeper continued, "during the Kang Dynasty, the Keepers used the Simulation to pluck the brain regions responsible for sight and sound during prisoner interrogations. It was considered . . . more humane. But when the dynasty fell, the traditional methods came back into favor. There's something about having a blinding light shone into one's eyes, and a braying song played into one's eardrums, that simply cannot be duplicated by direct visual and auditory stimulation."

She bent down in front of me and whispered in my ear. "But pain, well now, that's an entirely different matter. Direct pain, we all know how wonderful that is. Are you ready to experience the blissful release of direct pain, Floor?"

She slid the pronged tip of the Snake down my chest, somewhat erotically. I was just waiting for her to activate it. Dreading it.

"Of course," she whispered seductively. "If you tell me the password to your embedded ID, this can all end."

"I am Rade Galaal," I said, staring at the floor. "Petty Officer Second Class. Navy MOTH. Embedded ID number 527892540."

"Look at me," she said. "Look at me!"

I didn't. "I am Rade Galaal. Petty Officer Second Class. Navy MOTH. Embedded ID number 527892540."

"As you wish, Floor."

"I am Rade Galaal. Petty Officer Second Class. Navy—"

She set the prong of the Snake directly beneath my chin.

And gave me pain.

I won't describe what happened in the next few hours. No one likes to read about torture. All I'll say is that by the time she was done, my heart had to be restarted three times, courtesy of the portable defibrillator she'd brought along specifically for that purpose, and I nearly choked on my own vomit twice.

I never looked at her directly, not once. Never gave her that honor. Though I caught enough glances to know she was dressed in tight-fitting, blue-and-gray digital camos.

When it was finally over, she used the pulley to raise me up off the floor once more, then secured the rope to the metallic loop in the wall. My body stank from my voided cavities, but I was too far gone to really notice.

"I have heard MOTH training prepares a man for anything," she said. "And yet, do you know, I interrogated two MOTHs before you, using all the techniques of the Sino-Korean Keepers we have absorbed. Eventually, both MOTHs cracked. You knew them, I believe. Angus and Mortar of Bravo platoon."

"Impossible," I said. It had to be a lie. Those two had died on Geronimo, with most of Bravo platoon.

"The great MOTHs," she continued. "Who thought they were more than men, proved to be little more than weeping children in the end. Sniveling, groveling children, begging to obey. Begging to answer my every question."

"I don't believe you."

A hint of humor tinged her voice. "You have proven to be most resilient, Floor. But in the end, I will break you, as I broke them. As I broke Hijak."

She left. The door slab sealed, and the bright lights and blaring music returned.

I knew she had lied. Hijak would never talk. Nor would any other MOTH. It just wasn't possible.

Even so, another realization slowly dawned on me:

My platoon wasn't coming.

Either my brothers couldn't get to me, or they couldn't find me. Otherwise, they would have arrived already.

They are not coming.

I told myself these sessions were no different than what I had endured in training. That it was simply Trial Week all over again. I just had to buckle down and see it through.

But it *was* different. Because in training there was an end in sight, a glimmer of hope. But for this torture, the only release was submission. I had wanted to die as a MOTH, but not even death was an option, because the Keeper kept me alive no matter how many times my heart stopped.

If there was a hell, this was what it was like. I pitied the damned in that moment.

I pitied myself.

I held out for a week. Longer than could reasonably be expected.

My broken molar became infected. My hands swelled in the harness. But that pain was minor compared to the agony of the Snake.

I repeated Shaw's mantra when I came close to cracking, alternating it with the Code of Conduct answers for Missing-Captured personnel. "Remember me in the deepest, darkest hours, when you think you can't go on . . . I am Rade Galaal. Petty Officer Second Class . . ."

I had told myself MOTHs never gave up. That it just wasn't possible.

But in the end, no mantra, no mere words, could save me.

I had said I would die before I surrendered.

Well, I did die. I did.

My spirit, anyway.

The Keeper returned each day, and on the seventh, she seemed to have sensed something was different about my demeanor, because she lowered my body entirely to the floor and freed me from the harness.

When the bright afterimage faded from my vision, I stared at my swollen hands. My purple fingers were so distended I couldn't move them.

The Keeper cradled my head in her lap, and she fed me the gruel she had brought.

Thus far, I had never once looked at her face, even when the light levels were low like this.

I glanced up to meet her eyes for the first time.

She had an exquisite, chiseled face, reminding me of an ancient Greek sculpture of Athena I had once seen, though with Asian features. There was gentleness and concern written into her eyes.

"You're so beautiful," I said.

She smiled compassionately as she combed the matted strands of hair from my face. She truly cared about me.

"What is your password?" she said softly.

"Alejandro has his own star 5248241," I said simply.

There was pride in her eyes, the same pride a parent feels when she witnesses her child walking for the first time, I thought. The Keeper pressed her lips together and blinked away tears.

"Thank you." She released me and stood up. "Thank you." She went to the entrance. "You are a hero to your race. Your courage and loyalty will be remembered for generations to come."

She turned around, and before she left, I saw for the first time the long bar of metal grafted into her back. It ran along her neck from the base of the skull (the hair around it was shaved) and passed beneath her outfit, where I could see the bulge of the bar reach to the small of her back.

In the neck region, red droplets were scattered across the exposed surface of the metal: the glowing condensation of a Phant.

I blacked out.

I awoke, lying on a bed of some kind. The telescoping, spider-like limbs of a Weaver hovered above my pillow. The sensor light of the medical robot flashed blue.

I tried to sit up.

Tight straps bound me in place.

I resided in a crude, box-like metal compartment. Empty steel beds covered in foam mats faced me. There was no EKG. No IV tube jammed into the dorsal venous network of my hand.

This was a poor man's Convalescence Ward.

The rotten molar in my mouth had been replaced. I glanced at the thick straps that bound my torso and arms. My hands were no longer swollen from the wrists down. There were stretch marks along the skin of my hand, and crisscross scars where the harness had dug into my wrists, but otherwise I was healed up.

Physically, at least.

I heard the distant ambiance of a ventilation fan. That could indicate any number of things, though I had a tendency to believe it meant I was on a ship. Whether that was good or bad, I didn't know.

I glanced to my left. More empty beds.

I turned my head to the right.

Hijak lay there.

He was strapped down like me, two beds away. His face was very, very white, and his hands, like my own, had marks from previous swelling, and dark scars crisscrossing the wrists.

He was unconscious.

Hijak.

My heart went out to him. Forget our differences. Hijak was my platoon brother. My comrade-in-arms.

"Hijak," I said. "Hijak!"

His eyelids fluttered opened, and a long moment passed before his gaze focused on me with any recognition.

"Rage," Hijak said finally. His voice sounded raspy, like he hadn't sipped water in days. "I thought . . . you were dead."

"I thought I was dead, too."

"She said . . . she said she'd killed you. And she promised my parents were next." Hijak started weeping. "She said all the money they had wouldn't save them. She said she'd hang them up like pigs and skin them. I had to tell her, Rage. I had to."

The bastards. Torturing me was one thing, but torturing my platoon brother? That positively enraged me.

And yet I couldn't shake the terrible guilt I felt.

They broke me, too.

"It's okay now, Hijak. It's okay." I wanted to tell him I'd betrayed the platoon as well. And our country. But I couldn't. I was too ashamed.

His features twisted by shame, Hijak turned away from me. I saw he had a metallic knob attached to the back of his head, just like me.

Hijak. My brother.

The door to the ward opened.

Jiāndào stepped inside in all her dark splendor. She was wearing full makeup today, eyes outlined in dark purple, lips a pale red, forehead perfectly bronzed, cheeks rouged. The camos had been replaced with a sleeveless black dress with a low neckline that accentuated her breasts.

She had two military robots with her. They were the same as the MA (master-at-arms) robots the UC had, and looked similar to Centurions, but minus any uniforms. Their polycarbonate skins were a black tint, and around the rectangular boxes on the chests, where the brain cases resided, I saw the telltale blue droplets of Phant possession. Rifle stocks protruded from the holsters behind their heads.

"How sweet," Jiāndào said. "The two of you broke on the same day."

She leaned against the wall, a panther stretching her well-used claws. Jiāndào eyed us casually for a moment, resting the Snake comfortably in the crook of one arm.

My heart rate doubled just looking at the Snake, and I broke into a cold sweat. When I heard Hijak's breathing quicken beside me, anger and indignation abruptly overrode any fear I felt.

No one tortures my platoon brothers.

I was ready to spring at the tormenting bitch.

Unbind me. I dare you.

Jiāndào smiled slyly. "Don't worry, there is no pain today. If you behave." She glanced at the MA robots. "Prepare them."

The robots unstrapped me and Hijak from the beds.

I tried to lunge at Jiāndāo, but the robot was quicker. It slammed me down with inhuman strength and promptly electrocuffed me.

The same thing was done to Hijak beside me. No plasticuffs for us. Only the good stuff.

I scowled at Jiāndāo the whole time, but she affected not to notice.

We were escorted into the corridor outside. This was definitely a ship of some kind. SK make, judging from the Korean-Chinese characters outside the door.

Jiāndāo confidently took the lead in her low-cut dress.

My eyes were drawn to the metal bar drilled into her spine. I had thought I'd imagined the thing back in the brig, but it was very real. As were the drops of glowing red condensation scattered up and down the metal.

"You're one of them," I said.

She glanced askance, the hint of a smile on her lips, but she didn't say anything.

The metal bar reminded me of the knob attached to my own brain. How far was I from a fate similar to hers?

"Where are you taking us?" I said.

"The Guide wants to see you, Floor," she answered.

"The Guide?"

"Yes. The envoy to humanity."

Out here the main lights were dimmed, and the emergency system provided most of the illumination. The long twin tubes of blue LEDS built into the seams between the deck, bulkhead, and overhead gave everything a skeletal, wire-frame feel. It felt a bit like I was touring the insides of a liquid-cooled computer with all those gaudy tubules.

Otherwise the corridor wasn't so different from those found on UC starships, albeit a bit tight. The cramped metal bulkheads allowed Hijak and me just enough space to walk abreast. It was very claustrophobic. Shaw would have hated it.

There weren't any human crew about—theoretically, they would all be at duty stations. We did squeeze past a few unfriendly looking masters-at-arms robots on patrol.

We turned past a T intersection and ascended to an upper deck. Since my Implant was active, and logged in, I brought up my HUD map. On it, the ship's blueprint was represented by a black mass, with previously visited corridors filled out cookie-cutter style by the mapping software. Ahead of my position, the blueprint updated with each step I took. The software based the bulkhead delineations on my stereoscopic vision. When I glanced down side corridors, the software completed partial areas.

A few moments later I found myself on the bridge.

A man dressed in a captain's blue-and-white uniform stood before the main view screen. He faced away from us, his hands folded behind his back.

Wait a moment. This was no man, but an Artificial. SK variant.

The High-Value Target.

I noted its feet were fully repaired and intact. On the back of its neck, above the collar, I saw the telltale condensation of alien possession. Glowing, fat, purple drops.

Purple.

A purple Phant had killed my best friend, Alejandro.

The remaining members of the bridge crew included robot guards and a handful of humans, all SK. Nearly all the humans had long metal bars embedded in the back of their skulls and spines, and just like Jiāndāo, droplets of red condensation glowed from the grotesque grafts. Only two humans seemed unmodified, one an astrogator and the other a tactical officer, judging from their duty stations. These latter two very carefully refused to meet my eyes.

"Guide," Jiāndāo said. "I have brought them."

The Artificial known as the Guide did not shift its attention from the view screen, which was starless and black. Darker sections painted the blackness, delineating peaks, valleys, and craters. I thought it might be a planetoid that filled the view.

I glanced at where the tactical display should have been in the center of the room, but the holographic representation of the battle space was currently inactive, and all I saw was empty glass. Who knows, maybe it wasn't the tactical display at all—I wasn't on a UC vessel, after all.

"Humans are such easy things to break," the Guide abruptly said.

I exchanged a glance with Hijak. This was the envoy to humanity, and that was the first thing it had to say?

"Take something like this rock," the Guide continued. "Floating before us in space. Inanimate. Steered by the whims of gravity. Lifeless. No sentience whatsoever. And yet it requires such a vast amount of energy to break in two.

"One-tenth of that energy is needed to break a human being. Mostly, all one needs is time. Of all the species I have had the pleasure of vanquishing, humanity has proven the easiest thus far. Both physically, and mentally."

The Guide finally turned around. The Artificial appeared to be the spitting image of the Paramount Leader. Big lips, oily and pocked skin. Matted, balding hair. Entirely underwhelming, just like the real man. Indeed, the face was so realistic that it made me wonder if the Paramount Leader himself was an Artificial. Even the eyes were correct, with just the right amount of moisture, and that gleam of certainty all great leaders had. There was no "uncanny valley" here, that fine line between real and fake that caused repulsion in a human being if an Artificial's face was even slightly incorrect.

"It took me the longest time to understand human vocal patterns," the Guide continued. "Let alone speak. The engrams stored in the neural net of this Artificial helped, of course . . . the fibrillary random access memory had Korean-Chinese, English, and the more common languages of your race installed. I much prefer the original Korean-Chinese I have to admit, but English does have its charms. There are so many words for describing killing in English, just as if the language were specifically designed for the task. Slaughter. Butcher. Massacre. Assassinate. Exterminate. Slay. Raze. Destroy. Eradicate. Extinguish. And on and on. A warrior's tongue. Still, the inflections and phonemes feel unusual to me. In any case, once I had a solid grasp on the main languages, it was relatively easy to transmit my knowledge to the Learned, such as Jiāndāo. And then interpreting your documents and machinery became so much easier." The Guide took a step toward me. "I see the question on your face. Ask it."

"What are you?" I said, staring at the condensation on its neck.

"Ah. You refer to my composition in this universe, as it were. A gas when exposed to the void of space. A liquid within the pressurized environment of humankind. The simple answer is I am a multi-universe entity. What you see here in this liquid state, via the photons emitted to your ocular units from the constituent atoms of my form, is but a small fraction of my entire being, which spans countless dimensions that humanity cannot begin to fathom.

"Though we are not dissimilar from most life in the universe. Humans themselves are multi-universe entities. Your physical bodies comprise merely a tenth of your actual forms, but you don't even realize it: humanity has a way of blinding itself to the truth, relegating it to the level of an inconvenient headache. In any case, your species has developed a theory of matter called dark fluid. Tell me, have you heard of it?"

"No."

"I have," Hijak said quietly.

The Guide's eyebrows shot up. "Do tell."

Hijak gave me a hesitant look. "Dark fluid hypothesizes that the fabric of spacetime acts as a fluid. It coagulates, compresses, expands, and flows just like any other fluid, and when the fluid of spacetime contacts matter, it slows down and coagulates around it, amplifying the forces of gravity near it. The effect is only noticeable when you look at obscenely large masses, like galaxies—spacetime collects around those masses, and helps hold them together. But in places where there's hardly any matter, like the voids between the galactic superclusters, the dark fluid of spacetime relaxes, and starts stretching away from itself, becoming a repulsive force. Imagine three rocks representing galaxies in a shallow vat of molasses. The syrup—the dark fluid of spacetime—collects around the rocks, and in between them it stretches thin. That's dark fluid in a nutshell. The theory supersedes the theories of dark matter and dark energy, making them irrelevant."

"Bravo," the Artificial clapped mockingly. "Well done. Dyson Xang, is it? You have a keen mind. You will make a fine host. In any case, the space between Slipstreams is dark fluid. And that, in essence, is what we are."

"Your race exists in the space between Slipstreams?" I said.

The Artificial smiled patiently. "No. We *are* the space between Slipstreams."

I didn't fully understand, however, if I ever got home, maybe this tidbit might help the fleet scientists get a better handle on what we were dealing with.

"What about her?" I nodded at Jiāndāo. "She is human? Or alien?"

"Both. The physical part is human. The cognizant part is not. Somewhat similar to myself."

My eyes drifted to the metal bar grafted onto Jiāndāo's spine. "So she's a slave then. Her human part."

"A slave?" The Guide rapped its thumb against its chest. "Worse than a slave, I would say. After installing the necessary biomechatronic grafts to provide integration with the nervous system, the host body is ours to do with entirely as we please. Without the grafts, the bodies of most species in this universe incinerate on contact.

"When integrated via the graft, the host is still alive, though not in command of its mind and body. Its consciousness has effectively been replaced. It cannot think, nor move of its own accord. It is an experience similar to one of your fully immersive vids. Life plays before the eyes of the host, but the host itself is a spectator, nothing more.

"After the integration, we have access to some memories, but mostly it is a fragmented jumble. That's where the embedded IDs found in human beings come in quite handy. Your IDs store visual and auditory data from your Implants and external aReals in a fashion readily understandable by us, allowing us to retrieve the data at our leisure once we are in control of your bodies. Which is why we prefer to break a human before integrating him or her.

"By integrating with the members of a species, we can better understand how to vanquish them. But there is also a wonderful side benefit. As you may have noticed, we do not possess bodies of our own in this universe. It is a sublime thing to experience a species from their point of view. The galaxy is so much more vivid, and interactive, when you have a vessel capable of touch, of emotion, of taste."

"Except you're a robot," I said.

"This is merely one of my hosts," the Guide said.

"Why have you come?" I wondered how much more I could ask this "Guide," and why it was willing to entertain my questions in the first place. I had to remind myself that it had an entirely different way of thinking. Maybe some alien code of honor required the

Guide to brag about the capabilities of its race and reveal its intentions to every lifeform it planned to kill or integrate, I don't know. But as long as the Guide was receptive to my questions, I was going to keep asking them. "Why do you attack our worlds?"

"Isn't it obvious?" the Guide said. "Geronium. We feed upon it, and use it to power the great industry of our ships. Those entities you call Burrowers are engineered from the biomatter of this universe, yet exist partially in our own. We call them the Great Formers, and they have one specific purpose in mind: transform the crusts of planets into Geronium."

"Don't you have enough planets to transform in your own region of space?"

"The transformative process requires a planet populated by sentient lifeforms, as the multi-universe fields produced by such organisms are a major part of the process. These fields linger some Stanyears after a population has been terminated, and the Burrowers use them to process the crust into Geronium. In essence, the Burrowers digest what humanity would call the lingering 'souls.'

"When a suitable planet or moon is chosen for harvesting, a compatible species must first be assigned to the planet and bred. Terraforming or bioengineering is almost always involved, because while some species are better suited to certain planets than others, there is usually some disqualifying factor. Atmospheric pressure is too high, temperature is too low, gaseous ratios are off, and so forth. The process of terraforming and populating can take centuries. So, when we find a race that has done the hard work of colonizing planets for us, we are exhilarated. There is no better find. Of course we're going to come. Of course we're going to conquer. Thanks to humanity, we will have this whole region producing Geronium in under ten years. That will give us enough stores to last the next twenty thousand years, if you include the cache on our side of the galaxy.

"But humanity does not have to die out as a species. Obey us, and twenty percent of you will live: the twenty percent who contribute eighty percent of your societal output—the artists, engineers, scientists, and so forth. The remaining eighty percent of humanity, the unnecessary, superfluous dead weight, shall perish. We are doing you a favor, in actuality. Trimming away the fat, as it were."

Stunned, I just stood there for a few seconds. "Only twenty percent of humanity will live?"

"Yes. If you surrender. Otherwise less than one percent will be spared, to be used solely as breeding matter for Geronium production, and our entertainment."

I had to snicker at that. "Let's say we listen. We surrender. What happens to that twenty percent? The elite of humanity. Where will they live? Will they become hosts? Integrated, as you call it?"

"They will remain entirely human, and will live in peace on a designated planet. Perhaps your current homeworld, Earth. They will be given technology to increase their lifespan and quality of life. Everyone will be equal. All that we ask is the survivors obey us when the time comes, and let us draft capable men and women into our service. Do these things, and your place in the galaxy is secured."

I laughed. "So that you can eventually kill us or our descendants off for fuel? No thanks. Humanity will never agree to that."

"Some of you already have," the Guide said, nodding at the astrogator and tactical officer, who very carefully did not look back. As I mentioned, neither man had a steel bar grafted to his spine. "Why would you want to resist, anyway? Humanity will thrive under our tutelage. You will know an era of peace and prosperity unlike any you have ever experienced before."

"Yeah, as disposable breeders."

"When the time comes we will assign a small portion of your race to appropriate planets for breeding purposes, via a fair lottery. But that will be an age from now."

"The governments of humanity will never agree to any of this," I said. "Let me guess: you're going to take away our Gates, and our starships too?"

The Guide nodded. "You will be restricted to the designated home planet as part of the agreement."

I shook my head. "You can't take a space-faring people and knock them back to the stone ages. And you can't kill eighty percent of their population. The governments of humanity won't submit to either scenario. I'm sorry, this surrender isn't going to happen."

"Do you speak for all of humankind?" the Guide said, then nodded to itself when I didn't answer. "I thought not. If humanity surrenders, the quality of life enjoyed by your race will improve by a factor of ten. Billions of your people currently live in starvation and poverty, while billions more enjoy the comforts of limitless food and advanced technology. These 'haves' essentially live off the 'have-nots,' expending needless resources on such endeavors as colonization, when the time and energy could be better spent solving the problems of your homeworld.

"By reducing your population to twenty percent, we solve all these societal issues in one blow. In any case, a twenty-percent survival rate is much preferable to one percent. As the months pass, and the population of humanity continues to dwindle, the system governments will agree with my assessment. And they will surrender."

The Guide sat down in the captain's seat, and swiveled the chair toward me. "No doubt you have wondered why I have allowed you, a mere peon, to ask these questions. The answer is simple: I will let one of you go, so that he may report everything he has seen and heard. The one who returns will give his superiors full access to the data recorded in his embedded ID, and thus inform the United Countries and other empires of Earth they have one Stanyear to consider my offer. Meanwhile, my race will continue its advance, taking your colonies, making them our own. And if your people flee these colonies in excessive numbers ahead of our advance, we may steer toward the most populous planet in the region early. Yes: Earth. We want inhabited worlds, remember."

The Guide put his hands behind his head. "So. Now you have a choice. A dilemma, perhaps. Who will remain behind and become a host? And who will go free and spread the word of our generous offer? Choose, quickly. Or I will choose for you."

I stepped forward immediately. "Take me and let my brother go."

The Guide opened its mouth, but before it could say a word, Hijak came to my side.

"I'm not leaving you behind," Hijak said.

"You are." I gazed into his eyes. "It has to be me. You know it does. You're the caterpillar."

"I have a callsign now. Don't do this."

I swallowed. I realized I had to tell him why I was doing it or he'd never let me go. This was going to be hard. "I . . . I haven't treated you very well these past few months. I didn't think you deserved to be here. I was wrong. I had this coming, Hijak. Karma's a bitch."

Hijak shook his head. "You had every right to treat me the way you did. I had to prove myself. I'm still proving myself this very moment. When I signed up, I knew that someday I might have to make the ultimate sacrifice for one of my platoon brothers. I choose to make it now. I'm ready. Let it be me, Rage. *Me*."

"I can't. I won't." I raised my electrocuffed hands and gripped Hijak by the shoulder. "I have to do this. Besides, I outrank you. So I'm ordering you to stand down."

Hijak twisted from my grasp. "That's bullshit and you know it. We're the same rank. Sir."

"True. But I attained my rank before you. Seniority in grade, bro."

Hijak shook his head.

"Look, Hijak," I said. "You know why it has to be me? I was going to transfer to a different Team anyway. Probably quit, after that. My heart's not in this job, not anymore. We need real MOTHs. People like you. People ready to fight and die for what they believe in. People with *heart*. I don't have that anymore. My warrior spirit died with my friends."

Hijak wouldn't stand down. "And I'll tell you why it has to be me. I broke when the Keeper interrogated me, Rage. Broke. Betrayed the platoon. I can't live with what I've done. Not if I let you die, too. Let me do this. You have to. You deserve to live. Besides, you never know, maybe I'll be able to learn something about the enemy while I'm integrated. It'll be like an extreme undercover op, except with some crazy body modification. When you and the platoon come back for me, I'll have some stories to tell."

I shook my head. "You don't get it do you? There is no coming back from this. A steel bar grafted to your skull and spine, with a Phant shoving its incorporeal tendrils into your brain? No, Hijak, there's no return. You heard the Guide. You'll become worse than a slave. Look at these people. They're hardly more than machines now. I'm sorry, I've made up my mind." I turned toward the Guide. "I volunteer. Let him go."

"Very well," the Guide said.

"Sorry, sir," Hijak's voice came from behind me. "But you're forcing me to do this."

Something struck the back of my head with enough force to jar my teeth, and I fell to my knees. I groggily shook the stars from my vision.

I was vaguely aware as Hijak stepped past me. Even with his hands electrocuffed, he could still hit pretty hard.

"Take me and let Rage go," Hijak said.

The Guide spoke. "Well played, Dyson Xang." To the robots: "Take the one left standing."

I watched two masters-at-arms robots grab Hijak. "No." I said weakly.

The Guide ignored me, and glanced at Jiāndāo. "Oversee his integration."

Jiāndāo inclined her head.

"Hijak," I said, pleading.

Hijak glanced over his shoulder at me. "It's all right, Rage. They can't harm me now. No one can."

And then he was gone, led off the bridge by Jiāndāo and the combat robots.

I slumped.

"Rade Galaal," the Guide said. "Your jumpsuit will be returned, and you will be vented from an airlock. Once outside our ship, you will activate your Personal Alert Safety System. If you are lucky, one of your ships will pick you up before your oxygen runs out. If you are unlucky, you will die, and the UC will retrieve your body anyway, along with your embedded ID. Your military has the technology to access the ID without a password. A technology I will have very soon." The Guide smiled ironically. "It has been a pleasure."

Two robots led me from the bridge.

I didn't see Hijak in the corridor outside. However his Implant, like my own, was still active.

And he was logged in.

I watched his progress on my HUD map. He retraced the exact path we had taken from the Convalescence Ward. The dot representing Hijak descended to the lower deck, turned left onto the T intersection, and entered the closed-off hallway containing the ward. He proceeded into a side compartment across from the ward, and stayed there.

ISAAC HOOKE

Wards on UC vessels had similar layouts. Across from the recovery area there was always a small compartment set aside for intensive surgery.

I shut my eyes.

Hijak was going to be integrated with the Phants in a surgical process that would essentially kill who he was.

And it was my fault. I shouldn't have turned my back on him. Shouldn't have let him get the jump on me.

I arrived at a storage locker.

The robots opened the locker and tossed out the contents.

My jumpsuit.

"Dress," one of the robots commanded.

My electrocuffs clicked open and fell off.

I just stared at the jumpsuit. I couldn't take my mind off Hijak, nor the magnitude of my betrayal. I was leaving him behind. He was going to die.

The robots drew their rifles and trained them on me. "Dress."

I zipped on the "liquid-cooling and ventilation" undergarment. When I got to the actual jumpsuit, I activated my PASS device immediately, pretending it was part of the suit initialization procedure. It was questionable whether the signal would pass through the shielded hull of the vessel, and even if it did, the interference emitted by the Phants likely reduced the range. If the signal *was* detected, it would be quite a while before any nearby ships reached this location anyway.

When I was fully suited, I attached the life-support and jump-jet assemblies.

The robots led me to an airlock.

So this was it.

I was going to be unceremoniously flushed from the ship.

I would live.

And Hijak would die.

This wasn't right.

I couldn't leave him.

I couldn't abandon him.

Despite our differences, he was my platoon brother.

Abandonment wasn't part of our creed.

I surreptitiously unclasped the main buckles of my jetpack, and let the device hang over my jumpsuit by the shoulder straps alone.

The robots shoved me inside the airlock.

Before they could close the hatch, I turned around, slipped off the jetpack, and swung it toward them.

"Catch!"

I activated the jetpack remotely with my Implant, applying full forward thrust to double its momentum.

The jetpack slammed into the robots like a sledgehammer of steel and fuel.

The machines crashed into the opposite bulkhead.

I cut the power and the robots crumpled to the deck.

They didn't get up.

I glanced one last time at Hijak's location on my HUD map, doing my best to memorize the route. Then I thought the words to deactivate my Implant, because I knew a crippling burst of EM radiation from the Phants would probably fill my Implant with garbage data any second.

Zulu Romeo Lima.

The Implant shut off.

I opened my face mask and stepped from the airlock.

Drops of glowing liquid trickled onto the deck from the robot that had taken the brunt of the blow.

Keeping my eyes on the liquid Phant, I knelt to retrieve the disabled robot's rifle—

A hand abruptly wrapped around my boot and tripped me.

The other robot.

It was pinned beneath the first, but as I lay facedown on the deck, it reeled me in, drawing me toward it and the Phant.

I got in three good kicks with my strength-enhanced suit, and dented the robot's head enough for it to release me.

I scrambled away and hauled myself upright.

The robot tossed aside the deadweight of my jetpack and the second machine and started to rise.

It still carried its rifle.

If the weapon fired, regardless of whether the bullet hit or not, I was screwed because the ship's gunfire alert would sound.

Before the robot finished standing, I closed the distance between us, stepped down on the rifle with my strength-enhanced suit, and shoved the robot into the bulkhead.

The weapon tore from the robot's grasp and bounced on the deck. The tip of the barrel was now uselessly bent. It would still fire of course, though at forty-five degrees to the actual gunsights.

The robot launched itself on me, its fist aimed squarely at my unshielded face.

I managed to turn my head at the last moment, and the outer rim of my helmet absorbed most of the blow. I lurched backward and hit the bulkhead just behind me.

The robot launched another blow.

I dodged.

A small crater appeared in the bulkhead where the robot's fist struck.

I threw myself at the robot, hurling the two of us to the floor.

I landed on top.

I managed to grab its left arm and, putting the weight of my suit behind my grip, pinned the robot.

Its right arm came swinging in, aimed for my face.

I tilted my head to the side in expectation of a blow that did not come.

Instead of slamming its fist into me, the robot wrapped its polycarbonate fingers around my head and began pushing my helmet toward the deck.

I thought it was trying to break my neck, but when my cheek touched the deck, I realized the robot's intention: the glowing blue liquid from the first Phant seeped toward my face. I had maybe fifteen seconds before contact.

I shoved frantically against the polycarbonate arm, but the robot had me good. I couldn't move.

I slid my free hand along the robot's face, searching for one of the camera lenses by touch. I could feel the recesses and projections through my gloves when I pressed hard enough.

There. A lens.

Military-grade lenses were made of thick glass, so I wouldn't be able to break it with a mere glove, strength-enhanced or not.

But I had something else in mind.

I pointed the surgical laser in my fingertip into the lens. I got lucky, because this was my good glove. The other one had a melted laser port, courtesy of my encounter with the ATLAS 5 back in the ruins of Shangde City.

"Laser pulse, 1500t," I said. My helmet picked up the request, and the laser in my finger pulsed for 1500 trillionths of a second, right into the heart of the camera lens.

I slid my finger down to the second lens, and repeated the command.

In theory, I had taken out both its vision sensors.

But the robot didn't lessen the pressure on my helmet.

Maybe those weren't the lenses . . . I couldn't actually see its face from where I was. Or maybe it just didn't care that it was blind.

The liquid Phant was almost upon me.

I slid my boot sideways, and found purchase against the bulkhead. I pushed off, finally slipping from the robot's grip.

With nothing to press down against, the robot's arm slammed into the deck with a loud clang.

I rolled back, and stood up.

The blind robot fumbled about, searching for me.

I danced away from it and the Phant, picking up the bent rifle the robot had dropped. Then I repeatedly bashed the stock into the brain case area of the robot. Dents appeared. A lot of them. I hoped the weapon didn't accidentally fire and set off an alarm.

Eventually the robot stopped moving and collapsed. Glowing blue liquid seeped out, joining the first Phant on the deck.

I discarded the bent weapon and, stepping around the two Phants, I returned to the first disabled robot and retrieved its rifle.

No Klaxon filled the corridor, which meant neither robot had contacted Security. Maybe the Phants possessing them didn't know about the security systems they could tap into. Or maybe they'd triggered a silent alarm.

I hauled both robots into the airlock and shut the door. Then I backtracked down the corridor at a run.

In my head I visualized the ship's blueprint, doing my best to recall the many corridors from the map. I'd always found it mildly confusing to navigate from the top-down perspective of a HUD given the isometric vantage point of real life, but it was even more disorienting when done from memory. I had to backtrack several times, taking detours to avoid any masters-at-arms robots I spotted. None of the robots seemed on high alert, I noted.

Hang in there, Hijak.

My PASS device was still on. I was slightly worried the Guide might use it to track my whereabouts, but since the UC devices operated on a different band from the SK ones, if the bridge crew didn't specifically look for the signal, I'd be invisible. Besides, if the Guide really wanted to track me, he could use the security cameras that decorated the overhead. I realized a while ago no one was manning the ship's security station, at least not properly, because I'd passed several of those cameras without raising an alarm. Perhaps the unintegrated human being who I had thought operated the tactical station was in fact handling Security.

And perhaps he was giving me a chance.

It gave me hope for the future of humanity yet.

One deck down, I eventually reached the T intersection that led to the closed-off hallway I sought.

I slowly peered past the edge of the intersection.

Rifles in hand, two guard robots stood watch in front of the target hallway. The same robots that had escorted Hijak here, I thought.

The ship-wide firearm sensors could only be triggered by the motion of fast-moving projectiles. If I could bring my rifle right up against the brain cases before I fired, I could avoid setting off the alarm.

Now I just had to figure out how I'd get close enough to unleash two shots like that.

I ducked behind the bulkhead and retreated far enough to unload a spare magazine without drawing attention. I approached the T intersection, carefully peered past the edge to confirm the robots remained in position, and then threw the magazine down the opposite corridor.

I ducked against the bulkhead and held my breath.

The clang of polycarbonate-on-metal echoed down the intersection. I didn't dare look, but given the loudness of each tread, I was certain both robots approached in unison.

Not good.

I had counted on one of the robots staying behind.

This was highly unusual.

Obviously, these aliens didn't give a damn about proper watch tactics.

The clangs grew louder. My heart beat in time to each polycarbonate footfall.

I reviewed the map in my head, trying to remember if there was a way I could double back and come at the corridor from another direction while the two robots were distracted.

No. This was the only access point.

I had to deal with them here and now.

The clangs became nearly overwhelming—

The robots passed the bend.

I jabbed my rifle into the brain case of the first robot and fired.

I was already flowing toward the second robot—

Which trained its rifle on me—

The barrel of my weapon touched its brain case first—

I fired.

The robots toppled one after the other.

The firearm Klaxon didn't trigger.

I'd evaded detection yet again. My luck wasn't going to last forever though. If I hadn't been wearing a strength- and speed-enhanced jumpsuit, I would have lost that battle. Another one of my nine lives used up.

I dragged the robots around the bend, to a storage alcove containing firefighting equipment.

I noticed a Phant was slowly oozing from only one of the bodies, toward me. The other robot didn't exhibit any signs of alien possession. It must have been reprogrammed then. I was lucky it hadn't contacted Security. Or maybe it had . . . I hoped my friend on the bridge kept quiet a little while longer.

I gave the liquid Phant the finger, then hurried down the T intersection to the now-unguarded hallway. I dashed toward the door directly opposite the Convalescence Ward.

It irised open when I approached. Normally these doors would open only to those with proper clearance, but I suspected the security protocols had been disabled. Probably a good thing, because I had neither a SACKER privilege escalation kit handy, nor the know-how to use it. I promised myself I'd fix that glaring hole in my spec-ops arsenal when I got back.

I stepped inside.

A sickly, septic odor immediately assailed my nostrils.

My eyes were drawn to a Weaver, which had been wheeled to the central operating table. One of its telescoping limbs operated a bone saw. Spinning at high speed, the saw approached the table . . .

. . . Where Hijak lay restrained, facedown. Naked from the waist up, he struggled frantically—his skull and spinal column were directly in the saw's path.

Weavers were stand-alone units, and could be attached or detached to gurneys or tables as the operator saw fit. I hurried across the lab and, giving the bone saw a wide berth, I unlocked the Weaver from the table. The saw immobilized instantly. I wheeled the medical robot to the far wall, where I parked it and tentatively stepped back.

The machine didn't attack me.

It wasn't possessed then, but merely following the surgical procedures input by its operators.

I returned to Hijak. Bindings wrapped his hands and feet, and a steel vise secured his head to the operating table. His hair was shaven around the previously installed metallic knob.

I set the rifle down and removed my glove assemblies, knowing my own nimbler fingers would undo his binds faster.

Hijak couldn't tell who I was, as he still lay facedown. He was whimpering, and from the smell I knew he'd soiled himself.

"Hijak, it's me," I said quietly.

"Rage!" The raw emotion in his voice got to me. It sounded like he was crying. I almost did, too. "Oh, Rage. Thank you. Thank you!"

"Make sure your Implant is off," I said.

"It's off, it's off," he said. "Thank you. I owe you everything."

"You're welcome, bro. I'd never leave you behind. You know that."

He forced a laugh through his tears. "Of course you wouldn't. I knew you'd come back for me. I knew it." His body stiffened like a board. "The woman—did you—"

I had just finished unbinding his feet when the pain came. Jiāndāo.

I don't know where she was hiding, but she'd bided her time well. She got me right when I was at my most vulnerable.

I lay curled up on the floor. The pain went right through my jumpsuit, thanks to the steel knob installed in my skull.

When the fog of pain finally lifted, I heard her voice.

"You have returned to the fold, Floor," Jiāndāo said. "I must say, I am glad you came back. Oh, what joy we will have together. I will step on you, and step on you again until your little heart stops and you are dead. Then I will chuck your lifeless body from the airlock so your UC friends can find you and manually extract the contents of your embedded ID. This last session will be my gift to you, and to them. Do you have anything to say before we begin? Or should we continue your friend's operation first, so you can enjoy his last sentient moments? Maybe once he is integrated he can help torture you to death."

Jiāndāo emerged from the far corner of the room, and pointed the Snake at my groin. I almost pissed myself just thinking of the coming pain.

No! a part of my mind yelled. *You're more than this! You're more than a man! You're a MOTH!*

I wasn't going to go out this way. Cowering like some dog in a corner.

I was going to go out roaring.

I turned my head to look at Hijak.

No one tortures my platoon brothers.

I started singing the marching cadence I'd learned in Basic.

"Everywhere we go-o!"

She cocked her head in amusement, and activated the Snake.

I gritted my teeth.

No pain. There is no pain. I am a MOTH.

Through the red haze of torment, I spotted a Weaver connected to a gurney behind Jiāndāo. One of the many medical robots in the room, this Weaver didn't possess a bone-saw attachment.

Still, it would do for what I had in mind.

I continued the song, though the words came out slurred by agony.

"People wanna know-o."

I stood up.

Jiāndāo increased the pain level to some of the worst I'd ever felt. Heart-stopping.

But my heart beat on.

There is no pain. I am a MOTH.

I took a step toward her. It helped that I wore a jumpsuit. I wouldn't be able to do this with my tortured body alone.

She pointed the Snake at my gut, one the most sensitive regions of the torso, obviously trying to stop me.

But she couldn't.

Not now.

"Who we are-r!"

The pain was all in my mind.

It wasn't real.

I flung myself upon her.

She applied the Snake frantically now, concentrating on my heart, trying to stop it.

But I ignored it all. Even ignored the frantic fibrillations of my heart.

I just had to live a little longer . . .

I wrenched the Snake from her and hurled it aside. Then I shoved her backward, onto the gurney, and turned her over.

"So we tell them!"

The agony began to subside, though I knew the ghost pain would linger for some moments. It always did when the intensity was so great.

Jiāndāo struggled beneath me on the gurney.

I hauled myself on top of her. Studiously avoiding the Phant-covered bar, I dug my knees into her back, and flipped open the control panel of the Weaver connected to the gurney.

I had limited knowledge of medical robots. I'd taken a corps-man course in MOTH training, though it was mostly battlefield training. I always regretted not taking the advanced version, but I knew enough about Weavers to do what I needed.

"We are the Navy!"

The touchscreen menus were labeled in Korean-Chinese, but seemed to contain the same number of options as a UC Weaver. I flicked through the unreadable options by memory until I reached the procedure I desired. At least, I hoped it was the procedure. If the menu positions were different, or if my memory was wrong, I could seriously mess up her body.

Not that she didn't deserve it or anything.

All Weavers had the capability to perform low-invasive surgery by injecting a nanoprobe into the desired organ, such as the brain, eye, or heart. The probe was manipulated via a set of eight tightly coiled electromagnets.

I had turned on those electromagnets without actually injecting a probe.

Full power.

"The motherfucking Navy!"

I slid off Jiāndāo, who still lay facedown on the gurney.

The electromagnets only needed a few seconds to reach their full
charge potential, and when they did, Jiāndāo slammed upward into
the magnets. The metal bar embedded in her spine was glued fast.

I collapsed to the floor, my breath coming in ragged heaves, like
an old man who'd just been stabbed in the heart. The pain came now
in weak, sporadic waves, and I knew it would soon cease. Just a few
more moments.

Jiāndāo remained quiet the whole time, silently flailing her arms.
I guess the alien parasite was entirely unable to comprehend what I
had done. Or maybe it was too shocked to say a word. Jiāndāo didn't
weep, didn't scream, didn't even beg. She just thrashed.

"No one . . . tortures . . . my platoon brothers." I rose drunkenly
to my feet and opened the remainder of Hijak's binds.

"Rage," he said, giving me a hug.

"We're not free yet," I wheezed. "Don't go all celebratory on me."

"Are you all right?" he said, glancing at my arm.

I was clutching at my chest, near my heart, though I hadn't even
realized it. I lowered my arm. "Yeah. Fine. Just a little out of breath."

Hijak nodded at the woman. "What are we going to do with her?"

Behind me, Jiāndāo was still flailing, though less vigorously.

"Nothing," I said.

Abruptly she slumped, and ceased all motion.

Intrigued, I walked toward the gurney. Beneath the electromagnets, I saw condensation pooling on the bar grafted into her
spine. The liquid sweated directly from the metal, drawing into an
ever-expanding line down the middle of the bar.

I thought the magnet was drawing the Phant out at first, but as the liquid continued to aggregate, moving toward the center of the bar, I realized that was not the case. In fact, it was going to spill off soon.

Right onto Jiāndāo's skin.

"Must be some sort of fight-or-flight mechanism," Hijak said. "And because you've trapped it, the Phant is choosing flight."

Some of the drops had already seeped over the side of the metal, and slowly drizzled down toward Jiāndāo's skin. I wasn't sure if a single drop would burn through her flesh like acid, or whether her whole body would dissolve on contact.

I didn't want to find out.

Even after everything Jiāndāo had done to me, I couldn't let the Phant incinerate her. I knew the real owner of that body hadn't been responsible.

My eyes lingered on the inside of her wrist, where, for the first time, I noticed a small eagle inked onto the skin. A symbol of hope and freedom, it only reinforced the notion that this person had been something other than a Keeper before her "integration."

I disconnected the Weaver from the gurney.

"Rage, what are you doing?" Hijak said.

I slid the gurney aside so that Jiāndāo floated in midair.

"Rage?"

I grabbed the Weaver's handhold and tilted the swivel arm of the main unit, slanting it and Jiāndāo slightly downward and to the side.

The liquid Phant flowed across the surface of the metal bar and began dripping from the lower segments, pooling on the deck below. Some of the liquid spilled down the sides of the bar first, coming dangerously close to Jiāndāo's skin before trickling off.

"Is this a good idea?" Hijak said.

When the last few drops leaked onto the deck, the pool began moving.

Toward me.

I stepped around the glowing liquid and wheeled the Weaver—and Jiāndāo—away from the Phant. I deactivated the magnet.

Jiāndāo dropped to the deck like a deadweight. She remained motionless, even on impact.

"Help me move her," I said.

Hijak reluctantly grabbed her legs and together we lifted her onto the main operating table.

"We can't leave her here," I said. "The Phant will just take her again." I gave her a gentle pat on the cheek. "Jiāndāo. Get up. Jiāndāo."

Hijak scooped up the rifle I'd set down, and trained it on the woman.

"Forget her, Rage," he said. "Like you said, there's no coming back. She's had an alien species living inside her head for weeks, maybe months. Even if her mind is intact, she won't be who she was before. You can't go through something like that and expect to be normal. Plus she's an SK. We know how trustworthy they are."

I ignored Hijak, giving her a harder pat. Still nothing.

The Phant continued to approach.

I pinched her earlobe. Her head recoiled slightly, but she didn't open her eyes.

I grabbed a light pen and held her eyelids open. I angled the pen so that it shone into both eyes at once, and I noted her pupils constricted equally, right away. I turned off the pen, and both pupils dilated back to baseline. According to my corpsman training, the brisk reaction of both eyes was a good sign, and indicated she hadn't suffered complete neurological shutdown. Jiāndāo, or whoever she was before, was still in there somewhere.

I searched the drawers beside the table.

"It's getting closer, Rage," Hijak said.

I found an epinephrine autoinjector, a rectangular device about the size of a pack of playing cards. The black bar indicated the inject side, and was protected by a red guard in the middle. Normally reserved for treating anaphylactic reactions, the epinephrine in the device would certainly give her a kick.

I applied the injector to her thigh. The thing didn't activate.

"If you are ready to inject, please remove the red safety guard," came the voice from the device.

That's right.

I did so.

"Place black end against outer thigh. Press firmly and hold in place for five seconds."

I held the device to her outer thigh, above the fabric of her clothes, and the device counted out the time necessary for the drug to diffuse into her bloodstream.

"Five.

"Four."

"Rage," Hijak said. "Let's go!"

"Three.

"Two.

"One. Injection complete."

I tossed the device aside.

"Please seek emergency medical attention," the device intoned from the corner of the room.

Hijak had stepped back, and his gun was aimed downward now. "It's climbing the table."

I pinched the woman's earlobe again.

This time she jerked upright and looked directly into my eyes. "You."

"Me."

Hijak tensed beside me, and he lifted the rifle, aiming it squarely at the woman's head.

"How?" She glanced at her surroundings, taking in Hijak, and the Weavers.

"Magnets," I said. "We set you free."

"Then if I am free," she said, "why is he pointing a rifle at my head?" Her tone was different now. Less assured. More accented.

I nodded at Hijak. "Lower it, bro."

His eyes flicked toward me, then back toward her. Finally, reluctantly, he lowered the weapon.

He gazed at the deck and took another step back. "Rage . . ."

The woman followed his eyes, leaning forward to peer over the operating table.

She exhaled with a hiss and shoved me violently away.

Fear mixed with anger on the woman's face as she leaped down from the table and grabbed one of the mobile IV drip stands. She lifted the long steel rod like a weapon.

"Stand down," Hijak said. "Stand down!"

But she wasn't even looking at him.

I intervened. "Hold, Hijak! She's not attacking you, bro!"

He kept the weapon trained on her, and we both watched as the woman spun toward the operating table. She repeatedly bashed the IV stand into the glowing liquid at the base of the table, as if she could somehow harm the Phant. She wielded the thing like a sledgehammer, but it was no use, because all she did was displace the liquid. Glowing droplets splashed dangerously close to her feet.

I wrapped my hands around her upper body and pinned her arms. "Jiāndāo. Stop. You're not harming it. Jiāndāo. Please . . ."

I dragged her away.

She was breathing hard, her body tense in my arms. Abruptly she relaxed and let the IV stand fall to the deck.

I released her, and she turned toward me, keeping her eyes lowered.

She rubbed the eagle tattooed to the inside of her wrist. "If it pleases you, my name is Lana," she said. "I'm a pilot. At least I was. Not a Keeper. You must understand, they made me assume that role, using the memories of another. I was not in control of my body. You must believe me."

"Lana," I said. "I believe you."

"I'm not a Keeper!" she said, her voice borderline hysterical.

I grabbed her by the shoulders. "Lana. *I believe you.*"

She met my eyes for the first time, and her rapid breathing slowed. Our faces were only a handspan apart. I'd told her she was beautiful before, when she was my Keeper. Now that I was even closer to her, I realized she was more than beautiful: there wasn't a flaw anywhere on her face under that makeup.

"You're UC?" she said.

"I am."

Her brow furrowed. "But you saved me."

"I did." I could lose myself in those eyes.

"Uh, Rage?" Hijak said.

I looked away, feeling embarrassed.

"The Phant . . ." Hijak continued.

I glanced at the deck. The red liquid had abandoned the table, and was approaching Lana and me.

I released her shoulders, snatched my gloves from the table, and backed away with Lana.

"These beings can communicate telepathically," Lana said. "My former possessor is most likely communicating what it sees, and what we have done, to the others at this very moment."

"If that's true, then why hasn't the Guide raised an alarm?" I thought of the robots I'd terminated along the way here. The Phants had definitely seen me before now.

"The communication is queued, and takes a minimum of twenty Stanminutes to process, even if the Yaoguai are in close proximity."

"That's gotta make coordinating in combat difficult."

"They can communicate faster with the Mara, those you name the Workers. And the Burrowers. They can use them to exchange signals. They—"

"Let's roll," I interrupted her, turning toward the exit hatch. "You can tell me all about them later. We're cutting it close here as it is. I want to head to engineering. See if we can take over the ship with your help. We have a friend on the bridge too, I think. Otherwise I would've set off security alarms ages ago."

"You'll never take engineering," Lana said. "The liquid demons flood that deck."

"Oh." So much for that plan. "Then I guess we'll eject through the airlock, and just get the hell out."

"Only one of us can escape through the airlock." Hijak looked directly into my eyes. "You know that."

I scowled at him. "I'm not leaving without you two."

Hijak pressed his lips together. "The Guide only expects you, Rage. If we all go, he'll shoot us down. Just leave us. We'll hide out, try to survive. Cause what damage we can."

"We all go through the airlock," I said. "Or none of us do. No more arguing. Let's get you two suited up."

"Your friend is right," Lana said. "The Guide will hunt for us, at least initially. He will want me, especially. I have much knowledge of them. Too much." She glanced at the Phant in disgust.

"I'm not letting you stay," I said. "For exactly that reason. Humanity needs what you know."

Lana bowed her head. "If it pleases you, I do hope to come. But there is a better way to escape than by ejecting from an airlock."

I frowned. "Well, speak, woman."

"The hangar bay," she said simply.

"The hangar bay? Why? You want to take a shuttle?" I could see that. She was a pilot after all. "Won't that make it even easier for the Guide to shoot us down?"

"No," Lana said. "We take the mechs."

I snickered. "It's a nice thought, but Hijak and I aren't even provisioned to pilot SK mechs."

"If it pleases you, in fact you are. The ATLAS mechs on this ship have their provisioning systems disabled. Anyone can pilot them. I disabled them myself, or rather, my possessor did. It wanted to give all the Learned the ability to use the machines of humankind, regardless of the qualifications of the original human host. Door security ship-wide was disabled for the same reason. Why do you think every hatch opens for you?"

She did have a point about the hatches.

"Okay, but that still doesn't solve the little problem we'll have once we leave the hangar bay," I said. "Specifically, how to avoid becoming easy targets for the point defense system of this starship."

"If it pleases you," Lana said. "We reside in the ring belt above the gas giant Tau Ceti III. Do you realize what this means?"

I did: rocks, and a whole lot of them.

"Though the Guide hunts us," Lana continued, "we can remain hidden in the ring belt for days. Maybe weeks. Enough time for a rescue party to arrive. The Guide will not stay overlong, and risk discovery."

I glanced at Hijak.

"Up to you, Rage," he said. "Though to be honest, I still don't trust her."

"If we can't take over engineering, then one way or another we have to get off this ship." I edged away from the red Phant. "And if we really are inside a planetary ring belt, jetting out of here in ATLAS mechs is a hell of a lot better than doing it in jumpsuits, or even a shuttle."

"Not ordinary ATLAS mechs." Lana had a knowing glint in her eyes. "*ATLAS 6* mechs."

That sealed the deal.

I was excited for all of two seconds, because the door irised open and ruined my mood.

A guard robot stood outside.

Its rifle was pointed directly at me.

CHAPTER FOURTEEN

Shaw

Looking down, I watched the glowing vapor pass through Battlehawk's chest area. The Phant seeped directly into the ATLAS 5's brain case. It was almost as if the alien entity intuitively knew where the AI resided, like it could somehow detect the quantum residue produced by machine consciousness. Or perhaps the Phant merely had experience with human tech.

Either way, I remained very still, wondering the whole while if the alien vapor would incinerate me in the process.

The tunnel became strangely quiet. The eager clatter of countless alien limbs fell silent.

"I am afraid," Battlehawk said.

Machine consciousness was a prickly issue. Just because a machine was self-aware didn't mean it was really alive, the humanists argued. Emotions were delete-able subroutines, and therefore any entity whose personality and feelings could be added or subtracted piecemeal could not be sentient, the argument went. I wasn't so sure about that, because I'd met more than a few sentient-seeming robots in my life.

Anyway, neural programmers had the ability to bestow the full gamut of emotions on robots and Artificials, but some emotions were strictly illegal outside the lab, such as anger. The only emotion most machines were allowed, especially in the military, was fear. It aided in self-preservation, they said.

Though right now I wished the ATLAS programmers had deleted all fear.

"Forgive me," I told the AI.

"I understand why you do this," Battlehawk said. "Still, I will miss . . . sentience."

There wasn't really anything I could say to that. I couldn't shake the feeling I was making a mistake.

The last of the vapor vanished within Battlehawk's brain case.

It was done then.

Battlehawk was gone.

The crabs had formed tentative half circles on either side of Battlehawk, and gave the mech room, apparently uncertain whether this tower of servomotors and steel was friend or foe.

The hydraulically actuated joints of the ATLAS 5 abruptly engaged of their own accord, and dragged my body along. The inner cocoon twisted and bent around me, and all I could do was surrender to the movements.

Battlehawk squeezed a fist in front of its vision sensors, as if the Phant in control was relishing in its newfound power. The mech turned toward the beasts without taking any hesitant first steps—I suspected the Phant within had possessed an ATLAS before.

An unsaid understanding passed between Battlehawk and the beasts, because the latter began an organized retreat. The slugs became immaterial; the crabs retrieved their dead and shuffled away.

Most of the Phants receded too, satisfied that one of their kind was now in control.

Two alien mists remained behind however, and came up along-side Battlehawk. The vapors merely floated there, and I felt somehow exposed, as if the Phants were peering right through the outer shell of the mech at me. I half-expected the cockpit to eject me into their deadly embrace, or for the vapors to seep through the ATLAS and incinerate me. Maybe the mists would kill Fan as well. Or instead.

But none of those events transpired. The two Phants merely floated past, moving deeper into the tunnel, toward the small cavern that contained the teleportation disc.

Battlehawk followed.

My sound and vision feeds remained intact. Either the Phant in control of Battlehawk didn't know how to shut them off, or it wanted me to see and hear everything. I noticed there was no "blue tint of possession" overlaying the vision feed, like there had been while reviewing Battlehawk's archives. The tint must be introduced during the recording process.

When Battlehawk passed the dismembered carcass of Queequeg, I had to close my eyes. My chin quivered, and I knew if I looked at the body I'd break down in tears. I had to be strong and clearheaded now of all times. My life depended on it.

Good-bye, Queequeg.

The ATLAS 5 returned to the small cavern and approached the metallic disc set into the bottom of the cave.

One of the escorting Phants hovered over the device—

Then it was gone.

There was no flash. No sound. The glowing vapor merely vanished from existence.

The second mist moved over the disc—

It too blinked from this world.

I still didn't understand why my Improvised Explosive Device hadn't teleported earlier. Perhaps the disc was monitored remotely in some way. But as Fan had scolded me, I had no idea how the alien tech worked.

Speaking of Fan . . .

"Now might be a good time to make your exit," I sent over the comm. "Fan?"

Either he was ignoring me, or couldn't hear me. Perhaps he was already gone.

Or dead.

Battlehawk stepped onto the disc.

My pulse quickened.

This was it.

Just like when jumping from one solar system to another via Gate, I felt nothing. One moment Battlehawk and I were surrounded by the natural walls of the Geronium cavern, and the next we stood in a corridor.

The bulkheads and overhead were made of black pipes overlapping at different depths and densities to form a solid surface, while the deck was a raised gangway formed from the confluence of said pipes. The only light came from the headlamps of my mech. A metallic disc similar to the one in the cavern lay beneath me.

I'd observed all of this before via Battlehawk's archives, so as the ATLAS trod the surreal passageways it was almost like I was reliving a dream. One thing I hadn't noticed in the video was that those black bulkheads seemed to writhe sinuously as we advanced, just as if they were comprised of living vipers. Indeed, when we got close to one bulkhead, I saw that the pipes bent in random directions along their lengths in real time.

We passed different-colored, gaseous Phants occasionally, as well as alien beings in various jumpsuits. They all seemed to be moving with purpose. The jumpsuit aliens were bigger than humans for the most part, but the tallest only came up to Battlehawk's chest. Some wore translucent helmets, and I saw features—most of them hideous—that ran the gamut from insectile to algal. Metallic objects, bars, maybe, were attached to the back of most of the visible heads, with either glowing red vapor or droplets of red condensation congregated about the metal.

Phants?

If so, that didn't bode well for me. Not at all.

Battlehawk entered the alien menagerie I remembered from the vid archive.

The chamber I feared.

Glass holding tanks lined either wall, filled with different creatures. Alien Weavers hung from the ceilings of most tanks, and drilled metal parts and chips into the sedated lifeforms. Willing participants of cybernetic alteration, or forced? The latter, most likely.

When Battlehawk reached the midpoint of the chamber, a spherical robot of odd design floated forth to intercept us. Rectangular bars of varying lengths protruded from the robot's entire exterior, vaguely reminding me of caricatures of Earth I had seen where exaggerated skyscrapers crowded out the continents. The black object was about the size of a volleyball and floated a meter off the deck.

A blue cone of light erupted from the sphere, and bathed Battlehawk. The robot proceeded to revolve around my mech. Scanning it?

The robot made a bleep-blurp noise and retreated.

An alien approached, one of the jumpsuit cyborgs. It nearly matched my ATLAS 5 in size, and its jumpsuit was all tubes and spheres and servomotors. It had three legs and seven jointless arms (four tentacles in front, three in back), and its torso was capped by a glass dome. It was the same type of alien jumpsuit I'd seen in the defile on Geronimo, except this one was actually occupied.

As the alien neared, I discerned the head inside that translucent dome. It reminded me of an octopus or squid more than anything else, though with four eyes and two very long beaks. There wasn't any water inside the helmet, just a subtle, violet mist. I had the impression it was the kind of lifeform that might exist within the upper atmosphere of a gas giant.

The alien reached up with one of the trunk-like appendages of its jumpsuit and plucked a squirming Fan from his hiding place between Battlehawk's jetpacks and upper back.

"No!" Fan's voice came over the comm. "Shaw, help me!"

I strained my muscles against the inner cocoon of the cockpit, but I couldn't move.

"Why are you still here? I told you to go!" I fought against the cocoon. I wanted to help.

But I couldn't.

The alien carried Fan away. "Shaw!"

"Cockpit, open!" I said.

Nothing.

"Inner shell, release!"

The mech ignored my command words. There was a manual hatch-release switch somewhere in the cockpit, but I couldn't reach it if the inner cocoon wouldn't open.

The Phant wanted me to stay inside.

Not that I'd be able to do a thing if I got out anyway. The only weapon I had was the knife tucked into my utility belt. I didn't even have a working jetpack. Nor did Fan.

I watched helplessly as the alien carried Fan to an empty tank. The twin plates of glass composing the front face of the tank slid aside, and the alien tossed Fan within.

Fan rushed forward, trying to get out before the glass sealed, but he didn't make it. The top was still open, so he leaped up and grabbed onto the rim.

Mechanical arms were already lowering a slab of glass from the overhead, and Fan collided with the slab as he hauled himself up. He fell back, losing his grip. The slab contacted the other surfaces with a resounding thud, sealing Fan inside the tank.

The ominous shape of an Alien Weaver resided in the upper corner of the tank. The robot seemed dormant for now, its limbs curled around its black body.

Fan ran to the far side of the tank, away from the Weaver, and pounded at the surface with his fists. "Let me out!"

Battlehawk proceeded into the glass tank across from Fan's. Twin plates of glass sealed the entrance behind the ATLAS 5, and a similar slab lowered from above, trapping me and the mech inside. I spotted the dormant Alien Weaver built into the roof of this tank, and shuddered.

In Fan's tank, white mist now vented inside from floor ducts. The mist became transparent as it diffused the tank, and I realized an atmosphere of some kind was being prepared.

The Alien Weaver in Fan's tank abruptly dropped down and spread its appendages, like a giant spider encroaching on its prey. A tube of wiring connected it to a black box on the tank's roof, and as the Weaver approached Fan that tube uncurled behind it.

"No!" Fan said over the comm. "No!"

"Fan!" I transmitted. "Cut its wiring if you can! Fan?"

The Alien Weaver must have communicated something to Fan, because he spouted some strange words in Korean-Chinese over the comm. Using the aReal in my helmet, I translated them.

"My password is The dragon will rise 954. The dragon will rise 954!" He repeated the phrase again and again, his voice becoming a shriek.

His embedded ID password, no doubt. Not really something you'd want to fall into enemy hands, and yet he'd given it up just like that. I couldn't really blame him though, not when he faced that iron monstrosity. I didn't think I would hold up much longer when my turn came.

The Alien Weaver gripped Fan by the neck, and one of its telescoping limbs pressed into his jumpsuit.

Fan stopped struggling. He'd been injected with something, I thought, which meant these aliens were already familiar with human physiology. They must have captured a few SKs from the original party sent to Geronimo.

Invisible lasers cut into the tough fabric of Fan's jumpsuit, leaving behind charred black lines. The Alien Weaver promptly ripped away the suit around those lines, and then tore off his undergarments. The robot set Fan's naked body on the floor, facedown.

Fan still breathed—the atmosphere within the tank had reached the necessary temperature, pressure, and composition required for human life, then. These beings had definitely captured some of us before. *More* than some.

The Alien Weaver produced a metallic bar and a bone saw.

I shut my eyes. I wasn't going to watch as he was converted into some alien cyborg.

I had promised Fan he would live.

I never imagined it would be like this.

I'd betrayed him.

This was my fault.

I was the one who'd insisted we try to plant explosives on the teleportation device. He had only come along because of me. And I'm certain he could have escaped back there in the cave, but he'd stayed. For me.

"I'm sorry, Fan. I'm so sorry."

I bowed my head.

I probably faced a similar fate. Or worse.

I should've fought to the end.

I don't know what possessed me to surrender.

I thought I could save Fan.

Instead, I doomed us both.

This is why you never surrender, a voice inside my head told me. *This is why you never give in.*

I heard the bone saw spinning at high speed, even through the glass slabs of the tanks that separated us. I flinched as the pitch changed, and I didn't have to look to know the saw was cutting into him. I trembled in my cockpit, my breath coming in ragged spurts.

What have I done?

The noise of the bone saw ceased, replaced by another sound. A quiet, squishy sound: the murmur of microchips pressing into neural tissue.

I decided right then I had to watch this. I had to observe with my own eyes exactly what I'd done to Fan. This would be my punishment.

I opened my eyes in time to watch the Alien Weaver power-drill the metal bar into the back of Fan's skull. The robot's limbs jerked horizontally down his spine, methodically grafting the remaining sections of the bar to Fan's spinal column. Medical lasers cauterized the tissue along the edges.

When it was done, it looked almost like his spine itself had been yanked on top of the skin and transmogrified into metal. The crude rivets and bolts on the outskirts of the bar revealed the truth of the graft, however. It was horrifying either way.

Spider-like, the Alien Weaver swiveled Fan so that he resided on his back, leaning slightly to one side with the metal bar touching the floor. Then the Weaver retreated to the rooftop of the tank, folded its limbs, and returned to dormancy.

A glowing, red liquid seeped into the chamber. A Phant.

It carefully steered around Fan's unconscious body and pooled beside the metallic graft. The liquid diminished in size, seeping into the bar until none remained on the floor. A scatter of glowing red droplets remained on the surface of the metal, held in place by some unknown force.

Fan opened his eyelids.

Except it was no longer Fan. There was a dull light to his eyes, reminding me of someone who had been heavily drugged. He examined his arms and legs and, pressing one hand against the glass wall of the tank for support, clambered to his feet. He glanced through the tank at Battlehawk, but there was no recognition in his eyes. Nor emotion of any kind. It was the kind of look people had when they were inside their Implant.

What had I done?

Movement drew my eyes to the right, to my own dire situation.

At the edge of my vision, a dark green, gaseous Phant floated into my tank, very fast. For some reason I had been expecting a red one.

I waited for Battlehawk to eject me, and for the Alien Weaver to drop from the roof of the tank. I waited for my own inevitable surgery to commence.

But the cockpit did not open.

I realized the inner atmosphere of the tank hadn't changed, because the encroaching entity remained in vapor form.

Was I to be incinerated, then?

The blue Phant inside Battlehawk began to vent from the ATLAS 5's brain case.

Then I understood.

They were attempting a swap, as I had seen in Battlehawk's vid archives: the blue one vacated so that the green one could take over.

Battlehawk had escaped when they tried this before.

Would I be able to do the same?

I'd exhausted all of Battlehawk's weaponry. I had only my fists. Still, if it came to it, I'd bash my way out.

I was leaning against the cockpit's inner cocoon when the actuators abruptly yielded beneath me.

Control of the mech was mine again.

This was my chance.

Excitement rose within me as I took three quick steps toward the nearest glass surface.

But the dark-green vapor of the Phant was already seeping inside my ATLAS. It was fast.

Too fast.

I managed to raise my arm, but before I could strike the glass, the cocoon froze up.

No.

I slumped, leaning heavily against the unyielding actuators. I felt such sheer disappointment.

Apparently the Phants weren't going to make the same mistake a second time.

"Cockpit, open," I said, defeated. "Inner shell, release."

I struggled briefly against the cocoon, but it was no use.

The brief opportunity of escape had passed.

"Do not be afraid," the AI's deep voice intoned.

I blinked in disbelief. "Battlehawk?"

"No."

I swallowed. "Who . . . who are you?"

"I am Azen. You are safe now."

The glass slabs in front of me slid aside, and the mech emerged from the tank. Fan stared blankly past me the whole time.

I'm sorry, Fan.

The ATLAS 5 left behind the horrors of the alien menagerie, and we continued down the tight corridor of interlinked pipes.

I was spared, but to what end? Likely a fate far worse than Fan's awaited me.

The passageway eventually fell away, and we stood on the edge of a vast, cylindrical shaft. Below, a pit descended into the murk, while above the concave bulkheads vanished into the darkness before ever reaching a ceiling. I could barely make out the far side of the shaft, but I thought I saw openings to other corridors there.

I was starkly reminded of the insides of a Forma pipe, and I suspected the hollow, cylindrical shaft passed through the entire ship, like some inner core. Assuming we were even on a ship . . . I hadn't seen any windows yet.

Battlehawk, or Azen I supposed, stepped out into the shaft's empty void—

And was immediately lifted upward.

This was a grav elevator of some kind, though on a massive scale. Humanity had the tech to build smaller such elevators, though most were constructed for research purposes or marketing gimmicks. I'd never seen anything like this.

The minutes ticked by, and our speed slowly increased until the shaft and its offshoot corridors became a blur. I was taken aback by the sheer immensity of it all. We must have been traveling at least a hundred kilometers an hour. And still there was no end to the shaft in sight.

The occasional Phant or alien jumpsuit traveling in the opposite direction blurred by; amazingly we never collided with any of them.

The mech began to slow, and finally came to a halt. It just hovered there, motionless in the shaft. Abruptly we drifted to the left, traveling horizontally along the concave bulkhead.

We stopped before an opening and floated toward it. The ATLAS 5's feet touched the solid gangway inside, and then the mech proceeded forward under mechanical power once more, leaving the shaft behind.

We were in a corridor that looked much the same as the previous one, replete with elevated gangway and undulating bulkheads.

"Where are you taking me?" I said.

Azen answered immediately. "My homeworld."

We reached a wide, spherical chamber. A series of raised, concentric ribs spread from a central point in the deck, and curved up the bulkheads to the ceiling. Between each rib, a passageway led in and out.

A metallic disc, larger than any I had seen before, rested on a dais at the center of the chamber, at the confluence of those ribs.

Gaseous Phants of four colors—red, purple, blue, gray—traveled to and fro between the disc and the many entrances. Those that hovered over the disc vanished. Others materialized from thin air above the disc and drifted toward the passageways.

The incoming vapors queued along the outer rim of the disc. No two Phants ever floated onto the disc at the same time: a single Phant would advance over the disc and vanish; a different-colored Phant would appear shortly thereafter and leave the disc; then the next Phant would move forward.

"What if I don't want to go to your homeworld?" I whispered.

"You have no choice."

Azen advanced, and the Phants cleared a path for the mech. The ATLAS 5 waited by the edge of the disc until a Phant materialized in the center. When the alien vapor hovered aside, Azen marched onto the device.

The bulkheads winked out.

CHAPTER FIFTEEN

Rade

I stared into the barrel of the rifle, waiting for the guard robot to fire.

Hijak raised his own rifle, and the robot immediately swung its aim toward him.

Lana stepped smoothly between them.

"Lower your weapon," Lana said to the robot. Her tone and posture had changed—she was Jiāndāo all over again.

The robot lowered its weapon.

"You will escort us to the hangar bay," the woman continued. It was kind of frightening how easily she had resumed the mannerisms of Jiāndāo, and for a moment I thought the Phant had repossessed her.

"I will escort you to the hangar bay," the robot repeated, vacating the entrance.

"That's some Jedi mind shit right there," Hijak said.

I glanced over my shoulder to confirm that the glowing Phant was still on the operating room floor, and not inside Lana.

We stepped outside, and the robot marched us through the tight corridors.

I gave Lana a questioning look. "Lana?"

"Yes, it's me," she said quietly, answering my unasked question. "I programmed this robot myself. Or my possessor did, anyway."

I couldn't see glowing condensation anywhere on the robot, and I realized it wasn't possessed. The Phants didn't *have* to possess every single robot, not if they knew how to program them.

That probably wasn't a good thing. Or maybe it was, if it meant they'd obey Lana.

We reached the hangar bay. Two more robots, also not possessed, guarded the entrance airlock.

Thanks to Lana, they let us pass.

Lana ordered all three robots to wait outside.

"Do not let anyone enter, no matter what happens," Lana instructed the robots.

We entered the airlock, sealed it behind us, then opened the inner hatch to the hangar bay.

The first things I noticed when I stepped into the bay were the ATLAS 6s.

There were eight of them, arrayed in a line against the far bulkhead. So tall that even in their storage postures—with upper bodies hunched forward, legs bent, and shoulder rotors folded away—they barely fit the confines of the hangar.

I felt my heart beat with excitement just looking at them.

"The two of us will get suited up," Lana said.

I nodded absently as she led Hijak to the jumpsuit closet.

This was going to be quite the joyride.

I was already wearing a UC jumpsuit. When I sealed the helmet, the aReal in my faceplate outlined the mechs in red (as enemies), with generic *ATLAS 6* labels.

That wasn't going to work.

I hurried over to Lana and Hijak at the jumpsuit closet, and exchanged my UC helmet for an SK version. The fit was perfect. That was one of the nice things about having the jumpsuits manufactured by the same company: interoperability.

Strict regulations prevented that company—Nova Dynamics—from selling to anyone but official governments, but my platoon had found company gear on privateer ships numerous times during missions. The serial numbers were invariably erased, but the Chief suspected involvement at the manufacturer level. UC investigators were looking into it, but unfortunately, the matter wouldn't be resolved any time soon, given that most of our resources were now redirected toward more important matters.

I sealed the SK-version faceplate. The HUD (Heads-Up Display) built into the lens had the usual familiar layout, except for the Korean-Chinese characters.

"Command language: English," I said as the internal atmosphere stabilized.

Instantly, the characters switched to understandable words.

I should have issued that command when I was working with the SK Weaver back in the operating room. Ah well, I had to cut myself some slack: I *had* been subjected to a lot of pain back there, and I hadn't had the clearest of thoughts at the time.

I eagerly turned toward the ATLAS 6s. The mechs were outlined in green now, and no longer had generic names. I saw the Chinese characters representing their callsigns, and below them the English equivalents. Hopper. Fang. Tiger. Ox . . .

"What secure comm channel should we use?" Hijak said.

"One-five-nine." I tuned my comm to one-five-nine. Always a good idea to agree on a secure channel before you started transmitting.

I picked out a jetpack from the rack in the closet and shrugged it on. I'd left my old one behind after using it to take out the robots. The integration was perfect.

I sprinted across the hangar toward the ATLAS 6s.

"Hopper, unlock!" I activated my new jumpjets as the cockpit hatch of the designated mech fell open, and I landed inside.

The cockpit's elastic cocoon pressed into my body, forcing my posture to match the curled-in-a-ball storage position of the mech. My knees pressed into my chest with enough force to squeeze the breath out of me.

The hatch sealed, leaving me staring at the mech's innards. Without my Implant, all weapons-related commands would be vocal, just as control of the mech would be via the pressure sensors lining the cocoon. It would feel a bit like trudging in muck at first.

Then the mech's audio and visual feeds routed to my helmet, so that I heard and saw the world from the heights of the ATLAS 6.

"Hopper, load weapon patterns seven and five!"

"Unrecognized weapon pattern," a female voice intoned from the cockpit.

A female AI. That was interesting. Mechs were traditionally considered the epitome of masculinity, with voices to match. I guess the SKs viewed their mechs differently . . .

"Load serpent launcher into left hand," I said.

The serpent launcher swiveled into position.

"Load Gatling into right hand."

The Gat swung up and into place.

"Guns in hand," I said.

The weapons swiveled so that the triggers were directly above my fingers.

Unable to stand to my full height within the tight confines of the hangar bay, I lumbered toward the hangar doors. Try doing a buttocks-to-calves squat sometime, then shamble forward, and you'll get an idea of what that was like. The movement was made all the more difficult by the fact that without the Implant it felt like I was wading through a swamp.

I glanced at Lana and Hijak. They had just finished suiting up.

"This is Rage, comm check," I sent over the agreed-upon frequency. "One. Two. Three. Four. Five. Over."

"Hijak to Rage," Hijak sent. "Comm check. Five of five. Over."

"I heard both of you," Lana transmitted. "Five of five. Is that what you want me to say? Over."

"That'll do. By the way, Lana, you sure you can operate one of these mechs?"

In answer, she sprinted across the hangar toward the ATLAS 6 labeled "Ox" on my HUD. The hatch fell open as she ran, and she jetted inside. The cockpit sealed behind her.

Ox turned toward me, Gatling guns swiveling into its hands.

"Nice," I said.

Hijak chose Tiger beside her.

I switched to the backup comm system in the ATLAS 6, and repeated the comm test. The mechs passed with flying colors.

One less moving part to worry about.

"Open the hangar doors, Lana," I said.

The door interface could be accessed remotely via aReal. Right then I realized I could've probably opened it myself, as the Phants had likely disabled the security protocols on these doors, too. We were all one big, happy Phant family.

Abruptly I heard gunfire from beyond the airlock. Our three guard robots were obeying Lana's instructions to the letter, apparently.

A ship-wide Klaxon sounded.

The Korean-Chinese equivalent of General Quarters sounded over the hangar's main circuit.

"Uh, Lana?" I sent over the comm. "The hangar doors?"

"The doors won't open *now*," Lana transmitted.

"That's fine. No problem." I lifted my Gatlings toward the doors and opened fire.

Since we didn't have a chance to vent the atmosphere first, shooting the hangar doors triggered an explosive decompression in the bay—loose equipment and tools hurtled past and smashed into the doors, widening the gaps torn by my Gat fire. I heard what sounded like hammer blows around me as some of those objects struck my ATLAS on the way out.

My mech didn't shift at all, and neither did the other ATLAS 6s or the lone shuttle. The hangar's artificial gravity remained active despite the rupture, and the decompressive forces were far too weak to counter the weight of the heavier objects.

I glanced toward the inner airlock, and beyond the portal saw SKs in jumpsuits piling inside. I turned my Gatling toward the airlock, and they immediately piled right back out again.

Good.

I proceeded toward the damaged hangar doors and barreled my way through the gaps in the metal.

Hopper passed from the ship's artificial gravity field and into the weightlessness of the void. There was a chance I'd suffer from decompression sickness, since ordinarily I was supposed to wait an hour for my body to adapt to the pressurized environment of a jumpsuit, but it wasn't like I had a choice in the matter. The nausea I felt now definitely wasn't decompression sickness though, but rather the directionless disorientation of space.

There was a huge, floating rock in front of me. I'd seen it on the bridge view screen earlier, and back then I'd thought it was a planetoid of some kind, but now I realized it was one of the larger specimens of the Tau Ceti III ring belt. Smaller rocks drifted past all around me.

I jetted toward the big rock and released a lateral burst to swing my body around by 180 degrees.

The receding ship swept into view. As expected, it was an SK vessel, triangular overall, with crowded, box-like superstructures erupting at sharp angles from the surface. Frigate class, judging from the size—roughly half as big as the large rock. Likely the frigate used the gas giant on the one side and the rock on the other to mask its thermal signature from the rest of the system.

Lana and Hijak followed close behind me in their ATLAS 6s, dwarfed by the ship. Lana seemed quite capable in regards to mech operations. Walking in a mech was relatively easy, but firing off the jumpjets with pinpoint precision to steer herself through space? Not so easy. I suspected her little stint as a Phant host had something to do with her abilities.

"We should get behind that rock, Rage," Hijak sent. "Before the ship comes about for an attack vector."

I didn't think the frigate needed to come about for an attack vector at all. Already I saw a battery of turrets, part of the frigate's point defense system, swiveling toward us.

"You guys go ahead." I jetted upward immediately, wanting to draw fire away from the others.

"Rage . . ." Hijak transmitted.

"That's an order! I know what I'm doing." *Not really.* "I'll be right behind you." *I hope.*

Piloting an ATLAS 6 out here, I was basically the equivalent of a large, Avenger class starfighter, but with more firepower. And I was going to take advantage of that fact.

I targeted the turret battery with my serpent launcher and told Hopper, "Override friendly fire protection."

"Friendly fire protection disabled," Hopper answered.

I made sure the recoil dampening was dialed down to zero, then I fired off three rockets before the enemy turrets could come to bear.

The rockets struck, as indicated by three bright flashes of light.

A lucky shot: I'd taken out the entire battery.

The SK frigate activated its starboard thrusters, trying to bring more weapons to bear.

I spotted another collection of turrets farther along the hull and I let loose a second rocket barrage.

Too late.

Those turrets unleashed hell, detonating my rockets in bright flashes.

The parallel threads of turret fire continued slicing through the void—deadly, silent ribbons of light that swiveled straight toward me.

Crap.

I jetted downward and swung Hopper around to face the large rock.

I activated my horizontal jumpjets at full burn, cut the flow after two seconds, then followed up with a half-second lateral burst.

Turret fire streamed past just to my left, noiselessly continuing onward to smash into the rock in front of me.

I released another half-second burst, directly vertical, further altering my trajectory, and followed up with a countering burst so that I swung around the rock in a wide, elliptical trajectory.

I glanced over my shoulder and watched the ship and its deadly fire vanish from view behind the large mineral body.

Hijak and Lana were waiting for me on the other side.

"Nice driving," Hijak said.

"Let's go."

Everywhere I looked, the countless rocks of the Tau Ceti III ring belt floated past. According to the aReal in my helmet, the belt was roughly eighty thousand kilometers wide, with a local height-density ranging from as little as twenty meters to as high as two kilometers. Imagine a ring-shaped disc whose thickness varied along the edge.

The rocks themselves ranged in size from one centimeter to a hundred meters. Some were made of ice tinged with tholins such as methane, while others were composed of silicates.

The entire belt was dimly lit by the Tau Ceti G-class star, which was a pinpoint in the distance. The swirling purple-black vapors of the gas giant Tau Ceti III provided a constant backdrop below.

I jetted forward, dodging the larger rocks, putting as many targets between me and the frigate as possible.

I glanced at the HUD map on my helmet. Other than the green dots of Hijak and Lana, I didn't see anything else except the enemy ship, which was also marked in green. It hadn't moved.

"Switch to war-game mode," I transmitted. "We're the only friendlies. Leave everything else red."

Since we were all operating SK gear out here, by default the ship and any other SK units would be marked in green—friendlies. We would exchange telemetry data, constantly updating our positions with all other SK units in range. Though right now we were probably too far from the ship to share any meaningful telemetry data. Even so, if any other SK units approached, we would instantly know their positions, and they would know ours.

War-game mode changed all that. It was very useful in training, for obvious reasons.

As it was useful now.

"Hopper, initiate war-game mode," I said.

"War-game mode initiated."

Every unit on my HUD map became red, including Hijak, Lana, and the distant frigate. I immediately tagged Hijak and Lana as friendlies, and their icons returned to green. I left the frigate in red, so that we no longer exchanged telemetry.

"Do you know how to activate war-game mode, Lana?" I sent over the comm. A small rock bounced away from my chest piece.

"Done already," she replied.

"Nice," I sent. "Now then, all that's left is to set up an early warning system." To my mech: "Hopper, launch ATLAS Support System."

Hopper didn't reply.

"Hopper, launch ASS."

Still nothing. Either the ATLAS 6 didn't have an ASS, or the scout was launched via an entirely different command.

"Trying to get your ASS in gear are you?" Hijak jetted past me, and applied a vertical burst to avoid hitting an ATLAS-sized rock.

"Funny." I followed suit behind him, shoving off from the boulder. "Hopper, how do I launch the provided ATLAS Support System drone?"

"The ATLAS Support System drone assigned to this unit has been jettisoned," the female AI intoned.

Ah.

"Hijak, see if you can fire a support probe."

"Already tried," Hijak answered. "Looks like someone launched it on this mech already. And it never returned."

"Damn. Mine too. Lana, what about yours?"

"I'll check," she returned.

I glanced over my shoulder, scanning for pursuers. I saw only the endless floating bodies of the ring belt behind me. Even the thermal band was blank. If the frigate had left cover, I would've seen its thermal signature by now.

Even so, we weren't out of this yet. Not by a long shot.

"Got it," she transmitted. A small HS3-type probe ejected from her mech, and maneuvered behind one of the larger rocks. "I've switched the probe to the war-game setting, and marked the three of us as friendlies so we'll all receive updates. I'll leave it here in stealth mode, set to squawk on the approach of any nonmineral objects."

"Perfect."

I continued onward, moving from rock to rock, bumping into the smaller ones, avoiding the larger. We followed the orbital path of the ring belt, continuing to put distance between ourselves and the enemy. I looked back occasionally, but still there were no signs of pursuit. I saw only the endless panorama of slowly drifting rocks. On the map, Lana's drone remained in place, the only other dot between us and the frigate.

"Lana," I transmitted. "You've never actually piloted an ATLAS 6 before today, have you?"

"I've never piloted any sort of mech," she admitted.

"Doesn't that freak you out?" I sent.

"Not at all."

"Well it freaks me out!" Hijak interjected. "You had a Phant tinkering with your brain. You're a cast-off alien host. Who can say what they did to you?"

"I am what I am," Lana sent. "I have memories of another life. And I will use them." She tried to put on a brave front, but I heard the uncertainty and sadness in her voice. She'd never really be quite human ever again, would she?

"I find Dyson Xang's rancor disturbing," Lana transmitted suddenly. "You, I could understand, Rade Galaal. But him? He has Sino-Korean ancestry, doesn't he?"

"Don't go there," Hijak sent. I could almost hear the growl in his voice.

"It doesn't help that you interrogated and tortured us for the past week," I said. "Sure, it wasn't you. At least you say it wasn't. The Phant may be gone now, but who knows how deep its tendrils reached into your mind, and what remnants of the alien personality are still inside? You just admitted you have memories of another life. How do you even know you're yourself again, when who you were was overwritten?"

"Tell me how I can prove that I am who I say I am. That I am free of alien influence."

"That's the question of the day, isn't it?" I thought for a moment. "It would help if you told us how you ended up on the ship in the first place."

She didn't answer right away. When she did, her voice was quiet, reflective. "I was on Tau Ceti II-c. It was after a spaceline flight. It happened so suddenly. The skies blackened. The deadly rain fell. People died in the streets, melted away. Then the robots started attacking. It was my birthday. *My birthday.* I shouldn't have even been there, but the spaceline called me in to cover for a sick pilot." She sobbed.

One thing I couldn't take was a woman crying. It just ripped at my heartstrings. I wanted to hold Lana and tell her everything was going to be all right. But of course I couldn't do any of that out here in space.

"I made it back to my hotel room," Lana continued, "where I was captured, and brought to one of the sports arenas, which had been converted into a holding facility. That's where I met the Artificial. It called itself *Zhödöo,* the Guide. It promised that if we surrendered, we would be part of the twenty percent who were spared. That we would receive the technology of the Guide's people and bask in their enlightenment. And that we would serve them. It was very similar to the promise the Guide made to you.

"Like most people in the arena, I surrendered, and gave up the password to my embedded ID. But if I had known then what surrendering truly entailed, I wouldn't have done it. I would have chosen death instead. Because you see, I was brought to a room beneath the arena, where I discovered that my 'enlightenment' was to be integrated with the alien species.

"The Yaoguai had possessed our Weavers, and used them to graft metallic devices to our skulls and spines, which allowed the demons a conduit to our minds. When all the occupants of the arena were converted to appropriate Yaoguai conduits, the demons abandoned many of the robots, preferring the sensual pleasures of human flesh.

"It's the oddest feeling, observing your body doing things of its own accord, with your mind reduced to the capacity of a mere observer. And that's really all I was—I couldn't think, not in the usual way, not with words and images anyway. But the observer part of my mind was still active, and I was aware of everything. So that's what I did. I observed. Watched the debasing acts that were done to my body, and the disgusting things my body did in turn.

"When the demons tired of their sensual explorations, they delved into the knowledge gleaned from our embedded IDs. Soon they learned to program the robots to their whims, and no longer needed Yaoguai to possess the machines. They learned how to operate our shuttles and city defense systems.

"But the passage of knowledge wasn't only one way. I too learned things during this time. The enemy communicate telepathically, as I have told you, and once one demon learns something, that knowledge is passed on to every other demon of the same class, regardless of where the others are located, galaxy-wide. It does take time to propagate this knowledge, and I am not sure of the exact mechanism, but all I know is the more people we lose to them, the quicker they learn how to defeat the rest of us. We are not the first species to face the demons. And if we do not stop them, we definitely will not be the last."

I glanced over my shoulder. Still no sign of pursuit. Maybe we were going to get away after all.

We were quite far from the support probe now, but it still transmitted telemetry to my HUD, which meant reception was surprisingly good out here. Though the Skull Ship wasn't in orbit around this particular gas giant, its EM signals could travel system-wide, and we should have experienced at least some interference. Maybe the planet shielded us from the signals. Either way, I resolved to enjoy the improved range while it lasted.

"So you're saying you had no affiliation with Dragon platoon?" I said over the comm. "The SKs sent down with us to the moon? Do you even know what I'm talking about?"

"I do," Lana sent. "And no, we weren't part of Dragon platoon. Though we were in the warehouse, firing at Dragon platoon right alongside the robots. That's right. Firing at our own people. You see, we were protecting the Guide. We purloined the glass container from the SK platoon when we realized it was bulletproof, and we planned to use it to safely transport the Guide away. When you two showed up, that was an unexpected bonus. We had our chance to integrate more members of the UC. The much-vaunted MOTHs."

"Why was the Guide on the moon in the first place?" I said.

"To observe the proceedings firsthand," Lana sent. "And gather as much data as it could on humanity. The Guide reports directly to an entity known as the Observer Mind."

"And what the hell is that?" I was getting a bit of a starvation headache, and I ordered my suit to prepare an MRE (Meal, Ready-to-Eat, or more commonly, it's not a Meal, it's not Ready, and you can't Eat it).

"I honestly don't know," Lana answered.

The MRE nozzle jammed into my mouth, and I took a huge gulp of banana-flavored gruel. Not bad tasting, actually, if you could get over the texture. "This invasion is getting better and better all the time. An alien empire, which can communicate telepathically galaxy-wide, led by some ominous being known as the Observer Mind. What's next, an entire army of Skull Ships?"

"Hey, don't jinx us," Hijak transmitted.

"Hijak, I don't think anything I say at this point can make things any worse than they are."

An alert sounded, and five red dots appeared on the HUD map at my six, as relayed by the support probe Lana had planted behind us.

"You were saying?" Hijak sent.

"*Mierda.*" I dismissed the MRE nozzle. A glob of banana-flavored gruel trickled down my chin.

"What do you think?" Hijak transmitted. "Torpedoes? Mortars? Or fighters?"

"None of the above. Frigates don't have fighters. Mortars are too easy to dodge. And torpedoes couldn't navigate this mess worth a damn. So Lana, what the hell are they?"

"I'm getting a visual now . . ." Lana responded. "Oh, no."

"What?"

"We're being pursued by the other ATLAS 6s. All five."

"Damn it," I said. "We should have ordered the mechs to come with us."

"Too late now," Hijak sent. "Should've thought of that before."

"Yeah well, it was kind of hard to think with that Klaxon blaring in the hangar bay."

But he was right. I should've thought of it. This was my fault.

Damn it to hell.

Well, nothing we could do about it now. We'd just have to deal with them.

"Rage, is your PASS device still on?" Hijak sent.

"Yeah, why?"

"Nicely done," Hijak transmitted. "They're obviously using it to track us. Turn it off, bro."

"No," I said. "First of all, if I turn it off now, it will just alert the pursuers that we're on to them. Secondly, it doesn't matter. Atomic-powered machines like mechs leave a radiation trail. Not to mention the heat signatures we're emitting at this very moment. No, my friend, we're leaving a bright and shiny trail for them to follow regardless of whether the PASS is on or off."

"Okay fine," Hijak transmitted. "One thing I can't figure out: Why wouldn't the Guide just nuke the whole area?"

"Even if the Guide didn't want the UC to recover us anymore, there are too many rocks between us and the ship to fire a nuke now." I switched to direct communication, cutting out Lana.

"Protecting Lana has to be our top priority, understood? She knows things about the enemy. She could be the key to winning this war. You have to put aside your differences, Hijak. Forget for a moment she's SK. Forget for a moment she was an alien host."

Hijak didn't answer right away. When he did, his voice seemed resigned. "I'll do my best. But if it comes to you or her, I'm choosing you, Rage."

I was going to counter him, but decided not to. Nothing I could say would change his mind. If it came down to it, I wasn't sure who I'd pick between them, either.

"I'm having the ASS follow the targets at a safe distance," Lana transmitted. "And I'm keeping its stealth mode active. I've instructed the drone to move from rock to rock via small thruster bursts. No constant emissions."

"Good." That was exactly what I would have done. It was kind of scary how much knowledge the Phants had assimilated about human technology and tactics already. Knowledge that was imparted to Lana.

The ASS drone was battery powered, and didn't have a radiation signature. The heat profile was relatively small too. As long as it stayed well back, and hid behind appropriately sized rocks, it could remain undiscovered for quite a while.

I studied the red dots on the HUD map and considered our options. We had a significant lead on the pursuers. We could continue onward through the ring belt for several hours, maybe even days if we switched our mechs to autopilot while we slept. But we wouldn't be able to outrun them indefinitely. Eventually we'd run low on jetpack fuel, and we'd have to fight.

Better to face them now, on our own terms, while we still had an active scout on their six.

But first I wanted to clear up some things regarding the offense and defense capabilities of the mechs. "These ATLAS 6s have built-in ballistic shielding around the cockpit area. But what about the fuel canisters?"

"Those are shielded, too," Lana volunteered.

"And the visual sensors?"

"Those we can take out," Lana sent. "Assuming the target doesn't block our shots with its shield arm."

"ATLAS 6s have shields?" I cycled through the weapons in my left arm to confirm. Yep. Half-length body shields. When I had faced an ATLAS 6 on the battlefield before, it hadn't used a shield. "Seems a bit extraneous. But I guess it can only add to the defensive capabilities. So what this all tells me is that our Gatlings are basically useless."

"Not true," Hijak sent. "A Gatling will still get through the cockpit eventually. Just takes a little longer."

"Yeah, assuming we can convince the target to let us shoot it in the same spot for fifteen seconds. I think we're going to have to rely on serpents more than anything else. Too bad a planetary ring belt isn't the most conducive environment for that. We'll have to wait until the targets are close before launching, otherwise we risk premature detonation."

"How close are we talking?" Lana said.

"I would say at least ten to twenty meters."

"What about the energy axes these ATLAS 6s have?" Hijak said.

I'd forgotten about that.

I rotated through the weapons of my right hand.

Incendiary thrower.

Gatling gun.

Serpent launcher.

Ax mount.

"Weapon in hand," I told Hopper's AI.

As soon as the ax locked into place, I felt a jolt run through my right arm, and blue bolts of energy sparked up and down the surface of the weapon. The blade was three times as tall as a human body. Rediscovered wootz steel, with sheets of microcarbides within a tempered pearlite matrix, afforded one of the hardest substances known to man. I zoomed in and observed that distinctive banding pattern reminiscent of flowing water caused by the graphene molecules interlaced throughout the metal.

I examined the shield, which was still mounted to my left hand. Like I'd told Lana, it seemed kind of extraneous to me. When I zoomed in, I saw the same wootz banding pattern. Maybe not so extraneous . . .

"These shields are designed to defend against the axes?" I said.

"Exactly right," Lana responded. "While the ballistic shielding around the cockpit is for, appropriately, ballistics, an energy ax will penetrate ballistic shielding relatively easily, especially with the strength of an ATLAS 6 behind the blow. But place the wootz shield between the hull and the ax, and you buy yourself a bit of time."

"All right. Thank you." I scanned the immediate area, looking for rocks that would suit the purpose I had in mind. "This is what we're going to do."

After I finished explaining the plan, I jetted behind the boulder I'd picked out. It was about three times as big as my mech.

Why did I need a rock roughly three times as big as Hopper?

Space consists of a hard vacuum of low-density particles, mostly hydrogen and helium, with an average background temperature of 2.7 Kelvin. It's a cold, dark, empty place.

The atomic generator found at the heart of a mech produces roughly four watts of waste heat for every watt of electricity. That heat has to be shed, which is done via the radiators placed beneath the heat vents on the top and bottom of the liquid-cooled reactor. Those radiators dispose of around thirty-five gigajoules of waste heat every sixty seconds.

Add in the waste heat generated by a jumpsuit's life-support system, which is also transferred to the mech's hull, and you get a heat signature in the megawatt range—which, if left unmasked, is detectable up to three million kilometers out, or twenty AUs (one Astronomical Unit is the distance from the Earth to the Sun). This doesn't count the heat from the mech's jetpack, which obviously increases when the thrust is active.

Even with the thermal masking and obfuscation tech built into the ATLAS, the waste heat gives it an aura roughly six meters in every direction under the infrared band. Therefore, I had to choose a rock big enough to shield not just my mech, but its heat signature too. A rock with a surface I could readily grip, as I needed the ability to reposition it at will.

Lana and Hijak found similarly sized rocks and brought them back.

"Are you sure I can't convince you to continue on ahead without us, Lana?" I sent over the comm. "You know how valuable you are to us."

"Not on your life," she transmitted. "I'm going to fight with you. Because if you die, I'm dead anyway."

She was probably right on that point.

I opened the cockpit and detached the PASS device from my jumpsuit. I tossed it into the void along our previous trajectory, and watched it drift forward through the ring belt, where it would continue indefinitely—at least until it collided with something.

I resealed the cockpit.

The decoy was in place.

The three of us jetted apart, separated by two klicks (signal reception was still quite strong, and our HUD maps updated perfectly). We formed the points of a slightly skewed triangle, and proceeded back toward the enemy. After traveling four klicks, we halted, staying behind our rocks.

The trap was set.

On my vision feed, I had rad mode turned on. This allowed me to see the radiation trails produced by the ATLAS 6s. When we had moved apart, I'd watched the three main radiation trails of our old trajectory diminish to nothingness. I couldn't discern the radiation even now, but I knew the trails remained at the center of the triangle our new positions formed. This was good, because it meant the enemy wouldn't see our new trails, at least as long as the pursuers kept reasonably close to the old trajectory. I couldn't see the fresh trails made by Hijak or Lana—their mechs were too far away. The sole rad trail I *could* see was my own receding behind me. The only reason I knew Hijak and Lana were still out there was because of the dots on my HUD. Just as I knew the enemy was out there.

To this enemy, it should look like the three main rad trails continued onward, past our current positions, which was consistent with the receding PASS device. Only when the enemy mechs were well within our sight lines would they realize the trails branched back.

It was the perfect ambush.

You'd think the periodic updates transmitted by our aReals would give us away, but like our verbal comms, the signals were extremely weak, and utilized obfuscation tech to appear as background radiation. So there was no chance of discovery on that side of things.

I double-checked that the recoil buffers on all my weapons were set to full absorption while I waited. I didn't want unexpected kickback to send me hurtling backward when I fired my first shots.

I remained very still. The mech's atomic reactor automatically switched to low power mode, which further reduced my heat signature.

The moments passed. On the HUD map, I watched the red dots representing the enemy targets slowly approach.

More dots abruptly appeared, and rapidly spread far apart, fanning out ahead of the others.

Damn it.

The enemy mechs had launched support probes to cast a wider search net.

They sensed a trap.

"Rage, do you see that?" Hijak transmitted.

"I do. Guess we'll be engaging sooner than we thought. Be ready."

The red dots on the HUD map froze. That could mean only one thing: the enemy had discovered our trailing probe.

Things were getting better all the time.

"Just lost contact with my ASS," Lana sent.

"Hope you wiped, first," Hijak joked.

"Focus, people," I transmitted. "We should be seeing their probes any second now."

Extrapolating from the last known positions on my HUD, I realized that the probe on the far left of the enemy search net would pass close to me. The one on the far right would drift by Hijak. Lana was positioned well below the search plane, and probably would avoid encountering any of the probes.

Soon an enemy probe appeared, floating fifty meters diagonally down and to my left. I picked it out from the surrounding rocks by its tiny heat signature.

With the help of the targeting overlay built into my HUD, I trained my Gatling gun on it and fired.

"First probe, down," I transmitted.

"Second probe, down," Hijak sent.

"I haven't spotted anything yet," Lana sent.

"Forget the other probes," I returned. "They know we're here now. Engage."

I loaded the serpent launchers into both my hands, crawled to the edge of my hide, and peered past.

I saw nothing but floating, revolving rocks.

"Hopper, emphasize heat signatures."

Nothing.

No probes. No ATLAS 6s.

That was odd.

Then I spotted the two radiation trails, thin ethereal lines that fanned upward along my vision field and traveled far overhead . . .

I glanced up.

Two ATLAS 6 mechs bore down on my position.

The incoming missile alarm sounded.

On my map, I saw seven serpent missiles. All homing in on Hopper.

I thrust backward, abandoning the rock. While it might protect me from one or two missile blows if I could reposition myself fast enough, it definitely wouldn't hold up against seven.

I let off a lateral burst and swung around toward the missiles. My momentum continued to carry me backward, and I heard the patter of small rocks on Hopper's hull behind me.

I launched the Trench Coat. The metallic pieces surged forward and detonated two of the incoming missiles.

I swiveled Gatling guns into both hands and fired at the remaining missile cluster. Such a tactic was only feasible in the void, due to the nature of space combat, where one could jet away from a missile long enough to face it and shoot it down.

Got one. The explosion took out another beside it.

The missiles closed—

Another serpent detonated prematurely when it struck a small rock. The hot gases set off the missile beside it.

That left one last missile . . . less than ten meters away and closing fast.

The serpent proved a straightforward target at this range, and I easily took it down with my Gats.

But at that moment I came to a sudden dead stop.

I'd slammed into a large rock, cutting my momentum to zero.

The expanding gases of the detonating missile hit me, and Hopper hurtled backward, hitting the rock again, which had been sent flying back from my previous impact. The temperature inside the cockpit spiked to 50 degrees Celsius.

The missile alarm immediately sounded again.

My HUD map alerted me to another barrage of eight missiles. Damn it.

I swiveled sideways and shoved off from the rock, away from the serpents. I switched my rear thrusters to full burn and released the Trench Coat. Once. Twice.

Flashes behind me told me that some of the coat pieces had struck. I deactivated my rear thrust and applied a lat burst to spin around, wanting to gauge the situation behind me.

The lead missile was only two body-lengths from me.

I shot it immediately with my Gatling, and the cascade effect of the explosion took out the remaining three.

The shockwave sent me reeling backward. The temperature spike in my cockpit approached 70 degrees Celsius this time. Not good. The loud whir of cooling fans nearly drowned out the heat alarms.

I activated gyroscopic thrusters to stabilize.

Only to hear the missile alarm activate yet *again*.

Five missiles on my tail, and gaining.

I swiveled around to face them. Small rocks constantly struck the back of my mech as momentum carried me away. I was basically clearing a path through the ring belt for the pursuing missiles. The impact of a larger rock forced Hopper's head forward, a motion that was translated to the inner shell of the cockpit and jolted my own neck forward.

I launched the Trench Coat, detonating two of the missiles. I shot down two more with my Gats, and the final one blew up collaterally.

The missile alarm didn't sound again, thankfully.

I pivoted in place, trying to get my bearings. My eyes alighted on a nearby rock, one of the biggest in the general area at four times the size of my mech.

I thrust straight toward that rock, taking cover behind it, noting the position of another large rock along the way.

"Sit-rep," I sent over the comm.

"Engaged but fine," Hijak answered.

"Busy," Lana returned.

I couldn't see Lana and Hijak of course, but the green dots on my HUD map told me exactly where they were. Hijak had two red dots on his tail, while Lana dealt with only one, along with the smaller dots of missiles.

Hijak and I had agreed to protect Lana. Leaving her with only one enemy to face was the best we could do right now. She'd just have to hang in there. If I went back to her at this moment, all I would do was lead the two ATLAS 6s on my tail straight to her.

Speaking of those ATLAS 6s, their red dots on my HUD hadn't updated since the second missile barrage, and I had no idea where they were.

I positioned myself near the edge of the rock that formed my impromptu hide, scanning the battle space.

Other than the occasional flashes in the far distance, which revealed the general locations where Lana and Hijak fought, I saw nothing else between the drifting rocks. No heat signatures. No rad trails (save my own).

The gas giant and its ring belt were my sole companions.

For a moment I feared the pursuers had abandoned me to pursue either Lana or Hijak. It would be a simple matter to follow the remote flashes that marked the combats of my friends, after all.

But then a sixth sense told me to look down.

In the distance, between my legs, I saw two ATLAS 6s accelerating toward me, led by threads of white light . . .

Gatling fire.

The bullets drilled into Hopper's hull at the incredibly deadly rate of one hundred rounds per second. I heard the constant ricochets from the cockpit. If I had been in an ATLAS 5, whose hull was not ballistically shielded, I would be dead.

I swung my body up and away, over the topmost edge of the rock, placing the mineral body between myself and the mechs.

The rock shook beneath me as the Gatlings ate into it, and then the entire structure broke apart.

I felt constantly on the defensive out here. All I could do was run and hide, never getting any shots in.

There had to be a way to get the upper hand . . .

I spotted the other large boulder I had seen in the vicinity.

And I had an idea.

One piece of the broken rock was as big as my mech, and I dragged it along as I jetted away. The rock didn't conceal my heat signature, and of course the inevitable thread of Gatling fire followed me.

I loaded the serpent launcher into my right hand and leaned slightly beyond the rim of the rock.

I loosed four rockets.

As expected, the enemy ATLAS 6s initiated evasive maneuvers, launching their Trench Coats. Four flashes told me my rockets had been destroyed.

I launched four more, and used the distraction to steer my mech toward the other large boulder. I continued to drag the smaller rock along with me.

When I reached the boulder, I sheltered Hopper behind it, launching four more missiles.

"Guard," I told Hopper.

I opened the cockpit and ejected.

I thrust behind the smaller rock I'd brought here, which concealed my jumpsuit entirely.

I gave the rock a shove and, staying behind it, used it to float away from Hopper and the bigger boulder. I kept my body stationed on the far side, away from the sight lines of the other mechs, using their last known positions to guide me.

I felt extremely vulnerable out there, but my heat signature would be way smaller now, and I knew it wouldn't be visible beyond the confines of the rock.

At least, I hoped it wouldn't.

I didn't dare fire off my jumpjets again, not yet. The extra heat could give me away.

The rock continued to drift from the larger one, where Hopper remained in "Guard" mode.

A flash of metal caught my eye, and I saw an enemy ATLAS 6 approaching Hopper from below.

I glanced up, searching for the other enemy mech, knowing they'd try to outflank Hopper. I spotted it far above, almost exactly where I expected it.

Hopper received the telemetry from my helmet aReal, and initiated offensive action, launching six serpents at either mech. I cringed inside, because that was the remaining missile loadout of the ATLAS 6. When I got back, I wouldn't have any more serpents.

Stupid, stupid AIs.

In any case, the enemy mechs were suitably distracted, and both initiated evasive maneuvers, activating their Trench Coats.

Tightly gripping the small rock, I fired off several quick bursts from my jetpack, shadowing the movements of the leftmost, closer opponent.

The enemy ATLAS 6 employed the same tactics I had, and used its Gatling gun to take down the remaining missiles.

My shadowing had carried me to within twenty meters of the enemy mech. A quick check of my HUD told me the other ATLAS 6 was two hundred meters to the right.

With my helmet aReal, I zoomed in on each of them in turn. Both enemy units had their backs toward me, and were concentrating on Hopper.

I fired off a quick burst of my jumpjets, carrying myself and the small rock toward the closer opponent.

The enemy mech confidently fired three missiles at Hopper.

I didn't wait to see how Hopper reacted; I only hoped my ATLAS wouldn't accidentally shoot me while it responded to the threat.

I fired my jets at full burn, fast approaching the enemy mech from behind. I still ported the rock—I was just another mineral body as far as the external sensors of the target were concerned.

I kept my course centered on the enemy as rocks flitted past. Some hit me, and though a few of the impacts were sizable, none of them perforated my jumpsuit. One of the pebble-sized objects managed to make a big chip in my faceplate, however.

I closed with the target and released the rock—

With a final burst of thrust, I landed on the enemy mech's jetpack.

Though the jumpjets of ATLAS 6s were twice the size of the previous models, the fuel lines threading between the tanks and jets, like the older ATLAS 5, were readily accessible and unarmored. I used my favorite tactic, and severed the main line.

Jet fuel spurted out, boiling and desublimating at the same time, forming a cloud of fine, frozen crystals, similar to mist.

I sheathed my utility knife and pulled myself up into the seating area above the jetpacks, behind the head. I sat in the leftmost seat (the ATLAS 6s had two passenger seats, unlike the single seat of the ATLAS 5s). I'd seen the mech fire its Trench Coat earlier, so I knew no electro-defense mechanisms were installed.

Even so, before I could strap myself in, the enemy ATLAS 6 launched into a series of evasive maneuvers, and nearly shook me off.

I grasped the seat buckle for dear life. Behind the mech, a stream of fuel crystals formed a spiraling trail.

The ATLAS couldn't get me, not while I hung there, but the other enemy obviously could—I just hoped Hopper kept the second ATLAS engaged.

The mech's jets abruptly cut off.

Out of fuel.

I felt the hull shudder beneath me.

I turned around in time to see a jumpsuit-clad SK thrust himself toward me from the open cockpit.

He held a pistol.

I released the seat belt and activated my lateral jets, full burn—

And spiraled at high speed around the entire mech—

Coming at the surprised SK from the opposite side in under half a second.

Before he could react, I plunged my knife into the rib region of his jumpsuit.

My momentum carried the two of us away from the mech. Without fuel, the abandoned ATLAS 6 receded behind us, unable to bring its Gatlings to bear.

As the stars spiraled past at a dizzying speed, I bashed the 9-mil from the SK's grasp. The pistol spun away.

I started to withdraw the knife I'd plunged into the SK's jumpsuit, but he forcibly wrapped his hands around my gloves, keeping the weapon embedded. He didn't want to lose suit integrity—his jumpsuit had obviously sealed around the blade. If I removed the knife, I'd probably create a gap big enough to depressurize the entire suit.

I was starting to feel nauseous from all the rotating, and I fired some gyroscopic stabilizers. But the SK activated his own jumpjets, messing up my equalization attempts.

I strove once more to remove the knife, but I couldn't budge the weapon, not with his gloves wrapped around mine. I tried twisting the blade. No good. Our jumpsuits gave us equal strength, and he countered my every attempt.

I stared into my foe's helmet and saw the fearless, emotionless visage of a man who didn't care if he lived or died.

He was definitely controlled by a Phant.

I managed to pry one hand free from his grasp and I lifted my glove toward his helmet, hoping to open his locking assembly.

He took advantage of my slackened hold to kick me in the chest.

I lost my grip on the knife and drifted away from him.

The SK withdrew a second pistol from his belt.

Wonderful.

I jetted in reverse, activating my lateral thrusters at random intervals so that I moved in an unpredictable, three-dimensional spiral. Just like I was taught.

The ballistics alarm triggered inside my helmet.

"Hopper, pick me up!" I sent my mech.

I glanced at the HUD map. Hopper wasn't far.

I couldn't see or hear the 9-mil bullets, but I knew they were out there because of the muzzle flashes. Hidden, silent bullets sliced through the void, ready to perforate my suit and kill me. All it would take was one lucky shot.

"Hopper!"

I kept up the evasive maneuvers, trying to jet in the general direction of my mech. Then I felt a strong burning sensation in the back of my shoulder.

The SK had finally shot me.

The skin and muscle of my rear deltoid would be sucked outward because of the pressure differential, and would partially close the small perforation in my jumpsuit. The coagulating blood from the injury itself would complete the seal. At least, that's how it was supposed to work.

I felt the throbbing pain, and did my best to ignore it, reminding myself that I had experienced far worse at the hands of the Keeper.

My mech neared, moving erratically. Long threads of Gatling fire from the other enemy ATLAS forced Hopper to constantly evade. A single strike from one of those threads to my jumpsuit would mean instant death.

"Hopper, attacker on my six," I sent as my mech grew near. "Defend."

A stream of Gatling fire erupted from Hopper, silently slicing into the void behind me.

On my HUD map, the red dot indicating the SK behind me turned dark.

"Hopper, steady," I transmitted.

Hopper ceased the evasive maneuvers and headed straight toward me.

I positioned myself between Hopper and the remaining mech so that I was shielded from the enemy Gatlings. Hopper faced away from me, shooting at the pursuing mech.

I jetted toward Hopper at maximum thrust. Small rocks pummeled my suit.

"Hopper, reposition for dock."

Hopper ceased firing and swiveled around.

The mech's cockpit unlatched. There was no gravity to complete the opening out here, so Hopper used a metallic hand to yank the hatch the rest of the way down.

I dove inside.

I flinched in pain as the inner cocoon wrapped around me and pressed into my injured shoulder.

When Hopper's vision feed kicked in, I found myself staring at the SK I'd just escaped from. His jumpsuit spun lifelessly, ten meters away, and the blue mist of a Phant vented from his neck.

The sound of Gatling bullets hitting Hopper's right arm drew me back to the situation at hand, and I jetted my mech hard to the left.

Turning around, I realized the enemy ATLAS 6 held a Gatling in one hand and an energy ax in the other. That told me it had run out of serpents.

Good. So we were on relatively even footing now.

I double-checked my own serpent missile inventory. Yep. Empty.

I swiveled the wootz shield into my left hand and brought the energy ax into my right.

I held the shield toward the enemy. The wootz worked wonders against the Gatling gun, easily deflecting those bullets. I saw slight dents appear on the backside. Not invincible, then, but definitely better than ordinary ballistic shields.

I landed on a large boulder and dug in, waiting for my foe.

The dents stopped appearing on the back of the shield and I knew the enemy mech had ceased firing. Maybe it had exhausted its ammunition.

I tentatively peered past the rim of the shield.

The enemy ATLAS 6 had replaced its Gat with a shield of its own. It was coming toward me at ramming speed, and had lifted its blade far back, poised to strike.

I timed my moment precisely, smoothly jetting upward, bringing my ax down in a decapitating blow.

The enemy ATLAS managed to raise its shield in time, blocking my blade.

It immediately thrusted toward me, ramming its shield into my body, sending me spinning away.

I pummeled through a cluster of smaller rocks, then stabilized myself.

The enemy ATLAS 6 jetted toward me—

I moved aside—

We swept past each other, like medieval jousters in space, exchanging glancing blows. The impact jolted my wounded shoulder, and I winced in pain.

I turned about, and accelerated to meet the mech full-on this time—

We collided, shield on shield.

I kept accelerating, as did my opponent, and neither of us made any headway. I couldn't reach around with my ax; the shield was too wide.

I eased off on the thrust and tilted my shield to the left, letting the enemy ATLAS 6 roll past.

We could go on like this for hours. I needed a way to win. *Now*.

I jetted backward, swiveling both the shield and the ax out of my hands so that I appeared weaponless.

I held up my empty palms, as if indicating surrender. I winced, because the movement aggravated the gunshot wound in my shoulder, and my whole deltoid region throbbed anew.

As anticipated, the enemy ATLAS 6 jetted toward me.

I hadn't expected mercy.

Nor was I going to give it.

My opponent hoisted the energy ax far back as it approached—

And sliced horizontally toward my cockpit—

I accelerated upward and forward, swinging my entire body up so that my hips and legs were higher than my head.

The enemy's blade tore through empty space—

I moved over my opponent in a parabolic arc—

I passed the enemy's shield, reached down, wrapped my hand around its head, pulled myself in, and jabbed my fingers into the visual sensors.

I felt the glass give beneath Hopper's unrelenting strength.

The enemy mech swung its ax upward, and before I could counter, it sliced Hopper's arm off below the elbow.

I jetted backward, the stump of my arm sparking. I watched my severed appendage and all its swappable weapon loadouts, including the energy ax, drift end over end into space.

Of course, my real arm was safe inside the cockpit.

The enemy pilot, now blinded, spun his ATLAS 6 wildly, randomly cutting at the air with the ax.

I loaded a Gatling gun into my left hand and aimed at the chest piece. I fired, striking the armor. The blinded, panicking pilot activated his thrust at full burn, in a random direction that just so happened to hurtle his mech toward the planet.

The pilot didn't have to be blind. All he had to do was swivel one of the Gats back in hand, and transfer the scope vid feed to his cockpit. That was the first thing I would have done. But I was a skilled mech pilot, and for me the ATLAS was an extension of my own body. This "pilot" likely had a completely different occupation before today. The Phant that possessed him probably had the necessary knowledge buried somewhere inside it, yet actually putting that knowledge to use during the pulse-pounding heat of battle was a completely different story. If the Phant hadn't internalized that knowledge to the point where it could act without thinking, then the information was useless. Assuming of course that the consciousness of a Phant was even remotely similar to a human being's, though I suspected that when integrated with a human host, they behaved closer to us than anything else.

I fired off some subsequent shots for good measure, and the enemy pilot applied more thrust. If he kept that up, he'd find himself in a decaying orbit around the gas giant. Without booster rockets, he'd never get out again.

I followed the enemy mech for a ways, waiting for the pilot to eject. Ready to gun him down.

"Warning: approaching inescapable gravity well," Hopper's AI intoned.

The enemy pilot didn't eject.

His mech passed the point of no return.

I pulled up before I, too, became irrevocably trapped in the massive gravity well.

It was done.

I unleashed several long bursts of thrust, returning to the higher, safer orbit of the ring belt. Then I made my way toward Lana and Hijak. I was running low on jumpjet fuel at this point, and used my thrust sparingly.

Now that the life-or-death dance of battle had ended, the pain in my shoulder returned full-bore. I shrugged it off. There was no atmosphere present in the cockpit, and I really should have repaired my suit to reduce the swelling in my shoulder, but there wasn't time.

My friends needed me.

According to my HUD map, Hijak still faced one enemy opponent, in a battle just as desperate as mine had been. His dot was bright green and zigzagging. Lana had taken out her own single opponent, but her dot was darker, stationary.

I pulled up her vitals. They were fluctuating.

"Lana, do you copy? Lana?"

No answer.

I considered making a beeline toward her but decided against it.

I had to help Hijak, if I could.

Lana would just have to wait.

I hadn't been sure whose life I'd choose to save when the time came.

But I was sure now.

My platoon brother had top priority.

"I'm coming, Hijak," I said.

When I was halfway to Hijak's position, the red dot representing his target abruptly winked out.

"Hijak, you all right? I'm almost there."

"Bit late, Rage," he said, his voice coming in a painful wheeze. "Nothing to see here. Better . . . better check on Lana."

On my HUD, I saw the green dot representing his mech proceed toward Lana. We were about equidistant from her now, and would reach her at roughly the same time.

"Tell me you're okay, Hijak." I glanced at his vitals on my HUD. They seemed weak, but not critical.

"I took . . . a few good hits." Hijak sounded groggy. "I'll live. You?"

"Got it good in the shoulder, but otherwise I'm fine." I checked Lana's vitals again. She was alive. Barely.

I loosed a long, desperate burst of thrust, but I was already close to the maximum momentum I could attain out here. "Did you see what happened to Lana?"

"She ate four rockets."

That meant she probably had more than a few shrapnel wounds. And maybe she'd lost suit pressure.

Not good. Not good at all.

"It's my fault," I sent. I felt overwhelmed by guilt.

"It's no one's fault, Rage. We did our best. We were outnumbered five to three. It's lucky she lasted as long as she did."

I know his words were only meant to help me, but they didn't. "I should've ordered the mechs to come with us, back in the hangar bay."

"And I should have reminded you," Hijak sent.

We found her mech, Ox, floating lifelessly amid the rocks. There were dents all along the outer hull, with sections fused together or melted away entirely. Ox's left leg was missing, and its right arm was bent far back, almost torn off.

I opened my cockpit and left Hopper, closing the distance to Ox in my jumpsuit.

I grabbed her mech, and pulled myself around to the front.

"Lana," I transmitted. "If you can read me, open your cockpit. Lana?"

I knocked on the hull with my glove.

"Lana, I'm going to need you to—"

Her cockpit unlatched, and opened a crack.

"I'm coming in, Lana. Everything's going to be all right."

Without gravity, the unlocked hatch didn't fall open on its own. However, no matter how hard I struggled with it, I couldn't pry the hatch open—the edges were too dented.

"Hijak, a little help here, bro."

Hijak came over in his mech. He put one knee on Ox's hip, gripped the hatch with his hand, and pulled.

He tore the metal right off. "Whoops."

I went inside the cockpit.

The cocoon had released Lana, and she floated lifelessly within. She had multiple pieces of shrapnel embedded in her suit. Her faceplate was cracked, but intact. She still had internal suit pressure, as far as I could tell.

"Lana?" I held her in my arms, so that she wouldn't float off into space.

Her eyes fluttered open. "Rade Galaal."

"Tell me where it hurts."

"Everywhere."

"You're going to make it," I told her.

She smiled wanly. "Liar."

"Please, Lana, hang in there. We need you. You have important knowledge of the enemy. You can't die."

Her smile faded, and her eyes became distant. "You don't need me alive. All you need is my embedded ID. Everything . . . everything you need to know is in there. My password is 'soaring eagle 9000-2.'"

Those words tore me up inside. "We *do* need you alive. You're going to live, goddammit. I don't care about your embedded ID. To hell with it. I care about you. We're going to get through this, Lana. We're going to make it. You can't die, not after everything you've been through. You're a survivor. No one endures what you've endured, only to die now. It doesn't make sense. The universe won't allow it. Your will is too strong."

"A pleasant thought," she said. "If entirely untrue."

"I'm going to remove some of the shrapnel, all right? Then attach some SealWraps, and see if I can close your major wounds. Which one hurts the most?"

"They *all* hurt," she said.

I reached into the left cargo pocket of my jumpsuit, and retrieved my suitrep kit.

"No," Lana said, shoving my hand away. "It's too late."

"Lana—"

"Please." She gazed imploringly into my helmet. "Let me die in peace. Without false hope. Don't say I'm going to live, when you know I won't. Don't say you can help me, when you know you can't.

446

I want to die, remembering all I loved about this life, rather than dismissing those thoughts because of some false hope that I might awaken from the coming eternal sleep." She placed her gloved fingers around mine and squeezed. "Don't grieve. Remember me in the deepest, darkest hours, when you think you can't go on. Remember me in the storm."

I stared at her, stunned. "Who taught you those words?"

She smiled sadly. "You did." Her gloved fingers tightened around my own. "Forgive me. For all I have done to you."

My eyes were stinging. "You haven't done a thing to me."

"I have. And I'm forever sorry for it. I deserve this, for what I've done. I should've resisted my possessor, somehow. I should've been stronger. I'm sorry, Rade Galaal."

I squeezed her hand back. "You couldn't have resisted an enemy like that, Lana. None of us could."

"I was wrong, you know. About the UC. I thought you were all bigots. I—"

And then she was gone. Her eyes just stared straight ahead. Her mouth remained open.

If I'd approached her first instead of Hijak, maybe she might've stood a chance. If I'd—

No. I wasn't going to second-guess myself. Not in this.

Still, I wished . . . I really wished . . .

I closed my eyes.

I always lost everyone I ever cared about.

I heard the comm activate, and I waited for Hijak to say something. Instead, all I heard was violent coughing.

Feeling a sudden rising panic, I turned toward him. "Hijak, what's wrong?"

More coughing.

That's when I noticed the thin, dark gash in the cockpit of his mech, just beneath the arm. The mark of an energy ax impact.

"Nothing's wrong, bro," Hijak said. "Well, unless you count the small fact that I'm dying."

"No. Not you too." I ordered Hopper to guard Lana's body, then I jetted over to Hijak's mech. "Open her up."

"No point," he answered.

"Open it! Now!"

He popped his cockpit hatch.

I opened the hatch just as his inner cocoon released him.

Hijak looked up, and forced a smile. The entire lower half of his face mask was covered in blood. He coughed again, sending fresh crimson splatters onto the lens.

I saw the jumpsuit patch he'd applied under his armpit. "What happened?"

"Damn thing plunged its energy ax into my ATLAS," he said, between coughs. "Went right through the cockpit. I jetted away, but not before the tip got me. Good thing my arm was raised high up, or I would've lost the limb. Still, the ax pierced my right lung pretty bad. Seems I have a knack for attracting mortal wounds. I'm getting good at it. I'll make the doc proud."

"I'm going to apply a bandage."

"Bad idea," Hijak managed. "It's a chest-sucking wound. Lung . . . filled with blood."

Damn it.

I didn't have my medbag, which contained a special type of occlusive seal with a one-way flutter valve specifically designed to let the air and blood escape. The suitrep kit contained jumpsuit patches, a few bandages, one IV, a SealWrap, some clotting agents, all-purpose tape, a bag of plasma volume expander . . . nothing I could really use to create a chest seal.

I saw his vitals darken on my aReal, and I had a sickly feeling in my stomach, the kind I got when one of my platoon mates died.

A feeling I'd just experienced with Lana.

I was going to lose Hijak and there was nothing I could do about it. Not while I was out here, alone, billions of klicks from civilization.

Like I said, I always lost everyone who got close to me.

It seemed to be some universal rule.

Why did the universe hate me so?

"Rage." Hijak pawed at my face mask, like he was suddenly desperate to tell me something. "Rage."

"Save your breath, Hijak." Was he going to die now? At this very moment?

"Have to . . . say this." Hijak coughed more blood into his face mask. "You want to leave the Navy? Because you don't have heart anymore? You're wrong. You have heart. More than anyone I've ever known. I've seen you fight, Rage. You have this uncanny ability to read and anticipate the flow of battle. Like you were born to fight. And you never give up. No matter how badly the odds are stacked against you. That's heart, brother. That's true courage. It's why you can't leave the Navy. The MOTHs need people like you. *Humanity* needs people like you. Promise me you'll stay." He gripped my gloved hand, and squeezed hard. "Promise."

I stared into his eyes. "I . . . I'll stay, Hijak. I swear I will."

And so I floated there in the void of space, holding Hijak's hand as he slowly choked to death on his own blood.

I'd gone back for him, on the enemy ship. I'd refused to leave him behind.

But it was all for nothing.

All of it.

I couldn't save him.

I was done.

Hijak said I never gave up? He was wrong.

Because I put my head down and gave up right then.

No one was coming for us.

I knew that in my heart.

No one except the enemy.

And Hijak was going to die.

For some reason, as the two of us lay drifting in the ring belt, my mind kept returning to the contents of the suitrep kit. *You missed something*, a distant part of my mind told me.

I dismissed that voice in scorn.

You didn't miss anything. You've failed Lana. And you've failed your brother, Hijak.

But that distant voice kept coming back, stronger and stronger, no matter how many times I told it to go away. It read out the contents of the kit in my head:

Jumpsuit patches, bandages, an IV, a SealWrap, clotting agents, all-purpose tape, a bag of plasma volume expander . . .

Wait a second.

A bag of plasma volume expander.

I hurriedly fetched the kit from Hijak's cargo pocket.

"What are you doing?" Hijak said weakly.

"Quiet."

I secured a SealWrap to my wrist, choosing the glove with the working laser. Then I grabbed a bag of plasma volume expander and cut it open with Hijak's utility knife. The contents vaporized and desublimated, forming a cloud of very fine crystals. The discharge was beautiful, but I didn't have time to admire it.

The deflated plastic bag formed a square in my hands. I applied tape to three sides, parallel to the borders, so that half the adhesive protruded over the edges. I folded the bag in two, keeping the sticky portions of the tape facing outward, and I wedged it between the ring finger and pinkie of my glove, within the SealWrap.

I lifted Hijak's arm assembly.

Incredibly, he shoved it right back down again.

"Raise your arm," I told him sternly.

"No."

"Goddammit, Hijak. Stop behaving like a caterpillar. You have to let me try."

"No I don't. Maybe I want this. Maybe I deserve it for what I've done. Betraying my team. Betraying my country."

"You betrayed no one, Hijak. Now lift your arm before I kick your ass. You're a MOTH. You never give up. Or is your weak Chinese half finally asserting itself?" Ordinarily I'd never say something like that, but I wanted to get a rise out of him. I wanted him to fight.

It worked, because he lifted his arm, glaring at me the whole time from beneath his helmet.

I secured the SealWrap to his suit, atop the patch he'd applied beneath his armpit. Then I cut through the fabric of both the patch and the jumpsuit, using the surgical laser in the index finger of my glove. The SealWrap puffed out as the inner atmosphere of the suit expanded to fill it.

I slid aside the circular fabric I'd cut away. The blood from the chest wound trickled outward because of the lack of gravity. I had to work quickly before that blood hampered my efforts.

I placed the empty plastic bag directly over his injury and applied pressure, securing the three taped sides to his bare flesh. Because the blood had been floating directly outward, there wasn't too much plasmatic fluid around the edges of the wound, so the tape held.

I watched as the bag sucked inward with each inhale, sealing the chest wound; when he exhaled, the excess air and blood spurted out the untaped section.

Job complete. One makeshift flutter valve applied.

Meatball surgery at its finest.

Hijak's vitals stabilized. For now. It was only a temporary solution, I knew. Hijak needed to see a surgeon as soon as possible. But I had bought him some time, at least.

I wrapped the fingers of my other hand around the neck of the SealWrap, crimping it just below my fingers, and then I carefully extracted my wrist. I turned the adhesive dial, converting the Seal-Wrap into a stand-alone jumpsuit patch.

"Thanks, Rage." Hijak sounded much better. "I got something I want to say." He gripped me by the arm.

"Say it."

He swallowed visibly. "I'm going to make it. I'm not going to die out here. I refuse. Not after all you've done for me."

"That's the brother I know."

Hijak grinned for the first time all day, though it looked macabre with all that blood splattering his face mask. "When we get back, I owe you a beer."

"I get told that a lot."

I hoped he got the chance to buy me that beer. I really did.

"There's one thing I still don't get," he said, releasing me. "Back on the ship. Why did you come back for me?"

"Because you're my brother."

"I thought you hated me."

It was my turn to clasp his arm. "Actions speak louder than words, bro."

With difficulty, I began repairing the rear-shoulder puncture in my jumpsuit, because although the swelling skin and coagulated blood of the wound formed a temporary seal, if I didn't patch the suit I risked the whole area necrotizing.

When I finished, my shoulder wound temporarily reopened as the swelling subsided. It would clot again on its own. I just hoped I wouldn't lose too much blood in the process.

I secured Lana's body to the passenger seat above Hopper's jetpack, then Hijak and I went inside our respective ATLAS 6s and continued onward.

We aimed to put as much distance between ourselves and

the frigate as possible. We didn't know if the Guide was planning another attack of some sort, and we certainly didn't want to hang around to find out.

An hour passed. We let the mechs proceed on autopilot through the ring system. The only sounds I heard were my own breathing and the occasional thud of small rocks against Hopper's hull. I fell in and out of sleep.

Silent sparks continued to erupt from the stump of Hopper's right arm. I thought of another time I'd lost the arm of an ATLAS mech. Bender had really loved it. In fact, he would probably mock me for months when he found out I'd lost another arm, this time in an *ATLAS 6*.

Bender. Would I see him, and the rest of the platoon, ever again?

Hijak called a stop shortly into the second hour.

"What's wrong, bro?" I transmitted.

"Nothing. Just . . . I want to see the stars one last time."

He pivoted his mech, swinging away from the gas giant that consumed most of our vision.

I glanced at his vitals on my HUD. They were darkening again, and a hint of red was showing through. The tape must have come loose.

Well, there was nothing for it. Though I was weary to the bone, I'd just have to make him another flutter valve.

I opened up my cockpit, and the inner cocoon released me. I reached for my suitrep kit.

It was gone.

I'd lost it somewhere along the way. I remembered taking it out in Lana's cockpit. I must have forgotten it there . . .

Maybe I could just re-tape the existing flutter valve. Except the SK suitrep kit in Hijak's jumpsuit only had one SealWrap, and I'd used it already. Without the SealWrap, there was no way I could get access to his wound without permanently depressurizing his entire suit.

He was going to die for real this time.

Then I remembered Lana. She would have a suitrep kit as part of her jumpsuit.

I exhaled in relief.

I jetted to the passenger seat that held her body.

Incredibly, her left cargo pocket was empty. I checked the right pocket.

Empty as well.

So that was it, then. I'd lost.

It was all for nothing.

I jetted to his side and wrapped my glove around his. I watched the stars with him, waiting for him to die.

I thought I was hallucinating when I heard the incoming communication.

The words were in Italian, so I didn't understand them at first. I was too far gone to even accept the translation proffered by my helmet aReal.

Then the words came again, in English.

"This is the *Furlana*, H-class shuttle of the Franco-Italian battle cruiser *Tarantella*. Do you copy, over?"

Stunned, I didn't answer.

Then I saw the soft angles of the Franco-Italian shuttle as it crested the fringe of the ring belt. The distant Tau Ceti sun shone from precisely the right location behind the shuttle, giving the craft a beautiful yellow halo.

I cried tears of joy.

That the Franco-Italian warship was nearby to pick us up was a stroke of luck, because any longer and Hijak would have died. The FIs had detected the PASS device, along with the thermal signatures of our mechs. It helped that the explosions from our little space battle had lit up sensors halfway across the system—well, those sensors not occluded by the gas giant anyway.

I told them about the SK frigate, but when the Captain of the *Tarantella* sent probes to investigate, the enemy vessel was long gone. A rad trail led toward the opposite side of the planet, but Captain Andino elected not to pursue. He explained that he was under direct orders to proceed to the other gas giant in the system, Tau Ceti II, where the *Tarantella* would provide much-needed reinforcements for the fleet. He didn't really understand when I tried to convince him of the Guide's importance—he probably thought I was suffering from a touch of space insanity.

Lana's body was packed in cold storage, while Hijak and I were summarily dispatched to the Convalescence Ward.

The Weavers patched the wound in my rear deltoid, removing the bullet and replacing unsalvageable tissue with bio-printed variants. I only spent half a day in the ward, with most of that time in detox, where I was repeatedly scanned for the presence of alien germs. Hijak was still recovering, so that night I was debriefed alone over a secure vid node with Lieutenant Commander Braggs and two unidentified fleet officers.

The *Tarantella* was still quite far from the *Gerald R. Ford* and the rest of the fleet, so the communications lag was about four minutes between each question and answer. The Lieutenant Commander had me spawn a background process to upload the most recent audio and video archives from my embedded ID since my capture, and that only further degraded the connection. That said, the Intra-PlaNet node on the *Tarantella* was working surprisingly well, given the system-wide EM interference from the Skull Ship. It helped that the *Gerald R. Ford* was on the opposite side of the gas giant from the Skull Ship, as was the *Tarantella*.

When the debriefing began, the very first thing I admitted was that I'd been broken. I'd given up the password to my embedded ID and the enemy had downloaded everything.

I told them of the torture sessions with Keeper Jiāndāo, and how she had turned out to be a pilot named Lana. I told them what Lana had revealed about the enemy: how the Phants communicated telepathically, and obeyed some "Observer Mind." I also shared the full details of my conversation with the possessed Artificial, including how the Guide promised to "spare" twenty percent of humanity in exchange for our surrender.

When I was finally done, I gazed at the blank screen, waiting for the next transmission from the Lieutenant Commander to appear.

The four-minute latency mark came and went.

Six minutes passed.

Ten.

The blank signal that stared back at me told me everything I needed to know. I'd messed up. Big-time. I'd revealed all our secrets to the enemy, and sabotaged our chances of winning this war.

When the vid feed finally kicked in fifteen minutes later, the faces of the Lieutenant Commander and the fleet officers were grave.

"Thank you, Mr. Galaal," the Lieutenant Commander said, rather stiltedly. "We have everything we need for now. Good to have you back. Rest up. Oh, and please leave the secure connection active overnight, so we can finish downloading your embedded ID recordings."

The vid feed cut out.

Mr. Galaal.

Not Rage.

Yes. I'd betrayed them all right.

The next day I underwent additional surgery to remove the metallic knob grafted into the back of my head. It was an SK technology familiar to the Franco-Italian doctors and was supposed to be easy enough to remove. But apparently I'd suffered complications, because I ended up waking an entire week later.

After that I was sent to PTSD (post-traumatic stress disorder) therapy.

The military psychologist assigned by the Franco-Italians assured me I had done the right thing. The best of us would have broken under the same situation, he said.

I wasn't so sure. But I nodded my head and pretended I was fine, though inside I was falling apart.

Hijak and I berthed alone in the guest quarters, which was good, because I wasn't in the mood to fake camaraderie with the rest of the FI crew. When the two of us visited the mess hall to eat, we always took a table apart from everyone else. When we went to the gym, we worked out together in our own little world, again ignoring everyone else.

It was funny, because although Hijak and I hung out all day, the two of us hardly exchanged more than a few words.

We did have one real conversation, however.

About three days after we'd started PTSD therapy, shortly after lights out, I found myself staring at the ceiling. Unable to sleep.

Again.

"You awake, Rage?"

"Yeah, Hijak," I said.

"You never told me. Did they break you?"

The Keeper had said she'd broken us, in front of me and Hijak both. But Hijak was apparently too out of himself at the time to remember.

I didn't answer him for a long moment.

"Yes." I closed my eyes, and a tear trickled down my cheek. I was glad for the darkness. I didn't want Hijak to see me, not like this.

"I told you what she said, didn't I?" Hijak sounded close to tears himself. "That she'd hang my parents up like pigs and skin them alive. That all their money wouldn't save them."

"You told me," I agreed.

"It was bullshit, wasn't it? There was no way she could've reached my parents, or anyone else on Earth. Not from here. Yet I believed her."

"I don't have an answer for you, Hijak," I said.

"What kind of MOTH am I," Hijak continued. "Betraying my platoon, my *nation*, like that? What kind of *man*?"

"A damn good one," I said. "One of the best I know."

"I feel like such a traitor. A failure. Like I've gone against all the tenets MOTHs hold true. We never give in, no matter the cost to ourselves. We go through hell, and we keep going, and we never back down. *We never back down.*"

"Hijak. We were tortured. They broke us. Probably had us doped up on truth serum or scopolamine and whatever the hell else. That's something you can't fight: someone messing with your brain chemistry."

Lana, when she was Jiāndāo, had told me I was resistant to scopolamine. I didn't want to believe her; it was far easier to pretend a chemical had broken me.

"That's no excuse," Hijak said, refusing to take the easy way out. "We should've been stronger."

"Well we broke, and there's nothing we can do about that now except bounce back," I said. "We're returning to the Teams. We have to fight on. Live by the tenets of the Navy, and the MOTHs. Honor, courage, commitment. Truth to ourselves, our country, and our brothers. We can't give up. We can't let what they've done destroy us. If we do that, we've let the enemy win. Two more MOTHs, killed in the line of duty, and the enemy didn't even have to fire a single bullet. No, Hijak, we're going to hit back. We're going to have our vengeance for what the enemy did to us. Let their crimes stoke the fire of your spirit, and your rage, because we won't let them go unpunished. We'll show the enemy what it means to be more than men. We'll show them what it means to be MOTHs."

Hijak didn't answer for so long that I thought he'd gone to sleep. Just as I closed my eyes, he said, "Thank you, Rage."

My speech may or may not have helped him, but to be honest, I was more the intended recipient of those words. And it worked, for that night anyway. But the next morning when I woke up I felt hollow inside all over again.

When I killed more of the enemy, I'd feel better I was sure. But until then . . .

The *Tarantella* finally rendezvoused with the *Gerald R. Ford* above Tau Ceti II, near orbital station *Lequ*, our forward operating base. Hijak and I took the first shuttle to the supercarrier, and once aboard I was forced to undergo yet another week of counseling. Other than Hijak, the therapist wouldn't let me see anyone from the platoon. Not even Tahoe. On a ship as big as the *Gerald R. Ford*, that wasn't hard to arrange.

After some soul-searching, and a few intense sessions where I shed more than a few tears, the therapist finally cleared me for duty.

I was eager to get back to work.

I was eager to have my revenge.

They'd killed Alejandro. Taken Shaw. They'd captured me, stripped away who I was to the core, and broken me. And when I'd freed my captor, Lana, they'd murdered her.

Oh, I would have myself some payback, I can tell you that.

The black blood of the enemy would flow in wide, screaming rivers.

And that wasn't merely empty rhetoric or bombast. I meant every word, from the depths of my being, from the depths of the hell the enemy had sent me to.

Hijak had been cleared for duty a few days before, but he'd been confined to the berth the two of us shared. The therapist didn't want either of us to rejoin the platoon alone.

So when the time came for us to return, we did it together.

That first morning, neither of us could meet anyone's eyes for long. The welcomes and smiles seemed fake somehow, at least to me. Though neither the Chief nor the Lieutenant Commander had told them, my platoon brothers knew I had betrayed them. I could see it in their eyes.

How could I expect them to forgive me, or respect me, if I couldn't forgive or respect myself?

It was good to see that Tahoe had made a full recovery from the injuries he'd taken in Shangde City. But seeing him was the only bright spot in a morning that, for me, was full of shame.

Chief Bourbonjack took me aside after PT.

"Rage," he said. "You're home now. You're among brothers. You don't have to be ashamed about what you think you did, or did not, do."

"Who are you to talk about shame?" I blurted out. I hadn't actually meant to say that, but the deed was done. I guess I just wanted to deflect the blame for my actions away from myself, even though I was the only one responsible for what I had done.

I lowered my eyes. "I'm sorry, sir."

"No, no," the Chief said. "Go on. Speak your mind."

I glanced at him. His usually piercing eyes seemed softer somehow. "Well, it's just, the platoon didn't come for us. You didn't come."

The Chief nodded slowly. "No, we didn't freakin' come." He couldn't meet my gaze.

I waited for the explanation, which I sensed was forthcoming. I wanted him to reveal what had happened on his own time, and if he didn't, then so be it.

He sighed. That weatherworn face seemed suddenly older. "Honestly, boy? We had no idea where you were. We tracked the rad trail of the SK drop shuttle that took you. The trail ended in orbit near the Skull Ship, and we couldn't pursue any farther, not without risking attack. At that point, we didn't know what to think.

We weren't sure if the Skull Ship had blown the shuttle to smithereens, or if the craft had flown right by it, or what.

"If you *had* made it past, that likely meant our SK 'allies' had captured you. So we tried ordering them to hand you boys over, but the SKs repeatedly denied any involvement in your capture and insisted Dragon platoon had been shot at, too, down there, by what appeared to be rogue SKs. They produced vid evidence. Which we thought was doctored.

"So we waited, hoping you'd find a way to contact us. But you never did. I tried to get clearance to send a covert fire team over to the main SK battle cruiser to perform some recon, but I couldn't get it. If you were the Captain, or the Lieutenant Commander, would you risk upsetting the alliance with such a blatant show of mistrust? It was a damn good thing we didn't go too, because if we had, you might've returned to find the alliance in shambles.

"Anyway, we didn't know where else to look. Since our arrival, we've detected the heat signatures of multiple ships in the area, from the refugees constantly fleeing the local moons. The signatures are consistent with passenger liners. Nothing unusual there. Even after your capture, we didn't detect any strange vessel classes out there. Unfortunately, the thermal signature of an SK frigate is similar to a common liner, and we suspect that's how your kidnappers sneaked past. We didn't have the resources to set up proper checkpoints to intercept all those fleeing liners, but we did send messages, and received what seemed appropriate responses, with appropriate clearances. We had to assume you weren't on any of those ships. We were wrong. We made a mistake. I'm sorry, Rage. I really am.

"The Gate customs officials have been notified to remain on the lookout for a rogue SK frigate. We've also contacted the Brass, and they've promised to send additional battle cruisers to shore up the Gate defenses, both in Gliese 581 and SK space. We'll catch this Guide bastard, I promise you."

I was silent for a moment, trying to absorb everything the Chief had said.

"So you did try to come." That made me feel immensely better.

"We did, Rage."

There was one thing I still needed to resolve, though.

"I squealed, sir," I said. "I ratted out the platoon. I gave the enemy my embedded ID password. Betrayed my country. I don't deserve to be a MOTH anymore. Everyone knows what I did, Chief. Everyone."

"Maybe if you stopped acting so goddamned guilty—" Chief Bourbonjack cut his gruff comment short. He exhaled, then rested his hand on my shoulder. "You know what? I'm going to tell you something that I've never told a soul." He stared at me intently with those dark, judging eyes of his. "I was captured in Mongolia, a long time ago. I was brought to a stone cell, and introduced to the concept of the Keepers. And guess what? They broke me. It took fifteen days, but they did it in the end. I gave them my embedded ID password." He rolled up the sleeves of his camos, revealing the sickly, crisscrossing scars on his wrists underneath. "These arms have been shot off and replaced numerous times, but always the scars of the Keeper's harness return. You never lose them. Not the physical scars. Not the mental. All I can tell you is, the guilt ebbs every day. One day you'll forgive yourself, Rage. And maybe someday, I'll forgive myself too."

Those words lessened my guilt somewhat, because if a man of Bourbonjack's character could break, then that meant any of us could. I still wasn't proud of what I'd done, but I swore I wouldn't be so hard on myself from now on.

The Chief paused on the way out of the gym. "One question. Do you still want me to put in your transfer request?"

I thought about what Hijak had told me about heart when he almost died, and the promise I had made him. *The Navy needs men like you.*

I thought about what Chief Bourbonjack had just said. *I was captured in Mongolia. And guess what? They broke me.*

And lastly, I thought about my unrealized vengeance. *There will be rivers of screaming blood.*

"Rage?" the Chief pressed. "Do you still want out of MOTH Team Seven?"

"Not on your life, sir."

———————

Nothing had changed in my absence. The Skull Ship remained in orbit above Tau Ceti II-c. Other than a few warships from the Franco-Italians, including the *Tarantella*, significant fleet reinforcements had yet to arrive. The prevailing orders from Earth were to sit back, observe the enemy, and wait for reinforcements. Further instructions would be forthcoming.

The waiting proved unbearable. My platoon brothers and I threw ourselves at PT, working ourselves beyond exhaustion each day. We were at war, and yet we were doing nothing. It was maddening.

A week after my reintroduction to the platoon, Lieutenant Commander Braggs assembled us to share the latest bad news.

"The war, gentlemen, has taken an unexpected turn for the worse," the Lieutenant Commander said. "We've just received word on a secure node. Above our sister moon, Tau Ceti II-b, another Skull Ship has appeared."

EPILOGUE

Shaw

I sat alone on a high platform made of some sticky resin, suspended by physics I didn't understand in the upper atmosphere of a gas giant.

My mech had been confiscated, but I still had my pressurized jumpsuit, and my life. Not to mention my mind: I hadn't been lobotomized into some human-alien hybrid. Not yet.

My oxygen tanks had been refilled, as had my water canisters, and my stock of meal replacements had been replenished. Unsurprisingly, the MREs concocted by the alien entities were even more tasteless than the human versions. Still, I would last out here for quite a while if the aliens kept up this treatment.

Unless of course I chose to step off the platform and end it all.

I was seated on the edge of said platform even now, gazing at the city far below, which was nestled amid the gas giant's swirling red-orange clouds. The city's layout was utterly alien—then again, maybe not so alien, because it reminded me of the beehives my parents used to keep on our farm in France. From my elevated perch, I could peer right into the innards of that city, just as if I were looking into the cross section of a massive beehive. Hundreds of tall, parallel plates, probably made of the same resinous material as my platform, were situated equidistant apart. Each plate contained thousands of decagonal cells, and Phants in gaseous form drifted between them, as did other, aquatic-like beings. The jellyfish of Earth were probably the closest comparisons, except of course jellyfish resided in oceans, whereas these beings lived in gas.

A vast energy sphere enclosed the city, sheltering the denizens (and me) from the atmospheric winds. The sphere was a translucent, shimmering yellow; its hue varied across the surface, depending on where the winds were currently gusting strongest. Beyond the sphere, perpetual bolts of sheet lightning flashed, cast by the planetwide storm.

The upper winds of gas giants roared with more than twice the power of the strongest hurricanes on Earth, which meant that without the protection of the energy field, the hive city would've been ripped to shreds. Though I suspected the Phants and jellyfish would've endured regardless.

The edges of the hive city ran right against that sphere, where metal rods had been built to draw the lightning. Strategically placed wind turbines, which looked like jet engines, jutted through the sphere as well. Power generators.

Humanity had experimented with vaguely similar generators on Jupiter and Saturn. Our research ships deployed turbines into the gas giants from high orbit, with incredibly lengthy lines linking the turbines to the ship. Though these "power lines" were interlaced with graphene, one of the strongest forms of carbon known to man, within a Stanweek the lines invariably snapped. Either that, or some other component of the turbines failed.

Anyway, so there I was, on the far side of the galaxy, a prisoner on an alien world. *The* homeworld of the Phants, if my captor was to be believed.

I chuckled to myself. I seemed to have a penchant for getting myself tangled in hopeless situations.

I closed my eyes, thinking of Fan and Queequeg. Especially Queequeg. The animal had been with me through so much. He was my best friend.

And now he was gone.

He had died for me. As had Fan.

I understood now the agony Rade had endured when he'd lost Alejandro. When you lost someone that close, it just ripped a hole right through your heart, into the very essence of who you were as a person.

Whenever I thought of Queequeg or Fan, and how horribly either of them had died, I just . . . well . . . broke apart inside.

Queequeg was only a pet, I told myself. Just an animal.

Yet another part of me knew he was so much more than a mere pet.

I miss you, Queequeg.

As for Fan, there was no dismissing what had happened to him. He was a human being. And now he was gone. Everything he had been was destroyed and taken away. Replaced by . . . something.

Forgive me, Fan.

I'd lost so much. Yet I'd come so far.

This was fate. It had to be.

I was meant to come here. I had a purpose.

And I would see that purpose through.

I banished all thoughts I had of hurling myself from the platform.

No matter what happened, I wouldn't give up.

I wouldn't give in.

I would endure.

I would survive this.

No matter what they did to me.

I've been through worse.

I'm Shaw Chopra. UC Navy Astrogator.

And I would see Earth again.

———

I heard a distant humming, slowly growing in volume.

What now?

A figure approached from the hive city below. It flew straight toward me.

Maybe I would finally learn what my captors wanted.

I brought my legs over the rim of the platform and rose from the sticky surface.

A human being wearing a jetpack landed on the far side of the platform. The absence of a jumpsuit was conspicuous, as was the dark green, glowing vapor that surrounded the visitor's upper body.

This was no human being, but a possessed Artificial.

I edged away from the thing, moving toward the opposite end of the platform.

The Artificial wore the blue-and-gray digital pattern of an SK Navy uniform. It had the face of an SK too, and looked almost human, save for the eyes, which resided firmly in "uncanny valley." The orbs were too dull, and lacked the shimmer of life. I supposed it was because of the harsh atmosphere, which would've vaporized the moisture from its eyes.

"You will not be harmed," the possessed Artificial said.

I shook my head. "What about my companions? My pet, mutilated. And the man with me . . . you lobotomized him, drilling spare parts into his skull and spine so you could possess him. That's rather harmful, wouldn't you say?"

Those dead eyes bored into me. "This man, he came to the ship with you?"

"What do you think? We were in that twisted menagerie of yours when one of your servants took him and threw him into a tank for the robots to operate on."

The Artificial appeared genuinely saddened. "Then we cannot retrieve him. He is *Cáichön* now. Property."

"Property." I nearly spat the word. "Not so different from me. What do you want?"

"It is I, Azen."

"I don't care who you are." I smiled sardonically. "You've migrated from my mech to an Artificial. Am I supposed to be impressed? Tell me what you want."

The Artificial returned my smile, though it was not sardonic.

"I want to save your race," Azen said.

POSTSCRIPT

You can keep in touch with me or my writing through one—or all—of the following means:

Twitter: @IsaacHooke
Facebook: http://fb.me/authorisaachooke
Goodreads: http://goodreads.com/isaachooke
My website: http://isaachooke.com
My e-mail: isaac@isaachooke.com

Don't be shy about e-mails, I love getting them, and try to respond to everyone!

Thanks again for reading.

ABOUT THE AUTHOR

Isaac Hooke's experimental novel, *The Forever Gate*, achieved Amazon #1 bestseller status in both the science fiction and fantasy categories when it was released in 2013, and was recognized as Indie Book of the Day.

He holds a degree in engineering physics, though his more unusual inventions remain fictive at this time.

He is an avid blogger, cyclist, and photographer who resides in Edmonton, Alberta.

You can reach him at isaachooke.com.